A young woman disappears.
A husband is suspected of murder.
Stirring times for all the neighbourhood in

THE STEEPWOOD

Scandals

VO

When the debauched Marquis of Sywell won
Steepwood Abbey years ago at cards, it led to the death
of the Earl of Yardley. Now he's caused scandal again by
marrying a girl out of his class – and young enough to
be his granddaughter! After being married only a short
time, the Marchioness has disappeared, leaving no trace
of her whereabouts. There is every expectation that yet
more scandals will emerge, though no one yet knows
just how shocking they will be.

The four villages surrounding the Steepwood Abbey
estate are in turmoil, not only with the dire goings-on at
the Abbey, but also with their own affairs.
Each of the eight volumes in THE STEEPWOOD
SCANDALS contains two full novels that follow the
mystery behind the disappearance of the young woman,
and the individual romances of lovers connected
in some way with the intrigue.

THE STEEPWOOD
Scandals

Regency drama, intrigue, mischief...
and marriage

THE STEEPWOOD
Scandals

Anne Herries & Elizabeth Bailey

*Harlequin Mills & Boon Limited, Eton House,
18-24 Paradise Road, Richmond, Surrey TW9 1SR*

First published in Great Britain in 2001

THE STEEPWOOD SCANDALS © Harlequin Books S.A. 2006

Lord Ravensden's Marriage © Harlequin Books S.A. 2001
An Innocent Miss © Harlequin Books S.A. 2001

Special thanks and acknowledgement are given to Anne Herries and Elizabeth Bailey for their contribution to The Steepwood Scandals series.

ISBN-13: 978 0 263 854954
ISBN-10: 0 263 85495 7

052-1106

*Printed and bound in Spain
by Litografía Rosés S.A., Barcelona*

Lord Ravensden's Marriage
by
Anne Herries

Anne Herries, winner of the Romantic Novelists' Association ROMANCE PRIZE 2004, lives in Cambridgeshire. She is fond of watching wildlife, and spoils the birds and squirrels that are frequent visitors to her garden. Anne loves to write about the beauty of nature, and sometimes puts a little into her books, although they are mostly about love and romance. She writes for her own enjoyment, and to give pleasure to her readers.

Look for Anne Herries' brand new novel

A WEALTHY WIDOW

Available from Mills & Boon Historical Romance®
in February 2007!

Chapter One

October, 1811

'Courage, Beatrice! Are you to be daunted by tales of dragons and witches? No, certainly not,' she answered herself, unconsciously speaking the words aloud. 'This is nonsense, sheer nonsense! Papa would be ashamed of you.'

Beatrice shivered, pulling her cloak more tightly about her body as the mischievous wind tried to tug it from her. She was approaching the gates of Steepwood Abbey from the eastern side, having just come from the village of Steep Abbot, which clustered outside the Abbey's crumbling walls at the point where the river entered its grounds.

In the village behind her lay the peaceful beauty of gracious trees, their bluish-green fronds brushing the edges of an idyllic pool in the river's course. Ahead of her in the gathering dusk was the great, squat, brooding shape of the ancient Abbey, its grounds almost a wasteland these days. It was not a pleasant place at the best of times, but at dusk it took on a menacing atmosphere that was as much a product of superstitious minds as of fact.

'There is not the least need to be nervous,' she told herself as she peered into the shadowy grounds. 'What was it Master Shakespeare said? Ah yes! *Our fears do make us traitors*. Do not be a traitor to your own convictions, Beatrice. It is all careless talk and superstition…'

But there were so many tales told about this place, and all of them calculated to make the blood run cold.

The land had been granted to the monks in the thirteenth century, and the Abbey had been built in a beautiful wooded area bordering the River Steep. Its origins were mystical, and it was held in popular belief that there had once, long centuries past, been a Roman temple somewhere in the grounds. Some of the stories told about the goings on at the Abbey were enough to make strong men turn pale.

So perhaps it was not just the chill of autumn air that made Beatrice shiver and turn cold as she paused to take her bearings.

'Foolish woman! This is autumn,' Beatrice scolded herself, 'and you ought to have remembered the nights were pulling in. You should have left half an hour sooner!'

It was now the fourth week of October, in the year of Our Lord 1811, and the nights had begun to pull in more quickly than she had imagined possible. She ought in all conscience to have set out on her journey home to the small village of Abbot Giles at least half an hour sooner.

Most sensible females who lived in one of the four villages that lay to the north, south, east and west of the Abbey would not have considered crossing the Abbey's land after dusk, or—since the Marquis of Sywell had taken up residence some eighteen years earlier—during the day for that matter!

Beatrice Roade, however, was made of sterner stuff. At the age of twenty-three she was of course a confirmed spinster, the first flush of her youth behind her (though not forgotten!), all hope of ever marrying denied her. She was tall, well-formed, with an easy way of walking that proclaimed her the healthy, no-nonsense woman she was. Attractive, her features strong, classical, with rather haunting green eyes and hair the colour of burnished chestnuts, she was thought slightly daunting by the local squires, who did not care for her cleverness—or her humour, which was oft-times baffling.

'Miss Roade,' they were wont to say of her as she was seen walking between the four villages, 'bookish, you know. And as for looks—not the patch of her sister Miss Olivia. Now she is a beauty!'

And this from men who could hardly have caught more than a fleeting glimpse of Miss Olivia for the past fifteen years! But Miss Olivia took after her mother, and *she* had been beautiful. Miss Roade was like her father's family no doubt, and known to be sensible.

So what was the very sensible Beatrice doing poised at the gate to Steepwood's boundary walls, a gate which lay drunkenly open and rusting, useless these many years? Could she really be contemplating taking a short cut?

If they entered the grounds at all, most local folk stayed well away from the Abbey itself, taking either the path which led past the Little Steep river and the lake, or skirting Giles Wood—though only the braver amongst the villagers went near the woods.

There were odd goings on in the woods! Nan had told her that people were talking about it. Lights had been seen there at night again recently, and the gossips were saying that the Marquis was up to his old tricks—for it was firmly believed that when he had first come to the Abbey, Sywell and his friends had cavorted naked with their whores amongst the trees—and they had worn animal masks on their heads!

'Scandalous! That a nobleman of England should behave in such a manner,' Nan had said only that morning as she polished the sofa table in the parlour until the beautiful wood gleamed so that she could see her reflection. 'I dread to think what may be going on there.'

'Nan, you intrigue me,' Beatrice had teased. 'Just what dire things do you imagine are happening up there?'

'Nothing that you or I should want to know about,' her aunt had told her with a look of mock severity.

Really, the Marquis's behaviour was too disgusting to mention—except that life was sometimes a little slow in the villages, and it did make such a delightful tale to whisper of to one's friends.

Ghislaine and Beatrice had laughed together that

very afternoon, though Ghislaine had been inclined to dismiss the rumours.

'The Marquis of Sywell is too old for such games,' she said, her eyes dancing with mischief. 'Surely it cannot be true, Beatrice?'

'I would not have thought so—though there must be something going on. The lights have been seen by several villagers.'

'Well, I imagine there will be some simple explanation,' Ghislaine had said, and Beatrice nodded. 'I dare say the lights are but lanthorns carried by some person with business on the estate.'

'Yes, I am sure you must be right—but the gossips invent so many stories. It is amusing, is it not?'

Amusing then, but not quite so funny when Beatrice was faced with a walk through the wasteland that was now the Abbey grounds.

Some might whisper of devil-worship and the black arts, but others spoke of pagan rites that were firmly rooted in the history of ancient Britons. It was said that in the old days virgins had been sacrificed on a stone by the lake, and their blood used to bring fertility to the land. Naturally Beatrice was too intelligent to let such tales weigh with her. Really, what did go on in the minds of some people!

Besides, the Abbey had long been the home of an old and respected family—it was only since it had fallen into the hands of the Marquis of Sywell that it had become a place of abomination to the people of the four villages.

Beatrice took heart from the sensible view of her friend. Strange goings on there might be, but they were unlikely to be anything that could bring harm to her.

'It is foolish to be frightened just because it is becoming dark,' Beatrice murmured to herself. 'If I but walk quickly I shall be home in less than half an hour.'

Beatrice glanced up at the sky. Storm clouds were gathering. If she took the longer route, she might be caught and drenched by the rain that was certainly coming. She was not to be frightened by rumour and superstition. She would take the shorter route that crossed the Marquis's grounds close to the Abbey itself. It was a risk, of course, because she would have to pass close to that part of the building which was now used as a private home.

'Nothing ventured, nothing gained.' Beatrice murmured one of her beloved father's maxims, conveniently forgetting that he had so often been proved wrong in the past. For it was Mr Bertram Roade's tendency to plunge into the unknown that had led to his losing the small but adequate competence which had been settled on him by his maternal grandfather— Lord Borrowdale. 'What can *he* do to me after all?'

The *he* she was thinking of was, of course, the wicked Marquis himself, of whom the tales were so many and so lurid that Beatrice found them amusing rather than frightening—at least at home and in daylight.

'Be sensible,' Beatrice told herself fiercely as she began to cross the gravel drive which would take her past the Abbey—and the dark, haunting ruins of the Chapter House, which had been destroyed at the time of the dissolution of the monasteries and never restored. 'He couldn't possibly have done everything they say, otherwise he would have died of the pox or some similar foul disease long ago.' She smiled at the inelegance of her own words. 'Oh, Beatrice! What would dear Mrs Guarding say if she knew what you were thinking now?'

It was because she had spent the afternoon at Mrs Guarding's excellent school for young ladies that she was having to risk venturing right to the heart of the Abbey grounds now.

It had been so pleasant for the time of year earlier that afternoon. Beatrice had visited her friend Mademoiselle Ghislaine de Champlain, who was the French mistress at Mrs Guarding's school, and had stopped to drink tea with her.

Beatrice had been fortunate enough to spend one precious year as a teacher/pupil at the school, where she had studied with Ghislaine to improve her knowledge and pronunciation of French, in return for helping the younger pupils with their English—the happiest year of her life.

It was, of course, the only way she could afford to attend the exclusive school, her education having been undertaken by her father at home, which might account for some of the very odd things she had been taught.

She had been twenty during that precious year spent at the exclusive establishment. Beatrice had hoped to make a niche for herself at the school, because she very much admired the principles of the moral but advanced-thinking woman who ran it.

However, family duties had forced her to return to her home.

Thinking about the illness and subsequent death of her dearest mother occupied Beatrice's thoughts as she walked, banishing all lingering echoes of orgies and dire goings on at the Abbey. Mrs Roade had been an acknowledged beauty in her day, and, as the only sister of the wealthy Lord Burton, had been expected to marry well. Her decision to accept Bertram Roade had been a disappointment to her family.

Beatrice's musings were brought to an abrupt end as she heard the scream. It was the most blood-curdling, terrifying sound she had ever heard in her life, and she whirled round, looking for its source.

It had seemed to come from the Abbey itself. Perhaps the chapel or the cloisters...but she could not be certain. It might have come from somewhere in the grounds. Yes, surely it must have been the grounds—an animal caught in a trap perhaps? So thought the sensible Miss Roade.

For an instant, Beatrice considered the possibility of a dreadful crime...possibly murder or rape. Vague memories flitted through her mind; there was a tale of a girl caught inside the grounds one night when the monks still lived there: it was said that the girl had been found dead in the morning!

Beatrice shivered and increased her pace, her nerves tingling. All the stories of the Marquis's atrocities came rushing back to fill her mind with vague fears of herself being attacked by...what?

Long dead monks? Ridiculous! What then? Hardly the Marquis? Surely she was not truly afraid of him?

He was after all married at last, to a rather beautiful, young—and if the little anyone knew of her was anything to go by, mysterious girl. All Beatrice knew of her was that her name was Louise, and that she had been adopted as a baby by the Marquis's bailiff, John Hanslope. It was whispered that she was his bastard, but no one knew the truth of the affair.

The scandal of the nobleman's marriage to his own bailiff's ward had both shocked and delighted the people of the four villages. Despite his terrible reputation, it was still unthinkable that a man of his background should marry a girl who was after all little more than a servant. 'Quite beyond the pale, my dear!'

Beatrice's own sympathies lay with the unfortunate girl who had married him, for surely she must have been desperate to do such a thing?

A sudden thought struck Beatrice—could it have been the Marquis's wife who had screamed? She glanced at the brooding, menacing shape of the Abbey and crossed herself superstitiously. What could *he* have been doing to her to make her scream like that?

'No, no,' she whispered. 'It could not have been her—nor any woman. It was an animal, only an animal.'

He *was* said to be in love…after years of wickedness and debauchery!

Even a man of the Marquis's calibre could not be capable of hurting the woman he loved—or could he?

Beatrice tucked her head down against the wind and began to run. Perhaps it was her anxiety to leave the grounds of the Abbey that made her careless? It was certain that she did not see or hear the pounding hooves of the great horse until it came rushing at her out of the darkness. She was directly in its path and had to throw herself aside to avoid being knocked over.

Her action led to her stumbling and, having the breath knocked from her body by the force of her fall, she could only continue to lie where she was as the rider galloped by, seemingly unaware or uncaring of the fact that he had almost ridden her down.

Beatrice caught only a glimpse of him as he passed, but she knew it was the wicked Marquis himself, riding as if the devil were after him. He was a big man, wrapped about by a black cloak, his iron-grey hair straggling and unkempt about his shoulders. An ugly creature by all accounts, his features thickened and coarsened by his excesses—though she herself had never caught more than a fleeting glimpse of him. He was a bruising rider, and she had sometimes seen him in the distance on her walks—but they were not acquainted. The Roade family did not move in his circles, nor he in theirs.

'That was not well done of you, sir,' Beatrice murmured as he and his horse disappeared into the darkness.

She rose to her feet a little unsteadily, her usual composure seriously disturbed by what had happened that night. It was certain that the Marquis was in a black mood, perhaps drunk, as the gossips said he often was. Beatrice shuddered as she thought of the young woman who had married him the previous year. How terrible to be trapped in marriage with such a monster!

What could have possessed her to do such a thing?

Beatrice had never met the young Marchioness, or even seen her out walking. As far as Beatrice knew, no one had seen much of her since the wedding. People said she hardly left the Abbey—some said she was too ashamed, some murmured of her being kept a prisoner by her wicked husband, others that she was ill…and there was little to wonder at in that, married to such a brute!

She could only have married him for his money. Everyone said it, and Beatrice was sure it must be the truth—but had the Marquis been the richest man in England, *she* would not have married such a monster!

Beatrice had stopped shaking. She resumed her walk at a more sensible pace, keeping her head up so that she was aware of what was in front of her. There was little to be heard but the howl of the wind, which was eerie and unpleasant.

She would be glad to be home!

'You're soaked to the skin, my love,' Nan said, fussing over her the moment she entered her father's house. 'We have been on the look for you this past hour or more. Whatever do you mean by worrying your poor father so?'

They progressed to the parlour, Beatrice having left her sodden cloak in the hall. She moved closer to the fire, holding her hands to the flames until she had stopped shivering, then went over to the large oak and upholstered Knole settee, carefully moving her aunt's embroidery before sitting down.

'Have I worried Papa?' Beatrice thought it improbable. Her father would most likely be in his study, working on one of his inventions—the marvellous, wholly useless objects he was forever wasting his time on, which he believed were going to restore his fortune one day. 'I think *you* were worried, Nan. Poor, dear Papa can hardly have noticed. Now, if I were not here for dinner—then he might begin to worry. Especially if it meant waiting for his meal.'

'Beatrice!' Nan scolded. 'Now that is unkind in you. I know your humour, my dear—but it sounds harsh in a young woman to be so cynical. It is little wonder that...' She broke off, biting her lip as she saw the look in her darling's eyes.

'Yes, I know I have driven them all away—all my suitors,' Beatrice said ruefully. 'I really should have taken Squire Rush, shouldn't I? He has three thousand a year, I dare say...but he has buried three wives and that brood of his was really too much!'

'There were others,' her aunt said. Mrs Nancy Willow was a widow in her early forties: a plump, comfortable, loving woman, who was extremely fond of her eldest niece. She had come to her brother's house only after her husband (a soldier turned adventurer) had died of a fever. She sometimes thought it would have been better if she had been there before her lovely but slightly bird-brained sister-in-law had died, but she and Eddie had been in India at the time. 'I understand there was a suitable admirer once...'

'And who told you that, aunt?'

Nan frowned. Beatrice rarely called her 'aunt' in just that way: she was clearly touching on a sore place.

'Well, well, it doesn't matter,' she said. 'But should another suitable young man come along…'

'I could not leave Papa,' Beatrice said at once. 'Besides, it will not happen. I am nearly at my last prayers.'

'Now that you are not!' Nan said. 'You have many qualities, Beatrice. A discerning man would know that the minute he laid eyes on you…'

'…and fall instantly in love with me?' Beatrice said, amused by her aunt's romantic notions. 'Only find me this suitor, Nan dearest—and, if he is not too dim-witted, which I think he may have to be, I will engage to do my best to snare him.'

'You and your wicked, wicked tongue,' her aunt said, smiling even as she shook her head. 'And as for not being able to leave your papa—you know that is not so. You were obliged to give up all thoughts of marriage when your mama fell ill. To have left your father then would have been careless in you—but my brother has been kind enough to offer me a home for the rest of my life…'

'Unless *you* receive an offer of marriage, Nan!'

Her aunt pulled a wry face. 'I could not be tempted. I am comfortable here, and here I shall stay. Since it does not take two of us to run this house, you are free to do as you wish…'

'Yes, I see that it makes a difference…' Beatrice looked serious. 'It might be better if I started to look for a position…Papa's funds are limited, and since…'

'He would never hear of it, and nor should I,' declared Nan roundly. 'If anyone should look elsewhere, it must be me.'

'No!' Beatrice spoke quickly. She had been afraid her aunt would take that attitude, which was why she had not spoken her thoughts aloud before this. 'You do not understand, Nan. I am not speaking of hiring myself out as a governess or a companion…I would only leave here if I could go back to Mrs Guarding's school as a teacher.'

Her aunt stared at her, eyes narrowing. 'Is that why you have been so long this afternoon?'

'No, indeed, for I have not yet spoken to Mrs Guarding about my idea. I went to see Ghislaine de Champlain, who, as I told you, is the French mistress there. We spent some time talking, and then had tea together in her room, which overlooks the river. It really was most pleasant.'

'You speak of Mademoiselle Champlain often—and of the time you spent at the school,' Nan said. 'Would it really make you happy to return there, dearest?'

'Yes, I think so,' Beatrice replied, smothering a sigh. It wasn't that she was unhappy with her life in her father's house, but she sometimes longed for some stimulating company—a friend she could sharpen her wits on now and then without feeling that she was either hurting or bewildering that friend.

She briefly remembered her long-dashed hopes, which had been destroyed when she was a girl of nineteen—just the same age as her sister was now!—but their situations had been very different. Olivia was in London enjoying a brilliant season, and engaged to one of the best 'catches' of the Season. For Beatrice there had been no Season, and only one suitor she might have taken—if he had asked. However, after toying with her hopes and affections for a whole month one summer, he had taken himself back off to London and proposed to an heiress!

'Pray do not look so sad, my love,' Nan said. 'Come, sit by the fire and let me dry your poor feet. You look as if you have had a tumble in the mud!'

'As a matter of fact, I have,' Beatrice said, forgetting her disappointments as she recalled what had happened to her that evening. 'I walked home through the Abbey grounds, Nan.'

'You never did!' Nan looked horrified. 'Never say that monster attacked you?'

'In a way,' Beatrice replied, then shook her head as Nan looked fit to faint. 'Oh, nothing like that. I heard something…a scream, I think…then this horse and rider came up out of the darkness and I was forced to throw myself out of his path. Had I not done so, I must have been crushed beneath the hooves of the horse. I am sure it was the Marquis himself, and in a fearful mood.'

Nan crossed herself instinctively. Neither she nor any member of her family were Catholics, but in a matter such as this, the action could be very comforting.

Beatrice laughed as she saw her aunt's reaction. 'I must admit to doing much the same as you when I heard the scream,' she admitted. 'It was the most horrifying sound imaginable…' She broke off as their one little maid came into the room, carrying a silver salver. 'Yes, Lily—what is it?'

'Bellows fetched this letter for you from the receiving office this afternoon, Miss Roade. It's from London.'

'Then it must be from Olivia,' Beatrice said, feeling a flicker of excitement. 'Perhaps it is an invitation to the wedding at last.'

The longcase clock in the hall was striking the hour of five as Beatrice took the sealed packet from her servant.

Beatrice had been anxiously awaiting the invitation since learning from her sister that she was about to become engaged to Lord Ravensden, the wealthy Lord Burton's heir. Not that Lord Burton's wealth was of any interest to his heir, who, according to rumour, already had far more money than any one person could possibly need.

Olivia had been adopted by their rich relatives when she was a child. She had been loved and petted by them ever since, living a very different life from her elder sister, who had been overlooked by Lord and Lady Burton when they agreed to take one of the children as their own.

The sisters' parting had devastated Beatrice, who, being the elder, had understood what was happening, and why. She had kept in touch by letter since the day Olivia was taken away, but they had met only twice since then, when her mother's sister-in-law had brought Olivia on brief visits. Having seen the engagement announced in *The Times*, which her papa continued to subscribe to despite his meagre funds,

Beatrice had expected to hear from her sister almost daily, and was beginning to think she was to be left out of the celebrations.

She ripped the small packet open eagerly, then read its contents three times before she could believe what she was seeing. It was not possible! Olivia must be funning her...surely she must? If this was not a jest...it did not bear thinking of!

'Is something the matter?' asked Nan. 'You look upset, Beatrice. Has something happened to your sister?'

'It is most distressing,' Beatrice said, sounding as shocked as she felt. 'I cannot believe this, Nan. Olivia writes to tell me that she will not now be marrying Lord Ravensden. She has decided she cannot like him sufficiently...and has told him of her decision.'

'You mean she has jilted him?' Nan stared at her in dismay. 'How could she? She will be ruined. Has she no idea of the consequences of her actions?'

'I think she must have.' Beatrice gave a little cry of distress as she read over the page something she had missed earlier. 'Oh, no! This is the most terrible news. Lord and Lady Burton have...disowned her. They say she has disgraced them, and they will no longer harbour a viper in their home...'

'That is a little harsh, is it not?' Nan wrinkled her brow. 'What she has done is wrong, no one could deny that—but I should imagine Olivia must have her reasons. She would not do such a thing out of caprice—would she?'

'No, of course not,' Beatrice defended her sister

loyally. 'We do not know each other well—but I am sure she is not so cruel.'

'What can have prevailed upon her to accept him if she did not mean to go through with the marriage?' Nan asked, shaking her head in wonder. Jilting one's fiancé was not something to be undertaken lightly—and a man as rich as Lord Ravensden into the bargain!

'She says she has realised that she cannot be happy as his wife,' Beatrice said, frowning over her sister's hurried scrawl. 'And that she was cruelly deceived in his feelings for her.'

'What will she do now?'

'Lord Burton has told her she has one week to leave his house—so she asks if she may come here.'

'Come here?' Nan stared at her in dismay. 'Does she realise how we go on here? She will find it very different to what she has been used to, Beatrice.'

'Yes, I fear she will,' Beatrice replied. 'However, I shall speak to Papa at once, and then, if he agrees, I shall write and tell her she is welcome in this house.'

'My brother will agree to whatever you suggest,' Nan said a little wryly. 'You must know that?'

Beatrice smiled, knowing that she always without fail managed to twist her father round her finger. He could refuse her nothing, for the simple reason that he was able to give her very little. Fortunately, Beatrice had a tiny allowance of her own, which came to her directly from a bequest left to her by her maternal grandmother, Lady Anne Smith.

Nan had given her a towel to dry herself, and Beatrice had used it to good effect. Her long hair was wild about her face, gleaming with reddish gold lights and giving her a natural beauty she had never noticed for herself. She handed the towel back to her aunt, and looked down at herself. Her gown was disgraceful, but her dear, forgetful papa would probably never notice.

'You realise Olivia will be an added burden on your father's slender income?' Nan warned. 'You have little enough for yourself as it is.'

'My sister will be destitute if we do not take her in,' Beatrice replied, frowning. 'I do not know whether they have cast her off without a penny—but it sounds as if they may have done so. It would be cruel indeed of me if I were to refuse to let her shelter in her own home.'

'Yes, and something *you* could never do,' Nan said warmly. 'I have no objections, my love. I only wish you to think before you leap—unlike my poor brother.'

'We shall manage,' Beatrice said, and left her aunt with a smile.

The smile was wiped out the instant she left the room. She had not mentioned anything to Nan, because it was still not clear to her exactly what her sister's rather terse words had meant—but clearly Lord Ravensden was not a man Olivia could love or respect. Indeed, if Beatrice was not mistaken, he was a hard, ruthless man who cared for little else but wealth and duty.

He had had the cold-hearted effrontery to tell one of his friends that he was marrying to oblige Lord Burton. Since the Burtons had no children of their own, the title and fortune would pass by entail to a distant cousin of Lord Burton. They had felt this was a little unfair on the daughter they had adopted, and so made their wishes known to Lord Burton's heir: it would please them if he were to marry the girl they had lavished with affection since she came to them.

Apparently, Lord Ravensden had proposed to Olivia, giving her the impression that he cared for her—and it was only by accident that she had learned the truth. It must have distressed her deeply!

No wonder she had declared herself unable to love him. If Beatrice were not much mistaken, it would push any woman to the limits to find a place in her heart for such an uncaring man.

She wished that she might have him at her mercy for five minutes! It would give her the greatest pleasure to tell him exactly what she thought of him.

Chapter Two

Beatrice fought her rising temper. She was slow to anger, but when something offended her strong sense of justice—as it did now—she could be awesome in her fury.

'If I could but get my hands on him!' she muttered furiously. 'He should see how it feels to be treated so harshly. I should make him suffer as he makes my poor sister.'

No, no, this would not do! She must appear calm and cheerful when speaking to Papa. He had so many worries, the poor darling. This burden must not be allowed to fall on his shoulders. As for the added strain on his slender income…well, it made the idea of her becoming a teacher at Mrs Guarding's school even more necessary. If she could support herself, her father would be able to spare a few guineas a year for Olivia to dress herself decently—though not, her sister feared, in the manner to which she had become accustomed.

Beatrice paused outside the door to her father's

study, then knocked and walked in without waiting
for an answer. It would have done her little good to
wait. Mr Roade was engrossed in the sets of charts
and figures on his desk, and would not have heard
her.

Like many men of the time, he was fascinated with
the sciences and the invention of all kinds of ingenious devices. Mr Roade was a great admirer of James
Watt, who had invented the miraculous steam engine,
which had begun to be used in so many different
ways. And, of course, Mr Robert Fulton, the
American, who had first shown his splendid steam
boat on the Seine in France in 1803. Bertram Roade
was certain that his own designs would one day make
him a great deal of money.

'Papa…' Beatrice said, walking up to glance over
his shoulder. He was working on an ingenious design
for a fireplace that would heat a water tank fitted behind it and provide a constant supply of hot water for
the household. It was a splendid idea, if only it would
work. Unfortunately, the last time her father had persuaded someone to manufacture the device for him,
it had overheated and blown apart, causing a great
deal of damage and costing more than a hundred
pounds, both to repair the hole in the kitchen wall and
to repay the money invested by an outraged partner.
Money they could ill afford.

'May I speak with you a moment?'

'I've nearly got the puzzle solved,' Mr Roade replied, not having heard her. 'I'm sure I know why it
exploded last time…you see the air became too hot

and there was nowhere for it to escape. Now, if I had a valve which let out the steam before it built up…'

'Yes, Papa, I'm sure you are right.'

Mr Roade looked up. Beatrice was usually ready to argue his theories with him; he was none too sure that his most recent was correct, and had hoped to discuss it with her.

'You wanted to talk to me, my dear?' His mild eyes blinked at her from behind the gold-rimmed spectacles that were forever in danger of falling off his nose. 'It isn't time for dinner—is it?'

'No, Papa, not quite. I came to see you about another matter.' She took a deep breath. 'Olivia wishes to come and stay with us. I would like your permission to write and tell her she will be welcome here for as long as she wishes.'

'Olivia…your sister?' He wrinkled his brow, as if searching for something he knew he must have forgotten. A smile broke through as he remembered. 'Ah yes, she is to be married. No doubt she wishes for a chance to have a little talk with her sister before her wedding.'

'No, Papa. It isn't quite like that. For reasons Olivia will make clear to us, she has decided not to marry Lord Ravensden. She wants to come and live here.'

'Are you sure you have that right, m'dear?' Mr Roade looked bewildered. 'I thought it was a splendid match—the man's as rich as Midas, ain't he?'

'That is a very apt description, Father. For if you remember, Midas was the King of Phrygia whose touch turned all to gold, and on whom Apollo bestowed the ears of an ass. Lord Ravensden must be a fool to have turned Olivia against him, but it seems, like that ancient king, he cares more for gold than the sweetness of a woman's touch.'

'Must be a fool then,' sighed a man who had loved his wife too much. 'Olivia is better off without him. Write at once and tell her we shall be delighted to have her home. Never did think it was a good idea for her to go away…your mother's idea. She wanted the chance of a better life for at least one of her daughters, and her poor sister-in-law was childless. Thank God the Burtons didn't pick you! I couldn't have borne that loss, Beatrice.'

'Thank you, Papa.' She smiled and kissed his forehead lovingly. 'You know, if you let all the steam go in one direction, it might pass through pipes before it finally escapes, and give some heat to the rooms. It would make the bedrooms so much warmer…as long as you could be sure the device that heats the water will not blow up like it did the last time.'

'Let the steam pass through pipes that run round the house.' Mr Roade looked at his daughter as if she had just lit a candle in his head. 'That's a very good notion, Beatrice. It might look a little ugly, I suppose. I wonder if anyone would put up with that for the convenience of feeling warm?'

'I certainly would,' Beatrice replied. 'Have you made any advances on the grate for a smokeless fire? Mine was smoking dreadfully again last night. It always does when the wind is from the east.'

'It might be a bird's nest,' her father said. 'I'll sweep the chimney out for you tomorrow.'

'Thank you, Papa, but I'm sure Mr Rowley will come up from the village if we ask him. It is not fitting for you to undertake such tasks.' *Besides which, her father would make a dreadful mess of it!*

'Fiddlesticks!' Mr Roade said. 'I'll do it for you first thing tomorrow.'

'Very well, Papa.'

Beatrice smiled as she went away. Her father would have forgotten about the smoking chimney five minutes after she left him, which mattered not at all, since she intended to send for the sweep when their one and only manservant next went down to Abbot Quincey to fetch their weekly supplies.

Seeing her father's manservant tending the candelabra on the lowboy in the hall, Beatrice smiled.

'Good evening, Bellows. It is a terrible evening, is it not?'

'We're in for a wild night, miss. Lily brought your letter?'

'Yes, thank you—and thank you for thinking to fetch it for me.'

'You're welcome, miss. I was in the market at Abbot Quincey and it was the work of a moment to see if any mail had come.'

She nodded and smiled, then passed on up the stairs.

It was possible to buy most goods from the general store in Abbot Quincey, which was much the largest of the four villages, and might even have been called a small town these days, but when anything more important was needed, they had to send Bellows to Northampton.

They were lucky to have Bellows, who was responsible for much of the work both inside the house and out. He had been with them since her father was a boy, and could remember when the Roade family had not been as poor as they were now.

For some reason all his own, Bellows was devoted to his master, and remained loyal despite the fact that he had not been paid for three years. He received his keep, and had his own methods of supplementing his personal income. Sometimes a plump rabbit or a pigeon found its way into the kitchen, and Beatrice suspected that Bellows was not above a little poaching, but she would never dream of asking where the gift came from. Indeed, she could not afford to!

Walking upstairs to her bedchamber to wash and change her clothes, Beatrice reflected on the strangeness of fate.

'My poor, dear sister,' she murmured. 'Oh, how could that rogue Ravensden have been so cruel?'

She herself had been deserted by a man who had previously declared himself madly in love with her, because, she understood, he had lost a small fortune at the gaming tables. She truly believed that Matthew Walters had intended to marry her, until he was ruined by a run of bad luck—he had certainly declared himself in love with her several times. Only her own caution had prevented her allowing her own feelings to show.

If she had given way to impulse, she would have been jilted publicly, which would have made her situation very much worse. At least *she* had been spared the scandal and humiliation that would have accompanied such an event.

Only Beatrice's parents had known the truth. Mrs Roade had held her while she wept out her disappointment and hurt…but that was a long time ago. Beatrice had been much younger then, perhaps a little naïve, innocent of the ways of the world. She had grown up very quickly after Matthew's desertion.

Since then, she had given little thought to marriage. She suspected that most men were probably like the one who had tried so ardently to seduce her. If she had been foolish enough to give in to his pleading…what then? She might have been ruined as well as jilted. Somehow she had resisted, though she had believed herself in love…

Beatrice laughed harshly. She was not such a fool as to believe in it now! She had learned to see the world for what it was, and knew that love was just something to be written of by dreamers and poets.

She had been taught a hard lesson, and now she had her sister's experience to remind her. If Olivia had been so hurt that she was driven to do something that she must know would ruin her in the eyes of the world… What a despicable man Lord Ravensden must be!

'Oh, you wicked, wicked man,' she muttered as she finished dressing and prepared to go down for dinner.

'I declare you deserve to be boiled in oil for what you have done!'

Lord Ravensden had begun to equate with the Marquis of Sywell in her mind. After her uncomfortable escape from injury that evening, Beatrice was inclined to think all the tales of *him* were true! And Lord Ravensden not much better.

A moment's reflection must have told her this was hardly likely to be true, for her sister would surely not even have entertained the idea of marriage to such a man. She was the indulged adopted daughter of loving parents, and had she said from the start that she could not like their heir, would surely have been excused from marrying him. It was the shock and the scandal of her having jilted her fiancé that had upset them.

However, Beatrice was not thinking like herself that evening. The double shock had made her somehow uneasy. She had the oddest notion that something terrible had either happened or was about to... something that might affect not only her and her sister's lives, but that of many others in the four villages.

The scream she had heard that night before the Marquis came rushing upon her...it had sounded evil. Barely human. Was it an omen of something?

After hearing it, she had come home to receive her sister's letter. Of course the scream could have nothing to do with that...and yet the feeling that the lives of many people were about to change was strong in her. A cold chill trickled down her spine as she wondered at herself. Never before had she experienced such a feeling…was it what people sometimes called a premonition?

Do not be foolish, Beatrice, she scolded herself mentally. Whatever would Papa say to such an illogical supposition?

Her dear papa would, she felt sure, give her a lecture upon the improbability of there being anything behind her feelings other than mere superstition, and of course he would be perfectly right.

Shaking her head, her hair now neatly confined in a sleek chignon, she dismissed her fears. There had been something about the atmosphere at the Abbey that night, but perhaps all old buildings with a history of mystery and violence would give out similar vibes if one visited them alone and at dusk.

If Beatrice had been superstitious, she would have said that her experience that evening was a warning— a sign from the ghosts of long dead monks—but she was not fanciful. She knew that what she had heard was most likely the cry of a wounded animal. Like the practical girl she was, she dismissed the idea of warnings and premonitions as nonsense, laughed at her own fancies and went downstairs to eat a hearty meal.

'Ravensden, you are an almighty fool, and should be ashamed of yourself! Heaven only knows how you are to extricate yourself from this mess.'

Gabriel Frederick Harold Ravensden, known as Harry to a very few, Ravensden to most, contemplated his image in his dressing-mirror and found himself disliking what he saw more than ever before. It was the morning of the thirty-first of October, and he was standing in the bedchamber of his house in Portland Place. What a damned ass he had been! He ought to be boiled in oil, then flayed until his bones showed through.

He grinned at the thought, wondering if it should really be the other way round to inflict the maximum punishment, then the smile was wiped clean as he remembered it was his damnable love of the ridiculous that had got them all into this mess in the first place.

'Did you say something, milord?' Beckett asked, coming into the room with a pile of starched neck-cloths in anticipation of his lordship's likely need. 'Will you be wearing the new blue coat this morning?'

'What? Oh, I'm not sure,' Harry said. 'No, I think something simpler—more suitable for riding.'

His man nodded, giving no sign that he thought the request surprising since his master had returned to town only the previous evening. He offered a fine green cloth, which was accepted by his master with an abstracted air. An unusual disinterest in a man famed for his taste and elegance in all matters of both dress and manners.

'You may leave me,' Harry said, after he had been helped into his coat, having tied a simple knot in the first neckcloth from the pile. 'I shall call you if I need you.'

'Yes, milord.'

Beckett inclined his head and retired to the dressing-room to sigh over the state of his lordship's boots after his return from the country, and Harry returned to the thorny problem on his mind.

He should in all conscience have told his distant cousin to go to hell the minute the marriage was suggested to him. Yet the beautiful Miss Olivia Roade Burton had amused him with her pouts and frowns. She had been *the* unrivalled success of the Season, and, having been thoroughly spoiled all her life, was inclined to be a little wayward.

However, her manners were so charming, her face so lovely, that he had been determined to win her favours. He had found the chase diverting, and thought he might like to have her for his wife—and a wife he must certainly have before too many months had passed.

'A damned, heavy-footed, crass idiot!' Harry muttered, remembering the letter he had so recently received from his fiancée. 'This business is of your own making…'

At four-and-thirty, he imagined he was still capable of giving his wife the son he so badly needed, but it would not do to leave it much later—unless he wanted the abominable Peregrine to inherit his own estate and that of Lord Burton. Both he and Lord Burton were agreed that such an outcome would not be acceptable to either of them—though at the moment they were agreeing on little else. Indeed, they had parted in acrimony. Had Harry not been a gentleman, he would probably have knocked the man down. He frowned as he recalled their conversation of the previous evening.

'An infamous thing, sir,' Harry had accused. 'To abandon a girl you have lavished with affection. I do not understand how you could turn her out. Surely you will reconsider?'

'She has been utterly spoilt,' Lord Burton replied. 'I have sent her to her family in Northamptonshire. Let her see how she likes living in obscurity.'

'Northamptonshire of all places! Good grief, man, it is the back of beyond, and must be purgatory for a young lady of fashion, who has been used to mixing in the best circles. Olivia will be bored out of her mind within a week!'

'I shall not reconsider until she remembers her duty to me,' Lord Burton had declared. 'I have cut off her allowance and shall disinherit her altogether if she does not admit her fault and apologise to us both.'

'I think that it is rather we who should apologise to her.'

After that, their conversation had regrettably gone downhill.

Harry was furious. Burton's conduct was despicable—and he, Harry Ravensden, had played a major part in the downfall of a very lovely young woman!

A careless remark in a gentleman's club, overheard by some malicious tongue—and he imagined he could guess the owner of that tongue! If he were not much mistaken, it was his cousin Peregrine Quindon who had started the vicious tale circulating. It was a wicked piece of mischief, and Peregrine would hear from him at some point in the future!

Olivia had clearly been hurt by some other young lady's glee in the fact that her marriage was, after all, merely one of convenience, that despite her glittering Season, and being the toast of London society, her bridegroom was marrying her only to oblige her adopted father. She had reacted in a very natural way, and had written him a stilted letter, telling him that she had decided she could not marry him, which he had received only on his return to town—by which time the scandal had broken and was being whispered of all over London.

Harry cursed the misfortune that had taken him from town. He had been summoned urgently to his estates in the north, a journey there and back of several days. Had he been in London, he might have seen Olivia, explained that he did indeed have a very high regard for her, and was honoured that she had accepted him—as he truly was.

Perhaps he had not fallen in love in the true romantic sense—but Harry did not really believe in that kind of love. He had experienced passion often enough, and also a deep affection for his friends, but never total, heart-stopping love.

He enjoyed the company of intelligent women. His best friend's wife was an exceptional woman, and he was very fond of Lady Dawlish. He had often envied Percy his happy home life, but had so far failed to find a lady he could admire as much as Merry Dawlish, who laughed a lot and seemed to enjoy life hugely in her own inimitable way. Even so, he *had* felt something for Olivia, and he had certainly not intended the tragedy that his carelessness had caused. Indeed, it grieved him that she had been put in such a position, for without fortune and friends to stand by her, she was ruined.

So what was he going to do about it? Having just returned from the country, he had little inclination to return there—and to Northamptonshire! Nothing interesting ever happened in such places.

Harry's besetting sin was that he was easily bored. Indeed, he was often plagued by a soul-destroying tedium, which had come upon him when his father's death forced him to give up the army life he had enjoyed for a brief period, and return to care for his estates. He was a good master and did not neglect his land or his people, but he was aware of something missing in his life.

He preferred living in town, where he was more likely to find stimulating company, and would not have minded so much if Olivia had gone to Bath or Brighton, but this village...what was it called? Ah yes, Abbot Giles. It was bound to be full of dull-witted gentry and lusty country wenches.

Harry's eye did not brighten at the thought of buxom wenches. He was famed for his taste in cyprians, and the mistresses he had kept whenever it suited him had always possessed their full measure of both beauty and wit. He believed the one thing that had prevented him from giving his whole heart to Olivia was that she did not seem to share his love of the ridiculous. She had found some of his remarks either hurtful or bewildering. Harry thought wistfully that it would be pleasant to have a woman by one's side who could give as good as she got, who wasn't afraid to stand up to him.

'What an odd character you are to be sure,' Harry told his reflection. It was a severe fault in him that he could not long be pleased by beautiful young women, unless they were also amusing.

Harry frowned at his own thoughts. It was not as if he were hiding some secret tragedy. His mother was still living, and the sweetest creature alive—but she had not been in love with his father, nor his father with her. Both had carried on separate lives, taking and discarding lovers without hurting the other. Indeed, they had been the best of friends. Harry believed he must be like his mother, who seemed not to treat anything seriously, and was besides being the sweetest, the most provoking of females.

No matter! He was a man of his word. He had given his word to Olivia, and the fact that she had jilted him made no difference. He must go after her, try to persuade her that he was not so very terrible. As his wife, she would be readmitted to the society that had cast her off—and that surely must be better than the fate which awaited her now.

'Beckett…' he called, making up his mind suddenly. 'Put up a change of clothing for me. I am going out of town for a few days.'

'Yes, milord,' said his valet, coming in. 'May one inquire where we are going?'

'You are going nowhere,' Harry replied with an odd little smile. 'And if anyone asks, you have no idea where I am...'

'Come in, dearest,' Beatrice said, meeting her sister at the door. It was some six days since she had received Olivia's letter, and her heart was pained by the look of tiredness and near despair in Olivia's face. Oh, that rogue, Ravensden! He should be hung, drawn and quartered for what he had done. 'You look cold, my love. Was the journey very tiresome?'

The road from London to Northampton was good, and could be covered easily enough in a day, but the country roads which led to Abbot Giles were far from ideal. Olivia had travelled down by one of the public coaching routes the previous day, and had been forced to find another conveyance in Northampton to bring her on. All she had been able to hire was an obliging carter, who had offered to take both her and her baggage for the sum of three shillings. A journey which must have shaken her almost rigid! And must also have been terrifying to a girl who had previously travelled in a well-sprung carriage with servants to care for her every whim.

How could the Burtons have sent her all this way alone? Anything might have happened to Olivia. It was as if her adoptive parents had abandoned all care for her along with their responsibility. The very least they might have done was to send her home in a carriage! Their heartlessness made Beatrice boil with anger, but she forced herself to be calm. It did not matter now! Her sister was here and safe, though desperately weary.

'Beatrice...' Olivia's voice almost broke. Clearly she had been wondering what her reception would be, and Beatrice's concerned greeting had almost overset her. 'I am so very sorry to bring this trouble on you.'

'Trouble? What trouble?' Beatrice asked. 'It is with the greatest pleasure that I welcome my sister to this house. We love you, Olivia. You could never be a trouble to me or your family...' She smiled and kissed Olivia's cheek. 'Come and meet Aunt Nan, dearest. Our father is busy at the moment. We try not to disturb him when he is working, but you will meet him later. He has asked me to tell you how pleased he is to have you home again.'

At this the sweet, innocent face of Miss Olivia crumpled, the tears spilling out of her bright blue eyes.

'Oh, how kind you are,' she said, fumbling for her kerchief in the reticule she carried on her wrist. She was fashionably dressed, though her pelisse was sadly splashed with mud, and the three trunks of personal belongings she had brought with her on the carter's wagon would seem to indicate that the Burtons had not cast her out without a rag to her back. 'I know you must think me wicked...or at the very least foolish.'

'I think nothing of the kind,' Beatrice said, leading her into the tiny back parlour, in which a welcoming fire was burning. It was usually not lit until the evening, neither Beatrice nor her aunt having time to sit much during the day, but this was a special occasion, and the logs they were using had been a gift from Jaffrey House, sent down specially by their very wealthy and illustrious neighbour the Earl of Yardley.

The Earl had a daughter named Sophia by his second marriage, of whom Beatrice imagined he was fond. The girl was near Olivia's own age, and very striking, with black hair and bright eyes. Beatrice knew her of course, though they seldom met in a social way.

Mr Roade did not often entertain, nor did he accept many invitations, but the Earl's family were seen about the village, and Beatrice was sufficiently well acquainted with Lady Sophia to stop and speak for a few minutes whenever they met. She thought now that it was a pity her father had turned down some of the kind invitations the Earl had sent them over the years. It would have been nice for Olivia to have made a friend of Sophia Cleeve.

'My dear Olivia,' Nan said, bustling in. She was wearing a mob cap over her light brown hair, and a dusting apron protected her serviceable gown. 'Forgive me for not being here to greet you. I was upstairs turning out the bedrooms. We have only the one maid, besides the kitchen wench, and it would be unfair to expect poor Lily to do everything herself.'

Olivia looked amazed at the idea of her aunt having been busy working in the bedrooms, then recollected herself, blushed and seemed awkward as she went forward to kiss Nan's cheek.

'Forgive me,' she said. 'I fear I have caused extra work for you.'

'Well, yes, I must admit that you have,' Nan said, never one to hide the truth. 'However, I dare say the room needed a good turn-out—it was your mother's, you know, and has not...'

'Nan doesn't mean that you are a bother to us,' Beatrice said as she saw her sister's quick flush. 'The room you have been given was our mother's private sitting-room, not her bedroom—that is where she died, of course, and I felt it might distress you to sleep there.'

'I was about to tell Olivia that,' Nan said. 'We've been waiting for the bed to arrive—it was ordered from Northampton, but arrived only this morning on the carter's wagon. Had we not needed to wait, your room would have been ready days ago.'

'It was time we had a new bed,' Beatrice said smoothly, with a quick frown at her aunt. 'The one we have in the guest room, which is at the back of the house and depressingly dark, is broken in the struts which support the mattress. It is still there, of course, though since no one ever comes to stay, it does not matter...'

'I see I have caused a great deal of trouble,' Olivia said. 'You have been put to considerable expense on my account.'

'Nothing of the sort,' replied Beatrice. 'Take off your bonnet and pelisse, dearest. I shall ring for tea—unless you would like to go straight up to your room?'

Olivia looked as if she would dearly like to escape, but forced herself to smile at them.

'Tea would be very nice,' she said. 'I have a few guineas left out of the allowance my...Lord Burton made me earlier in the season, but I did not care to waste them on refreshments at the inns we passed. Besides, I was in a hurry to reach you. I shall give you what money I have, Beatrice, and you may use it for expenses as you see fit.'

'Well, as to that, we shall see how we go on,' Beatrice said, and reached for the bell.

It was answered so promptly that she imagined Lily had been hovering outside in the hall—a habit her mistress disliked but not sufficiently to dismiss her. Like Bellows, Lily did not complain if her wages were late, though Beatrice paid the girl herself, and usually on time.

'Tea please, Lily.' She turned to her sister as the maid went out again. 'That's right, dearest, sit by the fire and you will soon feel better. We shall talk properly later. For now, I want you to tell me all the news from London...that is, if you can bear to? We hear so little here, you know, except when neighbours return from a visit to town.'

'You know of course that the Prince was declared Regent earlier this year?' Olivia looked at her doubtfully.

'Yes, dearest. Papa takes *The Times*. I am aware that trade has been bad, because of Napoleon's blockade of Europe, and that unemployment is high. I didn't mean that sort of news…a little gossip perhaps, something that is setting the Ton by its ears?'

Olivia gave a little giggle, her face losing some of its strain.

'Oh, that sort of news…what can I tell you? Oh yes, apart from all the usual scandals, there is something rather exciting going on at the moment…'

She had taken off her outer clothing now, revealing a pretty travelling-gown of green velvet.

'There is a new French modiste in town. She is the protégée of Madame Marie-Anne Coulanges, who was herself once apprenticed to Rose Bertin—who, you must know, was a favourite dressmaker to Queen Marie Antoinette.' Olivia paused for effect. 'They say Madame Coulanges was once a friend of Madame Félice's mama, and that is why she has taken her up—anyway, she presented her to her clients, and Madame Félice has taken the town by storm.'

Beatrice smiled as she saw the glow in her sister's eyes. Her little ruse had worked, and Olivia had lost her shyness.

'How old is Madame Félice?'

'Oh, not more than two-and-twenty at the most, I would think. She has pretty, pale hair, but she keeps it hidden beneath a rather fetching cap most of the time, and her eyes are a greenish blue. I think she might be beautiful if she dressed in gowns as elegant as those she makes for her clientele, but of course it would not be correct for her to do so. Though no one really knows much about her…she is something of a mystery.'

'How exciting. Tell me, dearest, is she very clever at making gowns?'

'Oh, yes, very. Everyone, simply everyone, is dying to get their hands on at least one of her gowns—but she is particular about who she dresses. Would you believe it? I heard she actually turned down the Marchioness of Rossminster, because she had no style! She will dress only those women she thinks can carry off her fabulous gowns. Of course they are the most beautiful clothes you have ever seen. No one can touch her for elegance and quality.' Olivia dropped her gaze. 'She was very nice to me. I have one of her gowns and she was to have made a part of my wedding trousseau...' Her cheeks fired up as she spoke. 'I have the gown she made for me in my trunks. I will show it to you later, if you wish?'

'I would like very much to see it,' Beatrice said. 'If it is as smart as the one you are wearing...it must be lovely.'

She had been about to say that her sister would have little opportunity to wear her beautiful clothes now, but bit the words back before she was so cruel as to remind Olivia of all that she had lost.

'We shall talk of other things later,' she said. 'There is much to talk about, Olivia—but we have time enough.'

'Yes,' Olivia said, losing the sparkle she had gained when telling her sister the news about Madame Félice. 'Of course, London is thin of company now. I believe the Regent is to leave London for Brighton at the end of this month... Oh, that is today, isn't it?'

Her mouth drooped as though she were remembering that she would no longer be a part of the extravagant set that surrounded the Prince Regent and privileged society. However, the arrival of the tea-tray and the delicious cakes that Beatrice had spent the morning baking brought her out of the doldrums a little.

'These are delightful,' she said, choosing from the pretty silver cake-basket and chewing a small, nutty biscuit. 'Quite as good as anything I have tasted anywhere.'

'Beatrice made those for you herself,' Nan said. 'They are Bosworth Jumbles, but Beatrice adds her own special ingredients to the recipe, which some say was picked up on the battlefield at Bosworth in 1485, hence its name. Your sister will make some lucky gentleman an excellent wife one day.'

'Did you really make them?' Olivia stared at her. 'You are so clever. I have never cooked anything in my life.'

'I can teach you if you like, and there is a very good manual by Mrs Rundle, called *Domestic Cookery*,' Beatrice said. 'I know it may seem tedious at first, Olivia, but living in the country has its compensations. We have nut trees and fruit from our own orchards, berries from the kitchen gardens, and we make our own jams and preserves. It can be a rewarding way to pass the time.'

'Yes, of course.' Olivia lifted her head, as though wanting to show she was not above such things. 'Yes, I am sure I shall soon settle in…'

Chapter Three

Beatrice took her sister up to her room half an hour later. She had offered to help her unpack her trunks, being reasonably certain that Olivia had never had to do so for herself before. Olivia had accepted and was now showing her some of the lovely clothes she had brought with her.

'These are only a few of my gowns,' she told Beatrice. 'I left some of the more elaborate ones behind. I shall scarcely need the gown I wore to be presented to the Regent at my coming out…or most of my ballgowns. Lady Burton did say she would send them on…' Olivia blinked rapidly to stave off the tears gathering in her eyes. 'She was kinder than Lord Burton…she said she would be prepared to forgive me, but that he was adamant the connection must be cut.'

'Well, perhaps he will relent in time…'

'No.' Olivia's lovely face was pale but proud. 'I do not wish to return to their house…ever. What I did was right, and I shall not grovel to be forgiven.'

The subject was dropped, for Beatrice did not like to see her sister so upset. Instead, she exclaimed over the gowns they were unpacking, especially the one made by Madame Félice, the extraordinary French modiste who had suddenly arrived in town some months earlier.

'It is very lovely,' she said, holding it against herself. The jewel green of the fine silk actually became Beatrice very well, setting off the colour of her hair, and was, of course, far more stylish than anything she had ever made for herself. 'No wonder everyone is so anxious to order from her—but does no one know where she worked before she came to London? Was it in Paris?'

'No one seems to know anything about her before she set up her shop…but they whisper that she is the mistress of a very rich man.'

'Oh, why do they say that?' Beatrice looked at her curiously.

'They say she brought money to Madame Coulanges's salon. It stands to reason. She must have a protector—where else would she get the money to set herself up in a fashionable establishment? If she had no money, she would be desperate to take any order…'

'Yes, I see the reasoning behind such gossip,' Beatrice replied. She frowned. Her education had been to say the least unusual, and her opinions were strong in such matters. 'But I do not see that the money must have come from a protector. Why cannot a woman be successful for herself, without the aid of a man? Why must everyone always assume the worst? There could be other reasons why she was able to bring money to Madame Coulanges. Perhaps she inherited some from a wealthy relative, and used it to set herself up in business. She might even have won it in a game of cards.'

'It is intriguing, isn't it?' Olivia said. 'I dare say her story will come out eventually—and that will set the tongues wagging again. For the moment, she can do no wrong—no one would think the worse of her for having a wealthy protector. She does not mix in society, other than to dress her wealthy clientele, of course, and could never hope to marry into a good family.'

'Alas, I fear you are right. We are all too much governed by convention. I am sure we shall hear more in time,' Beatrice said. 'The news may be slow in filtering through to the four villages, but it arrives in due course.'

'The four villages…' Olivia stared at her in bewilderment. 'I am not sure what you mean?'

Beatrice laughed. 'Oh, I am so used to that way of speaking of our neighbours. I mean the villages that lie to the north, south, east and west of Steepwood Abbey, of course: Abbot Quincey, which is really almost a small market town these days, Steep Abbot and Steep Ride…which is tiny and remote, and lies to the south of the Abbey—and our own.'

'Oh, yes, the Abbey. We passed by its outer walls on our journey here. Is life affected much by what goes on there?'

Once again, Beatrice laughed. 'We have a wicked Marquis all our own,' she said. 'The stories about him would take me all night to relate, but I will only say that I cannot vouch for any of them, since I have scarcely met him—except for the night he almost knocked me down as he rushed past on his horse, of course.'

'That was very rude of him,' Olivia said. 'If he is so unpleasant I do not wonder that you do not care to know him.'

'No one cares to know the Marquis of Sywell—except perhaps the Earl of Yardley. I am not sure, but I think there is some story about them having belonged to the same wild set years ago, before either of them had come into their titles. It was a long time ago, of course. Before the old Earl, who was the seventh to bear the title, I believe, banished his son to France, lost the Abbey, which had been in his family for generations…since the middle of the sixteenth century…to the present owner, and then killed himself.'

'Indeed?' Olivia looked intrigued. 'Why was the son banished? Oh, pray do tell me, Beatrice—was it because of a love affair?'

'Have you heard the story?'

Olivia shook her head. 'No, but I should like to if it is romantic…to die for love is so—so…'

'Foolish,' Beatrice supplied dryly. 'Perch on the window-seat, Olivia, and I will sit here on this stool. It is a long story and must be explained properly or you will become confused with all the different Earls and not know who I mean.'

Olivia nodded, her face alight with eagerness. For the first time since her arrival, she seemed truly to have forgotten her unfortunate situation. Beatrice took heart, determined to make her story as interesting and entertaining as she could for her sister's sake.

'Well, the present Earl of Yardley, the eighth if I am right, was not born to inherit the title or the estate. His name when this story begins was Thomas Cleeve, and his family was no more than a minor branch of the Yardleys. It was then that he and his cousin (the last Earl before this one: I told you it was complicated!), some folk say, were both members of the rather loose set to which Lord George Ormiston belonged—he, to make things plain, is our wicked Marquis of today.'

'Yes, I see. He is now the Marquis of Sywell and he owns the Abbey,' Olivia said. 'Please do go on.'

'Lucinda Beattie, the spinster sister of Matthew Beattie, who was our previous vicar and died in…oh, I think it was eleven years ago…told our mother that Thomas Cleeve was disappointed in love as a young man and went off to India to make his fortune. That part was undoubtedly true, for he returned a very wealthy man. I know that he married twice and returned a widower in 1790 with his four children (twin boys of fourteen years, Lady Sophia, who I dare say you will meet, and his elder son, Marcus). He built Jaffrey House on some land he bought from his

cousin Edmund, then the seventh Earl of Yardley...
Are you following me?'

'Yes, of course. What happened to the romantic
Earl?' Olivia asked, impatient for Beatrice to begin
his tale. 'Why did he banish his son—and what was
his son called?'

'His son was Rupert, Lord Angmering, and I believe *he* was very romantic,' Beatrice said with a
smile. 'He went off to do the Grand Tour, and met a
young Frenchwoman, with whom he fell desperately
in love. It was in the autumn of 1790, I understand,
that he returned and informed his father he meant to
marry her. When the Earl forbade it on pain of dis-
inheritance, because she was a Catholic, he chose
love—and was subsequently banished to France.'

Olivia was entranced, her eyes glowing. 'What
happened—did he marry his true love?'

'No one really knows for certain. Some of the older
villagers say he would definitely have done so, for he
was above all else a man of honour, others doubt
it...but nothing can be proved, for the unfortunate
Lord Angmering was killed in the bread riots in
France...'

'Oh the poor man—to be thrown off by his father...' Olivia's cheeks were flushed as the similarity
to her own story struck her. 'But you said his father
killed himself?'

'As I have heard it told, the Earl was broken-
hearted, and when the confirmation of his son's death
reached him in 1793, he went up to town, got terribly
drunk and lost everything he owned to his friend the

Marquis of Sywell at the card tables. Afterwards, he called for the Marquis's duelling pistols and before anyone knew what he intended, shot himself—in front of the Marquis and his butler—the same one who remains in Sywell's employ today.'

'It was sad end to his story, but it had a kind of poetic justice—do you not think so?' Olivia asked. 'He blamed himself for the loss of his son and threw away all that had been precious to him...'

'It may be romantic to you,' Beatrice replied with a naughty look, 'but it meant that the people of the four villages have had to put up with the wicked Marquis ever since. And according to local legend, there was a time when no woman was safe from him. He has been accused of all kinds of terrible things...including taking part in pagan rites, which may or may not have involved him and his friends in cavorting naked in the woods. Some people say the men wore animal masks on their heads and chased their...women, who were naturally not the kind you or I would ever choose to know.'

'No? Surely not? You are funning me!' Olivia laughed delightedly as her sister shook her head and assured her every word was true. 'It sounds positively gothic—like one of those popular novels that has everyone laughing in public and terrified in private.'

'Dear Mrs Radcliffe.' Beatrice smiled. '*The Mysteries of Udolpho* was quite my favourite. How amusing her stories are to be sure. What you say is right, Olivia...but it is not quite as funny when you have to live near such a disreputable man.'

Olivia nodded. 'No, I suppose it would be uncomfortable. Tell me, did the present Earl inherit his title from the one who banished his son and killed himself?'

'Yes. After the death of the Earl and his son Lord Angmering there was no one else left—or at least, if Rupert left an heir no one has heard of him to this very day.' Beatrice shook her head. 'No, I am very sure there was no child. An exhaustive search was made at the time, I have no doubt, and no record of a marriage or a child was found. Had it not been so, the title could not legally have passed to Thomas Cleeve, and it was all done according to the laws of England, I am very sure.'

Olivia nodded, acknowledging the truth of this. 'Besides, even if Lord Angmering had by some chance had a son…what would there be for him to inherit if his grandfather had lost all his money gambling?'

'Nothing in law, I suppose. You may be certain, had there been an heir, he would have come forward long ago, to claim his title and anything that might still belong to his family.'

'I suppose so…' Olivia was reluctant to let her romantic notion go, and smiled at her sister. 'That was a fascinating story. I wish someone would come back to the villages and declare himself Lord Angmering's son, don't you?'

Beatrice threw back her head and laughed heartily. 'I should never have told you—you will be expecting something to happen, and I do assure you it will not.

No, my dearest sister, I must disappoint you. I think the Earl of Yardley is secure in his title—and since his fortune is his own, he does not need to prove anything.'

'No, of course not.' Olivia stood up and went to embrace her sister. 'Thank you for telling me that story—and thank you for taking me in with such kindness.'

'You are my sister. I have always loved you. I would not have wished for you to be in such circumstances—but I am happy to have you living here with us.' Beatrice looked at her intently. 'You have not regretted your decision to jilt Lord Ravensden?'

'I regret that I was deceived into accepting him,' Olivia replied, 'but I do not regret telling him that I would not marry him.'

'What did he say to you?'

'I—I wrote to him,' Olivia said, her cheeks pink. 'I could not have faced him, Beatrice. I was so…angry.'

'What made you change your mind about marrying him, dearest?'

'I was told by a rather spiteful girl…a girl I had hitherto thought of as my friend…that Ravensden was marrying me only to oblige Lord Burton, that he wanted me only as a brood mare, because he desperately needs an heir. He is past his green days, and no doubt imagined I should be grateful for the offer…'

'He could not have been so cold-blooded?' Beatrice was shocked. 'My dearest sister! I believe you have had a fortunate escape. Had you not learned of his callousness before your wedding, you would have been condemned to a life of misery at this brute's hands.'

Olivia took her hands eagerly. 'You do understand my feelings,' she cried, her lovely eyes glowing. 'I was afraid you would think me capricious—but when I realised what he had done...I realised I could not love him. In fact, I saw that I had been misled by his charm and his compliments.'

'His charm?' Beatrice frowned. How could this be? It did not equate with the monster she had pictured. 'Was he so very charming?'

'Oh, yes, I suppose so. Everyone thought so...but I found his humour a little harsh. Though of course he was toadied to by almost everyone because of his wealth, and the Regent thinks him a great wit.'

'It seems to me the man was eaten up by his own conceit,' said Beatrice, who had never met him in her life. 'I see what it was—you were the catch of the Season and Burton's heir. He wanted the fortune...'

'But most of it will be his anyway,' Olivia said, frowning. 'That is what is so particularly cruel. He had no need to oblige his cousin. Why propose to me if he did not care for me in the least?'

Beatrice saw that her sister was not so indifferent as she pretended. Whether it was her heart or her pride that was most affected, it was equally painful for her.

'Well, we shall talk of this again,' she said. 'Do not distress yourself, dearest. You will have no need to meet Lord Ravensden again, so you may forget him. One thing is certain, he will not dare to follow you here…'

Beatrice spent a restless night dreaming of disinherited heirs, pagan orgies and—inexplicably!—a man being boiled in oil. She woke early, feeling tired and uneasy. Which served her right for spending a great deal of the evening recounting stories of the wicked Marquis, making them as lurid as possible for her sister—who was clearly of a romantic disposition.

Had Olivia been other than she was, she might have settled for the comfort marriage to Lord Ravensden could provide, but she could not help her nature, and Beatrice could not but think she had made the right decision.

'Let me but get my hands on that creature,' muttered Beatrice.

Oh, he should pay, he should pay!

Olivia was certainly trying to settle to her new life, and had so far been very brave, but it was bound to be hard for her. They must all do whatever they could to lift her spirits in the coming months.

Such were Beatrice's thoughts as she left her father's house that morning, the day after her sister's arrival. It was the beginning of November now and a little misty. Mindful of the cold, she had wrapped up well in her old grey cloak, which was long past its best.

She had decided to visit the vicarage, her intention to ask the Reverend Edward Hartwell and his wife to dine with them the next week. She would also send a message to Ghislaine, and beg her to come if she could. It was the best she could offer Olivia by way of entertainment, though obviously not what she was accustomed to... The sound of hooves pounding on the hard ground gave her a little start.

She paused, watching as horse and rider came towards her at a gentle canter. This was not the bruising rider who had almost knocked her down a week ago, but a stranger. She had never seen this gentleman in Abbot Giles or any of the four villages.

His clothes proclaimed him a man of fashion, even though he was dressed simply for riding. As he came nearer, she could see that he looked rather attractive, even handsome, his features striking. He had a straight nose, a firm, square chin, and what she thought must be called a noble bearing.

Beatrice realised the rider was stopping. He swept off his hat to her, revealing hair as thick and glossy as it was dark—almost as black as a raven's wing. He wore it short, brushed carelessly forward in an artfully artless way that gave him a dashing air. He might have come straight from the pages of Sir Walter Scott's poems, some noble creature of ancient lineage.

'Good morning, ma'am,' the stranger said, giving her a smile that was at the same time both sweet and unnerving in that it seemed to challenge. 'I wonder if I could trouble you to ask for directions? I have lost my way in the mist.'

'Of course. If I can help, sir.' Beatrice glanced up into his eyes. So startlingly blue that she was mesmerised. Goodness! What a remarkable man he was to be sure. 'Are you looking for somewhere in particular?'

'I do not know the name of the house,' he replied. 'But I am looking for the Roade family of Abbot Giles…Miss Olivia Roade Burton in particular.'

An icy chill gripped Beatrice's heart. Surely it was not possible? She had been so sure that Lord Ravensden would not dare to come here. Yet who else could it be? This man was handsome, his smile charming—and *now* she looked at him properly, she could see that he was arrogant, too sure of himself and proud. A despicable man. Indeed, she wondered that she had not noticed it immediately.

Why had he come here? Beatrice's mind was racing frantically. If this was truly Olivia's jilted suitor, he must not be allowed to take her sister by surprise.

'Ah yes,' she said. 'I do know of the family—but I fear you are travelling in the wrong direction.'

'Is this not the village of Abbot Giles?'

'Has Ben turned the milestones round again? It really is too bad of him!' Beatrice said in a rallying tone. 'He will do it, poor foolish fellow. It all comes from the bang on the head, but it is most confusing for visitors.'

'Pray tell me,' the stranger said, a gleam in those devastating blue eyes. 'How did poor Ben come to receive such a damaging blow to the head?'

'It is a long story,' Beatrice said hastily. She pointed to the open gates of the Abbey grounds. 'If you follow that road, the narrow lane there, then keep on past the lake and turn to your right near the ruined chapel, you will come to the village in time.'

'That sounds a little complicated…'

'It is a short cut, any other route would take you miles out of your way.'

'I see, then I shall follow your instructions. Thank you, ma'am.'

The stranger looked at her hard for a moment, then set out in the direction she had indicated. Beatrice waited until he had been swallowed up by the mist, then turned on her heel and ran back to her home.

The visit to the Reverend Hartwell could wait. Olivia must be alerted to the fact that her abominable fiancé had come in search of her!

Beatrice found her sister at breakfast. A few pertinent questions confirmed her suspicions—no two men could have such blue eyes!

'I fear Lord Ravensden has come in search of you,' she told the startled and disbelieving Olivia. 'I managed to send him on a fool's errand—but he will find his way here before long.'

'I shall not receive him!'

'I do not see how you can refuse,' Nan said, frowning at both sisters. 'Beatrice, it was very wrong of you to misdirect his lordship. If he has come all this way to see your sister, he must be hoping to repair the breach between them.' Her gaze rested on the agitated Olivia. 'Are you sure you were not misled by the spiteful tongue of a jealous rival? Is it not possible that your fiancé has some real regard for you?'

Olivia was silent, then said, 'I do not think it

can be so, aunt. And even if it were…I have realised that my own feelings were mistaken. I cannot marry him.'

'For the sake of decency you should at least receive him.'

Olivia looked at her sister. 'Must I, Beatrice?'

Beatrice had had time to reflect. 'I think perhaps Nan is right. It will be awkward for you, dearest, but a few minutes should suffice—and Nan will stay with you.'

'Will you not be with me, Beatrice?'

'I think it best if Lord Ravensden does not see me,' Beatrice said, feeling slightly guilty now. Olivia's ex-fiancé must have ridden hard to reach the village so soon after her departure, and she had added an un-necessary detour to his journey. 'Be brave, dearest. Be dignified, and positive—and then you need never see him again.'

'Where are you going?' Olivia asked as she turned to leave.

'To complete my errand,' Beatrice replied. 'I must be swift. It would not do for Lord Ravensden to see me when he calls.'

She laughed, turned and walked quickly out of the house. Lord Ravensden was going to be very angry when he discovered the trick that had been played on him, and indeed he had every right. It would be much better if he never learned that the woman who had sent him on a wild goose chase was sister to the one he sought!

*   *   *

'Now what game might she be playing?' murmured Lord Ravensden to himself. 'Do my instincts serve me right, or have my wits been addled by the mist?'

Harry had the oddest feeling that the woman he had met a few minutes earlier had deliberately sent him in the wrong direction. Her story had been plausible, but somehow he had not quite believed in the village idiot who had a habit of turning milestones so that the arrow pointed the wrong way—dashed heavy things, milestones! Yet why should a young woman— and one who looked reasonably sane!—go out of her way to deceive him?

He had previously enquired the way of a man who could, in the politest terms, only be called a country bumpkin. The fellow had rambled on in some unintelligible tongue so that Harry had begun to wonder if he had inadvertently crossed the channel in the night, leaving him none the wiser as to his whereabouts. He had seen no signs of any kind for miles on end, and had been on the point of knocking at a house in the village he had just passed, when he had seen the young woman walking towards him through the mist.

She had looked to be gently born. Somewhat plainly dressed perhaps, but not without a pleasing air. He had judged her to be the wife of an impoverished squire—or perhaps the parson, since she seemed to be heading in the direction of the church he had passed some way back. Her speech had been soft, cultured, gentle on the ear. He had followed her directions, because he could not see why such a woman should lie to him.

Some ten minutes or so later, he was beginning to think he should have followed his instincts and continued straight ahead. It was difficult to get his bearings in this damned mist. He appeared to be following a narrow track, little more than a footpath, and on private land by the looks of it—that dark shape in the distance must surely be the Abbey that lay at the heart of the four villages. He was just considering whether or not he should turn back when he saw someone coming towards him.

The gentleman, for he was surely that, though carelessly dressed, was wearing a shabby black cloak which flapped in the wind. His hair was thinning at the temples—he wore no hat despite the inclement weather—and perched on the end of his nose was a pair of gold-rimmed spectacles.

'Good morning, sir,' Harry called. 'May I have a moment of your time?'

'Why certainly, sir,' replied Beatrice's father. 'We do not often have strangers in our village. Are you by chance lost? The rare visitors we do get often become confused about the four villages—which one do you seek?'

'Abbot Giles. I am seeking the Roade family. I am Lord Ravensden, and Miss Olivia Roade Burton is my fiancée. I am trying to find her.'

'Are you indeed? Well, now, what a fortunate chance that you should come this way.' Mr Roade beamed at him. He recalled Beatrice telling him

something about her sister's fiancé but could not remember the precise details. No matter, it was plain
enough what he ought to have known. 'You've come
to stay, of course. Olivia will be delighted to see you.
Not sure where we shall put you—but Beatrice will
think of something. She is nothing if not resourceful.'

'Beatrice?' Harry was beginning to think all the
inhabitants of this place were stark, raving mad. 'She
is…?'

'Of course, we haven't met. How remiss of me.'
Mr Roade reached up to offer his hand to Lord
Ravensden, who had to bend down to take it from his
position high on his horse's back. 'Bertram Roade.
Olivia is my youngest daughter…'

'…and Beatrice presumably the elder?' An appre-
ciative glint entered the blue eyes. 'Touché, Beatrice!'
Harry was no slow top and he knew at once why he
had been sent off in the wrong direction.

He dismounted, beginning to walk at Mr Roade's
rather fast pace. It seemed his host was in a hurry to
reach his home.

'You won't mind if I hand you over to the ladies
once we reach the house?' Mr Roade asked. 'It came
to me this morning, you see. I often see things more
clearly when I'm out for an early walk…something
about the air. Now I need to get back and work. I
forget otherwise. If I don't put my ideas on paper as
soon as they come, they slip away. It is most unfortunate.'

'Yes, I do see…' Many things were becoming clear

to Harry. 'Would you care to tell me about this idea, sir? Between us, we might remember it.'

'Capital notion! Beatrice thought of it, but she had it wrong, this time. She is a great help to me, excellent mind, you know. Let the steam pass through, was what she said—but it has to be the water itself. Beatrice wasn't thinking properly. I dare say she was worrying about having guests. Women do, don't they? We aren't used to entertaining. My fault, of course. I've let things slide since my wife died. Loved her, too much.'

'Yes, I understand,' Harry said, observing the deep sadness in his companion's mild eyes. 'But you were telling me about your idea…'

'Ah yes,' Mr Roade brightened. 'It will be pleasant to have a guest in the house again. Especially a man of sense. You've come to marry Beatrice, haven't you?'

'Olivia, sir,' Harry replied, eyes gleaming. The imp of mischief was sitting on his shoulder. 'Unless you would prefer me to marry Miss Roade, of course?'

'No, no, I remember now, it was Olivia. Mind you, Beatrice would make any man an excellent wife— very good at economy. Don't understand it myself. Trouble is, I'm not sure I could spare her. Looks after me too well, besides being an excellent companion.'

'Make sure any prospective suitor is as rich as Midas,' Harry suggested with an air of innocence. He was enjoying himself hugely. Indeed, he did not recall a time when he had been so well entertained. Had he really thought Northamptonshire would be boring? So far it was proving to be vastly diverting.

'Why do you say that?' Mr Roade looked at him, suddenly intent.

'Your son-in-law would then have a house large enough to accommodate Miss Roade, and any other member of her family she cared to bring with her.'

Mr Roade seemed struck by this. 'What I need,' he confided, 'is someone who would be willing to let me try out my ideas for gravity heating.'

'Gravity heating?' Harry's brows rose. 'What a very good notion! Yes, I do see the possibility. Very useful in old houses—if it could be made to work.'

Beatrice's father beamed at him. 'Exactly. It will make life so very much more comfortable. There have been some problems with overheating, you see—but I shall work them out in time. I suppose you do not happen to have an old and very draughty house?'

Harry chuckled. 'My dear Mr Roade,' he said. 'As it happens, I have far too many of them...'

Beatrice said goodbye to her friends and set off on the road home again. She had spent a good hour sipping Mrs Hartwell's rose cordial, and chatting about the gossip in the villages.

Mrs Hartwell had told her that her husband was worried about the stories of lights being seen in Giles Wood again.

'Edward fears that some kind of unpleasantness is going on there,' she said. 'I do hope he won't take it upon himself to investigate.'

'No, indeed,' Beatrice said. 'It might be dangerous.'

'I have tried to tell him,' the anxious wife said with

a sigh. 'But he feels it is his duty to his parishioners to keep an eye on such things...'

'Yes, of course,' Beatrice agreed. 'It must be a worry to him.'

The Reverend Hartwell had come into the parlour at that moment. He had been pleased to see Beatrice, who led the exemplary life he thought suitable for a spinster of her advanced age. At three and twenty, she would no doubt devote her life to her father, as was right and proper in the circumstances, and no more than her duty. He spoke kindly of her sister and promised they would all dine together the next Thursday. He had also promised to send his groom over to Steep Abbot with a note for Mademoiselle de Champlain, and to provide a bed in his house for her afterwards so that she need not walk all the way back to Steep Abbot on a cold, dark night.

'For I could not rest easy in my mind if the young lady were forced to go near the Abbey grounds after dusk, Miss Roade. There is no telling what might happen to any woman foolish enough to venture there alone.'

Beatrice agreed, feeling glad that he had no idea she had done so herself a few days previously. She took her leave of her kind friends, and set out to walk back to her home, which was at the outskirts of the village.

The mist had cleared now. Beatrice thought that Lord Ravensden must have found his way to Roade House long since, spoken with Olivia, taken his dismissal like any gentleman and gone. Presumably he

would already be on his journey back to
Northampton.

She entered the house by way of the kitchen, calling for her aunt. Nan was not in her usual place at
the table. Beatrice and Nan did all the cooking for
the household, though the kitchen wench, Ida, prepared the vegetables. *She* was sitting by the fire,
warming her feet—which always had chilblains in the
winter—and peeling potatoes for the mutton stew
they were to have that evening. Since the mutton was
likely to be old and tough, being the cheapest Beatrice
could buy, it would need a long, slow cooking over
the fire to make it tender.

'Have you seen my aunt, Ida?'

Ida wrinkled her brow and thought about it, then
her face brightened as inspiration came.

'No, Miss Beatrice—not since her went off in a
fluster, be an hour ago nigh on I reckon. There be a
gentleman caller…'

Beatrice nodded. Good, that meant their unwelcome visitor had found his way here—she had felt a
little guilty after she had sent him off in the wrong
direction—but she had wanted to prepare Olivia. She
was sure Lord Ravensden would have spoken to her
sister and departed by now.

'Where is Mrs Willow at the moment?'

'I think her went upstairs, miss. Her and Lily both.'

'And my sister?'

'In her room, miss. Her's locked herself in an'
won't come out never no more!'

'That is rather dramatic of her,' Beatrice said, hiding her smile. It appeared that more had been going on here than she had expected. 'I shall go and find my aunt and see what is happening.'

Ida's version of events was not to be trusted, since the girl was sometimes more than a little confused in her thinking. It was doubtful that anyone else in the villages would have employed her, but she worked for little more than her keep and was useful for the rough work in the kitchen. Besides, Beatrice had felt sorry for her when she came asking for work and looking as thin as a piece of thread that might snap in two. She did not look that way now, for Beatrice fed her servants on the same fare she offered to her family.

She would try the parlour first, Beatrice decided, since she could see no reason why both Nan and Lily should be required to tidy the bedrooms.

'I'm back…' The words died on Beatrice's lips as she opened the door and walked into the parlour. A fire had been lit, but only recently, and had barely caught hold. A man was kneeling before it, using the bellows in an effort to persuade the flames to rise. 'Good grief…'

The man turned to look at her, his blue eyes narrowing as he saw who was standing there. 'Miss Roade, I presume,' he said. 'Tell me, is it the custom in Abbot Giles to freeze your visitors to death? This damned fire does nothing but smoke and will not catch.'

'It will do so in a moment,' Beatrice said, 'but like the one in my bedchamber it does tend to smoke when the wind is in the wrong direction. Papa will invent something to stop it one day, but until then we can do nothing but endure.' She frowned, wondering why she was telling him this. 'Indeed *you* need not endure it, sir. I am surprised you have not already begun your journey back to London. You must know that you have no business in this house?'

'I am aware of no such thing,' Harry replied, his usual good humour unusually dented. He was cold and tired, and no one had offered him refreshments. His fiancée was in her bedroom, refusing to see him, and he was starving. 'I was invited to stay by Mr Roade—and I may tell you that I have every intention of doing so. At least until Olivia consents to see me. I have not come all this way to be sent off like a puppy with my tail between my legs.'

'Had you not destroyed my sister, you need not have come, sir. And as for leaving, Lord Ravensden, you would be well advised to do so at once. For I am told my sister will not see you. If you return to Northampton, you could find a decent inn where the chimney does not smoke.'

'You have already tried to be rid of me,' Harry said, glaring at her. 'Did you hope that I would lose myself completely and be found in some isolated wasteland frozen to the ground—or just that I would grow tired of wandering and take myself off?'

'I am sure I do not know what you mean,' Beatrice said untruthfully. 'Had you kept on the way I directed you and turned to the right by the chapel, the footpath would have led you back the way you had first gone, and you would eventually have come to the village.'

'Eventually, no doubt. Always providing that I did not freeze to death in the meantime.' He sneezed, as if to prove that there was a distinct possibility that he might have done so. 'At least, someone might have the decency to offer me a glass of wine.'

'Has no one done so?' Beatrice felt her cheeks grow warm. She was normally the most hospitable of women, and willing to share whatever she had with her guests. 'I shall attend to it myself, sir. We do not have a choice to offer you—but my father's sherry is tolerable.'

'Thank you,' Harry replied, eyes narrowing. She looked younger than he had thought when they met in the lane, and her cheeks had a becoming colour. Despite her drab gown, she had a natural elegance and was attractive in her own way. 'Oh, dash it, Miss Roade, need we be at outs with one another? This is an awkward situation, and some way must be found to set things right.'

'You owe my sister an apology!'

'Indeed, I do, Miss Roade. If she would but come out of her bedroom, I would make it—and then perhaps we could begin to sort this mess out.'

'You should have gone at once to Lord Burton, confessed that it was all your fault, and asked him to reinstate Olivia.'

'I was out of town. As soon as I returned, I went to see him. The fool is as stubborn as a mule. He declares that he will only forgive her if she marries me.'

'Oh…' Beatrice was at a stand. His answers were reasonable, and seemed to indicate he knew himself at fault—but clearly this was put on for her benefit. She remembered the tale that had been told to Olivia. The man was a rogue! 'You wretched man! How could you have been so careless as to say in public that my poor sister was fit only for a breeding mare?'

'No!' Harry was outraged. 'Dash it all! I shall not be accused of such a coarse remark. I may have mentioned it was not a love match to a friend…but the rest is simply a lie, added on by a malicious tongue.'

'And you expect me to believe that?' She glared at him, daring him to make another excuse.

'My dear Miss Roade,' fumed Harry. 'I neither know nor care what you may believe at this precise moment. I have been frozen half to death, left alone in an icy parlour with a smoking fire and no refreshment—and I am hungry. I meant to beg Olivia to reconsider, but now I am wondering if that would be wise. Obviously, her family are all quite mad—or I have partaken of bad wine and fallen into a nightmare from which I shall awake with a monstrous headache.'

Beatrice stared at him. Had he tried to ingratiate himself with her, she would have thought him a charlatan. Now she was torn between righteous anger and amusement, finding herself hard put not to smile.

'Indeed, you have been cruelly treated, sir,' she said in a softer tone. 'I do assure you that you have not been drinking bad wine, at least to my knowledge, for my father can afford so little wine that he buys only the best. Besides, as you have not been offered any, I cannot see that the opportunity was there. As to whether we are all a little mad in this household…well, you must decide that for yourself. I shall go at once to fetch sherry wine, bread and cheese. I fear I can provide nothing more until we dine, unless you would prefer almond comfits and a raspberry wine my aunt makes herself?' She saw his expression of disgust and was betrayed into a laugh. 'Do be seated, Lord Ravensden. I shall not let you go hungry for much longer.'

She left him staring after her and went back to the kitchen. There was bread freshly baked by Nan that morning, a good local cheese, pickles—and a decent sherry. No matter what else they lacked, Beatrice never let her father go without his sherry. They also had a few cases of good table wine in the cellar, bought in better times, and brought out on the rare occasions when they had dinner guests, but she was not about to open a bottle for Lord Ravensden. No, indeed! He could have sherry and ale, some bread and cheese—then he could take himself off back to London, where he belonged.

'Ah, there you are,' Nan said, coming down the stairs as Beatrice emerged from the kitchen with her tray. 'Oh dear, I should have seen to that. I quite forgot. I was upstairs, trying to persuade your sister to come down.'

'Pray take this to the parlour,' Beatrice said. 'The

fire may have caught by now and Lord Ravensden will be able to eat in peace. I shall go up to Olivia and see if she will come out for me.'

'She says she shall stay there until he leaves.'

'And he says he will not leave until he has seen her.'

Nan shook her head at such obstinacy and took the tray from Beatrice, who ran up the stairs and knocked at her sister's door.

'Olivia dearest, pray let me in.'

'Has he gone?'

'He is in the parlour having some bread and cheese. He wants to apologise to you.'

'I do not want to hear him. Ask him to go away.'

'He will not leave until you see him. He is the most tiresome creature ever. I do not wonder that you refused to marry him. Indeed, I should think you foolish if you did...'

There was a sound that might have been a laugh or a sob, then Olivia unlocked her door. She was pale and strained, but had not been crying. She pulled a wry face at her sister.

'Lord Ravensden led Papa to believe we are still to marry. He has invited him to stay—and he will. I know he will! Believe me, Beatrice, he will not be moved. He has the oddest notion of humour. He seems amused by this whole situation—at least, he was laughing when Papa brought him home.'

'He was not laughing when I left him. Do not worry, Olivia, I do not believe he will stay long. A man like that...he will find this house uncomfortable.'

'Yes, I dare say,' said Olivia, who was finding her own bedroom, where the fire had not been lit, less than cosy. 'Must I truly see him, Beatrice?'

'I think you must at least grant him a hearing. I believe he means to beg your pardon—and ask you to reconsider...'

'I do not want to marry him.'

'Nor would any woman of sense,' Beatrice said, 'though it seems he may not have said all the things you were told—but you need not fear, dearest. If after you have listened, you still do not wish to marry him, I shall support you. He may stay tonight, if he insists, then go back to town tomorrow.'

'And you will not try to make me marry him?'

'Is that what Lord Burton did?' Olivia nodded, and Beatrice felt anger at the foolish manner in which her sister's adoptive father had behaved. 'That was indeed bad of Lord Burton. Well, I shall not do any such thing. Wash your face and tidy yourself. I shall do the same, then we will go down together and beard the lion in his den. The sooner we set him to rights, the sooner he will leave us.'

'Yes.' Olivia looked slightly ashamed. 'It upset me to see him laughing with Papa. It was as if he were making game of me—but I dare say they were talking of something else.'

'Yes, I am certain they were. Papa would not laugh at you, dearest—and I do not believe Lord Ravensden would either, for all he is the most provoking creature.'

Beatrice smiled at her and went away to tidy herself.

Downstairs in the parlour, Harry had persuaded Mrs Willow to stay and drink a glass of sherry with him.

'Forgive me,' Nan said as he began to eat with a hunger that showed he was much in need of his breakfast. 'I should have offered food and wine. I was so startled by Olivia's foolish behaviour that it went right out of my mind.'

'Pray do not apologise, ma'am,' Harry said. 'I should have stopped to break my fast at an inn, but I was in a hurry to reach this house. All this trouble has been a dreadful misunderstanding.'

'I was sure it must have been,' Nan replied, smiling at him. 'I dare say it was no more than the spiteful wagging of a malicious tongue.'

'More than one, I fear,' Harry admitted. 'And my fault. I was away at the time it began. Had I been in town, much of this could have been avoided…'

'I knew it could not be as Olivia thought.' Nan looked at him with approval. He was in her opinion a very charming man, and in coming down at once to set things right had behaved in a proper manner. Olivia would be a fool not to take the opportunity he was offering her. 'I am sure my niece will see sense when you have talked to her…' She broke off as voices in the hall announced the arrival of Beatrice and Olivia. 'I must leave you now, sir. I have many tasks awaiting me.'

She rose to her feet as her nieces entered together,

their arms linked, then nodded to him, and smiled at the sisters in passing as she went out.

Harry was already on his feet. Olivia was looking pale and nervous. He was acutely conscious of his part in her distress. What a villain Burton was to behave so ill towards her!

'Forgive me, Miss Olivia,' he said at once. 'I startled you by arriving so suddenly. Yet I felt it was necessary to follow as soon as I returned to town and learned what had happened in my absence.'

'I was…upset,' Olivia said, her head going up proudly. 'But I should not have run away. It was good of you to come, sir, but there was really no need to put yourself to so much trouble. My decision was final. I fear you have had a wasted journey.'

Harry glanced at Beatrice, who had gone to the fire and seemed to be attacking the logs with a poker.

'Will you not at least allow me to apologise? My remarks were careless, but you have been told lies. I said only that it was not a love match. The rest has been added by another.'

'Surely that is enough?' Olivia said, her eyes meeting and challenging his bravely. 'Had I not believed you cared for me…'

'Oh, but I do…' Beatrice attacked the logs so fiercely that Harry could only think she was wishing it was him she was wielding her weapon against. 'I have a high regard for you, Miss Olivia. I am not a believer in romantic love, but I think we might have made each other tolerably happy. Indeed, I still believe it. It is my earnest wish to set things straight between us.'

There was a crackling sound behind him and then a great whoosh. Suddenly, the flames began to shoot up the chimney, throwing some warmth into the room at last.

'That is very much better,' Beatrice said with some satisfaction. She got to her feet, dusting her hands and brushing at her skirt. 'I think you should accept Lord Ravensden's apology, Olivia. Then he may go back to London and be at peace with himself.'

'Yes, of course,' Olivia said and smiled at him. She really was remarkably pretty when she smiled. 'I believe that you may have been misquoted—but it makes not the slightest difference...'

He moved towards her, reaching out to take her hand, but she stepped back, hiding her hands behind her back.

'Will you not at least try to forgive me?' Harry asked. 'Lord Burton has told me he will not relent towards you unless we marry... I never wished to bring you harm, Olivia.'

'But you have done so,' Beatrice said when Olivia was silent. 'My sister is too distressed to think clearly now. I pray you, sir, let her be. You have put your case, give her time to consider. If she should change her mind, she may write to you.'

'No,' Olivia said, her manner nervous but determined. 'I shall not deceive you, sir. I have discovered that we shall not suit. I was mistaken in my feelings.

Time will not make me change my mind. My answer will always be the same.'

'At least let me…' Harry sneezed three times in quick succession. 'Damn! Excuse me, ladies, but I fear I may have taken a chill.' He glared at Beatrice as though it were her fault. 'It must have been that wretched mist earlier. It was damp and chilled me to the bone.'

She stared him down. 'I shall make you a hot posset and then you may be on your way. If you leave at once, I dare say you might be home in time to sleep in your own bed.'

'Leaving? Surely not,' said Mr Roade, entering the room at that moment. 'Beatrice, what can you be thinking of? Ravensden has come to visit me. Asked him meself. Wanted you to see, Ravensden—I've started on the new drawings we discussed earlier. Come and have a look, give me your opinion, there's a good fellow.'

'Yes, of course, sir, delighted.' Harry inclined his head to the frustrated Beatrice. 'Excuse me, Miss Roade, Miss Olivia.' An odd smile flickered about his lips as he followed his host from the parlour.

Olivia looked at her sister in exasperation. 'You see—he won't go. He will keep on and on asking me to marry him until I say yes.'

'Is that what he did before?'

'Yes…though just in a teasing way so that I was not always sure he really meant it. I believe he thought I would keep on saying no. He was surprised when I finally accepted him.'

'Surely not?' Beatrice frowned. 'I would not have thought it of him. He seems genuinely to regret what happened. Do you not think you might reconsider…?'

'Please do not try to change my mind. You promised you would not, Beatrice.'

'And I shall not—if you are certain? You do realise that you may never get another chance to marry well? If you stay here with us, you may never marry at all.'

Olivia lifted her chin proudly. 'I do not wish to marry without love. I would rather take a post as a governess!'

Beatrice hid her smile. There was little chance of Olivia finding such a situation. She was far too pretty. Very few women would want to take her into their households in any position.

'Well, I dare say it will not come to that,' she said, and glanced out of the parlour window. 'It looks as if the fog has come down again. We cannot force Lord Ravensden to leave until that clears, which, by the look of it, will not be before the morning.'

Olivia glanced out of the window and pulled a face. 'Let us hope it has cleared by the morning. Perhaps he will realise the situation is hopeless and leave by then.'

'I am sure one night in our guest room will make Lord Ravensden eager to be on his way,' Beatrice said, a quiver of laughter about her mouth. 'I believe I did tell you that the bed has a broken support…'

Chapter Four

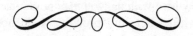

Harry heard the mattress strain ominously beneath him as he turned restlessly. The damned thing sagged in the middle! He had never been so uncomfortable in his life. If this was another of Miss Roade's stratagems to get rid of him… He groaned as he felt the ache in his limbs. It was not just the bed. He could not remember ever having felt this ill in his life. He was hot and cold by turns, his head going round and round.

'Mad…must be mad…mad to come to such a place…'

And still his feverish thoughts would not let him be! Having seen the obvious poverty in which the Roade family lived, Harry knew his conscience would never let him abandon Olivia to her fate. Somehow he must persuade her to marry him, and if he could not…it was a thorny problem, made more difficult by the fact that both the Roade sisters were damnably proud!

Yet he had brought this situation about, and somehow he must resolve it. He did not know why the look of accusation in Miss Roade's eyes pricked at him so much, but he could not seem to get her face out of his mind.

'Go away, woman,' he muttered feverishly. 'Let me be, will you?'

He would think of something…something that would ensure Olivia and her family did not suffer for his carelessness. If only the room would stay still for long enough for him to think properly! He groaned, searching for a comfortable spot in the bed and finding none.

He was ill, and must fetch help. Harry tried to struggle from the bed but found it too much for his spinning head, and fell back against the pillows with yet another groan.

Next door in her own room, Beatrice heard the moaning and frowned. Really, there was no need to make such a fuss! She imagined that the bed was a little uncomfortable, but it was his own fault. If he had not been so careless…*anyone can speak thoughtlessly*. The thought flashed into her mind unbidden.

Beatrice had soon realised that Lord Ravensden was not the monster she had imagined him on reading her sister's letter. He had been thoughtless and a little cruel, but perhaps he had not meant to be. She believed he was sincere in his wish to make amends.

Olivia seemed adamant that she would not have him, but only a few days had passed since Lord Burton had thrown her out. How would she feel when she began to miss her friends, and the balls she had found so delightful? She was trying to be brave, but Beatrice believed she must cry sometimes when she was alone. How could it be otherwise?

Hearing more groans, Beatrice frowned and put her pillow over her head. The man was impossible! Had he no consideration for other people? This was a small house, the bedrooms close to one another. If he kept this up, she would never sleep. She only hoped that one night in their guest room would ensure his early departure in the morning.

'Oh, Beatrice,' Nan said, coming in before she was properly awake the next morning. 'I am so sorry to disturb you, my love—but I think we shall have to send for Dr Pettifer. Lily went in to take Lord Ravensden's hot water this morning, and she says he was raving, quite out of his mind. I went at once to see for myself, and I fear she is right. The poor man has a nasty fever.'

'A fever—you mean he is ill?' Beatrice's conscience smote her. If their guest was ill, it was her fault. She had sent him out of his way in the mist, then he had been left in an icy parlour—and the guest room had not been used in years! Lily had lit the fire and put a warming pan to the mattress, of course, but it could not have been properly aired. 'I shall come at once.'

She slipped a dressing-robe over her nightgown, ran out into the hall and entered the next room without knocking. One look at Lord Ravensden's flushed face told her that Nan was right. He was ill. Very ill, by the way he tossed and turned restlessly. She walked over to him, laying her hand on his forehead.

'You poor man,' she said, as she found it hot and damp. 'What an unfeeling wretch I am to have let you suffer.' She looked at Nan with remorse. 'I heard him groaning during the night and imagined it was because of the bed. You must send Bellows for Dr Pettifer immediately.'

'Yes, I shall do so at once.'

Nan hurried away. Beatrice gazed down at the sick man. There was no question of his leaving them now, not for several days. She had an obvious duty to care for him while he was ill.

'You provoking creature,' she said in the scolding but teasing tone she would have used had her dear papa been ill. 'If I was not certain that you are ill, I would think you had done this deliberately.'

'Don't cry, Mama,' Harry muttered, tossing restlessly on the pillows. 'Poor Lillibet's gone…still got me. She's gone to Heaven where all the angels…should have been me! Little angel…gone to be with…' A shudder took him and he started up, clutching at Beatrice's arm. 'It should have been me. Damn it! Do you hear?'

He was clearly wandering in his mind. Beatrice stroked the dark hair from his forehead. He was very hot!

'Yes, of course I hear, you foolish man. I dare say it should have been you if you are so certain of it,' said Beatrice in a soothing tone, wondering who

Lillibet was. 'Rest now, my dear sir, or you will be with the angels yourself very shortly.'

He seemed to relax as he heard the scolding note in her voice.

'Yes, Merry sweetheart. Always do as you say...'

He was delirious, and thought himself elsewhere. Beatrice went to fetch a cloth and a basin of cool water. She soaked her cloth, then returned to the bed and began to bathe his head, face and neck. As she pushed the covers back, she saw that he was not wearing a nightgown. He must be completely naked beneath the sheets! She recoiled in shock. What ought she to do now? She had never in her life been near a naked man before this.

Beatrice's thoughts raced as she took stock of her situation. What was she doing here alone in Lord Ravensden's bedchamber? She must be mad indeed! She ought not to be here—but who else would nurse him? Lily could not be trusted, and her aunt had too much to do. There was no choice. Beatrice could not turn her back on a guest when he was in need of help, particularly as she felt partially responsible for his illness. Besides, he was in no case to ravish her at this moment.

'Do you know the trouble you are causing me, you wretch? I dare say it matters not a jot to you that my reputation will be ruined if anyone ever learns of this?' Beatrice chuckled as she realised that in truth it did not much matter. She almost never went into society, and she did not wish to marry—or at least, she did not wish to marry anyone who had ever asked her. 'The least you can do is to get better. I refuse to be compromised by a man who gives up without a fight. Do you hear me, sir? Die on me, and you will lie uneasy in your grave, I promise you.'

'What are you doing?' Olivia had come to the door in her dressing-robe. She entered cautiously. 'Is he really ill? Not simply pretending so that he may stay here longer?'

'Yes, I am afraid he is very ill,' Beatrice replied. 'I thought he was making a fuss last evening—for if you remember, he sneezed several times during dinner. However, I was wrong. He has a fever and will not be able to leave us for a while, dearest.'

'Well, I suppose it does not matter if he cannot leave at once.' Olivia sighed. 'He is not really so very bad, Beatrice. I liked him more than any other of my suitors, which is why I took him in the end. I thought I might come to love him, but I know now that I never could. He has no real sensitivity, no depth of soul. Ravensden finds everything amusing, and I did not always see the point of his humour, which was annoying. I would rather he didn't die, though.' She looked upset suddenly. 'Do you think this is my fault? Is he dying of a broken heart because I jilted him?'

'I very much doubt it,' Beatrice said. 'He has caught a chill, and it has turned to fever. I dare say the room was damp. If anyone is to blame, it is me. I should have let him take my bed and shared with you. In fact, when the doctor comes, I shall ask him if he can be moved to my room. He will be very much more comfortable there.'

'He would not have taken the chill if he had not chased after me.' Olivia looked repentant. 'I ought to have forgiven him kindly, offered to be friends. I shall do so if he recovers.'

'When he recovers,' Beatrice said. 'I have no intention of allowing him to die in Papa's house. Whatever would people say? Now go away, Olivia. It is not fitting that you should be in his bedchamber.'

Olivia laughed. 'It is too late to worry over my reputation. Not that I should be of much use in the sickroom. I have never done anything useful in my life.'

'Then you may start now, my love,' Beatrice said with a smile for her sister. 'Ask Lily to help you change the linen on my bed, please. It must be fresh and clean, ready for Bellows to take our patient there once Dr Pettifer has been to visit him.'

She watched as Olivia left the room, then turned back to her patient. He was so very hot, threshing restlessly from side to side in his fever.

'You poor man,' she said in a softer tone than she had used earlier. 'I must think of something to ease you...'

'So sorry, Lillibet,' Ravensden's hoarse cry disturbed Beatrice as she sat dozing in the chair by the fire. 'I didn't mean to kill you...'

Beatrice felt the chill trickle down her spine. What had this man done that haunted him so? Was Lillibet another unfortunate young woman he had somehow driven to her death? As Olivia might have been had she been less brave.

She got up and went over to the bed. He was burning up again. She felt a shaft of fear. What must she do to save him? She could not just stand by and watch him die. Something deep within her cried out against it.

He had seemed a little easier when she had earlier bathed his face and neck, but he was clearly hot all over, thrashing wildly in an attempt to throw off the light cover which was all that covered his nakedness.

Bellows had put a nightgown on him when he was moved, but it had become soaked through within an hour and it had been removed again. The sheets had had to be changed several times, which was making a lot of work for Nan.

'You poor, poor man,' Beatrice murmured, her heart wrung with pity for his pain. She went to fetch her basin and began to bathe his face. 'Does that feel good, my dear?'

'Yes, Merry. So hot…so hot…'

Beatrice glanced at the door. It was the middle of the night. No one was likely to come near at this hour…but just in case… She went over to the door and locked it, then returned to the bed.

'Oh, well,' she muttered. 'I suppose I may as well be hanged for a sheep as a lamb.'

She took hold of the cover and peeled it back, revealing Lord Ravensden's naked body. For a moment she stared, fascinated by its perfection despite herself. This man clearly kept himself in prime condition.

She turned away, blushing at herself and her most unladylike thoughts, and went to fetch her basin. She rinsed the cloth out in cool water and began to sponge his chest and arms.

'If you dare to wake and realise what I am doing, I shall die of embarrassment,' she scolded. 'You really are the most tiresome man! I have no idea why I am risking my good name for your sake. I dare not even think what the Reverend Hartwell would say…'

Beatrice slipped her arm behind her patient, lifting him a little so that he could swallow. She pressed the spoon against his lips. He was at least more comfortable now, though he was still in the grip of the fever, still unaware of where he was and who was tending him.

'Open your mouth, you stubborn wretch,' Beatrice commanded. 'Do not imagine I have all day to waste. I have more important work waiting. There are the walnuts to pickle, and a sheet to mend. If you imagine you are more important than such tasks, you much mistake the matter. Papa will be most upset if there are no pickles at Christmas.'

'Scolding harpy…'

The moment his lips moved, Beatrice had the spoon inside and the bitter medicine slipped down his throat. He made a gagging sound, as well he might. She had tasted a drop and it was foul, but she believed it had done him good.

'Serves you right,' she said. 'Next time you will

think before you speak. Had you done so in the first place, we should none of us be in this situation.'

She laid her hand on his brow. He was much cooler now. This was the third day of his illness, and she had scarcely left his side, sleeping in the chair near the fireplace so that she could hear if he cried out. She was not sure if he was really aware of anything, but she had discovered that he usually responded if she scolded him.

Nan had remonstrated with her for spending so much time alone with him, warning her what others might think if it came out, but Beatrice refused to be moved. Her aunt was right, of course, but it was more important for the moment to save Lord Ravensden's life.

'No one but us need ever know,' she said. 'Besides, he must be properly cared for. Dr Pettifer said he could die…'

That prospect had frightened Beatrice so much that she had lavished care and attention on him, doing everything that needed to be done for his comfort herself.

She bathed his forehead again now. Unknown to anyone else, she had three times washed his naked body all over. He had been so hot, and the cool water had seemed to ease him, as had the balm she had rubbed into his back to ease the aching she knew he must be feeling—and of course his natural bodily functions had had to be attended.

Some young, unmarried women might have found the task beyond them, but Beatrice had taken it in her stride, thinking only of what her patient must be suffering.

She washed and dried his arms, neck, shoulders and face, marvelling at the firmness of rippling muscles. She had never imagined a man could be so beautiful. His skin was like polished satin, with just a light sprinkling of fine hair on his legs, chest and navel. She turned him over, washing and then massaging his back—such a strong back, with such smooth skin!

'I hope you won't remember all this,' she murmured as she settled the clean covers around him. 'If you do, I shall deny it. I shall say it was Nan—or that you imagined it.'

'Yes, Merry,' he murmured. 'That feels good... thank you. Sleep now...'

Who was the woman he called Merry? He had spoken to her several times in his fever. Perhaps she was his mistress? He was bound to have one, of course. Unmarried, a man in his thirties...oh yes, there must have been women.

What did she care? Beatrice frowned at her own thoughts. She was being very foolish. It could mean nothing to her if he kept a dozen mistresses—except for Olivia's sake, of course.

Nursing him and attending to his needs had brought her close to him, but that was something she must quickly forget. A man like Lord Ravensden was not for her. Even if he were not engaged to Olivia, which he was—or would be if Olivia would have him back. Besides, he was the most frustrating, stubborn creature on this earth, and scarcely worth the trouble she had lavished on him.

No, no, that was not true. Beatrice knew she had misjudged him at the beginning. He had tried immediately to do the right thing by Olivia, and that must excuse him much.

She had heard him tell Olivia that he had the highest regard for her. He wanted to marry her, and it would be better for Olivia if she could be brought to see the sense of the arrangement. Not a love match perhaps, but one that could bring respect and content on both sides. It was as much and more than was granted to most women.

Olivia had been upset over his carelessness, of course she had, but these past three days, she had shown a very proper concern for her ex-fiancé. She had carried trays upstairs for her sister, and tried very hard to help with some of the duties Beatrice was neglecting for Lord Ravensden's sake.

Was it possible that she was beginning to change her mind, to think that perhaps she might marry him? It would not be surprising when you thought of the alternative. Surely Olivia must see that she would be happier married to this man than living in a house where there was never enough money for the necessities of life, let alone the luxuries she had been accustomed to?

Any sensible woman must realise that, and Olivia was certainly not a fool, for all her romantic notions.

Lord Ravensden might be a stubborn, frustrating

creature, but he was not a monster. Indeed, given a chance, he might prove a comforting husband.

Beatrice looked down at her patient once more. He was sleeping peacefully now. She believed he had turned the corner. He would recover, though he must be given time to rest. There was no question of throwing him out until he was ready to leave.

The fever had broken at last. He would rest now—and he must never know that it was she who had tended him throughout his illness.

She would go to the room she now shared with her sister, and in the morning Lily could bring him some good nourishing broth.

The slight noise brought his eyes open. Harry's gaze moved towards the fireplace. A maid was putting logs on the fire. He felt a flicker of annoyance as he realised she must have woken him. Dash it all! It was barely light. What was the wench doing in his room? His manservant Beckett was usually so efficient, always careful not to wake him after a late night—and by the way his temples were throbbing, it must indeed have been a late night! He could not recall ever having woken with such a head. Whatever had he been drinking?

He closed his eyes against the nagging pain, opening them again as he sensed the girl hovering near.

'Where is Beckett?' he asked, a note of irritation in his voice. Had the girl not been properly trained? She ought not even to be in his room. What was his housekeeper thinking of to allow it? 'Dash it, girl, what are you doing here?'

'The mistress said I was to make up the fire, then bring you some nourishing broth if you were awake…'

'Mistress?' There was no mistress in his home! Where on earth was he? Harry struggled to remember. He must have drunk a devilish amount the previous night. Good lord! This wasn't his room. He had never seen it before. He tried to sit up, groaned and fell back against the pillows. 'Dash it, I'm as weak as a kitten!'

'You've been ill, sir. These past three days and more.'

'Ill, you say?' Harry stared at her in bewilderment. 'Have I, be damned?'

He tried to gather his thoughts. Vague memories began to filter into his mind. He seemed to recall something. Soft hands bathing him, easing the terrible throbbing aches in his back…a voice scolding him, but not in an unkind way. No, the voice had not been unkind, indeed, it had seemed to carry a hint of laughter, as though its owner was deliberately needling him, forcing him to respond, pulling him through his illness by the sheer force of her will. It must have been Merry Dawlish. He knew of no other woman who would do such intimate things for him.

'Fetch Lady Dawlish,' he said to the girl. 'Pray ask her if she will attend me here as soon as possible.'

The girl gaped at him as if he had said something

odd. What could be the matter with her? Merry did not usually employ half-wits.

'Who, sir?'

'Why, your mistress, of course.' Harry frowned as she continued to stare at him in that odd way. 'I would speak with her, thank her for her care of me.'

'Begging your pardon, sir. I don't know Lady Dawlish.'

'Don't know her—then where the hell am I?' Harry's brow furrowed as he searched for some elusive memory at the back of his mind. 'Who has been caring for…?'

'That will do, Lily,' a voice from the doorway said, and it was Harry's turn to gape as a vision of beauty appeared in his bedchamber. A woman with wild, curling hair loose about her face and shoulders was standing just inside the door. Dressed in a wrapping gown of some soft green material, clearly in the middle of her toilette, she looked none too pleased at having been disturbed. 'I had thought you were better, Lord Ravensden, but it appears you are still unwell.'

Harry blinked as he suddenly recognised her and the mists parted in his mind. Of course, he was in the house of Bertram Roade…but this was not the room he had been shown to that first night. He was very certain of that. And the woman standing at the foot of his bed, glaring at him as if she would like to take her poker to him, was surely not Miss Roade. She was a goddess, some celestial beauty newly sprung from the heavens.

'Where did you come from?' he asked, bewildered

by the transformation. This vision was not the slightly dowdy young woman who had sent him on a wild goose chase, nor the avenging sister who had wielded her poker to such good effect, but a warm, sensuous, lovely thing who stirred his senses.

Beatrice walked towards him, laying a hand on his brow. It was quite cool, and the fever had gone from his eyes.

'I dare say you feel a little strange this morning,' she said, frowning at him. 'You were very ill, sir. The fever has gone, but it may take a while for you to gather your wits.'

'You have certainly sent them flying,' Harry said, catching hold of her wrist as she would have moved away. 'I presume that I have you to thank for the nursing that has brought me through this damned sickness?'

'Me?' Beatrice had seen a gleam in his eyes that bothered her. Once before, a man had looked at her in that way. Goodness! Did Lord Ravensden imagine that because she had tended him in his fever she was a loose woman? 'No, indeed, sir, you much mistake the matter. I have scarce been in this room at all, except when the doctor called...' She noticed Lily still hovering in the doorway, her mouth open wide as if she were catching flies. 'You may go, Lily.'

'Yes, miss.' She hesitated still. 'His lordship's broth, miss—should I bring it now?'

'Yes, certainly.'

'No, she shall not,' Harry said at once. His head was beginning to clear now, though he still felt weak.

'Beef, that's what I want. Slices of rare beef, mustard and pickles.'

'It may be what you want, Lord Ravensden,' Beatrice said, making a silent note to send to Northampton for more supplies: such a guest was not to be fed on the stews, pies and bacon puddings that made up their usual diet. 'However, I can neither recommend nor supply it for the moment. My aunt has made a restorative mutton broth for you, and there is some cold ham and a pigeon pie for supper. If you are feeling well enough to stomach a little solid food by then, we shall be pleased to serve you, either here in your room or downstairs in the parlour.'

'It was you, wasn't it?' Harry's eyes narrowed. The scent of her was right, and that scolding note…she was the woman who had cared for him so tenderly. 'I have you to thank…for saving my life, I dare say.' Had he been taken ill at some wayside inn, he believed he might well be dead by now. Only the devotion and skill of this woman had got him through.

'No, indeed, you have not,' Beatrice said, lying calmly. 'My aunt tended you, sir. I have far too much to do to be waiting on sickbeds…and I must be about my business now.'

'Don't go,' Harry said, holding to her wrist with surprising tenacity for a man so weak. 'Please, stay a moment longer. I swear you are in no danger from me. I am as harmless as a new-born lamb.'

'Lily will bring your broth,' Beatrice said. She hesitated, yet knew she must not give into his pleading. Any intimacy between them must cease this instant.

'Or, if you prefer, my aunt will tend you, though she has much to do and can ill be spared. We do not have many servants in this house, my lord.'

'I am accustomed to a manservant,' Harry said. 'Can your father's man not attend me?'

'Bellows is not used to serving guests,' Beatrice said, her brow wrinkling. 'But…if you prefer it…'

'Let him come—unless you would like to feed and shave me yourself?'

The glint in his eyes unnerved Beatrice, and the touch of his hand was sending hot shivers through her entire body. She might almost have thought she had taken the fever from him! 'I believe Bellows will manage,' she said, thinking it would serve him right if the man nicked him. 'I shall send him up directly.'

'Thank you, you are very kind.' A wicked smile tugged at the corners of his mouth. 'You will please convey my thanks to your aunt, Miss Roade. Tell her I have never been so kindly treated in my life before, and I do thank her most sincerely for her care of me. For *all* her care…'

A bright flush stained Beatrice's cheeks. She turned her head aside, afraid that she was betraying herself. He knew! He was mocking her. Very gently, and his thanks were sincere—but that gleam in his eyes! It was not to be borne. Gentlemen did not look at respectable single ladies that way. She had stepped over the boundaries of proper behaviour, and she had better step back quickly or both her reputation and her peace of mind would be lost for ever. She pulled back, and this time he released his hold on her.

'I shall be glad to convey your message, sir. Nan will be pleased that you are feeling better this morning.' She frowned at him. 'I realise you are not up to the journey back to London just yet. We are unfortunately not used to visitors staying, but we shall do our best to make you comfortable—until you can leave.'

'I see you still wish to be rid of me,' Harry said. His eyes narrowed in thought. His wits must be addled! Why had he not realised before? Of course she dare not admit to having tended his sickbed; her reputation would be ruined if anyone guessed what she had done for him. And Harry was well aware of the extent of her services: he was dying to relieve himself this very moment! However, the barriers of convention were in place and he could not mention such an indelicate subject to the very proper Miss Roade. 'It is most unkind in you, Miss Roade. I am far too weak to even think of leaving for the moment.'

'No, of course you must not think of leaving,' Nan said, coming in at that moment with a tray. 'Not for several days, or however long it takes you to recover your full strength. We should not dream of it. Now, sir, I have brought you some good broth. I want you to eat it all and I shall not take no for an answer. Beatrice, my love, your papa needs you.'

'Lord Ravensden has requested that Bellows attend him,' Beatrice said, seizing her chance to escape. 'I dare say he will take some soup from your hand, Nan—since you have already done so much for him while he was in the fever. As for myself, I have far too much to do to waste time here…'

'Pickled walnuts…' Harry murmured, his eyes narrowed as a fragment of a woman's scolding flashed into his mind. 'Yes, I must not detain you further, Miss Roade. And I will gladly take the broth from you, Mrs Willow—but I would prefer Bellows to shave me, if you won't think it ungrateful of me.'

Beatrice left them together. She heard Nan laughing at something he had said as she went back to her own room to finish dressing. What had she been thinking of to rush to his room in her dressing-robe? It was only that on hearing the odd note in Lily's voice she had feared he was ill again…but what could it matter? Lord Ravensden was nothing but an inconvenience in the house. She had done her duty by him, but now he was over the worst and it would be as well for her if she were to stay out of his way until he left.

In the meantime she must send to Farmer Ekins, who, she believed, had killed a pig some days ago. The beef must come from Northampton, because she did not care to buy from the market in Abbot Quincey, where she believed the quality to be inferior, though they seldom bought such luxuries for themselves. Instead, they relied on poultry, mutton and pork bought from neighbouring farms.

Beatrice frowned as she thought of the dwindling supply of her housekeeping. It had taken money she could ill afford to pay, first for the new bed for Olivia, and then there were the doctor's visits to consider. He had called three times to see their patient; she did not grudge the money this would cost, of course, but it meant that she would have to find some other way to economise.

She did not want to take Olivia's few guineas if she could help it, but her own quarterly allowance was almost spent. Perhaps Papa…but there was the wine merchant to be paid, and they needed some more sea coals for the kitchen, besides wax candles for the parlour. It was truly vexing the way money just seemed to be eaten up by this house. She had often thought they might do better in a small cottage, but dear Papa could not bear to leave the home where he had once been so happy with his wife, of course.

Oh well, she would manage somehow. She had been putting a few shillings by to buy material for a new gown from Hammonds, the general store and linen draper in Abbot Quincey, but the purchase could wait. Her old gowns would do for a little longer.

She sighed as she looked at herself in the drab grey gown she was wearing that morning. It made her look so—so old and staid, and she didn't in the least feel like either of those things, but the dress was serviceable, and perhaps she could trim it with a new ribbon.

Dressed, her hair confined in a strict coil at the nape of her neck, only a few rogue curls allowed to escape about her face, Beatrice smoothed the skirt of her dress and went downstairs in search of her father.

He was in his study, working, in not the slightest need of her services. He did, however, look up at her entry, to enquire how their guest went on.

'How is Ravensden, m'dear? Better, I dare say, or you would not be here.'

'He is over the worst now, Papa, but he cannot leave us yet.'

'No, no, that would be unthinkable,' Mr Roade said. 'Besides, I like the fellow, Beatrice. Excellent mind. I think I shall go up and see him later, take some of my drawings to show him.'

'I am sure he will enjoy that, Papa,' Beatrice said, and smiled, at this marked measure of her father's approval. 'But you must not tire him. I believe he still feels a little weak.'

'Almost certainly,' her father replied. 'Foolish to travel in such inclement weather. Mist is very dangerous to the constitution, you know—damp and cold, the worst combination.'

'Yes…' Beatrice felt the guilt strike her. If it were not for her unkindness, Lord Ravensden might never have been taken ill.

'Very fortunate it happened here,' Mr Roade said. 'If he had been staying at an inn he might not have been so well looked after. You were exceptionally good to him, m'dear.'

'I did very little,' she said, her cheeks warm. 'If you do not need me, Papa, I have things to do.'

'Of course, of course…' He waved her away, but did not immediately return to the contemplation of his drawings when the door closed behind her. Mr Roade might be absent-minded, but he was not a fool. He knew well enough what kind of a life his daughter had been leading these past few years. 'Truly, a fine mind…very like your own, Beatrice…'

Chapter Five

'Where is Bellows?' Beatrice asked her aunt as she went into the kitchen the following morning. 'He is needed to bring in more logs for the parlour fire. Olivia is mending a sheet—and it is a little chilly in there. We do not want her going down with a fever.'

Nan glanced up from her work. 'Bellows was with his lordship earlier, then he went off on an errand—I believe he took Lord Ravensden's horse.'

'Goodness!' Beatrice said, looking startled. 'I hope he had permission.'

'I imagine his lordship wanted him to do something for him,' Nan said. 'They have been getting on like a house on fire. Bellows says it is quite like the old days. Apparently, he has shaved gentlemen before. It is only since Bertram lost most of his money that he began to do the outside work.'

'Yes, I suppose it is,' Beatrice said, frowning. There had been a time when things were not so very bad, before Sarah Roade died, her income from her family dying with her, and before Mr Roade had made so many unwise investments. 'Can Lord Ravensden not shave himself yet? Is he still feeling weak? Really, it is such a nuisance, but I dare say he does not realise how much we rely on Bellows. So thoughtless of him to send Bellows off on an errand. But what can you expect of such a man? It is all of a piece!'

'I dare say he is accustomed to being shaved by his man, and to having servants on hand to run his errands,' Nan said, looking at her thoughtfully. It was unusual for Beatrice to be so out of humour. 'I will ask Ida to bring in the logs. She is perfectly capable of doing it.'

'Yes, of course.' Beatrice sighed. 'I was just wondering.'

'Why do you not go up and speak to his lordship for a few minutes?' Nan asked. 'He enquired for you earlier, my dear.'

'I am far too busy,' Beatrice replied. 'We have guests for dinner on Thursday evening, Nan. Had you forgotten? I must do some cooking in preparation.'

'That is tomorrow,' Nan replied with a lift of her brows. 'Is there really anything you need to prepare today, my love?'

'I suppose not—but I ought not to visit Ravensden in his bedchamber,' Beatrice said, not quite meeting her searching gaze. 'I wonder that you should suggest it.'

'Ah…' Nan smiled as she saw the frustration in her niece's eyes. 'No, of course not. It would be immodest in you, and is not to be expected, since you scarcely went near his lordship the whole time he was so ill…'

'Pray do not tease me.' Beatrice gave a reluctant laugh. 'I had to tell him that, Nan. Only imagine what he would think if he knew it was I who had…well, I think it best that I do not go up. Papa said he was in high spirits when he saw him.'

'Just as you wish, dearest. Lord Ravensden did say that he might get up later today and come down…'

'The foolish man! He is not yet well enough.'

'I did tell him that he ought to stay where he was for another day at least, but he said…' Nan shook her head. Better not to repeat the exact words Lord Ravensden had uttered. He was here to persuade her youngest niece to marry him, not to seduce the elder. 'He said he did not care for lying abed, and that he was feeling very much better.'

'Well, I shall go and tidy our bedrooms,' Beatrice said. 'Lily can do Lord Ravensden's room later…'

She picked up her dusters and the lavender-scented polish, which had been made with beeswax from their own hives and lavender she had ground herself to extract the oil.

It really was most frustrating, Beatrice thought as she polished the chest of drawers in her father's room. Conventions were so foolish. Just because she was not married, she was barred from dropping into Lord Ravensden's bedchamber as her father did whenever he felt like it. As though she was in any danger of being seduced! Why, she did not even like him…if she did not think he would be a good catch for her sister, she would not have bothered for one moment whether he was ill or not.

He had come to them on Friday the first of November, it was now the sixth, only five days since he had been found ill. *Only five days?* Why did she care that he was foolish enough to be thinking of leaving his bed so soon?

To be sure, it did not matter! Why should she care what the tiresome creature did? Yet he had been so very ill the first three days, and she could not help wondering if he really was better now. No doubt the stubborn man would rise from his bed too soon, then take ill again on purpose!

Leaving her father's bedroom, she paused to dust a table in the hall. She was frowning, her thoughts far from comforting as she worked, and did not notice the man walking towards her along the landing, his boots making no noise on the old, worn carpet, until he was almost upon her.

'You really are busy, aren't you?' Harry said, making her jump and look round. 'I thought Mrs Willow was not telling me the truth when I asked her why you would not visit me—but it seems I was mistaken.'

'Lord Ravensden!' Beatrice cried, her heart leaping unaccountably. From fright, of course, nothing else. The wretched man had sneaked up on her! 'What are you doing up so soon? Surely you are not fit to come down yet? You would do much better to rest, sir.'

'If you will not come to me, I must come to you,' Harry said. 'I am much recovered, besides, I could not lie there another moment, knowing that I must be causing so much trouble to your household.'

'Indeed, you are not, you foolish creature,' Beatrice said. 'I did not nurse you to have you risk yourself so heedlessly…' She stopped, furious with herself for having been caught out. 'I meant my aunt, of course. It was Nan who nursed you.'

'Of course…' Harry's eyes gleamed. 'It would have been quite improper for you to have nursed me, Miss Roade. And, since you will not come near me now, I see that you are indeed a very proper young woman.'

'Not so young, sir. I am three-and-twenty, not a green girl to be doing anything so foolish as to—to…'

'…bathe a naked man?' Harry's grin was despicable. 'Massage his back when it was aching so very much?'

'Indeed, I should not dream of it,' Beatrice lied, her cheeks flaming. 'You must have dreamt it in your fever, sir.'

'Indeed, I must,' Harry agreed, his eyes warm and admiring. 'Forgive me, mistress, I fear I have a shocking sense of the ridiculous. It is very bad in me. Mama has always told me so, and Merry is forever scolding me for my wicked levity.'

'Who is Merry?' Beatrice's curiosity overcame her. 'You called for her so often…'

'Did I? I wonder why?' Harry frowned. 'She is the wife of Lord Dawlish, Percy Dawlish. He is my closest friend, and Merry has always made me welcome in her house. I believe I must have thought it was she who tended me so kindly.'

'Yes, I see.' Beatrice smiled, oddly content with his explanation. 'My aunt said you mentioned Merry by name several times.'

'Yes, *of course*, your aunt. A remarkable woman, Mrs Willow—in many ways.' Harry frowned as he saw her pick up her dusters. 'Do you always work so hard, Miss Roade? Or is it because I have upset your routine?'

'I do not mind a little polishing,' Beatrice said. 'Lily has taken on some of Bellows's duties for the moment, so I am doing her work this morning.'

'I see. It was thoughtless of me. I sent him into Northampton this morning, to run some errands for me. Forgive me, I should have asked if it was convenient before commandeering your servant.'

'You are used to a house filled with servants,' Beatrice said, a faint blush in her cheeks. 'This must seem a very odd establishment to you, Lord Ravensden. I apologise that we cannot offer you more in the way of comfort.'

'You have no need to apologise for anything,' Harry said. He took her hand. She was wearing a pair of old cotton gloves. 'So that is how you protect your skin. You have soft hands, Miss Roade. I am glad you take care of them. It would be a pity if they should be spoiled doing work more fitted to others.'

'I have become used to it,' she said, withdrawing her hand from his swiftly. 'Though I am more often baking than polishing. I enjoy baking and preserving…making my own healing balms and simples. Most countrywomen do, my lord.'

'Yes, I see.' Harry smiled at her, taking her breath away. 'And what else do you do when you are not thus employed?'

'I read…play Mama's pianoforte when I have the chance, and sew,' she replied. 'When the weather is better, I walk a lot.'

He nodded, his eyes intent on her face. 'You do not ride?'

'I used to before…' She stopped, dropping her gaze for fear he should see too much. 'It is expensive to keep a riding horse, Lord Ravensden. Papa borrows a mount from Mr Hartwell's stable now and then, and I suppose I might too—had I a decent habit that would fit me.'

'Ah…yes, I understand. Mr Roade told me that some of his experiments had proved costly in the past.'

'Yes…' Beatrice would not look at him. 'You must not pity us, my lord. We are content, Papa and I…it is poor Olivia that you should be thinking of.' Her eyes swept up to meet his, full of condemnation. 'It is she who has lost everything.'

'Yes, I realise that.' Harry's face assumed a serious expression. 'The problem is—what can be done about it?'

'You must persuade her it is in her best interests to marry you, of course.'

'Must I?' Harry's brows arched. 'Yes, I suspect that

would be the correct and proper course of action. Where may I find Miss Olivia at this moment?'

'She is in the parlour, mending a sheet.'

'Is she indeed? Poor Miss Olivia. I should go to her at once.'

'Yes, please do.'

Beatrice turned back to her polishing cloths as he inclined his head and walked past, but a muffled oath made her look round almost immediately, and she saw that he had halted, his hand clutching the banister rail as if he had needed support. She dropped her cloths and went to him at once, looking at him in concern.

'You, foolish, foolish creature,' she scolded. 'I might have known this would happen. I dare say you imagine that if you fall and half kill yourself, it will gain you a bed here for yet more days. Well, let me tell you, your stratagem will not work. Take my arm, sir, and we shall walk down the stairs together. I shall not have you ill again.'

'No, that would be very bad of me, wouldn't it? Since you have given up your room for my sake.' Harry's eyes danced with laughter. 'Unless you mean to send me back to that disgusting bed in your guest room now that I have recovered enough to be moved?'

'Oh, pray do not,' Beatrice said, smitten by guilt. 'I dare say it was all my fault you were ill, Lord Ravensden. The room had not been used in years, and though the fire was lit as soon as I understood your intention of staying, it could not have thoroughly aired the chamber.'

'I quite thought you meant to drive me out,' Harry said. 'That was a dashed uncomfortable mattress.'

'The struts are broken,' Beatrice said. 'I must ask Bellows if he can repair them.'

'So you do mean to banish me?'

'Be quiet, you provoking man,' Beatrice said as they reached the bottom of the stairs. 'Of course I do not mean to send you back there. I am quite comfortable sharing with my sister for the moment.'

'I understand there is a bedroom not in use…next to Mr Roade…' Harry raised his brows. 'If the bed were aired, I might move there in a day or so. Or is that bed also broken?'

'No, it is a very good mattress,' Beatrice said. 'It was my mother's room. She died in that bed, and it has not been used since. Obviously, I could not expect Olivia to sleep there, as it was where Mama died— but if it would not disturb you?'

'I have no fear of departed spirits,' Harry said. 'If Mrs Roade was as generous as her daughter, I am sure I shall sleep quite satisfactorily in her bed. And it would mean that you could be comfortable in your own room again.'

Beatrice kept her face averted. Really, such consideration from a man who was supposed to be careless! What did he hope to gain by this? Or was she being too critical?

'Well, I shall have the room aired properly since that too has not been used for a while, but you need not think of moving for a few days,' she said, then wrinkled her brow. 'Were you thinking of staying long?'

Harry gave a shout of laughter. 'You heartless minx,' he said. 'How can you think of sending me away, when I have been so thoughtful of your comfort?'

Beatrice glanced up at him, then quickly away as her heart raced. Really, the man had too much charm. He imagined it would gain him anything, but he much mistook the matter if he thought she was to be twisted around his finger.

'Pray go in to my sister,' she said. 'I am not so heartless that I would send you away before you have had a chance to win back Olivia's affections—but I must tell you that I shall not force her to take you, and nor will Papa. You must fight your own battle, sir.'

'Oh, indeed, I intend to do so, Miss Roade,' Harry said, a glint in his eyes. 'By whatever means necessary. They do say that everything is fair in love and war, do they not?'

Beatrice gave him a speaking look and left him, as he tapped at the parlour door and then went in. His manner left much to be desired in a prospective bridegroom, but she would not try to influence her sister one way or the other.

Had she been able to send him packing the first day, that would have been an end to the whole affair, but circumstances had been against her. Now they were all caught in the coils of a mischievous fate and must play out the game until its end.

It was Thursday the seventh of November. Beatrice was in the kitchen when Farmer Ekin's boy came in at the back door. She looked up, a flicker of amusement in her eyes, as he entered, basket on arm. It was immediately clear to her from his expression that he had news. Ned visited many of the houses in the four villages, taking produce from his father's farm to their customers, and he usually had some titbit of gossip to offer.

'There you be, Miss Roade,' Ned said, setting his basket on the table. 'A leg of pork, and two plump cockerels—for the gentleman as is stopping here, I dare say. Ma says there's no need to pay her. She don't want money, says she should rather have some of your good shortbread when you have the time to bake it, and a jar or two of your pickled walnuts. Pa is proper partial to them.' He grinned at her. 'His lordship's Miss Olivia's fiancé so they say…she be stopping, too, I reckon. A houseful, you've got, miss, and no mistake.'

'Well, as to the matter of Lord Ravensden being my sister's fiancé, we are not sure if they are suited or not. Nothing is yet settled,' Beatrice said. She offered him a plate of buns she had baked earlier. 'Have you any news for me, Ned?'

He parked his backside on the edge of her table, taking a bite of the bun and looking as if he appreciated it. Miss Roade's baking beat that of any cook in the four villages that Ned had come across, and she was always generous.

'Well, miss…funny you should ask that,' he said, a sparkle in his eyes. 'I was up at the Vicarage, see. Mrs Hartwell wanted some eggs and a side of bacon, but when I got there she was in the parlour, and our Mary told me…' He paused for effect. 'It seems the Vicar was up at the Abbey early this morning. Went to see the Marquis, on account of his thinking it was up to him to make him see the error of his ways…getting on a bit his lordship, and like to burn in the fiery pit for his sins, I shouldn't wonder.'

'Yes, I dare say you are right.' Ned's sister Mary was cook to the Reverend Hartwell's household. 'What happened? Was the Marquis very rude?' She imagined that he might be, and wondered that anyone should risk the kind of reception such a visit would be bound to bring on a chance caller.

'Our Mary says he opened the door hisself…the Marquis, that is, miss. In a flaming temper…drunk like as not, I dare swear.'

'Where was his butler?' Beatrice asked. 'Surely it is properly Mr Burneck's job to answer the bell?'

'Our Mary says she heard the Reverend telling her mistress. It was the Marquis what came to the door, still in his dressing-robe, and carrying on something awful he was 'cos the Crow hadn't been back to the Abbey all night. Went over to Northampton to see his cousin the previous afternoon and hadn't come back.'

'The Crow…'

Beatrice smiled at the name, one often used by the

village folk to describe Solomon Burneck, the Marquis's butler. Burneck had been with his master for years, even before the Marquis first came to the Abbey. He was called the Crow because he always wore the same rusty black clothes, and because his nose was rather large and hooked like a bird's beak. His eyes were narrow set, his lips thin and pale, but despite his unfortunate looks, he was held in respect and some awe by local people. Solomon Burneck was a man of few words, but when he did speak it was often to quote something from the Bible, and he was thought to be a religious man. Why such a man should remain in the employment of a master such as the Marquis of Sywell was a mystery, but as Beatrice knew well, there was no accounting for loyalty.

'I did not know Mr Burneck had any relatives.'

'She came with the Marquis, worked for him for a few years,' replied the obliging Ned. 'You wouldn't remember but Ma does; it were a good many years ago when Mistress Burneck went off to be married…to a merchant with a house and shop of his own, so me Ma told me.'

'And Mr Burneck has not yet returned from his visit to his cousin? Well, that is odd,' Beatrice said. 'I wonder why he did not come back. Do you suppose he has left the Marquis's employ?'

'If he has done a bunk, he ain't the only one,' Ned said, hugely enjoying himself. 'The Marquis raved and shouted at the Reverend something awful, told him to clear off and never bother him no more—and…' Ned paused importantly. 'He said as her ladyship had cleared off and left him. Said the whole place were empty 'cept for him. What do you think of that then?'

'The Marquis said his wife had gone...' Beatrice felt an unpleasant shiver trickle down her spine as her memory flashed back to the night she had nearly been knocked down by the Marquis's horse. That scream she had heard...that terrible, unearthly scream! 'How long ago did she leave?'

'Dunno...mebbe a few days, mebbe longer...' Ned shook his head. 'Our Mary didn't hear no more...the mistress come out of the parlour, caught her earwigging and sent her back to the kitchen.'

'And there were no other servants up at the Abbey at all?' Nan had come into the kitchen in time to hear the last part of Ned's story. 'Well, I suppose that is not surprising—after the way he has behaved in the past. I am sure no decent woman would dream of working there. No wonder folks say it is all going to rack and ruin. A crying shame, that's what I call it. He is an important landowner hereabouts. He ought to employ a lot of people, and I dare say there's suffering in the villages because of it. It is a great shame he ever came here!'

'It is all very odd,' Beatrice said. The cold chill settled at the nape of her neck. She could not help thinking about the blood-curdling scream she had heard the night she crossed the Abbey lands. 'Where do you suppose the Marchioness could have gone?'

'I dare say she has run off,' said the practical Nan. 'Who could blame her? Married to such a man, and with the house falling into ruin about her, as it must be.'

'Yes…' Beatrice nodded, but something was not quite right. She felt uneasy as she considered what might have happened to the Marquis's young wife. 'But…'

Nan shook her head as if in warning, and Beatrice remembered they were not alone. There was no need to spread gossip unnecessarily.

'Well, thank your mother for me,' Beatrice said. 'Tell her I shall bring the shortbread down this weekend…and perhaps you would like another bun to eat as you go?'

Ned grinned from ear to ear as he took the offering, then went out of the back door. His cheerful whistling could be heard as he sauntered off, carrying his empty basket.

'I know what you are thinking,' Nan said. 'But a still tongue makes a wise head, Beatrice. We must consider carefully. It would not do to start a malicious rumour only to have Lady Sywell turn up next week.'

'No, you are very right,' Beatrice said. 'Besides, Ned may have got it all wrong. I shall be interested to hear what the Reverend Hartwell has to say this evening and…' She broke off as the back door opened and Bellows entered, carrying a large wicker hamper.

'His lordship ordered this, Miss Roade,' her man-servant told her. 'There's a rib of beef, various cheeses and a whole ham, besides the wines and brandy waiting to be brought in from the carter's wagon.'

'And how are we supposed to pay for these things?' Beatrice felt her temper rising. 'There is no way we can afford luxuries like this...' She had opened the hamper to find jars of Gentlemen's Relish, marchpane comfits and candied fruits, also several pounds of tea and sugar—and chocolate! 'Really, it will all have to go back!'

'No need to take on so, miss,' Bellows said in his bluff way. 'It was all put on his lordship's account...same as the carriage and horses he ordered from the livery stables, together with the services of a groom and driver. Said it was easier to hire than send for his own...' Bellows faltered as he realised his mistress was now more incensed than ever. 'And various other things for his personal use...'

'How dare he?' Beatrice fumed. 'How dare he be so—so condescending as to think I would be pleased for him to pay for the food he eats in this house!'

She began to take off her apron. Nan eyed her warily.

'Where are you going, dearest? Not to remonstrate with his lordship, I hope? I dare say he meant it for the best...'

'Meant it for the best?' The light of battle was in Beatrice's eyes. 'It is an insult, Nan. And I mean to tell him so.'

'Do pray remember that the poor man has been ill...' Nan called after her as she walked from the kitchen. 'You do not want him to suffer a relapse.'

Beatrice was not listening. How dare Lord Ravensden insult her so? The only reason she had not offered him the beef he so urgently required was that she would not give him inferior meat, and for quality it was necessary to go into Northampton…to the superior establishment Bellows had clearly visited. Had he only been patient, she would have provided proper meals once she had been able to buy the provisions she needed.

Lord Ravensden was sitting in the parlour when she entered, a book of poems in his hand. He had obviously been reading to Olivia, for she sat idle, her mending laid down on the table beside her. She flushed and looked guilty as she reached for the shirt collar she had been turning for her papa.

'Lord Ravensden was reading aloud—*The Rime of the Ancient Mariner* by Mr Samuel Taylor Coleridge,' Olivia said, looking at her sister uncertainly. 'It is a favourite with me.'

'How very pleasant,' Beatrice said. 'Olivia, dearest—would you run upstairs and fetch my shawl, please?'

'Yes, of course…' Olivia seemed startled by something in her sister's tone, but rose obediently and left the room.

'Lord Ravensden,' Beatrice began as the door closed behind her. Her eyes flashed with green fire. 'I dare say you are not accustomed to staying at such a house as this one…'

Harry had risen to his feet at her entrance. He eyed her warily as he caught the note of anger in her voice. What had he done now?

'Forgive me, Miss Roade. In what way have I offended you?'

'You sent my servant to Northampton without a by your leave, then you have the effrontery to order food and wines—and to put them on your own account. I am aware that I have not been able to offer you the sort of hospitality you are accustomed to, sir, but had you been patient another day or so...'

'Forgive me,' Harry said in a contrite tone that somehow took her breath away. 'I have been clumsy and I see that I have hurt your pride. I meant only to ease the burden I know my visit must have thrust upon you. Indeed, I have no complaints at the hospitality I have received here. I doubt that anyone has ever offered me so much...'

Beatrice was not to be so easily mollified. 'You have sent for a carriage and horses—does that mean you intend to leave soon?'

'No, indeed, for I fear I could not yet contemplate a long journey,' Harry said and was taken by a fit of coughing, which lasted some seconds. When he had recovered enough, he went on, 'It was just that I thought it might be useful to have some of my own servants...to run my errands. And to help do the jobs that Bellows would normally do outside.'

'Oh...' Beatrice found herself at a stand. She could hardly complain when he had obviously been at pains to alleviate his reliance on Bellows's services. 'I see...well, I suppose that might be a help.'

'And you will forgive me?' Harry asked, a soft, persuasive note in his voice. 'Please accept my small gift in the light in which it was offered, Miss Roade. I understand you have guests this evening. Perhaps you may find it of use for them if nothing else?'

'I dare say I may,' Beatrice replied and frowned at him. 'You are a very tiresome creature, my lord.'

'Yes, indeed, I know it,' Harry said, and took a step towards her. 'Miss Roade...'

Whatever he was about to say was lost as Olivia returned with her sister's shawl. She looked relieved to see that they had not yet come to blows.

'Is everything all right, Beatrice?'

'Yes...yes, of course.' Beatrice laughed, wondering why she had felt so very angry. 'It was all a mistake, I dare say.' She hesitated, then, 'We are to have visitors this evening, as you know. Before they come, I believe I ought to tell you both something I have learned this morning...'

Olivia looked at her as she hesitated. 'Pray do go on, sister. Have you some gossip to relate?'

'Well, yes, I have,' Beatrice replied. 'Do you recall we spoke of the Marchioness of Sywell the evening you arrived?'

'Yes, indeed...or at least, you said you knew nothing of her, that she was almost a recluse...'

'Well, it seems she has disappeared.'

'Disappeared?' Olivia stared at her, eyes opening wide. 'What do you mean?'

Beatrice related the story as it had been told to her, then drew her breath in sharply. 'You may remember I was almost knocked down by the Marquis as he rode past me one night...some two weeks ago now?'

Olivia nodded, her eyes beginning to glow with anticipation. 'Well, I had earlier heard the most terrible scream. I thought it must have been the cry of a trapped animal, but now…'

Olivia clapped her hand to her mouth. 'The poor Marchioness, she has been murdered by her wicked husband!'

'Well, as to that,' Beatrice said doubtfully. 'We should not jump to conclusions, Olivia…but it does seem a little odd.'

'How did the Marchioness's disappearance come to light?' Harry asked, the mischief beginning to dance in his eyes as he saw the gleam of excitement in Olivia's.

'The Reverend Hartwell made a visit to the Abbey,' Beatrice said. 'Mysterious lights have been seen at night in Giles Wood, and the Reverend Hartwell thought there might be some—some unpleasant things going on up there. It seems that he thought it his duty to remind the Marquis that he might be called upon to meet his Maker at any time and must repent his sins…'

'Of which there are many?' Harry asked, clearly enjoying himself. 'Tell me, what does he imagine is the significance of the lights? What has the Marquis been up to—surely not pagan orgies?'

Beatrice frowned at him in reproof. 'Well, you may not know of Sywell's reputation…but he has been denounced in the pulpit of every church in the county I dare swear. He is never sober, so they say…and no woman was safe from him, at least until he married.

She was much younger and very beautiful…though I do not recall ever having seen her myself. The adopted child of the Marquis's bailiff, she was educated by her stepmother, who was a governess—and she did not mix with the villagers nor go to school. She had been away from the village for some years, engaged in some trade, I suppose, but came back when her guardian died…and then the Marquis married her and carried her off to his home. After that, she has scarcely been seen again.'

'A very rogue!' Harry stated. 'It stands to reason— he must have done the dastardly deed.'

'Will you be serious, sir!' Beatrice gave him a speaking look from her wonderful eyes, which were themselves glowing like jewels. 'We do not yet know for certain that she is missing—nor that she has been murdered. She may have simply gone away for a visit.'

'If that were so, the Marquis would not have ranted of her absence to Mr Hartwell,' Olivia said. 'No, no, it is clear…he must have murdered her. And his anger at her disappearance was clearly to cover his own guilt. I am sure he has done away with her!'

'And buried her in the haunted chapel at dead of night,' said Harry helpfully. 'He must have got it from one of Fanny Burney's novels.'

'You rogue!' Beatrice cried, laughing at his tone. 'I liked *Evelina* excessively. Now if you had said dear Mrs Radcliffe…' Her eyes were bright with mischief. 'You have a wicked humour, sir. Why will you encourage Olivia in this nonsense?'

'How can you be sure it is nonsense?' Olivia asked. 'You did hear a scream—and you did see the Marquis rush past on his horse.'

'Yes...' Beatrice frowned. Olivia was more animated than she had been in days, her imagination clearly caught by the mystery of the young Lady Sywell's disappearance. 'The truth is, I cannot say what happened—and nor can any of us. I think we should wait and hear what the Reverend Hartwell has to say this evening...'

'A capital notion,' Harry said. 'I shall look forward to it eagerly.'

'Are you sure you are well enough to join us this evening?' Beatrice asked with an air of false concern. 'That cough was painful to hear, my lord—perhaps you should go to bed and I will ask Bellows to come and rub goose grease on your chest.'

'No, that you will not,' Harry said, and coughed again, twice. 'I shall drink a little of the excellent brandy Bellows ordered for...us...if I may, and hope that I may be well enough to come down to dinner.'

Beatrice fixed him with a look that would have slain lesser men.

'Pray go on with what you were doing when I arrived,' she said. 'I have no time to waste if we are to have a decent dinner this evening.'

Harry's smile made her turn hastily away. What did he mean by giving her such a look? He was here to persuade Olivia to marry him—not to make her spinster sister's heart behave in the most peculiar way imaginable.

Chapter Six

Beatrice glanced at herself in the mirror as she dressed for dinner. Her one evening gown was sadly worn and out of style. She had refurbished it with a fresh sash and trimmed the edge with green ribbons, but the colour did nothing for her complexion.

Olivia looked at her and frowned. 'I have more gowns than I need, Beatrice,' she said. 'I should have thought before…perhaps some of them could be altered to fit you?'

'I very much doubt it,' Beatrice said and laughed. 'You are a sylph, dearest, while I am what they call well-formed. Do not feel at all uncomfortable because you have a few pretty gowns. They may have to last you for a long time.'

'Yes, I know.' Olivia smiled at her. 'I do not mind that—but I wish I might share those I have with you.'

'It would be too difficult to alter them,' Beatrice said. 'Besides, I shall buy some material soon and make myself a new gown in time for Christmas.'

'Oh, well,' Olivia sighed. 'I do not suppose either

of us will often have much need of stylish gowns in future.'

'Are you feeling very unhappy, dearest?' Beatrice looked at her in concern. 'I know you must miss your friends—but there are some young women in the villages you might come to know in time. Lady Sophia, Annabel Lett, who is a widow and has an adorable little daughter—and Miss Robina Perceval. She is the niece of the vicar of Abbot Quincey and a very charitable and friendly young woman. She sometimes visits our village, and we stop to talk when we pass in the street. I shall invite her to take tea with us the next time we meet.'

'I am sure I shall find friends soon enough,' Olivia said, her blue eyes a little wistful. 'You must not worry about me, Beatrice.' She smiled and tucked her arm through her sister's. 'We ought to go down. Our guests will soon be arriving…'

'I cannot imagine why Mr Hartwell thought it a good idea to visit the Marquis in the first place,' said his wife at table that evening. 'Everyone knows what a dreadful man he is…'

The Reverend gave her a faintly reproachful look. 'I felt it incumbent upon me to make the effort, my dear. Sywell should make his peace with God before it is too late. As a Christian minister, I must do my duty as I see it.'

'Very right and proper,' Harry said, not a flicker in his eyes to betray him. 'Tell me, my dear sir, do you expect the Marquis's demise imminently?'

Beatrice gave him a darkling look. She glanced across the table at her friend Mademoiselle de Champlain. 'Tell me, Ghislaine, how do things go on at dear Mrs Guarding's school? Have you any new pupils?'

Ghislaine was an attractive woman in her late twenties, pleasant to look at but not pretty except for her dark eyes, which were very fine.

'They come and go, as you know, Beatrice,' she said. 'We have several young ladies coming to us after Christmas, and shall be in need of a new teacher to look after the little ones. Have you thought any more about returning to us?'

'I have not given it much thought of late,' Beatrice replied. She saw Lord Ravensden's eyes on her. 'As you know, I have considered taking up a position...if Papa could spare me?' She looked at her father, who was addressing his beef with the dedication of a man who had not eaten such a treat for a long time.

'What's that, Beatrice?' Mr Roade blinked at her. 'Excellent beef, my dear. You and Nan have excelled yourselves...visit Mademoiselle Champlain when you like, have her here to stay for Christmas. Why not? Always pleased to see your friends.' He beamed round the table happily, apparently lost in his own thoughts.

Beatrice would have turned the subject once again, but Olivia was before her.

'Is it true that the Marquis told you his wife had gone, sir?'

The Reverend Hartwell let his solemn gaze rest on

her. A man of forty-odd years, with thinning hair and brown eyes, he was very aware of his importance in the community. The world was full of sinners, and he knew his duty. Let it never be said that he had neglected the spiritual welfare of his parishioners, even one as disreputable as the Marquis of Sywell.

'I do not have to ask where that came from, Miss Olivia. It is unfortunate that Mary Ekins should have overheard me telling Mrs Hartwell…but the gossip will not be long delayed I fear. It is true that Lady Sywell does appear to have left her husband. No one has seen her for months…'

'Why would she do that, sir?' Olivia's blue eyes were wide and guileless, her manner that of a young girl begging for instruction. Mr Hartwell warmed to her at once. 'Do you think the Marquis was unkind to her?'

'How could it be otherwise?' asked the Reverend, frowning and shaking his head sadly. 'The marriage was doomed to fail from the start. Sywell is a disgrace to his class, Miss Olivia—I might say a disgrace to mankind. Far be it from me to condemn a fellow creature, but he was most damnably rude…told me I was an interfering, prosy busybody and…well, such language is not fit for a young lady's ears.'

'No, indeed it is not, Mr Hartwell,' said his wife and smiled kindly at Olivia. 'I dare say you are very shocked by all this, my dear. Pray tell me, have you come home to be married?'

'No…' Olivia blushed fiery red. 'That is…'

'Miss Olivia is not sure she will take me,' Harry

said. 'I have come to beg on bended knee, but she has never yet given me an answer.'

'But I thought it was announced in *The Times*?' Mrs Hartwell stared at him in surprise.

'That was a misprint,' Harry said without the slightest hesitation. 'Dashed awkward for Olivia, you know. I am thinking of suing them…'

'Indeed, you must not on my account, sir.' Olivia gave a strangled laugh, which she smothered behind her kerchief. Her eyes twinkled at him. 'It was simply a mistake, and since I have no wish to marry at all, it cannot make so very much difference in the end.'

'No wish to marry?' Mr Hartwell looked shocked. 'It is surely your duty to marry, my child? It is a woman's allotted purpose in this world, the reason for which all women were created.'

'Oh, but surely…' Beatrice began to protest, then stopped and blushed, remembering the Vicar was her guest, and the rules of politeness would not allow her to disagree with him.

'You wished to object, Miss Roade?' Harry asked, deceptively enquiring. 'I dare say you think a woman fit for other purposes than the rearing of a family?'

'I think a woman should be free to choose whether or not she cares to be married,' Beatrice said, frowning at him severely. 'But I have no wish to argue with our guest, whose opinions must naturally be respected.'

'Just so…' Mr Roade beamed at them all. 'Do we have one of your excellent puddings this evening, Beatrice?'

'Yes, Papa. I shall ring for Lily now...'

She got up and went over to the sideboard, giving Lord Ravensden a look as she passed. He raised his brows at her but she merely shook her head. He was the most provoking man, but she would not be drawn. Time enough for what she had to say to Lord Ravensden when their guests had gone!

'Well,' Olivia said when they were alone in the parlour later that evening, all their guests having drunk tea and left. Mr Roade and Nan had both retired, leaving the three free to speak their minds. 'I think the case plain...Lady Sywell has not been seen in an age. You may depend upon it, her husband kept her a prisoner, and now he has killed her...and this is his way of pretending to the world that she has gone off.'

'You are placing your reliance on the scream Beatrice heard when she was crossing the Abbey lands,' Harry said, nodding thoughtfully. He seemed not to be aware that he had used her first name and Beatrice did not want to be the one to point it out. 'But consider this—the Marchioness has not been seen in months, while Beatrice heard the scream only a few weeks ago. It may be that Lady Sywell found her position intolerable and ran away soon after her wedding.'

'Someone would have seen her,' Olivia said. 'Besides, I have a feeling...' She shivered impressively and looked grave. The great actress Sarah Siddons could not have done better herself had she taken centre stage. 'I am convinced that the Marquis of Sywell killed his wife and has buried her body somewhere...'

Beatrice frowned, remembering the night she had almost been knocked down by the Marquis, who had seemed half-demented. What Olivia was saying was possible. The man was clearly a brute, who cared for no one and nothing.

'Even if you are right...I do not see how it can be proved.'

'We must find her grave,' Olivia replied, a look of determination in her eyes. 'If he has killed her, she must be buried in the grounds of the Abbey.'

'Or the ruined chapel...' supplied Harry, and received a reproving look from both sisters. 'Forgive me, I am sure you are right, Miss Olivia.'

'We cannot look for the grave,' Beatrice objected. 'The Abbey grounds are private property.'

'That did not stop you crossing them...' Harry's eyes danced with wicked amusement, then he crossed his arms and looked penitent. 'But I shall be silent on that subject. What do you suggest, Miss Roade? Shall we call out the militia and demand Sywell be arrested this instant?'

'I told you he takes nothing seriously,' Olivia said to her sister, pulling a face of exasperation. 'How could I be expected to marry a man like that?'

'You could not, of course,' Beatrice said and glared at Harry. 'If you have nothing of sense to say, sir, you may take yourself off to bed. I dare say you are weary, and needing your rest. Shall I send Bellows up to you with a hot posset?'

'A large brandy would be more appropriate,' Harry said. 'But I shall leave you to work out our plan of campaign. You are more in command of the terrain, and I rely on you for instructions. I suppose we shall have to search at night? If we were seen in daylight it might be awkward…or is that a mere quibble?'

'Go to bed, sir,' Beatrice said sternly. 'I shall speak to you in the morning.'

'Yes, Miss Roade. Your wish is my command…' Harry smiled at both sisters and went from the room.

Beatrice looked at Olivia and laughed. 'You are quite right, dearest,' she said. 'He is impossible. I am sure no woman of sense would ever wish to marry him.'

'Perhaps not,' Olivia said, looking thoughtful. 'But for the right woman I suppose he might be an agreeable husband. He is charming, is he not?'

Beatrice turned away to make sure that the fire screen was in place. 'Yes,' she said, without looking round. 'He does have a certain charm, and in some circumstances I suppose a woman might be wise to accept an offer from Lord Ravensden.' She faced her sister, smile in place. 'Come, let us to our beds, Olivia. We must both sleep on all this, and in the morning we can decide what we ought to do…'

Harry smiled to himself as he undressed. His stay in Northamptonshire was proving most diverting. His sense of the ridiculous had made him go along with Olivia's outrageous suggestion, though his own more logical mind told him that it was unlikely they would find a grave...unless, he supposed, the lights in the woods might have a more sinister significance than he had first thought.

It was possible, he imagined, that there might actually be a woman's body buried somewhere on the estate. It was an unpleasant thought, and not one he wished to sleep on.

His mind turned towards the woman he had left downstairs. What was it about her that he was beginning to find fascinating? Far too fascinating for his peace of mind!

Sipping the brandy Bellows had brought him, Harry considered. Supposing Olivia continued to refuse him? He sighed. It was an awkward situation, and he could have wished that things were different. Somehow, he must find a solution to all their problems...

Why was it so impossible to sleep? Beatrice turned from side to side on her pillow, which was unaccountably lumpy. Olivia was sleeping, but as her sister moved she moaned and half woke.

This would never do! She must not wake Olivia. Slipping carefully from beneath the covers, Beatrice pulled on her wrapping-gown and left the room. She normally slept easily at night, but nothing was normal now. Lord Ravensden's arrival had turned their household upside down, and she sometimes wondered if anything would ever be the same again.

Now there was this mystery of the young Marchioness to plague her. Where had she gone? Had she truly been murdered by her cruel husband—or had she simply run away?

Alone in the kitchen, Beatrice poured herself a glass of wine, then saw the glacé fruits that had not been eaten after dinner and helped herself to two of them. They were quite delicious. She ate them both and licked the sweetness from her fingers, feeling guilty as she remembered that she had grumbled at Lord Ravensden for buying them...the provoking man.

How had he managed to get under her skin in this manner? He was constantly making her want to prick at him with words as sharp as needles, and yet she was always glad to see him.

A thought occurred to her, which was ruthlessly denied. Impossible! She could not be developing a *tendre* for him? No, certainly not...such an idea was out of the question. Especially after the way Olivia had spoken of him just before she went to bed. It was clear that her sister was beginning to reconsider...

Beatrice turned her head as the kitchen door opened. Her heart jerked as she saw Lord Ravensden standing there in his silk dressing-gown, his feet bare. He was probably naked beneath that very fashionable robe, just as he had been when she bathed him during the fever.

Beatrice felt her cheeks go warm. She should be ashamed of such thoughts!

'So you could not sleep either,' Harry said. 'May I join you?'

'Yes, of course.' The tray of brandy and glasses

stood on the table with the remains of the nuts and sweetmeats from dinner. 'Brandy is a help when one cannot sleep…and this is a very fine vintage.'

'I am glad you approve,' Harry said. God! Had she any idea of how very desirable she looked in that wrapping-gown? The colour became her so well. She ought always to wear those jewel colours. 'May I?' He poured himself a little brandy into a glass, warming it between his hands as he continued to look at her. 'Do you suppose Olivia is serious about searching for Lady Sywell's grave?'

'Yes, I think she is,' Beatrice said, wrinkling her brow. She was aware of some feeling flowing between them. It had been there for a while now, but she had tried to ignore it. That was easier to do in company than when they were alone, both wearing much less than they ought to be! 'I am not certain that her supposition is correct…but I suppose it could do no harm to look.'

'And if by some remote chance we were to find this grave?'

'Then we should have to call in the militia, Lord Ravensden. It would be a very terrible crime, and the perpetrator should be punished—do you not agree?'

'Your eyes are like emeralds in this light,' Harry said. 'I have never seen a woman with eyes the colour of yours, Beatrice.'

There, he had said it again! Her first name.

'You should not, my lord.' Her cheeks took fire. 'It is not fitting that you should say such a thing to me…'

'It is not fitting that we should be sitting here to-gether,' Harry said, his smile taking her breath. 'But I hope you do not mean to ask me to go away?' Beatrice shook her head. She ought to leave at once herself, but she did not wish to. 'I think we have gone beyond the bounds of conventional conversation, Beatrice. You are a beautiful woman, why do you pretend to be a dowd?'

'I am three-and-twenty, sir. I have no dowry, and I have driven away all the widowers who would have taken me for my usefulness as a mother to their moth-erless children. What use have I for pretty gowns?'

'It is a crime that you should wear grey and brown when you look best in green…or perhaps midnight blue…' Harry considered. 'But you could wear most deep colours.'

'Please be serious for a moment, sir.'

'I am very serious,' Harry said, and pulled a face. 'Must you call me sir? I am Ravensden—or Harry to those I love and trust.'

'To Merry and Lord Dawlish?' Beatrice asked, her eyes raised to his. She caught her breath at the burn-ing heat she saw there.

'And to a few others,' Harry said. 'Perhaps to you one day, Beatrice.'

'When you marry Olivia?' Her eyes challenged him. 'You do mean to ask her again, don't you?'

'I believe I must,' Harry replied and cursed softly. 'We are caught in a pretty coil, Beatrice, are we not? I think I am not wrong in suggesting that you too feel something…'

This conversation should not be taking place! It would not do. She had no idea whether what he had in mind was to offer her *carte blanche* or...but it could not be. He was promised to Olivia, and she believed that her sister would eventually claim her right to be his bride.

'I must go...'

As Beatrice rose so did Harry. He reached out, catching her wrist, making her pause to look back at him.

'I must leave now...'

She got no further, for she was in his arms, pressed close against him so that she could feel the heat of his body. He looked down at her for a moment, then lowered his head, touching his mouth to hers. For a moment his kiss was soft, hesitant, but then, feeling the response of hers, his kiss deepened, becoming passionate, fierce and demanding.

Then, when she thought she would swoon for pleasure, his mouth released hers, and she was free of his embrace. His face was twisted with pain and a hunger that shocked her. Did he want her so very much? No man had ever looked at her in quite that way before.

'Forgive me,' he said, his breath ragged with desire. 'I had no right to do that, no right at all.'

'No,' Beatrice said quietly. 'Nor I to let you. We both know that your duty lies with Olivia, my lord. You are fond of her, and she would make you a fitting wife. Your position demands that, and I have never mixed in society. I am a plain, simple countrywoman, with none of the social arts...'

'As if that mattered...you cannot think it, Beatrice?'

'I do not know what to think,' she said. 'Please, my lord, let me go now. I must return to my sister. To stay longer might prove dangerous for both of us.'

'Harry...' he said hoarsely. 'I beg you, let me hear my name on your lips this once...please.'

Beatrice swallowed hard. 'Harry...' she said, her heart twisting with sudden pain. 'Now, let me go, my dear. You know this is wrong, don't you?'

'Yes.' He stood back, his features harsh, unreadable. 'Had you been any other than Olivia's sister, I might still have found a way...but that is clearly impossible.'

Beatrice turned swiftly lest he should see the pain his words had given her. So he *had* thought to make her his mistress and not his wife. As well then that she loved Olivia too dearly to try and take her fiancé from her!

Harry let her go, and she left quickly, before she betrayed herself. She ran upstairs, feeling the pain too bitter to dwell on. She had brought this on herself, by allowing him too much freedom. He knew that she had done things no respectable young woman would dream of doing, and it had led him to think of her as a wanton.

Raising her head proudly, Beatrice fought down her desire to weep. There was nowhere she could be alone, and besides, she would not weep for such a cause. Had she not been taught a harsh lesson when she was a naïve girl?

It seemed that men were all the same. They used those who were foolish enough to allow them the freedom of their hearts and bodies, and married innocent girls—especially if those girls were heiresses.

She must watch herself in the future. She had let down her guard this evening, but she must keep it firmly in place from now on.

Beatrice watched Olivia and Lord Ravensden laughing together as their relationship developed. The transformation in her sister these past two days was nothing short of amazing. Olivia's imagination had been captured by the disappearance of the Marchioness, and since Lord Ravensden seemed determined to indulge her, she appeared to have lost her shyness with him. She had begun to speak to him in a manner that, if not flirtatious, was certainly that of an intimate friend.

Of course they must have been friends during the Season. Beatrice was beginning to know her sister better, and she sensed that Olivia must have liked Harry Ravensden a great deal or she would not even have considered accepting his proposal. Obviously she had been hurt and deeply distressed by the spiteful tales related to her. However, now that she knew Harry was innocent of the cruel things he was supposed to have said concerning his reasons for marrying her, and that he truly felt some regard for her, she had clearly forgiven him.

Beatrice spent some of her time with them, but she did not always join in their banter. She was trying to keep her distance, and often excused herself on the grounds that she was busy. On Friday and Saturday she attacked the linen cupboards and the pantry with such determination that both Nan and Lily were startled, while poor Ida locked herself in the scullery and would not come out until Beatrice begged her.

However, on Sunday morning she was persuaded to go to church with her sister and Lord Ravensden, and, somehow, on the way home, she found herself walking with Harry. Olivia had lingered to speak with Lady Sophia, who had detached herself from her father, the white-haired, very dignified, distinguished Earl of Yardley, and had come up to them after the service and introduced herself to Olivia.

Beatrice had been delighted that the young woman had shown so much kindness to her sister, and deliberately walked on ahead so that Olivia could spend a few minutes alone with her. She glanced at Lord Ravensden as he joined her

'You have been very busy of late,' Harry remarked, a thoughtful expression in his eyes. 'I must tell you that Olivia and I have worked out our plan of campaign in your absence.'

'Do you really mean to go through with this?' Beatrice raised her eyes to his, then looked away quickly as she saw his expression. He seemed to be reproaching her.

'Why not?' Harry asked. 'What harm can it do? Olivia is determined. I dare say she would go alone if we refused to go with her. Should there, by the merest chance, be any truth in this notion of hers, that might prove dangerous for her.'

Beatrice felt a chill at the nape of her neck. 'Yes, you are very right, my lord. It does seem improbable that the Marquis actually killed his wife, and buried her body...but people are beginning to talk and wonder. I took some shortbread down to Ekins' farm yesterday, and it is true that no one has seen the Marchioness for months.'

'So...' Harry's brow creased in thought. 'It is possible that she has been murdered. And I really do not care for that idea, do you?'

'No,' Beatrice admitted. 'I must say that I should feel both disgust and anger if I thought that she had died at her husband's hands.'

Harry nodded, his expression unusually grim. 'Yes, I imagine you would not wish the guilty man to escape punishment.'

'No, I should not.' Beatrice was thoughtful. 'What have you and Olivia decided?'

'We thought we should take it in turns to walk about the grounds in daylight. Sometimes Olivia and I, sometimes you and your sister, and...' He looked rueful. 'Do you think you could bear to accompany me? I know you must be angry with me for my thoughtless behaviour the other night.'

'Angry...' Oh, if only he knew how much she longed for him to kiss her like that again! No, she must not think of such things. He was forbidden to her by all the laws of decency and truth. She could not look at him as she replied stiffly, 'I am not angry, my lord.'

'Beatrice, you know that I…' Harry broke off with a muffled oath. 'Good grief! I do not believe it. That is Percy's curricle. I would know it anywhere. What on earth is he doing here?'

Beatrice glanced towards her house and saw the smart carriage with huge yellow wheels parked in the driveway. She paused as a man turned and began to wave excitedly at them. Goodness! What on earth was he wearing? His coat was unexceptional, being a very fine blue cloth and cut exquisitely so that it moulded to his slightly stout figure—but his waistcoat was striped in yellow and black, and his neckcloth was so extravagantly high that he must surely have difficulty in turning his head!

'Damn my eyes!' Lord Dawlish exclaimed, striding towards them, a smile that seemed as much relief as pleasure in his dark eyes. 'So there you are, Harry, safe and well. I knew it must be so, but Merry would have it you were ill…'

Harry clapped a hand to his forehead. 'I was engaged to her for Lady Melchit's ball. She will never forgive me. It clean went out of my head.'

'She would have it you were nearly on your deathbed,' Percy said indignantly. 'Made me drive all the way down here.'

'As it happens, she was right,' Harry said, smiling affectionately at him. Percy would not have taken much persuading if he believed his friend was in trou-

ble. 'If it were not for Miss Roade, I might very well
have died.'

'You don't say so! You mean Merry was right?'
Percy gaped at him. 'Well, I never. I made sure it was
all nonsense—but now you come to mention it, you
don't look all that clever. Merry would give me no
peace until I came to look for you. Your man said
you were out of town but refused to say where, and
you must know there has been some gossip. That fellow Quindon has been in town, and looking mighty
pleased with himself. I dare say he would be glad to
step into your shoes. People wondered when you went
off without a word, talk of suicide and such nonsense.
Never believed a word of it meself...it was Merry
who came up with the notion that you might be here.'

'How sensible of you to dismiss such gossip, and
how clever your beautiful lady is,' Harry said and
grinned wickedly. 'But you have not met Miss
Roade...Beatrice, this is my very dear friend Percy
Dawlish. I may have mentioned him before, and his
wife Merry? Percy, I want you to meet the lady who
saved my life.'

'It was no such thing,' Beatrice said with a frown
at him. 'My aunt nursed Lord Ravensden, of course.
I merely sent for the doctor.'

'Ah yes, of course. I forgot for the moment. It was
Mrs Willow who nursed me.' Harry's eyes gleamed.
'It would have been most improper for you to have
done so, Beatrice.'

'Yes, I should say...' Percy looked uncertainly
from one to the other. Miss Roade did not look quite

like the young women Harry usually set up as his flirts, but there was definitely something between them. One only had to look at their eyes, and the sparks were most definitely flying. 'Pleased to meet you, Miss Roade. I must thank you—or Mrs Willow—Merry would be devastated if anything had happened to this rogue here. Very fond of him, though as Merry says, he can be the most tiresome creature.'

Beatrice laughed. She liked this man, who was clearly very fond of Lord Ravensden. For some reason the shadow that had hung over her these past few days seemed to have melted away.

'I am always pleased to meet a good friend of Lord Ravensden,' she said. 'And one who clearly knows him so well.'

'Now, Beatrice,' Harry said, the promise of retribution in his eyes. He was about to say more but his words were lost as Olivia came up to them. 'Percy, you know Olivia, of course.'

'Of course, delighted to see you looking so well, Miss Roade Burton.'

'Miss Olivia, if you please, sir,' Olivia said. 'I do not care to use the name of my adopted family now.'

'Just so…' Percy looked uncomfortable. 'Deuced awkward affair. Can't think what Burton was about to do such a thing.'

'Not awkward at all,' Harry said before she could reply. 'It is all a misunderstanding, Percy. We shall come about, given time.'

Olivia seemed as if she wanted to speak, but changed her mind as Beatrice shook her head at her.

'You will dine with us, Lord Dawlish?' Beatrice said, going forward to smile at him. 'We dine at five and thirty on Sunday. Early I know, but we keep country hours here.'

'I should be delighted to dine with you,' Percy said. 'I noticed a decent inn on the Northampton road. Do you imagine they would put me up for a few nights?'

'A few nights, Percy?' Harry's deep blue eyes quizzed him mercilessly. 'Really? Can you bear it? Northampton, my dear fellow! Will Merry not worry about you?'

'I shall send word that all is right and tight,' Percy replied airily. 'But I think I shall break my journey for a day or two—just to satisfy myself that you are really recovered.'

'Can you be in doubt when I have good friends to watch over me?' Harry grinned at him. 'You always did have a nose for a mystery, Percy. Your curiosity will lead you astray one day, my friend—but if you are to stay, you may make yourself useful. Four of us will discover the grave more quickly—if it is to be found, of course.'

'Grave...' Percy's mouth dropped open. 'No, I say, Harry. Steady on, old fellow. What have you been up to now? Help you all I can, risk life and limb if you needed me—but don't like any of this havey cavey stuff, you know.'

'We are trying to discover if there have been some unpleasant goings on at the Abbey,' Harry said, as they all followed Beatrice into the house. 'Nothing unlawful, Percy...well, only a bit of trespassing.'

'We think Lady Sywell may have been murdered,' Olivia said. 'Pray do tell him, Harry!'

'Yes, I shall do so...' Harry smiled at her. 'It's like this, Percy...a young woman has disappeared in mysterious circumstances. There is a possibility that she may have been murdered...'

'And her body buried in the grounds of the Abbey,' Olivia supplied impatiently. 'All we are going to do is look for signs of her grave.'

'Disappeared...' Percy looked bewildered. 'Don't quite follow you.'

'Do have a glass of sherry and warm yourself by the fire,' Beatrice said, ushering them all into the parlour. 'The Marquis of Sywell is an unpleasant man, you see, and he married a girl out of his class a year ago...and no one has seen her for months.'

'Lady Sophia was telling me that the Marchioness of Sywell did not go into company at all,' Olivia put in. 'Lady Sophia too had heard that the Marchioness has been missing for several months.'

'Sywell...' Percy frowned. 'Know that name... damned unpleasant fellow. Caught him cheating at cards once, never sat down with the fellow again.'

'Did you challenge him?' Harry asked, frowning.

'Not worth the bother, old chap. Only lost a few guineas. Unpleasant thing, calling a fellow a cheat...no proof, of course, just a sense of what was happening.' Percy shook his head. 'Just the sort of chap would murder his poor little wife! Something should be done about it. Damn it all, can't be allowed to get away with that sort of thing. It ain't sporting, what?'

'We are going to try to discover the truth,' Olivia said, smiling at him. 'Would you help us, sir?' She tipped her head to one side, looking so charming that Percy coloured. 'Obviously neither Beatrice nor I can search alone—but if you would accompany me, Harry can protect my sister.'

Percy was irrevocably devoted to Lady Dawlish, but not above a little flattery from a pretty young woman. 'Delighted, m'dear. Of course I wouldn't dream of letting you go alone...if that wretched fellow is about you will need someone to take care of you, see you come to no harm. Delighted to be of service.'

'Thank you, I knew you would not desert me,' Olivia said, and received a wicked smile from Harry as payment for her subterfuge.

Beatrice was a little shaken by this revelation of her sister's society manners. Olivia was clearly nowhere near as vulnerable or as innocent as she had imagined. Her startled eyes flew to Harry, who very reprehensibly winked at her.

'And I shall make it my business to see that Beatrice comes to no harm,' he said, clearly well satisfied with the situation. 'So...when do we commence the search?

'In the morning,' Beatrice said. 'It would not do on a Sunday. Besides, I must see to the dinner. I shall have wine and biscuits sent in to take the edge off your hunger…'

She saw Lord Dawlish send a startled glance at Harry—she could not think of him as anything else since he had forced her to use his name!—and went away, smiling to herself. No doubt Harry's friend would think this a very unusual household…

Chapter Seven

Beatrice sat at the window of the room she shared with Olivia and gazed out into the darkness. Her sister was sleeping, but she had found it impossible to rest, and she dare not venture down to the kitchen in her dressing-robe again, not while they had guests staying.

Outside, the moonlight was turning all to silver, bathing the lawns, trees and hedges in its gentle glow. Beatrice could not help thinking of the evening just past, how pleasant it had been to have company in the house—the kind of company that she found so amusing. Both Lord Dawlish and Harry were great wits in their own way, though she had begun to sense that Harry went much deeper than anyone supposed. However, he was careful not to show his thoughts too plainly, and everyone had spent much of the evening jesting at each other's expense. Indeed, they had been a merry party.

Once, she had looked up to see Harry watching her, and the look in his eyes had made her heart stop and then race madly on. She smiled at her own thoughts, which were far from what a modest young woman's ought to be.

Her smile faded a little as her thoughts turned to the search they intended to make of the Abbey grounds. She knew that Olivia was convinced the young Marchioness had been cruelly murdered, but the idea seemed appalling to Beatrice.

How lonely the young Lady Sywell must have been, trapped in that great brooding house alone with her monstrous husband. Beatrice had never truly thought about it before, but now she felt guilt strike her to the heart. How unkind they had all been! Perhaps if some of the villagers had tried to make friends with her, instead of condemning the marriage…they might have brought comfort to that poor woman.

Sighing, Beatrice forced the unhappy thoughts from her mind and went back to bed. She must get some rest or she would be too tired to do anything in the morning.

'Somewhat neglected, ain't it?' remarked Lord Dawlish as the four conspirators gathered at the Western gate of Steepwood Abbey the following morning. 'Odd sort of place. Almost a wasteland by the look of things, a little sinister, what?' He patted the small but deadly pistol he carried in his capacious coat pocket as if to reassure himself.

'Beatrice and I will walk towards the lake,' Harry said. 'At least we have a good morning for it, no sign of mist or rain. I doubt the grave, should there be one, will be near the Abbey. Too obvious in open ground. No, I believe we should concentrate our search elsewhere.'

Percy glanced round doubtfully. Well enough to speak of searching in the comfort of a warm parlour over a good brandy, but where to begin in what looked to him very like a wilderness?

'Not sure this was such a good idea, Harry.'

'Courage, mon brave!' Harry said and smiled. 'It is a daunting prospect, but reflect, we are simply out for a walk to take the air. Apparently there is only one servant left in the Marquis of Sywell's employ. It is unlikely that we shall be troubled by anyone—and you know what to say if you should be challenged.'

'You and Olivia should try looking in the old herb garden,' Beatrice said. 'It is sadly overrun but still rather lovely, and peaceful. The walls have crumbled in places—but it is not so unpleasant as some of the outhouses, or as dangerous. Many of the older buildings are in danger of falling down.'

'Herb garden, you say? That sounds more the thing, Miss Olivia.' Percy looked more cheerful. It was a bright morning, the sun making the idea of such a walk quite pleasant, and they were all well wrapped up against the wind. He offered his arm to Olivia. 'At least it should be easy enough to spot if the ground has been disturbed. The whole estate has gone wild…disgraceful neglect!'

'Shall we?' Harry offered his arm as they began to

stroll in the opposite direction to their companions. 'Percy is right, you know. This plan was conceived in a spirit of adventure, but it will not be as easy to carry out as Olivia imagined.'

'My sister has not lived here since she was a child, and can have no idea what the grounds were really like,' Beatrice said. She had not taken his arm, she dare not, lest she betray herself. 'My mother's brother adopted her, as you may know. She was too young to understand why she was being taken from her mother, and she sobbed when they carried her away. It was heart-wrenching, so cruel. I have never forgotten the look of reproach in her eyes.'

'But you understood.' Harry's brows arched. 'It must have been a sad wrench for you, to lose your sister.'

'And for my parents. Mama wept for days. I have never really understood why she agreed. Unless...I believe Lord Burton may have paid some of poor Papa's debts. Oh, dear, that sounds terrible! But I think Mama truly believed it was for Olivia's own good.'

'As perhaps it was,' Harry suggested. 'Olivia has had many advantages you have not.'

'Yes, perhaps so, in some ways. We did not see her again for a long time, and when Lady Burton brought her to see us she seemed quite happy. It was only when she was about fourteen that she began to write to me, though I had written to her from the moment they took her from us. I believe, for several years, she was happy enough in her own way.'

'I am sure she was,' Harry said. 'Olivia has been spoiled and petted. I believe Lady Burton at least is genuinely concerned about what has happened. Indeed, I suspect it may have broken her heart.'

'Yes, I suppose it must be an unhappy time for her. It is a pity her husband could not have shown more compassion.'

'I dare say he felt Olivia had let him down. Burton is a proud man—and he had given her everything she could possibly want in a material way.'

'Yes, of course. I do see that—but I think if he had truly cared for her, he might have been kinder. Papa would never cast me off, whatever I did.'

'Perhaps Burton's disappointment was all the stronger, because he had lavished so much attention on her?'

Beatrice looked thoughtful as they approached what must once have been a collection of cottages used by those who served at the Abbey during the time of the monks. Some of them had tumbled down, allowing moss and brambles to grow through the debris. Over the centuries they had been rebuilt and repaired many times, until these past eighteen years when they had been allowed to fall into decay.

'Yes, I am sure of it. But you know, I have been truly loved. I do not think that was the case for my sister—for I am convinced that if they had loved her as they ought, they could not have treated her so shabbily now.'

Harry nodded, but made no further comment. His eyes went over the huddle of ruins with contempt.

What kind of a landowner allowed such wanton waste? He himself had vast estates, which took a great deal of management, but he would have been shamed to see such a sight on his land.

Beatrice saw his look and nodded. 'These have not been lived in for years. No one born locally would come to work or live here after the Marquis's reputation was known. He brought in servants from town for some time, but none would stay long. Even if he wanted to repair his buildings, he would not find anyone here who would work for him.'

'They look as if a good storm would blow them down,' Harry said, frowning at the hovels. 'I shall make a closer inspection. Wait here, Beatrice. I would not have you risk yourself.'

'I am not a child, sir. If you imagine I shall hinder you…'

'Acquit me of such thoughts,' Harry urged. 'Come if you must, but take care. The stones are loose and the ground uneven. I would not have you stumble and injure yourself.'

'Go ahead and I shall follow,' Beatrice said, picking her way over rubble and tufts of grass which had grown up between. A rabbit had started up ahead of them. She wondered suddenly if this was where the rabbits that appeared so mysteriously in her larder came from. It would certainly solve the mystery of the lights in the woods. 'Something has occurred to me, my lord,' she said as she caught up to him. 'I believe Bellows may know these grounds much better than any of us.'

'Now why didn't I think of that?' Harry murmured, a gleam of appreciation in his eyes. 'That was an excellent rabbit pie we had last night...' He looked up as a pigeon fluttered out of one of the ruined cottages and flew off. 'And those pigeons in red wine...quite delicious, and in plentiful supply, one would imagine.'

Beatrice frowned. 'I should have guessed long ago where Bellows was snaring his game, but it was useful and I suppose I did not wish to enquire too closely.'

'A resourceful man, our Bellows. I believe I shall take him into my confidence.' Harry raised his brows. 'You think his loyalty beyond doubt?'

'He has not been paid in three years,' Beatrice confessed. 'I tried to pay him something last Christmas, but he declares he will wait until my father makes his fortune. Which, I dare say, may be never.'

'Oh, I don't know,' Harry murmured wickedly. 'Percy was very taken by your father's idea for gravity heating. Dawlish Manor is very large and very cold. Percy won't go near it in winter.'

'Oh, I do hope Papa will not persuade him to let him try his experiments at Dawlish Manor. I believe it might prove quite expensive, and not at all what Lord Dawlish would expect.'

There was no sign of any suspicious mounds in the ruins of the cottages. After a few minutes, they continued their walk towards the barns and outhouses that had made up part of the monks' working community. During the years of the Yardleys' ownership these had been kept in good repair and used for storing produce from the various tenant farms that still belonged to the Abbey, but the barns too had been allowed to rot and there were gaping holes in the roofs. Some had no more than a wall left standing.

There was somehow a sinister air about the place, an oppressive atmosphere that hung over the huddle of ruins, the smell of age and decay—almost of evil. It was as if a curse lay over everything.

Beatrice shook her head at the thought. It was a foolish one, and should be dismissed at once.

After searching for some half an hour or more, Beatrice and Harry could find no sign of anyone having been near for years. They were reasonably satisfied that there was no grave to be found here.

Leaving behind the depressing huddle of rotting buildings, they began to walk towards the lake. Here there was a gentle undulation in the land, as in much of the county, and they climbed towards the rise, then breasted it to gaze down on the lake lying below. Even the years of neglect could not take away the beauty nature had bestowed on the scene spread before their eyes.

The waters of the lake were grey, reflecting the sky above, but there was a patch of silver far out where the sun had broken through and the surface rippled. Trees gathered about the banks, willows, stunted and shaped by the hand of a cruel wind, reed-beds sheltered water-birds, and beneath the water fish swam, lazily content.

'I have never stood here like this before,' Beatrice

said. 'Whenever I venture on to Abbey lands, which is not often, I always use the shortest route from Steep Abbot to Abbot Giles, and I do not stand and stare. It is very beautiful here…do you not think so?'

'This must once have been a fine estate,' Harry remarked. 'How came it into the hands of its present owner?'

Beatrice began the story, telling it as she had to her sister on the night of Olivia's homecoming, and in this manner they continued to walk, enjoying each other's company, thinking more of how pleasant it was to spend time in this way than anything else, yet taking note of all they saw.

And so it was that they spent nearly three hours exploring, without seeing anything that was in the least suspicious, entirely at one with each other and well content. If in the process they came to know each other's thoughts a little better, then that made the exercise all the more worthwhile.

It was as they retraced their steps towards the Abbey that they suddenly saw someone coming towards them. He was tall, thin, dressed in black, and even before they could see his face clearly, Beatrice knew him.

'It is Solomon Burneck,' she said to Harry. 'He will know me…'

Harry nodded. He linked his arm firmly with hers and went forward to meet the Marquis's servant.

'Good morning, sir,' Harry said pleasantly. 'Forgive me, I believe we are trespassing here?'

'You are on the lands of Steepwood Abbey, which

is the estate of my master the Marquis of Sywell,' Solomon replied, his narrow set eyes flicking to Beatrice and then back to Harry, who was so obviously a gentleman. 'May I enquire your business, sir?'

'Ravensden,' Harry said. 'Miss Roade and I were out walking my dog and the wretched creature gave us the slip and ran in here. I am afraid we came to look for her. We should perhaps have called at the house to ask permission, but we thought to find her before we could be a trouble to anyone.'

'A dog?' Burneck's expression did not waver. He knew true breeding when he met it, as well he might, and this man was clearly of noble birth. 'May I enquire what kind of a dog, sir?'

'A wolfhound,' Harry replied. 'A great, foolish creature but of the sweetest temper. I do not suppose you have seen her this morning?'

'*The way of transgressors is hard*,' said Solomon, his expression unreadable. 'There are many places where a creature might lose itself in this wilderness. It is a place of abomination in the eyes of the Lord. I fear the curse of ages past is upon this land, and those who usurp the rightful destiny of others.'

'Yes, quite,' Harry murmured, only the flicker of an eyelid giving Beatrice a clue to his thoughts at being addressed in this manner. 'Well, we must trespass no more. We can only hope the foolish creature will find its way home.'

'*A living dog is better than a dead lion.* Ecclesiastes, chapter nine, verse four,' Solomon announced, suitably grave. 'God shall punish the unjust and at the final judgement all men shall be equal in the sight of the Lord. *The Lord giveth and the Lord taketh away.*'

'Yes, you are quite right, it is very true,' Harry said and coughed behind his hand. 'But one must hope for the poor creature's sake that nothing too terrible has overtaken her.' He turned to Beatrice, his eyes alight with wicked mirth. 'Come, Miss Roade. I believe we must delay this gentleman no longer.'

Beatrice inclined her head to Solomon Burneck. She dare not utter a word lest she have a fit of giggles. She managed to contain herself until they had left the narrow lane leading from the Abbey grounds, emerging into a wider road that led either to the village or up the slope to Roade House, then she turned on Harry.

'You wicked, wicked wretch! I thought I should die back there. I do not know how I managed to contain myself.'

'Are you unwell, Beatrice? Where is the pain?' Her speaking look made Harry laugh. 'No, I shall not tease you. I thought Mr Burneck a most unusual man...'

'You must know that Solomon Burneck is well respected by the people of the four villages,' Beatrice said, serious now. 'They believe him to be deeply religious.'

'From his habit of quoting the Bible, one supposes?' Harry looked thoughtful. 'It was all rubbish, you know. Perhaps he does it for effect or...I sensed some deep resentment there beneath the surface, did

you? There is something about him, something that
seems a trifle unusual, even dangerous. Besides, it
does rather beg the question of why such a man
chooses to work for Sywell, does it not? If he were
truly religious he would surely have left Sywell's employ years ago. Perhaps his master has some hold
over him…' He frowned. 'What do you suppose he
meant by the curse of ages past being upon this
place?'

'How can one know? There are many rumours and
tales, but I do not know of a curse…though the history of the Abbey has been bloody and violent, and
many who have lived here have suffered tragedy in
their lives,' Beatrice said, suddenly realising how true
that was. She recalled the feeling that had come to
her as they explored the ruins of the old barns and
hovels and shivered. 'But Mr Burneck is an odd man.
No one truly knows him, except…I have recently
learned that he has a cousin, but she married years
ago and lives in Northampton. He visits her from time
to time, and must presumably care for her. I believe
she once worked for the Marquis, though many years
ago…'

Harry nodded, and looked thoughtful. 'Some form
of blackmail perhaps? The cousin was Sywell's mistress and Burneck stays to protect her reputation for
fear of her husband's temper? No, it will not wash,
Beatrice. I doubt Sywell would even remember the
woman was once his mistress, let alone bother to
blackmail her or his servant. No, I believe the man
may have some deeper, secret, more personal reason

for his loyalty. Something that makes him stay no matter what his master does…'

'Yes, perhaps…' Beatrice was struck by this, which she felt a little sinister. Solomon Burneck was indeed a mystery. She had always been inclined to laugh at the tales told of the Marquis and his evil ways, but now she was very certain that there was indeed something very strange about the Abbey and its inhabitants. She shuddered as the coldness trickled down her spine and spread through her body, then turned to Harry, needing to turn the conversation. 'But why are one's people loyal? I have remarked it on more than one occasion. And Bellows has been as faithful to Papa…'

'But for far more reason,' Harry pointed out. 'Your father is a man anyone would respect and indeed love.'

Beatrice smiled and nodded. She hugged his arm in a companionable way, and felt the chill of horror leave her as her mind returned to normal, happy things.

After leaving Solomon Burneck, she had not let go of Harry's arm and was finding it very pleasant to walk in such close contact with him. It gave her a warm glow inside to know that Harry held her father in such high regard.

'Yes, Papa is very lovable,' she said. 'I have been…' At that moment she saw Olivia and Lord Dawlish approaching from the opposite direction and remembered that Harry was—or ought to be—her sister's fiancé. She let go of his arm. 'Here is my sister…'

The four met, greeted each other with excited cries, then hurried inside the house to warm themselves in front of the parlour fire, which was burning merrily.

'Did you find anything?' Olivia asked. 'We explored the herb gardens—and we walked in the cloisters. We found an open door at the rear and no one was about, so ventured inside. It has the most marvellous arched roof, Beatrice, really very beautiful, but it looks as if it has been used to store broken furniture and rubbish these past years. I wanted to try exploring further into the main building, but Lord Dawlish would not let me.'

'Might have been awkward if we had seen anyone,' Percy said. 'Private house, after all. Wouldn't want anyone wandering into my house without a by your leave.'

'And the Marquis is so often drunk,' Beatrice said. 'You were very right, Lord Dawlish. Besides, I doubt he would have hidden his wife's body in the house itself.'

'Good lord, no! Most unpleasant,' Percy said. 'Enough to give one nightmares, too ghoulish by far.'

'We saw nothing suspicious,' Harry said. 'But we could only cover so much ground, though we walked as far as the lake and returned by another route. I think we need help if we are to succeed in this search. There is still the monk's cemetery and the woods…'

'…the infirmary, which has been used for many years as stables,' Beatrice put in, 'and of course the ruins of the church.' She smiled at Harry. 'Though there is not much more than one wall left standing, I am afraid.'

'If I were going to hide a body,' Olivia said, 'I think I would choose the graveyard...'

'One more soul amongst so many?' Harry nodded. 'Yes, you may well be...' He broke off as the door opened and Nan came in seeming flustered and obviously upset.

'So there you are,' she said, looking at Beatrice a little reproachfully. 'It was while you were all out...I did not know what to do. Bellows had not yet lit the fire in here, and I dare not disturb your father...'

'Whatever is wrong, Nan?' Beatrice looked at her in concern. It was seldom that her aunt's feathers were this badly ruffled.

'He was most put out because I asked him to come back later but I really could not ask him in...' Nan's worried gaze turned on Harry. 'A gentleman, my lord. He said he was looking for you, and when I told him you were out was...well, he was not polite.'

'What did this gentleman look like?' Harry asked, frowning. 'Pray describe him if you will.'

'He was shorter than you, my lord, and stout—and he had reddish hair cut straight about his ears, in the manner of the Puritans of old.'

'The abominable Peregrine!' chorused Harry and Percy together.

'He insisted he should be allowed to wait, and was not best pleased when I told him he could not,' Nan said, looking guilty. 'But I really could not spare the time to see to him. It was most inconvenient.'

'So you sent him about his business,' Lord Dawlish said. 'Well done, ma'am!'

'The gentleman you speak of was my cousin.' Harry smiled at her reassuringly. 'Sir Peregrine Quindon. Though what he is doing here, I cannot imagine.'

'Come to see if you're still alive,' Percy said with a knowing look. He tapped the side of his nose with his forefinger. 'You may depend he heard the gossip in town, wanted to discover if he was about to inherit your estates.'

'That is most unkind in you, Percy,' Harry murmured reproachfully. 'Peregrine is always most concerned for my health. He never fails to ask me if I am feeling quite well, or to point out that I am looking a little under the weather.'

Percy gave a snort of laughter. 'You may mock, Harry, but that cousin of yours cannot wait for you to die so that he may step into your shoes. If I were you, I should get myself an heir—several of them. Nip his ambitions in the bud, before he begins to get ideas above his station.'

'You do not imagine that Peregrine means me harm?' Harry raised his brows. 'My very dear Percy, you are letting your imagination run wild. My cousin is a bore, and not the most pleasant of companions—but he is far too much of a coward, and of a righteous turn of mind, to do anything violent. If he saw me drowning, he might turn away and pretend he had not seen, he would not murder me.'

'You are very sure, Harry?' Percy looked unconvinced and frowned.

Yes, I am,' Harry replied. He glanced at Nan. 'I must apologise for my cousin's behaviour, ma'am. I know that Peregrine can be tiresome when he chooses.'

'Well, he was rude, Lord Ravensden, but I was more worried that I might have upset a friend of yours.'

'You did exactly as you ought,' Harry reassured her with one of his most charming smiles. 'Tell me, did my cousin say where he was going when he left here?'

'Took himself off to an inn, sir. He says he shall return later.' Nan looked to Beatrice for guidance. 'Am I supposed to provide dinner for him? Only we shall be needing more supplies…'

'Allow me to make some provision,' Harry said, glancing at Beatrice, his brows arched. 'My family seems to have imposed itself on your good nature, and I really cannot allow this to continue. With your permission, Beatrice, I shall go myself to Northampton in the carriage this afternoon and bring back what we need.'

'I'll come with you,' Percy said. 'Good grief, yes. We must be eating you out of house and home, Miss Roade, and Peregrine likes his food, none better.'

Beatrice could only smile and thank them for their thought, her cheeks a little warm. 'If you will go, you must take some refreshment first,' she said. 'Excuse me, I shall go to the kitchen and see to it at once.'

Beatrice arranged the silver brushes on the chest of drawers in what had been her mother's bedroom, admiring the impressive Ravensden crest on the backs. She glanced around her. A fire had been burning non-stop for several days now, and the room felt warm at last. The bed was made up with fresh linen and well aired. Harry would take no harm here.

She had moved his possessions herself while he and Lord Dawlish were gone to Northampton. This time she had accepted his offer of help with a good grace. She really had no choice. She certainly could not feed so many guests. It had been difficult enough with one extra gentleman, but it would be impossible with three.

She surveyed her efforts with satisfaction. The mellowed gleam of old wood was somehow welcoming. This was undoubtedly the best bedchamber in the house, well furnished with a cheval mirror, a handsome dressing-chest, an elegant day-bed and a writing bureau; it had indeed been the heart of the house while Sarah Roade lived.

Harry would be comfortable here, and she could go back to her own room. It was not that she minded sharing with her sister, just that she had been restless of late, unable to sleep and worried that she might disturb Olivia.

Beatrice sighed as she gathered up her polishing cloths. Her heart and mind were much afflicted by what had happened these past few days. The time she had spent with Harry that morning had served only to make her realise how very much she liked him.

No, liking was not a strong enough word to describe her feelings for Harry Ravensden. This feeling she had was very much more than friendship or even affection. She knew that no man had ever stirred her senses as he did. She had only to look at him for her heart to leap wildly in her breast, and the touch of his hand made her breathless, weak with longing. She longed for him to kiss her as he had that night in the kitchen, to kiss her and go on kissing her, to take her to himself, to his bed, to possess her utterly and make her his own.

Yet it was not only passion he aroused in her— yes, she did truly like him as well. He made her laugh inside. She could share her thoughts with him as she never had with anyone, except sometimes with her dear papa. A flicker of his eyelids, a quiver of his mouth—that generous, soft, oh, so, kissable mouth!— and she would gladly have surrendered all.

How she wanted to feel his mouth on hers. Her body felt as if it were melting, as if she were already a part of him and he of her.

No, this would not do! Her thoughts were immodest. She must not allow herself to dwell on that wretched kiss. Harry was not hers to love and cherish.

How could she bear to see him marry Olivia? Beatrice knew that she must stand aside, she must let her sister choose whether or not she would have him—but if she did, Beatrice's own heart would break.

Her wandering thoughts were recalled as she heard a man's voice in the hall below. It was loud and complaining, and she knew at once that this must be the abominable Peregrine.

'Harry, you wretch!' she murmured to herself as she went down the stairs. How could he so name his only cousin?

'Ah, there you are, my love,' said Nan, looking at her with relief as she reached the hall. 'As you see, Sir Peregrine has returned...'

'How nice to see you, sir,' Beatrice said, smiling at him. Goodness! He did look very annoyed. 'I am so sorry that no one was here to receive you this morning. My aunt was too busy for visitors—but please, come into the parlour and warm yourself. It has turned colder of late and I dare say you feel the chill.'

'And you are, madam?' Sir Peregrine's gaze narrowed sharply.

'I am Miss Roade. You are in my father's house, sir.'

'Is my cousin here? It is Ravensden I have called to see—and very inconvenient it was, chasing all this way.'

'I fear Lord Ravensden has been called away,' Beatrice replied. 'He and Lord Dawlish will be here soon.' She looked at her aunt. 'Nan, will you bring sherry and biscuits, please?'

'Yes, of course.' Nan went off, clearly relieved to be about her business.

'Come, sir. You must be frozen to the bone,' Beatrice said, leading the way into the parlour. 'Please be seated near the fire.'

She took a seat for herself in a worn leather wing chair to one side of the hearth, gesturing for him to take its twin. Sir Peregrine ignored her invitation and stood in front of the fire, facing out into the room so that she was forced to stare at his profile. He looked about him, clearly contemptuous of all he saw: the shabby furniture, which was a hotchpotch of various styles and periods, worn carpet, faded drapes. Beatrice had grown used to them, but his expression reminded her of how poor her home must look to a stranger.

'It was kind of you to come all this way to see Lord Ravensden,' she said, feeling that some attempt at polite conversation must be made.

Peregrine turned his baleful gaze on her. 'My duty. Only duty, Miss Roade. Lady Susanna Ravensden, Harry's mother, came to see me in town. In quite a way. She had heard gossip. Ridiculous, of course. I told her how it would be. I was sure nothing had happened to Ravensden, and now you see I am right. It was a wasted journey, and in such weather!' He sounded disgruntled…disappointed.

Beatrice was silent. She did not feel inclined to tell this man that Harry had been very ill for three days.

'So…' Sir Peregrine glared at her. 'You are the

sister of Miss Roade Burton—and this is her family home.'

'Yes, sir. This is our home.'

'Quite a come-down for her. I dare say she regrets having jilted Ravensden now.'

Beatrice felt the anger rising inside her. How dare he say such a thing about Olivia? It was despicable. She was not sure how she would have held her temper had the parlour door not opened at that moment to admit Harry and Lord Dawlish.

'At last,' Sir Peregrine said, greeting his cousin with a jaundiced stare. 'I had almost given you up, Ravensden.'

'Had you, Peregrine? How unfortunate.' Harry's brows rose. His manner was cool, reserved. Beatrice was surprised. This was not the man she had come to know so intimately, but she suspected that it might well be the Eighth Marquis of Ravensden. 'Had you notified me of your intention, I might have saved you a tiresome journey. There was not the slightest need for you to come down here.'

'I said as much to Lady Ravensden—but she would have it that something had happened to you.' Sir Peregrine looked outraged. 'She very nearly accused me of having had a hand in your murder! As if I would dream of such a thing. I hope I know what is due to you as the head of the family, Ravensden.'

'I am perfectly sure you do, Peregrine—and I am just as sure that Mama meant nothing of the kind. You know she sometimes gets carried away when she is upset,' Harry said, but there was no laughter in his eyes, only a kind of hauteur. 'However, it was very good of you to concern yourself—and now you may rest easy in your bed, Peregrine. As you see, I am perfectly healthy and amongst friends.'

'Speaking of a bed...' Sir Peregrine frowned. 'The only decent inn in the district has nothing to offer me. I trust you can put me up for the night.'

'This is not my house,' Harry said. For a moment something flickered in his eyes. Beatrice sensed that he was very angry. 'But I believe there may be a spare room.'

Beatrice's eyes met Harry's. 'Do you mean *the* spare room?' He nodded and she almost laughed as she saw the sudden quiver at the corner of his mouth. What was he thinking? The wicked creature! To inflict such a punishment on his cousin! 'Reflect for a moment, my lord. What the probable consequences of lodging Sir Peregrine in such a room might be...'

'Why, what's wrong with the room?' asked Lord Dawlish, sensing their mischief. He had followed Harry into the parlour and they had now been joined by Nan and Olivia.

'It is haunted,' Olivia declared before anyone else could speak. 'By a headless spectre who rattles his chains at midnight and scares anyone foolish enough to sleep there half to death.'

'Ghosts!' Sir Peregrine said dismissively, and looked at Olivia with obvious dislike. 'I do not believe they would disturb me.'

'The room has not been used in years,' Beatrice said with slightly more truth than her sister. 'I do not believe it could be aired in time, sir. Besides, the bed has a broken strut. The last person to spend a night there was very uncomfortable.'

'And took a virulent fever,' added Nan, making everyone look at her in surprise. 'Besides, the sheets have just been washed and there are no dry ones.'

This was most unusual for Nan, and showed that she had taken Sir Peregrine in great dislike.

Sir Peregrine looked horrified. 'Then I shall not stay,' he said. 'I have a delicate constitution. No, Ravensden, I shall not be persuaded. You may give me dinner, I hope? Then I shall return to London. Better to drive though the night than sleep in a damp room.'

'Yes, I am sure you are wise, sir,' Beatrice said and her eyes were drawn involuntarily to Harry. He looked as though he might explode, though whether with anger or some other emotion she could not be sure. 'Now—shall we have our sherry?'

She stayed to drink a glass with them, then excused herself, going to the kitchen with Nan to help prepare their meal, which consisted of a roast, a pigeon pie and a baked carp...supplied by Bellows from where she did not dare think. She spent some time making rich sauces and a choice of puddings. Whatever else Sir Peregrine chose to sneer at in this house, he should not find fault with the dinner set before him.

'That was a splendid meal, m'dear. Splendid!' Mr Roade looked at his eldest daughter with affection. 'Once again you and Nan have excelled yourselves. Now, if you ladies would go through to the parlour, I wish to talk to our guests for a few moments.'

'Yes, Papa, of course.'

Beatrice placed the port and brandy on the table in front of him, then followed Nan and Olivia from the room.

'I shall be glad when that dreadful man has gone,' Olivia said a little later, when they were seated in the parlour drinking tea. 'I cannot like him, Beatrice. Did you hear some of his remarks at dinner? He was so offensive. He almost suggested that I had trapped Lord Ravensden into offering for me. I do assure you, I did not!'

'You should not let him upset you,' Beatrice said and frowned. 'He is clearly eaten up with conceit—and jealousy. Plainly, he hopes to drive a wedge between you and...' She broke off as Sir Peregrine came into the parlour.

'I have sent your man to tell my coachman I am ready to leave,' he announced pompously. 'I fear I cannot stay longer, Miss Roade. My compliments to your cook for an enjoyable meal. I have scarcely eaten better in town. I wonder that such talent is to be found in a village like this.'

His words were uttered in such a manner as to imply that he wondered any decent cook would stay in such a place. Beatrice held her breath and counted to ten. If he had not been Harry's cousin, she might have given him the rough side of her tongue.

'We have many talents in the country, sir,' she said, and stood up. 'I shall see you to the door myself.'

'You are very good, Miss Roade.' He stood back and allowed her to go before him. His cloak and hat were in the hall. He waited for her to hand them to him. She did not do so, and he was obliged to retrieve them from the wooden stand himself. He frowned. 'I must tell you I cannot approve this marriage, Miss Roade.'

'I beg your pardon, sir?' Beatrice curled her nails into the palms of her hands. She must not lose her temper. She must not! 'I fear I do not understand you.'

'The match between your sister and Ravensden was ill-judged. She has jilted him, and no doubt pride brought him here in pursuit of her—but he would be well advised to cut the connection. I cannot think well of Miss Roade Burton.'

'Your opinion of my sister is of no interest to me, sir,' she replied, as calmly as she could. 'If you have anything to discuss concerning Lord Ravensden's marriage, you should properly address it to him.'

'Well said, Beatrice!' Harry came out of the dining parlour. The expression in his eyes shocked her. He was furious. He looked as if he would like to strike his cousin, and was barely able to contain himself. 'Do you have something to say to me, Peregrine? If so, please speak now. But I must warn you, I am at the limit of my patience.'

'I—I must go,' Sir Peregrine muttered, his face pale. 'You are your own master, Ravensden, and have no need of advice from me.'

'Exactly. You would do well to remember that,' Harry said. 'Do have a safe journey back to town, cousin. Should you meet Lady Susanna, please tell her that I am in good health—and very shortly she will have the pleasure of meeting my fiancée.'

Sir Peregrine bowed his head and went out without another word.

'Forgive me for my cousin's disgusting manners,' Harry said, moving towards Beatrice. 'I do apologise for his having inflicted himself upon you. You look pale. What did he say to upset you so much?'

'Only that he could not approve of your intention to marry into my family.' She put her hands to her face, which was burning. 'I know we are not your equal…'

'Have I said that?' Harry looked at her, eyebrows raised. 'Have I ever given you any cause to think that either you or any member of your family was beneath me?'

'No.' Beatrice took a sharp breath. '*You* would not, of course, but I know…'

'What do you know?' Harry asked gently. He took her hands in his, gazing down at her in such a way that her heart went wild, beating against her ribs so madly that she could hardly breathe. 'Had I the freedom to speak as I would like, then you would know, Beatrice. Believe me…'

He was interrupted as Mr Roade and Lord Dawlish came out into the hall.

'Lord Dawlish has agreed to pay my debt to the blacksmith, Beatrice,' her father said, looking delighted. 'That means he will deliver the new parts I need for my experiment. Is that not good news, m'dear?'

'Yes, Papa.' Beatrice looked doubtful and Harry's eyes began to gleam with amusement. 'I do hope so…' she added as her father and Lord Dawlish went into the parlour, apparently on excellent terms. 'Oh dear, how unfortunate...'

'You seem anxious?' Harry looked at her. 'Any particular reason?'

'It is only that the last time Papa fitted his stove, there was an explosion. It blew a hole in the kitchen wall and it was an age before we were straight again.'

'Ah yes, I see,' Harry said. 'We must hope that the improvements work, must we not?' He smiled at her, holding on to her left hand and playing with the fingers. 'Are you feeling more like yourself now, Beatrice?'

'Yes, thank you.' She gave a small, rueful laugh. 'I must tell you frankly, Harry—I cannot like your cousin.'

Harry chuckled, his eyes bright with mischief. 'My very dear Beatrice. No one ever likes the abominable Peregrine. I would have thought it very odd in you if you had.'

'Oh, Harry!' Beatrice's laughter was free of shadows this time. 'You always make me feel so much better.'

'Do I, my dear? I am glad of that.' He let her hand go. 'I think perhaps we ought to join the others, or I might forget that I am a gentleman and must live by the code of honour to which I was born.'

'Yes.' Beatrice's heart raced wildly as she saw his expression. 'Yes, we should join the others...'

Chapter Eight

Beatrice was up early the next morning. She knew the rest of the household would not be stirring yet, and so she slipped out of the house to carry out some of her errands, which had been neglected since Lord Ravensden had followed her sister to Abbot Giles.

There were some elderly folk living alone in the village, in cottages barely fit for inhabitation, and she had always done her best to help where she could. As difficult as things were at times for Beatrice and her family, she knew that some others were far worse off and she always shared what she had; at the moment there were so many good things in the house that she had brought biscuits, cakes, sweetmeats, and some cheese for her friends.

The first cottage she called at was that of Miss Amy Rushmere, a lady who had been a companion to many rich employers during her long and interesting life. Beatrice always called on her at least once a month, staying to drink a little elderberry wine and gossip about what was happening at the houses of the local gentry.

Miss Rushmere opened her door with a smile of welcome. 'Oh, how good of you to come, Beatrice,' she said. 'You must have so much to do with all the company you have staying.'

'Lord Ravensden does not often rise much before noon,' Beatrice explained. 'I think he may be in the habit of riding early when at home, but he still has a slight cough, you know.'

'Yes, I heard that Dr Pettifer had been called out to see him three times,' the old lady replied, shaking her head in distress. 'He must have been very poorly.'

'We feared for his life at one period,' Beatrice said, frowning as she remembered how very ill Harry had been. 'But he is a strong man and I am thankful to say very much better now.'

'Yes,' Miss Rushmere smiled at her. 'I saw you walking together yesterday morning. What a very handsome man he is to be sure.'

'Yes, very.' She sat down at the table. Amy Rushmere was one of the oldest villagers living in Abbot Giles, and there were many things she could remember that no one else knew. 'Tell me, what do you think of the news that Lady Sywell has run off?'

'It is very curious, isn't it?' Miss Rushmere wrinkled her brow. 'Of course, one knew how it would be when he married her. The marriage was always a mistake. She was obviously the by-blow of John Hanslope—at least, rumour would have it so...'

'Have you some other thought on the matter?'

'No, no…I dare say the story is true in this case. I saw her a few times, you know…a pretty child.' Miss Rushmere smiled; her faded eyes seeming to be looking somewhere beyond Beatrice, into the past. 'As a child I used often to walk in Giles Wood, including that part of it which belongs to the Abbey. The estate was very different then, well tended and alive with people. There is a grove in the woods, on the Abbey side, that is said to be sacred, you know…'

'No, I did not know that,' Beatrice said, her interest caught. 'At least, I may have heard it, but I had forgotten.'

'Oh, yes, I know it well from my childhood, and I have been there more recently. It is a pleasant spot and always seems peaceful to me, as if it is blessed in some way. There is a stone, moss-covered, with some strange lettering on it.' Miss Rushmere wrinkled her brow as she recalled something. 'I once saw Lady Sywell sitting alone there. It was just after her wedding. She seemed so sad. I remember her hair was an unusual colour—and she had a delicate, vulnerable look. I spoke to her, but she only smiled. She reminded me of someone, but I am not certain who…I do hope she is safe.'

'Yes, I pray she is,' agreed Beatrice.

Miss Rushmere nodded. 'They do say that anyone who desecrates the shrine is for ever cursed…'

Beatrice felt the shiver trickle down her spine.

'But surely Lady Sywell would not…'

'Oh, no, my dear. I was thinking of her husband. He and his friends were often in the woods when he first came here, and the stories of his orgies are too unpleasant to relate. I think that the spirit of the woods…whoever she may be; I believe it is a woman…would choose to visit her anger more upon the Marquis than his innocent lady.'

'Yes, that would have more justice,' Beatrice said. 'But it is Lady Sywell who has disappeared.'

'Yes, indeed, and one wonders what can have happened to her. I remember the family who used to live there long ago…young Rupert as a boy…'

Beatrice nodded, letting the elderly lady ramble on as she would. She had wondered if Miss Rushmere could throw a little more light on things, and the story of the sacred grove was very romantic—Olivia would love it!—but it did not help to solve the mystery of the Marchioness's disappearance.

After leaving Miss Rushmere's cottage, Beatrice visited two more, but she did not stay to gossip for long, merely handing her gifts over at the door. She was in more of a hurry than usual, and did not at first respond when someone called her name, then she turned and saw the young woman walking towards her, holding a small girl by the hand. The child was perhaps two years old, a pretty little thing with reddish hair, her mother's very much darker and pulled back in a severe style that did nothing for her.

'Oh, Beatrice,' Annabel Lett said as she came closer. 'You walk so fast I thought I should not catch up to you. It is ages since I saw you.'

Annabel was a widow and lived in Steep Ride with only her cousin as a companion. Some people with nasty, suspicious minds whispered that she was not truly a widow, perhaps because her closest friend was Charlotte Filgrave, who the gossips would have it was a fallen woman, but Beatrice ignored such gossip. She liked Annabel and was always pleased to see her, though they did not often meet, unless it was on their walks.

'I have been visiting Miss Rushmere and others,' Beatrice said as Annabel came up to her. 'Now I must get back. We have visitors staying and there is so much to do…'

'Yes, of course, there must be,' Annabel replied. 'I came early because I wanted to ask Dr Pettifer's advice about something. When I go back I shall call on Charlotte Filgrave and Athene…'

'You could come up to the house and take a glass of sherry if you wish,' Beatrice said. She knew that Annabel's situation was very like her own in that there was very little money coming in, and often thought she too must be lonely at times. 'I am sure Olivia would love to meet you.'

'I should like that another day, providing I may bring Rebecca with me?' Annabel replied and smiled as Beatrice bobbed down to say hello to the child. 'I am expected by Charlotte this morning, but do tell your sister she is very welcome to call if she is over at Steep Ride.'

'Yes, of course—but you must come to tea with us one day, Annabel. Olivia will be glad to make your acquaintance. I shall send a note with Bellows.'

She left her friend, who had begun to walk in the

opposite direction and went up to the house. As she did so she was hailed by Lord Dawlish, who had just arrived and was being shown into the parlour. She hurried to take off her bonnet and pelisse and followed him, finding that both Olivia and Harry were already there, sherry wine and biscuits having been set ready on the table.

'Ah, Beatrice,' Harry said with some satisfaction. 'We were just wondering where you were.'

'I had some errands in the village,' Beatrice replied. 'Friends I must not neglect because we have company. I had hoped to hear something that might help us with our investigation, but I did not.'

'Well, I have some news,' Harry said. 'I have spoken to Bellows, and he has agreed to help us. Apparently, he has a few trusted friends. They are going to the Abbey grounds this very night and will cover much of the ground that we would find difficult.'

Olivia had been standing at the window. 'It has started to rain,' she said, coming to sit down on the sofa. She looked disappointed. 'We shall not be able to walk today.'

'I learned something this morning,' Beatrice said. 'It appears that there is a sacred grove in the woods, on the Abbey side. There is an old tale that says if anyone desecrates the grove they will be for ever cursed. Miss Amy Rushmere saw Lady Sywell there once.'

'A sacred grove?' Olivia was entranced. 'How I should love to see it! And a curse—how strange!'

'A sacred grove,' Harry nodded. 'And a shrine to the Earth Mother, I dare say. Perhaps there might also be the remains of a Roman temple somewhere on the estate?'

Beatrice looked at him oddly. 'Why, yes, I've heard it said the monks built on the site of an old temple—what made you say that?'

'One of my interests is the study of old manuscripts and ancient writings,' Harry said with a little smile. 'There are many forms of what are basically the same belief in the power of good and evil. And it is a strange but oft proven fact that the priests of what would seem to be entirely different faiths chose to build their shrines in the exact same places.'

'Why would that be?' Beatrice asked, fascinated more by this new insight into Harry's character than by the study of old religions.

'It is my own opinion that the forces for good and evil are both held within the air, earth, fire, water and indeed, the very stones that form hills and mountains—and that these twin forces are harnessed by us for either the benefit or the destruction of mankind. There may be certain places on this earth where these forces are more strongly concentrated, for instance where there are ancient woods and water...'

'Then do you deny God?'

'No, certainly not,' Harry said, 'for what is our God other than the greatest force for good known to mankind?'

'And the Devil?' asked Olivia. 'Is he also a form-less force?'

'You are thinking of the horned beast?' Harry nodded and smiled. 'I dare say this force could manifest itself in whatever form it chose—perhaps its most dangerous would be the shape of a beautiful woman. Think of Jezebel, Delilah and Salome…'

'You rogue, Harry!' Beatrice cried. 'I vow there have been as many evil men in history as women— you have only to remember that it was a man who condemned Our Lord to death, and a woman he chose to show himself to after the Resurrection.'

'I would not deny it,' Harry replied. 'The fact that God sent our Saviour to us in our own form only confirms my belief in the ability of these forces to take what shape they like. Our Lord came to show us the way, and his message was one of goodness and love. How better can any of us serve our fellow creatures than by doing good and treating others less fortunate than ourselves with kindness?'

Olivia was clearly much struck by his words. Could this truly be the man she had declared to have no depth of soul? Beatrice thought that perhaps his depth of soul and sensitivity was such that they needed to be protected from a mocking world, that perhaps Harry mocked the world lest the world mock him.

'I see I have given you food for thought.' Beatrice smiled. 'Well, I have work to do.' She turned as Harry coughed. 'Are you well, my lord? Were you comfortable last night? You have not taken another chill?'

'I was very comfortable, thank you,' Harry said, smiling at her concern. He had thrown off his serious mood and was once again the man of society manners. 'This cough is a little irritating, but I dare say it will clear in time. I am quite well now. I have a very strong constitution, you know. In fact I am hardly ever ill.'

'I have some syrup of rose-hips that may ease your throat,' Beatrice said. 'I shall fetch it at once.'

She went to the door and was met by Lily, who had been about to knock.

'A note has been sent down from Jaffrey House, miss. It is addressed to Miss Olivia.'

'You may take it in to her.'

Beatrice was thoughtful as she hurried away. If Harry was right…then the feeling of horror she had experienced in those tumbledown buildings at the Abbey might have more significance than she knew.

She shook her head, trying to rid herself of a feeling of foreboding. She had experienced it the night she first visited the Abbey, and it had come to her a few times since.

But this was all nonsense! Harry had probably been mocking them again!

Beatrice went to the stillroom and brought back a small blue bottle and a glass. She poured a measure into it, handing it to Harry, who sipped it cautiously then smiled as he found it both soothing and pleasant.

Olivia looked up from the note she had been reading, an expression of pleasure in her eyes.

'Lady Sophia has asked me to take tea with her this afternoon,' she said. 'Is that not thoughtful of her?'

'Yes, very kind,' Beatrice replied. She saw at once

how much the thoughtful gesture had meant to her sister. 'Perhaps Lord Ravensden will send you in his carriage if the rain keeps up?'

'Yes, of course Olivia may have the carriage,' Harry agreed and frowned because she had used his title, not his name. Now what bee had she got in her bonnet? 'Were you not also invited, Beatrice?'

'Lady Sophia is more Olivia's age,' Beatrice said, avoiding his intent gaze. 'In the past Papa has turned down many kind invitations from the Earl and his family. We could not repay their hospitality, you see, and Papa will not accept charity. Except for the logs, of course, which he does not know about, so cannot hurt him. Besides, I have much to do…'

'I have an errand in Northampton,' Lord Dawlish said suddenly. 'Will you bear me company, Harry?'

'What?' Harry seemed lost in thought. 'Yes, yes, of course, Percy.' He glanced at Beatrice. 'I dare say you will be glad of a few hours to yourself?'

'Yes…' She managed a smile. She could not say what was in her heart, so it seemed best not to say anything. 'Please excuse me.'

She left them and went upstairs to help Lily turn out the bedrooms. However, that done, Beatrice changed her gown and went back to the parlour. It seemed very empty. She thought wistfully how very pleasant the last few days had been with so much company in the house.

She would miss Olivia if she married Harry. Oh, she must not think of him that way! It could only increase her pain. And she was definitely in pain. She had allowed herself to love Harry Ravensden, and now she must suffer for it. What a fool she was!

It was time she wrote to Mrs Guarding and inquired if there might be a position at the school for her—perhaps in the spring. She opened her pretty black and red japanned writing-box and took out her pen, then dipped it into the ink. Having finished her letter a few minutes later, she read it through but did not seal it with wax. It might be best if she spoke to Papa before she sent it off.

She went over to the pianoforte, sat down on the stool and began to play a sad, haunting melody that made the tears rush to her eyes. She stopped abruptly as the feeling of hopelessness almost overwhelmed her. What was she going to do?

'Oh, why have you stopped?' a woman's voice asked, and she turned round, startled to see a stranger in the doorway. A very attractive, elegant lady in her autumn years. 'That was delightful, Miss Roade. You are Miss Roade, of course. Mrs Willow said I would find you here, my dear.'

Beatrice rose to her feet, a little disconcerted. She had never seen this lady before, but somehow felt she knew her…there was something about the eyes, and the soft, generous mouth.

'Forgive me…I do not know who…'

'How foolish of me.' The woman's laughter tinkled like wind bells on a summer breeze. 'Mrs Willow would have announced me, but I heard you playing and crept in so as not to disturb you. There was such feeling in your playing, I was caught by it. I am Ravensden's mother, Miss Roade.'

Yes, of course! She could see the likeness now.

'Lady Ravensden?' Beatrice was suddenly thrust into action. She went forward to welcome her guest. 'Oh, please, do come in. Where are my manners? You must be frozen. Thank goodness we have a decent fire to warm you. I dare say you are exhausted after your journey.'

'Please, no formality. By choice I am Lady Susanna to my friends.' Her smile lit up her face. 'What a sweet girl you are! I have descended on you with no warning, and yet you welcome me with open arms.'

'You were worried about Harry—I mean Lord Ravensden,' said Beatrice, tears stinging her eyes once more. How very missish of her. She blinked them away. 'Of course, *you* had to come.'

'Lady Dawlish sent round to my London house the moment she heard from her husband. She said my son had been ill?'

'Yes, indeed. He was very ill, distressingly so,' Beatrice said, all subterfuge gone as she saw the anxiety in Lady Susanna's eyes. 'I was very worried about him for a time. Pray do sit down, my lady. My aunt will no doubt bring us some tea in a moment— you would prefer tea to wine?'

'Yes, thank you, my dear. Please do go on. You were telling me about Harry's illness.'

'He caught a chill,' Beatrice said. 'He was ill during the night he first arrived, but we did not realise until the next morning. We sent for Dr Pettifer at once, and we did all we could to ease him. He was in a fever for three days, but then it broke and he recovered his strength very quickly. He still has a cough, but he is much better now.'

'Harry always was strong,' his mother said. 'He caught scarlet fever as a boy—from one of the grooms. He was forever playing in the stables! He was very ill and so was his sister Elizabeth. She…died, but Harry recovered and was none the worse. Thank God! I feared that I would lose them both.'

'Oh, so that's who Lillibet was,' Beatrice said as a flash of understanding came. 'In his fever he talked of her and said that it should have been him who died. It seemed to trouble him a great deal.'

'Did he say that he ought to have died in her place?' Lady Susanna stared at her. 'You are quite certain, Miss Roade?'

'Yes. Quite certain. Why? Is it important?'

Lady Susanna nodded. 'Perhaps. I have wondered if he might have blamed himself for his sister's death. He was so very fond of her. We all were, of course, but Harry worshipped her. They were inseparable as children, and I do not believe he was ever quite the same afterwards.'

Beatrice saw the sadness in her eyes. 'Yes, of course. You must all have felt it dreadfully…the loss of a child. Little angel, that's what Harry called her.'

'Indeed she was,' Lady Susanna said. 'I dare say

that's why she was taken so young—she was too good for this world.'

They sat in silence for a moment, then Lady Susanna smiled. Her smile was so very like Harry's.

'Well, it was a long time ago, Miss Roade. We must think of the future. Pray tell me what my son has done to make your sister cry off? I am sure he must have said something careless. He does have a wicked sense of humour.'

'Indeed, he does at times,' Beatrice agreed, with a look that betrayed much more than she knew. 'But it truly was not all his fault. You must not blame him too much. He told a friend in confidence that it was not a love match, but someone overheard and added malicious lies to the tale. Olivia was very upset.'

'Naturally, as any young lady would be in her place.' Lady Susanna frowned. 'I dare say we know who spread these lies. You may not have heard of Harry's cousin, Sir Peregrine Quindon. He is a most unpleasant man.'

'He was here yesterday,' Beatrice said. 'He told us he had come because you were anxious about Lord Ravensden and begged him to search for Harry.'

'Indeed, I was anxious when I heard all the stories circulating,' Harry's mother replied. 'But I did not ask that odious little toad to search for Ravensden. I would not trust him in such a case. He envies my son his fortune and title.'

'Yes, that was obvious,' Beatrice agreed. She liked Harry's mother, she liked her very much. 'I am certain Harry knows it…' She paused, blushing as she

realised she had used Lord Ravensden's name yet
again. 'Forgive me for being so familiar. You must
think it strange, but we have been living so
close…almost as a family. We are all on first-name
terms. But I ought to remember Lord Ravensden's
title when addressing a member of his family. It is
very wrong of me to presume so much. I do beg your
pardon.'

'No, no, my dear, not at all. It is pleasant to hear
that Harry has such good friends,' his mother said.
'Sometimes he seems to take nothing seriously—like
me, I fear.' She looked pensive. 'Yes, he can be very
like me at times.'

'There can be nothing to complain of in that, I am
sure.'

Lady Susanna shook her head. 'When the head will
not let the heart rule, much can be wrong,' she said.
'I must tell you in confidence…'

They were interrupted by the sound of voices outside in the hall, and then the door opened and Harry,
Lord Dawlish and Olivia came in together, all laughing and obviously on the best of terms. They all
halted and stared in astonishment as they saw Lady
Susanna.

'Mama!' Harry looked astounded as he saw her.
'What are you doing here?'

'Lady Susanna,' Percy said, seeming less surprised
than his friend. 'Glad to see you. Devilish cold out
this afternoon.'

'Lady Susanna…' Olivia blushed and made a slight

curtsey, obviously a little embarrassed by the unexpected encounter.

Harry crossed the room and kissed his mother's cheek. 'It was good of you to be concerned for me, Mama, but you should not have come all this way in this weather.'

'Won't like the inn I'm staying at,' Percy said with a frown. 'Very noisy in the mornings.'

'But Lady Susanna will stay here,' Beatrice said at once. 'You can take my room, Lord Ravensden. I shall move in with Olivia—and Lady Susanna may have your room. It is the best, so I am certain you will not mind moving once more.'

'It is not I who will suffer the inconvenience,' Harry said, his eyes warm with approval. 'But if you are certain you do not mind?'

'Of course not. We could not think of sending Lady Susanna to the inn. She will be more comfortable here with us.'

'Then I shall say no more,' Harry said. He smiled at her, then turned to his mother. 'I have been shopping this afternoon, Mama. I have discovered a very good linen draper by the name of Hammond in Northampton, and I have bought several rolls of material. I hope they will please you. I shall show them to you later.'

Lady Susanna looked surprised. 'That was very thoughtful of you, Ravensden.'

'I have also brought gifts for everyone here,' Harry said. 'I bought you a fan and a book of poems, Olivia. For Mrs Willow I have a roll of good woollen cloth in a deep blue colour. I do hope she may find it acceptable. For Percy I bought a pair of York tan gloves. For Mr Roade a case of good port and another of Madeira. For Lily and Ida there are warm shawls. For Bellows a new pair of boots, he gave me his size…' He paused and glanced at Beatrice. 'I bought Miss Roade a new gown. Mrs Willow lent me one of your old ones yesterday, Beatrice, and the seamstress altered something she had made up previously to your measurements. She assured me it would fit you perfectly.'

Beatrice blushed fiercely. Oh, the wicked, devious man! He had gone to so much trouble to cover his kindness, knowing that she would have refused such a gift had he tried to give it to her without having bought presents for everyone else. His thoughtfulness touched her, and she could only shake her head at him.

'You must have spent a great deal of money, my lord.'

'It was just something to do on a wet afternoon,' Harry said. 'Your family has received me—and my entire family—with such kindness and generosity. I wanted to give each of you some small token in return.'

'And so I should think,' Percy said, who had obviously been in on the conspiracy all the time. 'Bought a few gifts myself, Miss Roade. Just gloves and perfumes, you know. Not much good at choosing frippery. Usually leave all that to Merry. Very clever at it.' He looked thoughtful. 'Tell you what, dine with you all tonight, then leave for London in the morning. All right and tight now. Don't need me getting in the way, and Lady Dawlish will be missing me.'

'Yes.' Harry grinned at him. 'Another day and we shall have Merry dashing down here to see where you are. You had best go home and set her mind at rest, Percy.'

'Just what I thought,' his friend said and smiled a little secret smile to himself.

'Well, I must speak to Lily and make arrangements for dinner this evening,' Beatrice said. She glanced round the room at all the smiling, happy faces. 'How pleasant it will be this evening. We shall miss you when you leave, Lord Dawlish.'

'Sorry to leave, Miss Roade, but I dare say we shall be seeing each other often enough in future.'

She could not help feeling a little wistful. It had been so very pleasant these past few days, and the house would seem quiet when they had all gone.

Beatrice nodded but said nothing more as she went out. She supposed that Olivia might ask her to stay once she was married to Lord Ravensden. She must remember to call him by his title! No doubt she might meet both Lord and Lady Dawlish one day. But it would not be the same. Nothing would ever be the same after Harry married Olivia. She could not expect it.

Beatrice left Lily to finish the preparations for dinner and went up to the room she was once again sharing with Olivia. Her sister was already changing into a pretty blue gown. An emerald green silk gown was lying on the bed.

'That must have been made by a French modiste,' Olivia remarked. 'It is quite lovely, Beatrice, and it will suit you. Harry has chosen well—but he is known for having exquisite taste. His house in London is magnificent. I visited only once, but everything is so beautiful.'

Beatrice looked at the gown, then reached out to touch it reverently with her fingertips. She had never in her life owned or worn anything as elegant. Olivia watched her as she hesitated, seeming almost afraid to pick it up.

'Put it on,' she urged. 'He bought it for you. He wants you to have it. You cannot refuse when he went to so much trouble. That would be churlish, Beatrice.'

Beatrice nodded. She could not trust herself to speak, but went behind the screen to wash and change. Some minutes later, she emerged wearing the gown. She glanced at Olivia nervously.

'How do I look?'

'Beautiful.' Olivia laughed and pulled her in front of the dressing-mirror. 'Let me do your hair for you, dearest—and you may wear my amber beads.'

'Do you not want to wear them?' Beatrice asked as Olivia fastened the string of small beads on gold wire about her neck. 'They are so delicate and pretty.'

'I shall wear the cross and chain Mama sent me the year before she died,' Olivia said and bent to kiss her sister's cheek. 'You may keep these beads if you wish. They were a gift from a friend. I left my more expensive jewels with the Burtons. It may have been foolish, but I did not wish to bring them.'

'You were very right to do so,' Beatrice said, as Olivia began to dress her hair in a softer style than she usually wore, allowing curls to fall in charming disarray. 'Perhaps one day you will have pretty things again, dearest.'

'The fan Harry bought me is exquisite,' Olivia said, and showed it to her. 'See…it has gold filigree on the mounts.'

'Very stylish,' Beatrice agreed. She sneaked another glance at herself in the mirror. The gown fitted so well it might have been made for her. It had a dipping décolletage which showed the merest glimpse of her breasts, small puffed sleeves, a wide sash and a skirt that draped her figure so lovingly that it was almost indecent. 'Is this gown a little too revealing, Olivia?'

Olivia was searching in her trinket box. She frowned and pulled open all the drawers one by one.

'I cannot find Mama's cross…' She turned to look at Beatrice and laughed, mischief in her eyes. 'You should see the gowns some of the ladies wear in town; *that* is positively demure!'

Beatrice blushed. 'Sometimes I feel such a country mouse. It is years since I went anywhere.'

'You must have been lonely after Mama died.' Olivia frowned. 'I cannot think where I put the necklace she gave me. I was sure it must be here, but I cannot find it.'

Beatrice saw she was really worried. 'When did you last wear it, dearest? Can you not remember?'

'I am not sure...' Olivia thought for a moment. 'Oh yes, I remember touching it when we were in the herb garden... Oh, I do hope I did not drop it there!'

'Perhaps it is caught on the gown you were wearing,' Beatrice said. 'Leave it for the moment, Olivia, and we will both look tomorrow. If we cannot find it we will go to the Abbey and search for it together.'

'Yes. I would hate to lose it,' Olivia said. She fastened a string of seed pearls about her neck. Then looked at her sister, reaching out to pat one last twist of hair in place. 'You look stunning, Beatrice. I can think of no other word that does you justice.'

Beatrice looked shy as she nodded. Was that really her in the mirror? That elegant, rather attractive lady? Surely not!

'Shall we go down?'

'We must use a little of Lord Dawlish's perfume,' Olivia said, dabbing a tiny dot of perfume behind her ears. 'It was kind of him to think of us, was it not?'

'Yes, very kind.' Beatrice felt the butterflies start up again in her stomach as she and Olivia left the room together. She really felt most odd—like someone completely different.

Everyone had gathered in the parlour to await them. Olivia pushed her forward, making her go in and hanging back so that for a moment she stood alone.

'Oh, Beatrice,' Nan said, the first to speak. 'You look lovely, my dear. Doesn't she, Bertram?'

Mr Roade looked at her and nodded. 'Nice gown, m'dear. You look beautiful this evening—but then, I have never thought you anything else.'

'Exquisite…' Lord Dawlish breathed, clearly amazed by the transformation.

'Quite lovely,' said Lady Susanna. 'That colour becomes you, my dear. Harry has chosen well.'

Harry said nothing. He did not need to, his eyes said it all.

Beatrice blushed and looked away from his intent gaze. Be still her foolish heart! She must not let the gift of this wonderful gown give her hope. Nothing had changed. Harry was promised to Olivia. He must keep his word for the sake of honour, and her sister's happiness.

'Dinner is ready,' Lily announced from the doorway. Her mouth dropped open as Beatrice turned. 'Oh, lor! Oh, Miss Beatrice. You be a proper lady now.'

Beatrice smiled, the tension leaving her. 'Thank you, Lily. We shall come to table now.'

She watched as her father offered his arm to Lady Susanna. Lord Dawlish escorted Olivia, and Harry obligingly offered an arm to both Beatrice and Nan.

'Thank you,' she said softly as he set a chair for her. 'I have never worn anything as lovely.'

'The woman makes the gown,' Harry murmured, a wicked glint in his eyes. 'One day I shall prove it to you, Beatrice.'

Whatever could he mean? She could not look at him as he went to take his seat at the opposite side of the table. What was he suggesting? Did he hope that she would consent to be his mistress after he was married?

Wicked, wicked thing that she was! She was almost ready to agree to such an arrangement if it was the only way she could have him.

Beatrice spent the whole of the next morning baking. Lady Susanna's tray of hot chocolate and fresh, sweet rolls had been taken up to her, and she was not expected down before noon. Harry and Olivia had apparently gone out walking, though whether they were planning to visit the Abbey grounds she did not know.

It was as she was about to go upstairs and change her gown after the morning's work was finished that Harry came in alone.

She looked at him in surprise. 'Is Olivia not with you? I thought you were walking together?'

'I believe she had a prior engagement with Lady Sophia,' Harry replied, looking serious. 'May I speak with you, in private if you please, Beatrice?'

His expression made her nervous.

'Yes, of course, my lord. I shall come into the parlour. Is something wrong?'

Harry followed her into the room. 'You remember I said Bellows and his friends were going to search the grounds last night?'

'Yes, of course.' Beatrice felt a shiver down her spine. 'Has something happened?'

'They have found something in the woods, which

may be a grave. Bellows says that the ground has definitely been disturbed recently. He was up there some weeks ago and the mound of fresh earth was not there then.'

'Oh, no!' Beatrice felt her legs buckle and sat down on the sofa with a bump. She was shocked beyond measure, and the sickness rose in her throat. Although she had agreed to the search, she had never truly expected that they would find a grave. She gazed up at Harry, her face white. 'Do you think…is it really the Marchioness?'

'I do not know,' Harry said, looking anxious himself. 'I must admit it is a possibility now, but we cannot be sure until the ground has been dug over.'

'You are planning to…' Beatrice was filled with a sense of dread. 'Would it not be best to send for the militia and let them investigate?'

'I considered that, but if nothing untoward is found it could be awkward. Sywell is after all a man of some consequence, despite his disgraceful behaviour. I have decided that several of us will go to the site this evening. If we find a body I shall then call in a magistrate and the law will take over. If nothing is found, we may simply go on with the search or abandon it as we choose. But we might search for ever in such a place and never find anything.'

'Yes, I suppose…' Beatrice was uneasy, but she felt that events had moved on beyond her control. 'You will take care?'

'Of course.' He smiled at her. 'Nothing very terrible will happen, Beatrice. Bellows and his friends know the Abbey grounds intimately. They are undeterred by rumours of pagan rituals carried out in the woods centuries ago, and by the threat of being cursed for disturbing the old gods, who were there before ever the land belonged to the Abbey.' His eyes were bright with mischief. 'That is to say nothing of the spectres of dispossessed monks that are supposed to haunt the chapel. I fear our Bellows is somewhat of a rogue, though I believe he has his reasons.'

Beatrice smiled. She knew he was trying to make her laugh, to make her forget the true horror of what was going on.

'Bellows has helped to support us for the past three years,' Beatrice said. 'But now that I know...I cannot allow it to continue.'

'Indeed, I think it ought to be brought to an end before he is discovered and hung for a thief,' Harry said. 'But do not worry about it, Beatrice. I give you my word, before I leave Abbot Giles these things will all have been resolved.'

Beatrice lowered her gaze, her heart beating wildly. She could not bring herself to ask him what he meant, and so returned to the subject of the grave in the woods.

'Have you told Olivia that something has been found?'

'No—and nor must you, for her own sake.' Harry grinned ruefully. 'You know your sister. If she suspected what was planned, she would give me no peace until I allowed her to come with us. She is not above using all her feminine arts to gain her own way—as perhaps you may have observed?'

'Yes.' Beatrice laughed ruefully. 'I must confess, I was surprised at first, but she means no harm by her flirting.'

'Indeed not,' Harry agreed at once. 'Olivia is a lovely, charming girl. Why do you suppose half the men in London proposed to her?'

Beatrice smiled but did not answer. It was clear to her that Harry was very fond of Olivia.

'She must not be allowed to accompany you this night. It might make things more difficult...'

'I was thinking of her safety,' Harry said. 'Besides, it has turned bitterly cold. She will be far better in her bed—and should we discover the worst it will not be pleasant.'

'No, of course not.' Beatrice, gave a little shudder and looked at him. 'I suppose you will not allow me to come either?'

'I cannot forbid you,' Harry said. 'But I would prefer you to stay here, Beatrice. I shall tell you everything. Have no fear that I will hide anything from you—no matter what we find.'

'Then I shall do as you ask of me,' she said, and smiled at him. 'You must be hungry after your walk, my lord. I shall go up and change my gown, then a light nuncheon will be served in the front parlour.'

Chapter Nine

Beatrice found herself watching Harry all that evening. She could not get the idea out of her head that his life might be in danger. It was foolish of her to worry, she knew, and yet the strange feeling that had so disturbed her the night she crossed the Abbey lands alone at dusk had come back to haunt her. What was it about that place? The tales of fearful apparitions and ghostly happenings had always seemed improbable to Beatrice, and yet now she wondered if Steepwood Abbey and all who lived there were indeed cursed.

She was fearful, uneasy about what Harry and Bellows were about to do that night. Would the old gods be angered by yet another intrusion into their sacred places?

Oh, how foolish she was to be haunted by legends and myths. She was very sure that Harry was not, despite what he had said about the forces of good and evil being held to the earth in certain locations.

When everyone retired to their rooms at half-past

ten, she gave him a speaking look that he met with a lift of his brows. She shook her head. There was nothing for her to say or do. He knew her feelings, and he had asked her to stay home, and she must obey him in this. She had given her word that she would not speak of what was to happen to anyone, and no matter how anxious she was, must keep it.

It was, however, impossible to sleep. She lay staring into the darkness long after Harry had slipped out of the house. If only she could have gone with him! She longed to rise and follow him, but good sense told her that her presence would merely be a hindrance to the men as they went about their gruesome business. Harry was not alone. There were four strong men with him. What could befall him? Nothing, of course.

Yet she could not sleep. Something seemed to hang over her, a premonition of danger for Harry. She could not rid herself of the thought that some harm might come to him at the Abbey.

It was no good! She could not lie here next to her sister while her thoughts were with the men in the woods. She would get up and go downstairs.

It was with the intention of waiting in the kitchen that Beatrice rose, but her feet turned towards the room that had always been her own and was now being used by Harry. Perhaps he had already returned and she would find him there.

She hesitated outside the door, knocked softly and then went in, taking her chamberstick with her. The bed was empty. Harry had not yet returned. She took her candle to the mantle and lit two more, then sat down on a seat in the window. A few minutes passed and she was on her feet again, walking restlessly about the room, which seemed to carry the scent of him everywhere.

She touched his brushes, then picked up his dressing-robe, holding it to her face as she breathed in, inhaling the perfumes of sandalwood and leather. Oh, how she loved this man!

She had never expected to feel this way. It was beyond anything she had ever known.

Beatrice took Harry's dressing-robe with her to the bed and sat on the edge, holding it to her breasts reverently. In that moment she knew that she was ready to sacrifice all for love.

If Harry asked her to be his mistress, she would consent. She could not bear that he would leave and never see her again. No matter what his terms she must accept them, with the provision only that her sister would never know and be hurt by the knowledge.

Smiling to herself, Beatrice laid her head on the pillow. She would rest here and wait until Harry returned…

Harry followed Bellows into the kitchen, where the two men divested themselves of their muddy boots with the use of a very ingenious device, invented by Mr Roade, which only scraped the soft leather of Harry's boots a very little.

'I'll have these cleaned up by morning, my lord,'

Bellows said. 'No one will ever know we were up at the woods tonight.'

'The grave of a horse…' Harry shook his head ruefully. 'I must confess to feeling relieved when I realised what had been buried there.'

'It would have been shocking had we found the young woman, sir,' Bellows said. 'Do you wish the search to go on?'

'I think we must continue it for a while,' Harry said. 'If we abandoned it now, I could not rest easy in my mind. It may be that we shall find nothing, but at least if we have tried, we have done all we can.'

'We'll concentrate on the graveyard next,' Bellows said, nodding thoughtfully. 'In daylight it should not be difficult to spot if the stones have been moved. It would be easy enough to add another body and no one the wiser.'

'You must take no risks,' Harry said. 'I would not have your death on my conscience. Nor yet any of your friends.'

'Don't you worry about me, sir. There's only the Crow and the Marquis up there, and Lord Sywell is never sober these days.'

'Well, just be on your guard,' Harry warned. 'Sywell would be within his rights to shoot if he saw you…he must be aware that poaching has been going on in a large way on his estate.'

'There's folk needing food in the village,' Bellows said, and frowned. 'I do not excuse what we have done, for I know it to be unlawful, but—if the Marquis did his duty by the estate, there would be work for many as are near to starving. Besides, begging your pardon, my lord—the game is only going to waste.'

'I shall not judge you,' Harry said. 'You have been a good and faithful servant to Mr Roade and his daughter, and for that I respect and applaud you—but it must stop.'

'I dare say there will not be the need for it in future, my lord.' Bellows smiled. 'May I be the first to offer my congratulations?'

'As to that, I have not yet asked the lady in question.' Harry laughed. 'I see I have no secrets from you, my friend. Go to your bed now, and thank your friends for all they do. They shall be well rewarded, I promise.'

'Yes, sir. We all know that. Good night then.'

Harry nodded as the man went out, then helped himself to a glass of brandy, sipping it as he walked up the stairs. He was thoughtful, relieved that the night's work had not proved as gruesome as he had thought it might. Perhaps Olivia had it wrong; perhaps, as he had first believed, the young Lady Sywell had merely run away from her terrible husband. He hoped it would prove so, for the alternative was unthinkable.

The search would go on until the whole of the estate had been thoroughly covered, but he had no inclination to take a further part in it unless he was forced. If another grave was discovered he would need to be there, of course, to lend authority to the investigation. However, he was more interested now in sorting out this business of his engagement to Olivia. Things could not go on as they were…for everyone's sake. He had taken his time for reasons of his own, but he must do something soon.

Opening the door of his bedchamber, he checked as he saw the candles burning and there, asleep on the bed, Beatrice. How lovely she looked, her hair tumbling about her shoulders, face flushed in sleep. For a moment he wondered if he had come to the wrong room, but there was no mistake. She was fully clothed, lying on the covers. Beatrice must have come here to wait for him.

He set his brandy glass down besides the chamberstick she had brought with her, then walked softly to the bed. Why was she here? He could guess. She must have found it impossible to sleep, knowing what was going on, longing to be with them, yet knowing she would only be in their way. She had risen from her bed so as not to disturb her sister and come here…but why here? Why had she not waited for him in the kitchen?

He sat carefully on the edge of the bed, temptation overcoming his sense of right and wrong as he bent to gently kiss her lips. In seconds she was awake, gazing up at him, still caught in sleep, half dreaming.

'Harry, my love,' she whispered. 'You are safe…you have come back to me…thank God.' And then she put her arms up about his neck, and pulled his head down to hers, kissing him with such fervent passion that his desire for her overcame all scruples.

His mouth devoured hers hungrily. His arms were

about her, crushing her against him. He could feel the thrust of her nipples through the fine material of his shirt and knew that she was aroused. She wanted him as he wanted her.

Harry's tongue invaded her mouth, tasting its sweetness, drawing it into his own. He kissed her throat as her head arched back and she moaned with pleasure, then he pushed back her night-robe and found her breasts, his tongue flicking at the nipples, which were peaked and thrusting for his attention. He laid her back against the pillows, his breathing harsh as he buried his face into the softness of her navel, inhaling the warm, sensuous perfume of her skin.

'I want you so badly, Beatrice,' he muttered. 'God, you are so beautiful.'

'I am yours if you want me…'

He was so sorely tempted. Harry had never felt this way about a woman before in his life. He was burning to make her his own, but even as she lay looking up at him, her eyes drowned in passion, he knew he could not do this. She was as innocent as she was beautiful, he sensed that instinctively, and he could not take the gift she was offering him so sweetly. He had taken her by surprise and she had not thought beyond this moment. He could not take advantage of her.

'No,' he said, his voice made harsh by the wrench of self-denial. 'This is wrong, Beatrice. I will not shame you. I will not anticipate your wedding night by grabbing greedily for the sweetness you would offer me. It would not be right…'

Beatrice stared at him in horror. What was he saying? She had misread his feelings. He did not want her! He spoke of right and wrong, of shame…when all she had thought of was her desperate longing to be in his arms. She would have given all for one night of love, even if she could have no more—but he had spurned her offer. He was too honourable a man. He had drawn back, reminding her of the barriers between them, and she felt the sting of humiliation wash over her.

'Forgive me,' she said in strangled voice. 'I must have been dreaming. I did not know what I said…'

And then, before Harry could move to stop her, she rolled away from him, almost threw herself from the bed and fled from the room, never stopping until she reached the safety of the room she shared with Olivia.

He would not pursue her here, she knew. She had forgotten herself in the heat of passion, but Harry had behaved with all the true decency and honour she might expect from a man of his lineage. She believed he would do and say nothing to betray her…but how was she ever to face him again?

Beatrice leaned against the bedroom door and closed her eyes, her face burning. She was trembling, distressed, ashamed. Oh, why had she been so foolish as to throw herself at him? How could she have behaved in such a wanton fashion? What must he think of her?

After a moment, she crept back into bed, lying with her knees curled up to her chest as the memory of his rejection overcame her.

She was such a fool to think that Harry cared for her. Why should he? She was three-and-twenty, almost an old maid. Olivia was young and fresh and pretty, and she knew how to behave when a gentleman flirted with her. No man would prefer her to her sister! It was her own foolish heart that had led her astray.

Beatrice had lost her head as well as her heart. She had believed that Harry meant to offer her *carte blanche*. At first she had been upset that he could contemplate making her his mistress, but her desperation to be in his arms had made her deny her own principles.

Well, she was well served for her recklessness. She had made a fool of herself, and she must get through the next few days as best she could. To save them both embarrassment, she would try to keep her distance from Lord Ravensden as much as possible over the next few days.

'Oh, here you are,' Olivia said as she came into the kitchen, where Beatrice had hidden herself the next morning. 'I am sure I lost my cross in the Abbey gardens. Will you come with me to look for it? Please, Beatrice. It means so much to me.'

Beatrice glanced towards the window. It was a bright morning with no sign of rain or mist. She decided a walk would do her good, help to take away the headache that had been with her since she woke, besides, she had promised to help her sister look for the trinket.

'Yes, of course I will,' she said, taking off her apron. 'Let me get my cloak, dearest, and we shall go this minute.'

'Have you seen Harry this morning?' Olivia said as they both went into the hall. She waited as Beatrice put on a warm cloak and bonnet. 'Nan said he was up early and went out riding, but he must surely have returned by now. It is almost time for nuncheon.'

'No, I have not seen him,' Beatrice said. She had not ventured near the parlour all morning, and she did not intend to. She would find a task to keep her busy somewhere. But it was not her sister's fault that she was so unhappy. She linked her arm in Olivia's and smiled at her. 'Now, dearest, tell me how you are feeling. Have you settled now? You are not still angry with Lord Ravensden?'

'No, I am not angry,' Olivia replied. 'It was clearly a misunderstanding—and made worse by the abominable Peregrine. I like Harry. He is kind and considerate, and that careless humour is just a game with him.'

'Yes, I know,' Beatrice said. 'I believe he would make…a comfortable husband. You should think very carefully before you refuse his offer, Olivia.'

'Oh, I shall,' her sister said in a rather odd tone. 'I shall consider any offer Lord Ravensden makes me very carefully…'

Beatrice nodded, but did not reply. They had entered the Abbey grounds now, and were walking down the narrow lane they had taken before.

'You walk on one side,' Beatrice said, 'and I shall

take the other. If we both look carefully, we may find it.'

'I believe it may be in the herb garden, for I was touching it when Lord Dawlish and I stood there talking,' Olivia said, but she followed her sister's action, walking with her eyes downcast in case she should catch sight of a flash of gold. 'I should so hate to lose it, Beatrice.'

There was no sign of the heavy golden cross and chain in the lane that either of the sisters could find, but they continued to trace the path Olivia and Lord Dawlish had followed on that earlier occasion, both walking with their heads bent, eyes searching intently for the necklace Olivia had lost.

The herb garden was neglected, its once neat beds overgrown and forlorn, the walls almost completely gone in some places, but it still retained an air of the peace that the long dead monks must have sought here. The beds had been set out neatly between little hedges, separating the medicinal herbs from those used in cooking, but now it was impossible to tell where one began and another ended.

'We stood by the stone bench talking for a moment or two and I touched the cross…' Olivia gave a sudden cry and ran forward. She stooped down and picked something up, turning to wave at Beatrice who was still lagging some way behind her. 'I've found it…'

Olivia gave a little scream as she turned and saw why her sister had not followed her. She was being confronted by a man dressed in what must once have been a well-cut coat, but was now stained and hanging loose about him, the buttons torn from the cloth. His hair was wild about his face, and looked as if it had not been washed or cut in many months, and he was swaying on his feet, cursing in a loud harsh voice.

She had no doubt that this must be the wicked Marquis himself! Olivia was transfixed with terror as she realised that he was very drunk, and threatening her sister. He had some kind of gun in his hand, a heavy thing with a wide barrel that looked dangerous.

'Damned trespassers,' Sywell muttered drunkenly. 'I'll teach you to come poaching on my land… Hang the lot of you. Make an example to the rest…'

'We are not poachers,' Beatrice said. Her face was pale, but she held her head high. 'Be sensible, sir. We are two women out for a walk. We mean no harm…'

'Damned trespassers,' Sywell said, leering at her. He blinked, obviously too drunk to know what was going on. 'Had enough of this…teach you a lesson…'

He aimed his gun at Beatrice, clearly intending to fire. Olivia screamed loudly, and then suddenly both sisters heard a shout and the sound of thudding hooves.

Turning, Beatrice saw a horseman riding straight towards them. It was Harry! His horse jumped between the tumbled walls with ease, trampling on herb beds and whatever lay in its path as horse and rider charged straight at the Marquis. Harry clearly intended to ride Sywell down rather than let him fire at Beatrice.

She cried out in alarm as Sywell seemed to realise what was happening and swung round to face in the horseman's direction. He took aim once again, but as he did so, Olivia gave a great leap forward and threw herself at Sywell's back. The gun's heavy barrel turned skyward and the shots fired harmlessly into the air, but the noise had terrified Harry's horse and it reared up wildly, in an attempt to unseat its rider. Harry held on desperately for a few minutes, but was thrown violently to the ground, almost at the same moment as Sywell pitched forward in a drunken faint.

'Harry!' Beatrice screamed. She rushed to where he was lying, still and unmoving on his back, his eyes closed, colour white as death. She knelt on the ground by his side, running her hands over his face, forgetting all her feelings of shame and embarrassment in her concern for the man she loved. 'Harry, my darling,' she wept, the tears beginning to run down her cheeks. 'Oh, Harry. Please don't die…I love you so. Please don't die…don't leave me. I cannot bear it if you die…'

Olivia came to kneel down at her side. She looked down at Harry's still form. 'He must have been knocked unconscious by the fall,' she said. 'Stay here with him, Beatrice, and I will run and fetch help.'

Beatrice hardly heard her. She bent to press her lips to Harry's, the tears falling onto his face as she continued to beg him not to die. 'Please don't leave me,' she begged. 'Please live, Harry…live, my darling, live for me.'

Olivia glanced towards the Marquis, who lay where

he had fallen, face down in the herbs that had gone wild. He had not moved, and it seemed clear that he was too drunk to do any more harm.

'The Marquis has passed out,' she said, and got to her feet. 'Stay with Harry, Beatrice. I shall not be long...'

Beatrice was vaguely aware of her sister's words, but she did not turn her head as Olivia began to run. All she could think of was the man who lay so still and pale on the ground before her.

'I love you,' she whispered, stroking his cheek. 'I love you, I love you. Do not leave me, my dearest heart, for I think I shall die if you do. Speak to me, only speak to me...'

Harry's eyelids flickered. He made a moaning sound, then opened his eyes and looked up at her.

'What happened?' He sat up, then groaned as he felt the dizziness sweep over him. 'Now what have you done to me, Beatrice? I feel as if a coach and horses has fallen on my head.'

'You were thrown from your horse,' Beatrice said, sitting back on her heels. 'Do you not remember? The Marquis was threatening me with a blunderbuss and you rode straight at him. He was going to fire at you instead of me, but Olivia rushed at him and his shots went wide.' Beatrice drew a sobbing breath. 'She saved your life because of that, Harry. She saved your life...'

'Good grief! Yes, I think she probably did,' Harry said and sat up gingerly. 'What a brave young woman she is. I must thank her properly.' He glanced round and saw the Marquis lying on the ground. 'Where is she? And what is wrong with him? I do trust Olivia did not actually kill the fellow. That would be a trifle awkward, I fear.'

'I imagine he is in a drunken stupor—and Olivia has gone for help,' Beatrice said, biting her lip as she fought the urge to laugh. 'Will you never be serious, Harry? Do you not realise what might have happened here? I thought you were dead.'

'Did you indeed?' Harry smiled at her. 'Fortunately, that was not the case.' He held out his hand to her. 'Will you help me to rise, Beatrice? I am feeling most odd…most odd.'

She gave him her hand and he pulled himself up, but swayed unsteadily for a moment. 'I think I must put my arm about your waist,' Harry said, a gleam she did not miss in his eyes. 'I may be able to walk if you will help me.'

'Olivia will bring Bellows,' Beatrice said, belatedly remembering that she had meant to stay well clear of him. 'Perhaps you should wait, my lord.'

Harry glanced round. His horse was pawing the ground restlessly some feet away.

'Bellows can bring poor Rufus,' Harry said. 'He has never behaved so badly before, and it was truly not his fault. I think you must assist me, Beatrice.'

'Very well, if you lean on me, we can walk home together.'

'Slowly,' Harry said. 'I cannot walk fast, Beatrice. You must be patient and take your time with me.'

'Yes, of course,' she said, looking at him in concern. 'I think you may have cut your head, sir. There is a little blood trickling down your neck.'

'It feels as if I have split it wide open,' Harry said. 'I shall rely on you to nurse me if I am ill again.'

She had the oddest sensation that he was teasing her, deliberately reminding her of what had passed before. She blushed for shame. How could he? Surely he must realise how awkward she felt after what had happened between them the previous night?'

'I shall naturally bathe your head for you, sir.'

'So we are back to *sir* again,' Harry said and sighed. 'I quite thought we had gone beyond that, Beatrice.'

'Pray do not remind me of my foolishness,' she begged, wishing that she could run off as she had the previous evening but knowing that she could not desert him. 'I had been dreaming. I did not know what I was saying. You should take pity and not remind me of something best forgotten.'

'You dreamt of me, I hope?'

Beatrice turned her head towards him, but he had paused and his eyes were closed as if he were in some pain. 'Does your head hurt very much, my lord?'

'I must confess it does,' Harry replied. 'But I truly believe Sywell would have killed you had I not seen you enter the Abbey grounds. I was some distance away and followed—another moment and I might have been too late. Why on earth did you and Olivia come here alone? Were you searching for that wretched grave again?'

'No...' Beatrice blushed. 'It was for a gold cross

and chain, which were a present to my sister from our mother. She lost it here when she was with Lord Dawlish and was so upset that I agreed to come with her to look for it.'

'Did you not think it might be dangerous? Could you not have told me, allowed me to arrange a search? Consider, Beatrice—if we had found that grave, you would probably have been confronted by a murderer, rather than a drunken sot who was too far gone to withstand a push in the back from a woman.'

Beatrice bit her lip, knowing the rebuke was well deserved.

'From that I gather the grave did not contain the Marchioness's body?'

'It was the burial place of a horse.'

She nodded, relieved it had not been what they feared.

'Yes, I dare say the Marquis has buried more than one mount,' Beatrice said soberly. 'He is what is generally known as a bruising rider.' She looked up at him. 'You realise we must end the search after what has happened this morning? We cannot continue it now. Someone might die and that would help no one.'

Harry frowned. 'Yes, I think you are right. I had intended it to go on—but it is too dangerous. If the Marquis is ready to fire on a defenceless woman, then he would not hesitate to kill Bellows or his friends.'

'I was not defenceless, I had my sister.' Beatrice's sense of humour was coming to her rescue. The warmth of Harry's body pressed against her was making her feel things she had vowed she would never allow herself to feel again, but she could not help herself.

'Yes, I had forgot,' Harry murmured and smiled oddly. 'One more debt I owe Olivia.'

'You should not speak of your marriage as a debt,' Beatrice said, overcoming her own feelings in defence of her sister. 'Olivia is a lovely, generous person, and you have confessed several times that you are fond of her.'

'I do not deny it. I do feel a warm affection for your sister, Beatrice.'

Beatrice saw the hot glow in his eyes, and looked quickly away. How could she be mistaken in that look? Harry wanted her. His kisses had told her that last night, even as his words denied her. How was she to take him? This was unfair!

'You must not tease me, sir,' she said. 'I was foolish last night—but it was because of—of things you had said…'

'I know it,' Harry confessed, his expression becoming serious. 'You should feel no shame, Beatrice. This is all my fault, none of the blame can lie with you. I must make an end to this, put everything straight. This has gone on too long, Beatrice. I must speak to Olivia.'

'Yes, I…'

Beatrice stopped speaking abruptly as she saw Lady Susanna, Nan, Bellows, Lily and even Ida following on behind Olivia.

'It seems the whole household has turned out to rescue me,' Harry said and smiled oddly. 'Truly,

Beatrice, I have never known such devotion in my life, despite all the legions of servants I employ.'

'Are you badly hurt, my lord?' enquired Bellows, coming up to them at the double. 'Let me have him, now, Miss Beatrice.'

'Beatrice and Nan will help me,' Harry said, clearly in charge once more. If he had been feeling dizzy earlier, there was no sign of it now. 'You will find my horse wandering back there somewhere—and the Marquis of Sywell in a drunken stupor. You will oblige me by letting Mr Burneck know his master is lying on the damp ground unconscious, and then you can bring poor Rufus home...'

Harry had been about to say more when they all heard the most tremendous bang. Everyone turned round in time to see a little cloud of smoke issuing into the air from the direction of Roade House.

'Papa!' Beatrice cried. 'He must have fitted the new stove...'

'He was in the kitchen when we left,' Nan said, looking frightened. 'I warned him not to build the fire too high, Beatrice, but he said he wanted to test it to the limit.'

'Take Harry's arm,' Beatrice said, and as Nan did so, she let go herself and began to run towards the back of the house. 'Papa... Oh, let Papa be all right...'

Her heart was beating wildly. Oh, why would her father meddle with such dangerous things? She could not bear to lose him too. If anything had happened to her dear Papa...

As she drew near, she saw someone stumble from the gaping hole in the kitchen wall. His face was blackened with soot, and his clothes had been singed by the heat, but he called to her cheerfully as he saw her.

'No need to worry, Beatrice. I am not hurt. It was just as well everyone else had gone out, though. I think I've done more damage this time than I did before.'

'Oh, Papa…' Beatrice said and uncharacteristically burst into tears. She flung her arms about him, and clung to him sobbing her heart out. 'I thought you might be dead or badly injured…and I really could not bear that.'

'There, there,' Mr Roade said, patting her arm awkwardly. He seemed bewildered by her show of emotion. Beatrice was always so calm and sensible. 'No need to take on so, m'dear. It was just a little bang and some smoke, that's all.'

Beatrice shook her head. Now that the tears had started, she simply could not stop. She realised that she had not cried like this even after her mother died. She had held her grief inside then for her father's sake, but now it was pouring out of her, all the grief and hurt she had held inside her for so very long. Suddenly, it had all become too much to bear.

She turned, instinctively looking for Harry, and then he was there, taking her into his arms, bending to sweep her off her feet and carrying her inside the house and into the parlour, where he laid her on the sofa and knelt down on the carpet by her side.

'I am sorry...' Beatrice wept. 'I cannot seem to stop...'

'I am not surprised,' Harry said gently. 'You have been forced to carry too many burdens for too long.' He handed her his handkerchief, which was very large and very white. 'Wipe your eyes, dearest Beatrice. You have no more need to cry. I am here to take care of you now. You will never be so alone again.'

She looked up at him, her eyes drenched in tears. 'But you cannot mean it,' she said. 'You are promised to Olivia. You must marry her. It is the only proper and honourable thing to do.'

'It might be if I would have him,' Olivia's voice said from the doorway, and they both turned their heads to look at her. She was smiling, a hint of mischief in her lovely face. 'How can my sensible sister be so very foolish as to imagine I would marry a man who is not in the least in love with me? I have known for days that Harry was head over heels in love with you, Beatrice—but until this morning when I saw the way you acted when you thought he might be dead, I did not know how you felt about him.'

'Did you not?' said Lady Susanna, coming to stand beside her in the doorway. 'How odd. I knew it the first time I heard dear Beatrice say his name. And of course, I knew that Harry was in love with her when he bought her that gown.' Her laugh had a merry sound. 'It is the first time I have ever known my son to go shopping without being pushed into it. He must be utterly devoted to you, Beatrice.'

'Mama...' Harry warned, a glint in his eyes. 'No,

really, you go too far…what about that emerald neck-lace I sent you for your birthday?'

'Which I have no doubt you sent your agent to order from the very best jeweller in town…'

'*Touché*, Mama!' Harry laughed. 'Well, I must ad-mit I do not normally like to visit any commercial establishment other than my tailor or my club. Unless it is to buy a horse, of course.'

Beatrice was blushing madly, her cheeks on fire. 'I… Do you really not want to marry Harry, Olivia? I was sure you were beginning to change your mind.'

'No, honestly, Beatrice, I do not,' Olivia said. 'I have been hoping he would not ask me again, but my answer would still have been no had he done so, which he has not.'

Harry had risen to his feet. 'Would anyone care to hear my opinion of all this?' he asked. 'Or have you all made up your minds already?'

'Surely you are not going to deny you are in love with Beatrice?' his mother cried. 'Really, Harry, I cannot think what gets into you sometimes. If you throw away this chance of happiness I shall wash my hands of you. Please, I beg you. Do not be like your father. His father and mine arranged our marriage when we were born. Your father offered for me be-fore I was properly out of the schoolroom, because he felt it his duty. He did not love me—and I did not love him. Fortunately, we became friends in time, and we both found solace in other people.' She paused, her cheeks a little flushed. 'I was in love once.'

'Were you, Mama?' Harry was sidetracked by this

startling revelation. 'I never knew that…when?' He frowned, then nodded to himself. 'Was it with Lillibet's father?'

'Yes…' She smiled at him. 'If I seemed to show her favour, Harry, it was because of my darling Robert. We had a brief affair, and then he died. He left me his child as a farewell gift.'

'No wonder you were so distraught when she died,' Harry said and the sadness came into his eyes. 'That was my fault, Mama. If I had not played with the children of the grooms, it would not have happened. It should have been me who died that day.'

'No!' Lady Susanna crossed the room to where he was standing. She looked up at him for a moment, then reached up to stroke his cheek with her hand. 'I would have been equally as grief-stricken whichever of my children had died. I loved you both so much, though I fear I did not show it enough. I had learned to discipline myself, you see. It was the only way I could live. I was tied to a man who was my friend, but who did not love me—and the man I loved so very much was dead. How could I dare to show love? When Lillibet died, I felt that she had been taken from me in payment for my sins. If I had shown too much love for you, you too might have been taken from me…'

'Mama…' Harry stared at her. He was clearly very moved by this dramatic declaration. 'I never dreamed you felt this way…'

'How could you?' she asked, and smiled at him. 'You learned by my example, Harry. You learned to hide your feelings, to protect yourself against love…but I do most humbly beg you not to do so now. If you do not ask Beatrice to marry you, you will lose the most precious thing you are ever likely to possess in your life.'

Harry was silent for a moment. He looked down at Beatrice, and then at all the expectant faces. Behind his mother and Olivia were grouped Nan, Mr Roade and the servants.

'Bellows, you were sent to fetch my horse. Please do so at once,' he said, establishing his authority. 'Mrs Willow, you will oblige me by making some tea for Beatrice, and take Lily and Ida with you if you please…'

'Yes, of course, my lord.' Nan smiled and turned to shoo the gaping servants ahead of her.

'Mr Roade, I would much appreciate it if you could organise both Lady Susanna's coachman and the one I hired in Northampton. I believe we should all remove to my house in Cambridgeshire as soon as possible, for there will not be much comfort to be found here. As cold as my house at Camberwell is, we can reach there before nightfall and be assured of a warm welcome if I send a groom ahead. Bellows may stay here to arrange repairs, and the servants can send our baggage on with the carter tomorrow…'

'Ah yes,' Mr Roade said, his eyes brightening. 'Is that the house you told me was so very old and draughty?'

'I have several old and draughty houses,' Harry replied serenely. 'Do not despair at today's failure, sir. I dare say if we give the matter some thought, we shall discover where your calculations went a little awry…and in time we shall be sure to hit on the answer.'

'Yes, I am almost sure I know already,' Mr Roade said and beamed at him. 'I think we shall get on very well together, Ravensden. I see that you are a man of excellent sense. I knew how it would be the day you came. Did I not tell you that Beatrice would make an excellent wife?'

'Yes, indeed you did, sir.'

Mr Roade nodded as if he had arranged it all, looked kindly at his daughter and went out of the room.

'Miss Olivia,' Harry said and smiled at her. 'It is and has been my intention for some time to make you an offer…not of marriage, but of my friendship. I intend to settle ten thousand pounds on you, money that cannot be taken away from you should I suddenly lose my mind and decide I do not care for the colour of your gown. I do hope you will be kind enough to accept this offer. It sits ill with me that I have been the cause of your downfall and I must—I must!— make some reparation for my own peace of mind.'

'I thank you for your kindness, Lord Ravensden,' Olivia said, and dimpled prettily. 'I shall not refuse your generous offer, for it will make me independent—and you must know that I have made up my mind never to marry…'

'Olivia…' Beatrice said, looking anxious. 'Surely one day…'

'I shall not marry, unless I find a man I can love as much as my sister loves you, Harry,' she said and gave them her sweet smile. 'I shall go upstairs and pack a few necessities for our journey. Lily can help me. We will pack your things as well, Beatrice—and I am sure Nan will be pleased to help Lady Susanna.'

'Thank you, Miss Olivia,' Harry said. 'No, dash it all—why stand on ceremony? We have fallen into the habit of first names, why should we change it now?'

'Why indeed?' Olivia said, 'especially as I expect to hear that we shall be related by marriage very soon.'

'Olivia!' Beatrice protested. 'He has not asked me yet.'

'I have not yet had the chance,' Harry said. He looked at his mother as Olivia went out. 'If you imagine, Mama, that I intend to ask Beatrice to be my wife with you watching, you are very wrong.'

'As long as you do it,' Lady Susanna said. 'I shall take no other for my daughter-in-law, dear Beatrice.' Her laughter tinkled. 'And now I really must go or I do believe my son will lose his temper...'

'Harry...' Beatrice murmured and he looked down at her as his mother left and they were at last alone. 'You must not mind them. They are all so interested in what is going to happen, you see. Even poor Lily and Ida.'

'The house will be repaired as I have said,' Harry told her. 'The servants will have a place here—unless you choose to take them with you, of course. Others will be employed as Bellows sees fit. Mrs Willow will have sufficient money for all that is required to run the house properly. Your father will have a home with us, naturally, but he must also have this house so that he can feel independent and come here when he chooses…besides, I dare say it has many cherished memories for him.'

Beatrice reached for his hand and held it tightly. 'How thoughtful you are,' she said, her throat tight. 'But you do not really mean to let him experiment in your house?'

'My house in Camberwell is ancient and hardly worth preserving,' Harry said and grinned at her wickedly. 'Wait until you have experienced how cold it can get. Only Ravensden itself is bearable in the winter. I prefer my house in town. Believe me, my darling. Your father will do us all a favour if he manages to blow Camberwell up. We shall then be able to build a modern house, which will be very much warmer.'

Beatrice laughed. Her tears had all dried long since. She got to her feet, gazing up at him uncertainly. It seemed that she was to be given all her dreams, and she found it hard to believe even now.

'Do you really want to marry me, Harry?'

'How can you doubt it, my dearest?' He took her hand, carrying it to his lips to kiss the palm. 'I think I have loved you, if not from the moment we met, at least from the moment you came rushing into my bedchamber with your hair wild about your face. Indeed, I fell in love with you when you tended me as I lay so ill…'

'You called out for Merry,' Beatrice said. 'I wondered if she was your mistress, but then you told me she was Lord Dawlish's wife.'

'There have been women,' Harry said, his gaze narrowing as he looked at her. 'But none I loved. Mama was right. I chose not to let love into my life, because I was afraid of it. I loved Lillibet and she died. I thought that if I let myself love again…'

'Yes, I understand,' Beatrice reached up to touch a finger to his lips. 'I was hurt once when I was very young, and I thought that I would never love anyone again. I did not realise then that he had hurt my pride more than my heart. You taught me what real pain is, Harry. I thought my heart would break when I believed you would marry Olivia—and I was desperate when you were thrown from your horse this morning.'

'I heard you beg me to live.' He smiled tenderly at her. 'I must confess that I was not as badly shaken as I allowed you to believe.'

'Had you not recovered, I believe I should have died…but I knew it was your duty to ask Olivia, and that I had no right to love you.'

'At first I really thought I had no choice but to beg Olivia to be my wife,' Harry said. 'I had given my promise to your sister, and because of my carelessness, Lord Burton threw her out—but then I began to realise that I could not marry her when my heart belonged to you. And yet it was too soon to speak to you. I had to wait in all decency…' He gave her a rueful look. 'Besides, I was not even sure my feelings were returned. It was only when I kissed you and felt your response—then I knew that some other way of settling the affair must be found.'

'Oh, Harry…' Beatrice smiled through more tears. 'I ran away last night because I was so ashamed of what I had done…offering myself to you so shamelessly.'

'And I wanted to take your sweet offer,' Harry murmured throatily. 'I wanted it so badly, Beatrice—but I was ashamed that I could contemplate such a thing. I have always followed my own code of honour in these matters. I knew you to be innocent, and that is the way you shall come to me as a bride. Untouched and lovely as you are.'

'You have not asked me yet,' she reminded him, afraid that she might weep if she did not laugh.

Harry chuckled, and dropped to his knees. 'On behalf of myself, my mother and all other interested parties, I do very earnestly beg you to do me the honour of becoming my wife, Miss Roade. I have a very high regard for you, indeed the highest, and should you refuse, I shall be cast down into the depths of despair.'

'Will you never be serious, Harry?' Beatrice asked, giving him a speaking look. 'I have a good mind to refuse after such a proposal. Indeed, it would serve you right if I kept you dangling for months.'

'But you do not intend to do so, do you, dear heart?' asked Harry as he got to his feet. 'You do know that if you do not this instant consent to be my wife, I shall very likely take you upstairs by force and make love to you until you surrender.'

Beatrice gurgled with laughter. 'You tempt me, sir. If you make such threats, I shall very likely hold out just to see…'

Harry pulled her into his arms and kissed her so thoroughly that she could hardly breathe. She gazed up into his eyes as he released her.

'You are sure you want to marry me?' she whispered, a teasing note in her voice. 'You are not just saying this to please your Mama?'

'Beatrice…' Harry threatened. 'I am counting…'

'Oh, very well,' she cried. 'If it is the only way to save my virtue, I accept.' She laughed as his eyes took fire. 'I accept with all my heart, with my mind and my body…'

Chapter Ten

'You look beautiful,' Olivia said as she finished arranging the lace and veiling on Beatrice's bonnet. 'And your gown is lovely—as elegant I am sure as Madame Félice would have made it herself if she had not been too busy to oblige you.'

'Lady Susanna was most put out because she could not see me,' Beatrice said and laughed. 'But I did not mind. Madame Coulanges was kindness itself, and I am well satisfied with my trousseau. I have never owned so many beautiful things. Harry is always buying me something…a trinket or a jewel or some little thing that happened to catch his eye.'

'And why not?' Olivia said, sparkling at her. 'You deserve everything he gives you, dearest. For years you had nothing, and now you will have everything money can buy.'

'And more,' Beatrice said, her eyes glowing with the knowledge that she was truly loved. 'You will come and stay with us sometimes, Olivia?'

Beatrice looked anxiously at her sister. Roade

House having been restored, Olivia had chosen to live there with her father at their home in Abbot Giles. She had even declined to accompany Beatrice and Lady Susanna to London when Beatrice went up to buy her bride clothes.

'Of course I shall, often.'

Beatrice smiled as she looked round her old bedroom. She had chosen to be married in Abbot Giles, and her wedding was this very morning. Lady Susanna had wanted to give them a grand reception in town, but Beatrice had begged to be allowed a quiet wedding in her own village.

'I should like my friends to see me wed,' she'd said, a little shyly for her. 'Later perhaps, you could give a ball for us in town, Mama, and all your friends can attend that?'

'An excellent idea,' Harry agreed instantly. Beatrice must of course have her way. 'You could not deny Ida and Lily the privilege of attending you on your wedding day, could you, my love?'

'They will naturally want to see me leave for the church,' Beatrice replied, shaking her head at his levity. 'And to share a piece of the wedding cake, of course.'

'Shall you make it yourself, dear heart?'

Beatrice threw him a darkling glance. 'I shall not have time.'

'Indeed, you will not. The very idea!' cried Lady Susanna, scowling at her son. 'It will take us all our time to be ready, since my impatient son says he will wait no longer than Christmas to claim his bride—though how he expects to have everything ready by then, I do not know.'

'Sooner if I could persuade Beatrice,' Harry said. 'Gowns can wait. Beatrice has the rest of her life to visit the seamstress if she so chooses.'

Beatrice had merely smiled. Her wedding day had seemed an age away then, but the trip to town had been as hectic as it was enjoyable, and before she really knew it they were back in Abbot Giles.

And now it was her wedding day, the twenty-second of December. Beatrice glanced at herself in the mirror once more. Her gown was fashioned of a soft cream velvet and heavily trimmed with a slightly paler lace. Her rather fetching bonnet was trimmed with matching lace and deep blue ribbons.

Harry still preferred her in green, and indeed several of her new gowns had been made in varying shades of green. However, she thought that the soft cream was very suitable for her wedding—its purity reflecting her innocence. For she was still untouched. Harry had managed to restrain himself—though with mounting difficulty.

They were to spend their wedding night and the first few days of their married life at Camberwell, which Beatrice had found a very comfortable, pleasant house despite all Harry had said to its detriment. Harry had employed a small army of craftsmen to make the house as comfortable as possible for them.

'We shall visit each of my estates in the spring,' he had told her. 'But I dare say we shall spend much of our time in town. Unless you particularly wish to live in the country, my love?'

'I can be happy wherever you are, Harry.'

'Perhaps I shall build us a new wing at Ravensden,'

he said, and kissed her hand. 'We have our whole lives to decide.'

They did indeed have a lifetime to decide where they would make their home. Beatrice could hardly wait for the moment when their life together would really begin.

'Are you ready, dearest?'

Olivia's question recalled her wandering thoughts. She glanced at her reflection, touching the simple string of pearls that had been Harry's gift to her on their official engagement, besides the magnificent ring of emerald and diamonds that he thought fitting for his future wife. She knew that there were many precious heirlooms awaiting her in her husband's bank in London, but the pearls had been a personal gift, unworn by any other Ravensden bride.

'I chose them myself,' Harry had told her as he placed them tenderly about her neck. 'I did not send my agent, I promise you.'

Beatrice smiled at the memory. She looked at her sister and nodded. 'Yes, I am ready,' she said. 'Let us go down now.'

In the hall below, family and servants were gathered together to watch her leave.

'Lor, miss, you do look lovely,' said Lily.

'Her be a real ladyship now,' said Ida, sniffing. 'Her won't be with us never no more.'

'You must both stay here and look after Papa,' Beatrice said, smiling at them. 'Do not imagine you will never see me again. I shall return now and then to see all my friends, I promise.'

'You are beautiful,' Nan said, and pressed a posy of silk flowers tied with blue ribbons into her hands.

'I always hoped you would find a good man, my dear, and you have.'

'Yes, I know.' Beatrice smiled and kissed her cheek. 'And he is not in the least addled in the wits.'

She turned to her father. 'Papa, shall we leave?'

He offered his arm. 'Be happy, my dear,' he murmured as they went out to the carriage which was waiting to carry them to the church. It was a very smart affair with the Ravensden coat of arms painted on its side and was one of Harry's many gifts to his bride. 'But I know Ravensden will look after you.'

'You will come and stay with us often, Papa?'

'Most certainly. I have almost perfected my idea for gravity heating, Beatrice. I have promised Ravensden that I shall make Camberwell as cosy as you could desire. I dare say I shall be ready to begin work in a few months…just as soon as you two have had a little time alone together.'

Beatrice smiled. She faced the thought of her father's assault on Camberwell bravely. After all, Harry had promised that they would go on a tour of his estates as soon as the weather improved. That should take several weeks, and there was always the lovely and comfortable house in town.

Harry and Lady Susanna were guests at Jaffrey House. When the Earl of Yardley had heard that Ravensden and Beatrice were to be married in the church at Abbot Giles, nothing else would do for him.

'I knew your father, Ravensden,' he had told Harry. 'You and Lady Susanna will oblige me by staying here for a few days—and I shall be delighted to offer you my house as the venue for your wedding reception.'

Harry had accepted the offer in the spirit in which it was made, bringing in an army of his own servants and cooks to prepare the meal that was to be offered to their guests. Beatrice's quiet wedding had become rather larger than she had anticipated. However, since the guests invited were, apart from Harry's friends, to come largely from the four villages, she could not complain.

'We shall give food and ale to everyone who comes to ask,' Harry had said when telling her of his plans. 'Ours shall be a wedding that every man, woman and child in the four villages may enjoy if they wish.' He smiled and kissed her. 'I want everyone to share in my happiness, Beatrice. When I first came to this place, I expected to be bored—but I have never known a dull moment since I arrived. I am very grateful to the people of the villages for giving me my lovely bride.'

Beatrice had invited several children from the villages to be her bridesmaids, and Olivia would have charge of keeping them in order, something that would take some doing! Beatrice's wedding had set the four communities buzzing, and there was sure to be a great deal of talk about this day for months ahead.

There was a large crowd gathered outside the church to watch Beatrice arrive, despite the fact that it was a chilly morning. A cheer and then the sound of clapping greeted her as she stepped from the carriage. Inside the church there was not one spare seat to be had. Beatrice was more popular than she would ever have guessed, and everyone was delighted that she had made such a fortunate match.

Beatrice was vaguely aware of how many people had gathered to see her wed, but once she entered the church, her eyes were only for the man who stood waiting for her to join him. He turned as the organ music announced her arrival, and the love in his eyes brought her to the verge of tears.

She walked, head high, on her father's arm to join him.

'So…' Sir Peregrine said to Beatrice at the reception later. 'I must wish you happy, madam.' It was clear that the words stuck in his throat. 'At least Ravensden has chosen a sensible woman this time. I suppose I may be certain of a decent dinner should I choose to visit you.'

'Of course, sir,' Beatrice said and smiled. Even his poisonous barbs could not spoil her happiness this day. And all of Harry's other friends had greeted her with true pleasure, especially Merry Dawlish, who was already planning a long visit in the spring. 'Anyone Ravensden or I choose to invite to our home may be sure they will be welcomed in every way possible.'

She did not add that she would be glad to welcome him, and he gave her a sour look before walking off to speak with Lady Susanna.

Harry came up to her a moment later. 'What did the abominable Peregrine have to say?'

'Nothing that need make you frown so, my dearest Harry. You need not fear for me. I was vulnerable when your cousin stayed with us, but I can assure you, I am well able to deal with him now.'

Harry's eyes gleamed. 'You will oblige me if you

can persuade the abominable Peregrine not to visit us more than once every five years.'

'Harry!' she scolded laughingly. 'I hope I know my duty to your cousin better than that—however abominable he may be. He shall come and stay when Merry does, later in the spring.'

'But do you know your duty to me?' Harry asked, his eyes beginning to smoulder.

'I believe it is to love, honour and obey…' Her eyes met and challenged his. 'I shall try to be a dutiful wife, my lord.'

'Then do you think you could manage to say your farewells and slip away quite soon, Beatrice? I should like to be alone with my bride.'

'I shall do as you bid me, my lord.'

'I wonder…' Harry laughed. 'This is a new Beatrice indeed. It will be interesting to see just how long this meekness will last.'

She shook her head at him and went away to change her gown, refusing to be drawn. It would hardly befit the new Lady Ravensden to admit that she was as impatient as her lord.

Nan and Olivia were waiting to help her with her clothes. There were hugs and kisses, and good wishes, then Beatrice came down to where a little group of young women from the villages were waiting to see her leave. They looked at her expectantly as she held her posy of silk flowers out, then laughed and threw them in the direction of the young women, but it was Olivia who caught them neatly.

Harry, meanwhile, had been throwing handfuls of coins to the young urchins who had gathered in anticipation of the custom, and were now scrambling eagerly on the ground in pursuit of the silver and gold.

Beatrice laughed with sheer pleasure at the sight, then she was being helped inside the carriage, a final wave and they were on their way.

'At last,' Harry said as they stood together in the small, comfortable parlour he had requested should be made ready for them. A good fire was burning in the grate, throwing out a welcome warmth after the chill of the journey. A cold meal and wine had been laid on the table, and, except for Harry's valet and Beatrice's maid, the servants had retired for the night. 'Come here, Beatrice. I want to know just how willing you are to serve your lord.'

Beatrice laughed as she heard the teasing note in his voice. She was wearing a very elegant travelling-gown of heavy silk in a deep shade of green, and her hair was dressed into the loose curls her maid had spent so much time arranging earlier.

'Very willing,' she said, and stood laughing up at him. 'What is it you would have of me?'

Harry reached out and began to take the pearl-headed pins from her hair. He dropped each one carelessly on to the floor, letting each strand fall until it was free. Then he ran his fingers through her hair, satisfied only when it became a wild tangle.

'There,' he said huskily. 'That is the vision I saw when I came back from that hell of pain—the sickness that would undoubtedly have claimed me had you not saved my life.'

'I did only what any other woman would have done…'

'No! You did far more—more than I had any right
to expect,' Harry said, a look of tenderness in his
eyes. 'You gave me so much...even then, when you
scarcely knew me. Why? Why did you do that,
Beatrice? You had no reason to care whether I lived
or died.'

'I would not have had you die in Papa's house—
whatever would people have said?' Beatrice asked,
but the teasing look disappeared from her eyes as she
looked into his. 'Or perhaps I loved you from the
start. The first time I saw you—before I knew your
name.'

'But you tried to send me away...'

'You had hurt my sister. I denied my heart. I believed you must be the monster who had so carelessly
destroyed her.'

'When did you change your mind?' Harry looked
at her intently.

'When?' Beatrice began to smile, the wickedness
in her eyes. 'Why, my lord—I believe it was when I
pulled back the covers and saw you...' She paused
and blushed.

'...naked?' Harry laughed, his eyes taking fire.

'As nature intended.' She gazed up at him naugh-
tily.

'I believe I have got me a wanton wench!'

'I believe you may have done,' Beatrice admitted.
'Are you very hungry, my lord? Only I do not particularly wish for supper.'

'I am hungry only for you,' Harry said, and reached
for her. His kiss was both tender and passionate, full
of an aching yearning. 'I believe I should like to go

to bed, Lady Ravensden.' He smiled as he released her. 'Go up now, my love, and I will follow shortly.'

'Yes, my lord,' Beatrice replied, her manner so demure that his eyes gleamed with laughter, knowing full well that some wicked barb was to come. 'But I pray you—do not be long lest I fall asleep.'

There was no fear that she would fall asleep. Beatrice allowed her maid to help her into the gossamer-soft garment she had chosen for her wedding night, before dismissing the girl with a smile. She sat before her dressing-mirror, brushing her own hair as she had always done, then went to the bed and lay down.

When Harry entered the room, she closed her eyes. She did not need to see him to sense that he was near. He sat on the edge of the bed as he had once before, gazing down at her, then she felt the touch of his lips on hers.

Opening her eyes, she smiled up at him. Very slowly, she reached up and slid her arms about his neck, pulling him down to her. This time when they kissed, Harry did not restrain himself. His need was such that she felt the power of it, and when at last they drew apart, both were trembling.

'I love you, Beatrice,' he murmured huskily. 'I love you more than I can express in words. Will you let me show you in the only way I know how?'

Her eyes darkened and grew smoky with desire. 'I love you, my dear, dear Harry. Show me how to be a good wife to you. Teach me what you would have me know and be.'

'I do not believe you will need much teaching, my

wanton wench,' Harry murmured throatily as he
reached out for her. 'But I promise you, I shall be a
demanding master.'

Then he was pulling her gown over her head, discarding it with his own robe so that she was free to
touch the wonderful smooth skin she had once tended
so lovingly while he lay in his fever. There was no
need of tuition on either side, for they each knew
instinctively what would please the other.

'So lovely, so lovely,' he murmured huskily. 'As I
always knew you were beneath those hideous gowns.
It is the woman who makes the gowns, Beatrice, but
this skin is too lovely to be touched by anything but
pure silk. You are the goddess of my heart, and everything I have is yours to use as you will,' he vowed,
and buried his face in the sensuous satin of her flesh.

Breast to breast, thigh to thigh, they caressed and
kissed, playing each other like fine instruments to
make sweet music. Harry's lips and tongue sought out
the secret, sensitive places of her body, lavishing her
with such tender, loving caresses that she was swept
away with him to pleasure beyond all imagining. And
if there was a moment of pain when at last he entered
her, making her truly his own, she was scarcely aware
of it. She was a woman made for love and loving,
and she opened to him with all the warmth of her
being, feeling only the joy of being truly loved, of
belonging. They were joined as one: one heart, one
body, one mind, one soul, and both knew that to find
such completeness was a blessing from the gods that
was not given to all, and believed themselves the favoured ones.

And after their first coupling was over, they lay

entwined, talking long into the night as lovers will, confessing all their secrets that neither had ever told so that they were irrevocably bound. He came to her again and again during that night, taking her with tenderness sometimes, at others with a fierce passion that left them both exhausted, so that at long last they slept deep into the morning.

And their servants crept about the house and smiled to know that master and mistress were still sleeping.

My Lady Ravensden was sitting up in her bed amongst a pile of silken pillows. She had been married a month now, and was blissfully content. Her tray of hot chocolate and sweet rolls had been brought up, together with a small pile of letters.

Beatrice saw that most had come from the villages. There was one from Ghislaine, one from Olivia, and another from her dear papa. What a feast awaited her, for she knew that both Ghislaine's and Olivia's letters would be full of lovely gossip, and she was anxious to hear the latest news and whether anything more had been discovered concerning Lady Sywell's disappearance.

She opened Ghislaine's letter first. Her friend wrote such a clear precise hand, and her letters were always so entertaining. If anything had happened at the Abbey, she would be sure to have news of it. And indeed, it seemed that there were at the moment some very interesting happenings.

'Still abed, you lazy wench,' Harry said, coming in as Beatrice was about to reach the meat of Ghislaine's letter. 'It is far too good a morning to lie abed. Get up and come riding with your lord.'

'Yes, Harry, in a moment,' Beatrice said. 'I just want to read what Ghislaine says…'

Harry plucked the letter from her grasp. She tried to take it back, but he withheld it, so she sat back and looked at him, giving in to his mood of playfulness. He would no doubt return it in a moment.

'Ghislaine says there is news of the Abbey…'

Harry was not attending her. He had begun to fold the paper into a shape that looked rather like an arrowhead, sharp at one end and flaring out wider at the other. Lifting his arm, he drew back the paper dart then brought his hand forward and released the paper with a strong thrust. It flew straight across the room and into the open grate, where it was consumed in seconds by the flames.

'Harry!' Beatrice cried. 'I hadn't finished reading my letter.'

Harry's expression was one of astonishment. 'Did you see that, Beatrice? Did you see the way it flew straight and swift?'

'Straight into the fire,' Beatrice said. 'You wretch.'

'How wonderful it would be if man could build a machine that would fly…'

'You mean a balloon?'

'No…' Harry was still wearing that look of amazed wonder. 'Balloons travel at the behest of the wind, and are awkward, clumsy contraptions. I mean a machine with some kind of energy that man can direct and control…' He turned to her, suddenly excited. 'I recently bought a collection of papers from the estate of a man who had travelled widely; he was a scholarly man, well versed in ancient scripts—and among his papers I saw a fragment of parchment with what looked like the beginnings of a design for such a machine. I do not know where the paper came from, or who scribbled the few details upon it, but I believe it might possibly be made to work. I must write to Mr Roade at once and tell him of my idea before I forget.'

'A flying machine, Harry?' Beatrice looked at him in amusement. 'Would that not be rather dangerous?'

'Slightly less so than a stove that overheats and blows holes in the kitchen wall,' Harry said wickedly and bent to kiss her. 'Just think what fun Papa and I will have trying to discover if the contraption will fly.'

Beatrice smiled at his enthusiasm. She had little doubt that this would be the first of many inventions that Harry and dear Papa would waste their time on in the years to come, but as long as they were content, what did it matter?

'Now what is going on in your head?' Harry asked and bent to kiss her. 'I am going to write my letter; will you be long, dearest?'

'I shall join you in half an hour,' Beatrice promised. 'Go down now, my love, and let me finish my letters—what there is left of them.'

'I am very sorry that I threw your letter into the fire,' Harry said, and kissed her hand. 'Will you forgive me?'

'You are already forgiven,' she said and smiled as he kissed her hand once more, then walked over to the door. 'I shall not be long, Harry.'

Beatrice picked up her remaining letters as the door closed behind her husband, but she did not attempt to open them. She was so very lucky…but the letter from Ghislaine had reminded her, and she could not help thinking of the young Lady Sywell. They had not been able to find a grave, and the mystery of the Marchioness's disappearance was not yet solved, but Beatrice could not forget the unhappy young woman.

What had happened to her? Had her wicked husband murdered her—or had she left Steepwood Abbey of her own accord? Beatrice had no way of knowing. She would no doubt hear from one of her friends if there was any news, but she was no longer living in the villages and it must be for others to discover the truth.

Beatrice shook her head, dismissing the shadows as she rang the bell to summon her maid. It was time that she got dressed and went down to go riding with her beloved husband!

* * * * *

An Innocent Miss
by
Elizabeth Bailey

Elizabeth Bailey grew up in Malawi, then worked as an actress in British theatre. Her interest in writing grew, at length overtaking acting. Instead, she taught drama, developing a third career as a playwright and director. She finds this a fulfilling combination, for each activity fuels the others, firing an incurably romantic imagination. Elizabeth lives in Essex.

Chapter One

October, 1811

The tick of the large clock on the mantelshelf seemed to grow in volume as the silence lengthened. The younger man looked upon the elder with a growing feeling of chagrin. Could he have misheard? The shock of disbelief held every faculty in check as the grey eyes in Wyndham's lean-cheeked countenance grew cold.

A trifle above average height, his lordship was correctly attired for the occasion in a dark coat and black pantaloons, which overlaid the wiry strength of his slim figure with the elegance which must characterise any adherent to Brummell's decrees of fashion. But no one could accuse George Lyford, Viscount Wyndham, of being a dandy, despite the carefully windswept style of his dark brown hair. He was extravagant neither in dress nor habit, adopting none of the affectations of fashion such as a quizzing glass,

and at seven-and-twenty, he had all the weary cyni-
cism of a man of the world.

The last thing he had expected was to succumb to
the lure of an artless débutante with a mop of golden
curls. Still less had he supposed—though he was not,
he hoped, a coxcomb—that his pretensions to the
hand of Miss Serena Reeth would have been summarily rejected.

Wyndham knew not what to say to his host. The
blow struck at more than his pride, although he must
count that deeply wounded.

'Have I understood you correctly, sir?' he uttered
at length. 'You refuse my offer?'

Lord Reeth cleared his throat, and gruffly repeated
himself. 'My daughter, sir, is not for you.'

'But why?' burst from the frustrated suitor.

Reeth returned no answer, and the Viscount broke
away from the elder man's gaze to take an impatient
turn about the library. It was a roomy apartment, the
tall glass-fronted bookcases causing a trifle of gloom
to pervade the place. Or it might have been due to
the dank drizzle beyond the windows, uncomfortably
dull thus early in October.

Wyndham fetched up at the heavy oak desk, upon
which Lord Reeth had caused a candelabrum to be
set. In its light, the welter of papers and correspon-
dence bore witness to the Baron's industry. The
Viscount turned sharply back upon his host, who had
remained by the fireplace, one hand on the mantel.

Lord Reeth made an imposing figure, with that full
head of hair of burnished gold, and a Roman nose

that he had refrained—mercifully!—from bequeathing to his lovely daughter. He was of good height, and had the sense to dress in the sober suiting appropriate to his middle years. He adhered to dark breeches, though of fashionable cut, and the fit of his coat was dictated by comfort.

The strong round tones of Reeth's voice served his oratory well in his chosen field of endeavour—in which Wyndham had not the smallest interest. He felt he was grasping at straws as he put the question.

'Can it be that you reject me because I am inactive in politics?'

His host gave a short bark of laughter. 'If I cared for that, my dear boy, I dare say I should look in vain for a suitable *parti* for my girl.'

'And what makes me so unsuitable?' demanded the Viscount, aggrieved. 'I have no wish to puff off my consequence, my lord, but I am generally accounted eligible.'

He knew it to be an understatement. He must have thought himself a nodcock to imagine for a single moment that the heir to the Earldom of Kettering, already master of a handsome fortune, could meet with a rebuff from a mere baron. But he had met with one, and it had left him at a loss.

Reeth did not answer him, and Wyndham probed in another direction. 'Can it be a slur upon my character? Have you been told something to my discredit, sir? If so, pray enlighten me and allow me an opportunity to—'

'Nothing of the sort!' interrupted Reeth in an impatient tone. Wyndham saw his complexion darken as he came away from the mantel at last, moving to a table to one side upon which reposed a silver tray, heavy with the refreshments his butler had deemed suitable to the occasion. Lord Reeth picked up the decanter.

'Madeira?'

'Thank you, no.'

The Viscount watched his host pour out a glass of the ruby liquid and toss it off. All at once it occurred to him that Reeth was embarrassed. An explanation for his refusal leapt abruptly into Wyndham's mind. Unwelcome, and altogether distressing.

'If those items I have mentioned do not encompass your objections, sir,' he said slowly, 'then I am forced to the conclusion that it is Miss Reeth herself who—'

'Ah, yes!' Reeth suddenly slammed his glass down onto the tray with a force that nearly broke it. He turned quickly towards his guest, his air both apologetic and curiously eager. 'My dear boy, you have hit it! I did not like to say it outright, but I am afraid that my little Serena has indeed turned her face otherwhere.'

Wyndham had supposed that he had run the gamut of emotion during this unpleasant interview. He found himself mistaken, for a sense of bitter hurt rose up, followed immediately by a feeling of outrage.

'I protest I have had no small degree of encouragement from the lady!'

'Possibly you had, sir,' conceded Reeth, thrusting the Roman nose into the air. 'But my daughter, you will allow, is an innocent. She is barely eighteen, you must know.'

'I know, sir. It was that circumstance—'

He broke off, closing his mouth upon what Lord Reeth must find scarcely flattering. It could afford him no satisfaction to know that the Viscount had hesitated to lay his heart at Serena's feet only because she was so very young. He'd had no wish for a bride just out of the schoolroom, and to have fallen victim to Serena's pretty innocence had been an event so much outside his calculations that he had wasted almost the entirety of last Season persuading himself that it had not happened.

Only the summer without the delight of her presence had proved a barren desert. In fact, he had missed her like the devil, and had been wholly unable to enjoy a sojourn with his friends at his hunting-lodge at Bredington, even less a prolonged visit to his ancestral home at Lyford Manor in Derbyshire.

His mother—as might have been expected!—had shrewdly penetrated the reason for his abstraction. Unexpectedly, Lady Kettering had wholeheartedly approved Serena, and encouraged him to declare himself. It had been all the spur Wyndham needed. He had returned to town yesterday, knowing that Reeth must be in residence for the Parliamentary sitting, and presented himself without loss of time in Hanover Square. In vain, it would seem. He had hesitated too long.

Unconsciously echoing his thoughts, Lord Reeth spoke again. 'Had you come to me with this proposal in May or June, my lord, you might have met with a different answer.'

Wyndham set his teeth. 'You are telling me that Miss Reeth favoured me then, but that she has since transferred her affections to another?'

To his surprise, Reeth had occasion once again to clear his throat. What the devil was there in that to embarrass him? Unless he felt his daughter's emotions to be as fickle as did Wyndham himself. He had been so sure of Serena's feeling for him! It was her naïvety in this that had so enchanted him, for had she not worn her heart in those large pansy eyes? Deep brown they were, startling against the mass of gold locks. An oddity which lent a great deal to the sweet seduction of her charm. She was wholly unconscious of it, which had its own attraction.

Yet lovely as she was, she would have held the Viscount's attention but briefly had it not been for the refreshing lack of artifice. He had been at first amused, and then touched, when he had seen her unable to help showing her partiality for him. Or had he been indulging in misplaced vanity?

'She is very young, Wyndham,' said her father excusingly, drawing his attention back. 'It would be surprising if she was not to fancy herself in love with a number of gentlemen before her affections became fixed.'

'No doubt,' said Wyndham coldly. 'But I, my lord, have no wish for a wife whose heart proves thus inconstant.' He strode to the door, and executed a slight bow. 'I will bid you good-day, sir.'

Smarting unbearably, Wyndham left the room, and ran down the stairs in a mood of baffled rage.

From a hidden vantage point above, Miss Serena Reeth watched in bewilderment as Lord Wyndham shrugged on his greatcoat and received his hat from the butler. Had he not then come to make her an offer? The front door closed with finality behind the Viscount, and Serena ran back into the little parlour that had been her nursery and flew to the window.

She was in time to see his lordship climb into his curricle and drive away. Dismayed, she saw the carriage turn the corner of the square. A moment later, the Viscount was lost to sight.

Serena stood frozen at the window, a forlorn figure in a demure muslin morning-gown, with long sleeves ending in a little ruff at the wrists. This feature was repeated about the neck, which dropped into a V-shape, creating a suggestion of décolletage which admirably suited the young lady's slightly buxom form. Her golden hair, loosely confined with a ribbon, fell to her shoulders, and the brown eyes gazed sadly at the rain that drizzled in the empty square.

How could Wyndham have gone without seeing her? She had jumped violently at the knocking on the door—as she had done on each occasion since their return to London, hoping for just this visitor. When she had peeped from the window, her nose pressed to the pane, and had spied him on the steps, her heart had jangled in her chest, racing for all it was worth.

But Cousin Laura had not come to fetch her, as she

usually did when her attendance was required in the saloon, and Serena had at last ventured forth to seek out Lissett.

'His lordship is with Lord Reeth in the book-room, Miss Serena,' the butler had told her, a fatherly gleam in his eye.

Serena had gasped. 'Oh, Lissett, do you think—?'

'Now, now, Miss Serena, do you go and wait in the nursery—I mean, the parlour. Be sure his lordship will send for you, if there's any call for you to have speech with Lord Wyndham.'

But no summons had come from Papa, and Lord Wyndham had left the house—and in so precipitate a fashion! In growing disappointment, Serena came away from the window. She must have been mistaken. The Viscount had not after all offered for her. But what other business could take him to Papa?

The suspense was not to be borne! Serena left the parlour and made her way downstairs to the first floor, heading for her father's library. Outside the door, she was obliged to hesitate before lifting her hand to knock, for her breath seemed to have become tangled up in her throat.

She entered upon the echo of her knock and stood framed in the doorway for a moment, gazing in mute question upon Papa's stern features. Then she saw that Cousin Laura was in the room, had come most probably on the self-same errand.

The duenna was a faded lady of uncertain years, clad in a discreet gown of dove pearl silk made high to the throat, with a lace cap upon her greying hair and a pair of spectacles in her hand with which she was prone to fiddle when stirred. She did so now, apparently undecided whether to keep them on her nose or in her hand even as she swept forward to clasp her charge in her arms.

'Poor dear child! What an escape! And I have ever thought him so very gentleman-like.'

These words cast Serena into bewilderment. She put her cousin aside. 'What can you mean, Cousin Laura? You cannot be speaking of Wyndham!'

Cousin Laura tutted, shoving her spectacles back on her nose as she shut the door. Serena turned to her father, and discovered a portentous frown upon his brow.

'Papa, what is it she means? I had thought Lord Wyndham came to—to—'

'To make you an offer,' finished her father heavily. 'Indeed he did, my child. I am sorry to tell you that I was obliged to refuse my consent.'

Serena's heart plummeted. 'You *refused* him?'

'Dear child, you must not grieve,' came from Cousin Laura, as that lady tried again to enfold her in a fond embrace.

Serena shook her off. 'I cannot believe it. You know, Papa—you *knew* how much I…' Her voice failed and she hunted frantically for her handkerchief.

'Do not think me unfeeling, Serena,' said Reeth, still in that tone of deep solemnity. 'I am palpably to blame. Had I known—had I an inkling of Wyndham's true character, I should never have allowed you to know him well enough to form an attachment.'

But she had formed an attachment! And what in the world did Papa mean by this allusion to his character? Serena blew her nose and sniffed away the rising tears, tucking the handkerchief into her pocket.

'I do not understand you. He is the best of men—the kindest too!'

'He may be as kind as you please, Serena, but as to his being the best of men, you are deceived. As I have been. But you may believe that nothing will induce me to bestow my daughter upon a libertine who runs in the harness of such a man as the Marquis of Sywell!'

Cousin Laura was tutting in the background, but Serena hardly heard her. Wyndham a libertine? It was not possible! Besides, 'I know nothing of the Marquis of Sywell.'

'I should hope not!' uttered Cousin Laura. 'I do not believe a more evil creature lives upon this earth.'

'But who is he?' And what had Wyndham to do with him? But this she did not ask, for a swarm of butterflies danced in her stomach at the question.

She heard Cousin Laura clucking behind her, and was seized with trepidation as Lord Reeth sighed and moved to the fireplace.

'It is not a matter I should ordinarily discuss with you, my child, but I feel bound, under the circumstances, to give you a hint. Sywell, you must understand, has for years been the scourge of the area surrounding his home at Steepwood Abbey. Not a female has been safe since the early nineties when he came to live there. The tales of his debauchery are legion.

I will not distress you with the sum of them, but will say only that every ruinous vice known to man has been Sywell's downfall—and that of every young man whom he has seen fit to corrupt.'

'But not Lord Wyndham!' protested Serena involuntarily. 'Oh, it cannot be true!'

'I think you must accept that it is so. Wyndham owns a hunting-lodge at Bredington, but a mile or two from the infamous Abbey. Indeed, he spent this summer gone there, with a number of cronies, all of whom may be said to be in Sywell's set. You may be sure that the class of female who no doubt frequents Bredington on such occasions is not that with which I could wish my daughter to have acquaintance.'

Serena could bear no more. 'I don't believe it! I will not believe it of him!'

Turning from her father, she fled the room, choking on sobs. Hardly knowing what she did, she ran upstairs, seeking automatically for the solace of her nursery parlour. Slamming the door, she threw herself down upon the day-bed, unable for several bitter moments to control a fit of weeping.

That Wyndham was such a man she could not accept. Papa must be mistaken. How could he know these things? And why had he not known of them last season? It could not be true!

But a seed of doubt lay heavy on her heart. If it was not true, why should Papa have refused his consent? And Wyndham had offered! Despite all, a thrill shot through her at the thought. He had cared for her, after all. How she had despaired when he had not come up to scratch by the end of last season. Summer had been the most miserable time of her life. Or so she had believed. Remembering, she knew that her feelings then were as nothing to those she was now experiencing.

To know that the Viscount wanted to marry her, and to be forced to understand that he was unworthy of the feelings she cherished for him. Oh, this was misery indeed!

The door opened to admit Cousin Laura. Quickly, Serena sat up, dashing away the telltale tears. But it was to no avail. Her duenna came to the day-bed and sat down, possessing herself of Serena's hands.

'My poor girl, I do most sincerely feel for you.'

Serena met her eyes. 'Is it indeed true, cousin?'

Cousin Laura sighed, squeezing the hands she held. 'I am afraid that it is. You see, I happen to know a great deal about the doings of the Marquis of Sywell.'

Serena pulled her hands away, stiffening a little. 'How can that be, cousin?'

'Well, you see, my dear, my father was a clergy-man—'

'The Reverend Geary, yes, I know. What has that to say to anything?'

'I am just going to explain, my dear. I was sent in my girlhood to an academy which was frequented on the whole by daughters of clergymen. It happens that my dearest friend was Miss Lucinda Beattie. Her brother took up a living in Abbot Giles. He has passed on now, poor soul, but Lucinda still lives in a cottage there, and we have always corresponded with regularity, so you see—'

'But what in the world has all this to do with Lord Wyndham?' demanded Serena impatiently.

'Why, Abbot Giles is one of the villages surrounding Steepwood Abbey. So of course Lucinda knows all about the Marquis of Sywell. Indeed, she mentioned in her last letter that Lord Wyndham was known to be staying at Bredington along with several of his intimates. I thought nothing of it at the time, but now that—'

'Then how can you know that Wyndham has had anything to do with this Marquis?' Serena interrupted. 'Merely because he has been in the area—'

'Oh, there can be no doubt of there having been women of ill-repute staying at the hunting-lodge. I am sure it would not be for the first time. Lord Buckworth was certainly there, and he, my dear, besides being Wyndham's boon companion, is a notorious rake!'

'But Wyndham is not a rake. You cannot have heard anyone say that of him, for I certainly have not.'

'No, but we do not know how he conducts himself at Bredington. And Lucinda has frequently spoken of young men attending wild parties at the Abbey.'

Serena got up from the day-bed, crossing to the fireplace where she gripped the mantel until her knuckles shone white. She did not want to believe this! She fought to contain her rising temper as she turned to her duenna.

'For my part, cousin, I should suppose such stories to have been exaggerated. Have you not told me that there are aspects of a gentleman's life about which a wife should not concern herself? You have warned me often enough that I must take care to ignore it if I should find that my husband was engaged upon activities of which I might be supposed to disapprove.'

Cousin Laura drew herself up. 'There is a difference,' she said primly, 'between the peccadilloes to be expected of any normal man, and the depravities of such a person as the Marquis of Sywell and his companions.'

'Well, what is the difference?' asked Serena reasonably. 'Papa will not speak of these things before me, and if you will not tell me either, cousin, then how am I to judge?'

'Oh, dear. Now, Serena, you cannot expect me to—'

'Very well, I shall ask Wyndham himself!'

'Serena! You could not be so dead to all sense of shame as to… Besides, he would say nothing. No gentleman would sully the ears of a delicately nurtured female with such—'

'Well, if the Viscount is so nice in such matters, I shall not believe him capable of—of debauchery,' declared Serena defiantly. 'It must prove a good test if I were to ask him.'

Cousin Laura was moved to leap up from the day-bed in great agitation. 'Serena, I utterly forbid you to mention the matter to him! Lord, it sinks me even to think of it! What, will you accuse him of rape and seduction? Will you demand of him whether he has participated in the drunken orgies in which Sywell indulges? Perhaps you would even speak of the men and women who cavorted naked in the remains of a Roman temple in Giles Wood!'

Staring, Serena paled. 'Naked? Orgies?'

'There now, you have made me speak of them!' Cousin Laura sat down again, tutting and fiddling with her spectacles in a despairing way. 'Perhaps it is as well.'

Serena felt her knees shaking under her. Shifting to a chair to the left of the fireplace, she sank into it, feeling as if the pit of her stomach had vanished.

'Tell me, pray. If you don't, I shall only imagine worse.'

'I should hope your imagination was not of an order to conjure up such visions,' said Cousin Laura. She leaned forward a little, her features creasing into concern. 'My poor child, you do not know! Sywell quite scandalised the villages. Every woman employed at the Abbey was either seduced or raped. No one ever knew whether the women working there were maids or—to speak plainly—whores. And there is not a tradesman's daughter around who could count herself safe from his vile lusts. And all this, mark you, at drunken parties whose wildness shocked even the most liberal-minded of gentlemen. Men and women engaging in the most public displays of wantonness, in the most degrading postures. I tell you, Serena, there are no depths to which that man has not sunk. To say nothing of his reckless gaming. Sywell has been vilified from the local pulpits on Sundays for years since. The Reverend William Perceval, I am

told, attacks him regularly from his church at Abbot
Quincey.' She paused for breath, eyeing her charge
with a distress that Serena had never seen before. 'My
poor child, if there is even a suspicion that Wyndham
has been involved in these activities, your father did
right to reject him.'

Serena was inclined to agree. She felt quite sick,
revulsion superseding her distress. She would not
have thought it of Wyndham! So kind and teasing as
he had always been.

A snatch of memory came into her mind. She was
aware of Cousin Laura speaking to her, but she did
not hear what was said. For there were his lordship's
smiling grey eyes, on the first occasion that he had
danced with her.

Lady Sefton had presented him to her at Almacks,
and they had stood up together for two country
dances. Serena had been too shy to converse with him
at first as they came together in the movement of the
dance.

'It is customary, Miss Reeth, to exchange a word
or two with your partner upon these occasions.'

Serena had looked up and found those grey eyes
teasing and warm. She had broken into laughter.

'Well, but I cannot think what to say to you, sir!'

'Come, come, Miss Reeth,' had said Wyndham
gently. 'And you the daughter of a noted politician?
Surely you can enlighten me on some shrewd gov-
ernmental move.'

'I should think you know much more about such

things than I, my lord,' Serena had answered candidly.

'I, ma'am? But I am merely a dandy, you know. One of these worthless fribbles who follow Brummell.'

Serena had smiled at this sally. 'I cannot believe that you would follow anyone. And I do not think you are a dandy.'

'You flatter me, Miss Reeth.'

'Oh, no. I admire you very much, sir, but I would not flatter you.'

She had then blushed at the forwardness of her own remark. To her relief, however, the Viscount had laughed.

'But you are delightful, ma'am! I shall certainly sue for a dance another night.'

And he had done so, on several occasions. Serena had found him so comfortable to talk to, for he never scolded, however outspoken she became. And she was afraid that she had been outspoken. But Wyndham, so far from disapproving of her, had elected to enjoy her frankness. Not that she intended to speak so candidly, but she could not seem to help herself. She said whatever came into her head. She knew it to be her besetting sin, and had begged Wyndham not to encourage it.

'My dear Miss Reeth, you must hold me excused,' he had said lightly. 'I cannot be expected to discourage what gives me so much pleasure.'

'But it shouldn't do so, sir. You ought to be excessively displeased with me for the things I say.'

'Upon whose authority?'

'Cousin Laura's.'

'I beg Cousin Laura's pardon, but I cannot sub-scribe to her notions. I pray you will abate not one jot of your refreshing candour!'

Yet Serena doubted whether this large-mindedness would extend to her asking him impertinent questions about his gentlemanly excesses. Cousin Laura was right. She could not ask him. Indeed, she had no wish to do so.

Having spent the better part of the night fighting intrusive memories, Serena determined that she must spare no pains to suppress that *tendre* which she had foolishly allowed herself to feel for my lord Wyndham.

This determination proved more difficult than Serena had bargained for. When she made it, she had thought, in a nebulous way, that Wyndham could never come in her way again. This, she realised on Friday evening, had been foolish.

Not that she would have expected him to be present at the dull party given by one of the political hostesses in Papa's circle. But no sooner did she catch sight of the Viscount at a distance than she recollected that Lady Camelford was a noted society dame as well as the wife of one of Lord Reeth's associates in the government.

The thought passed swiftly, for the consciousness of his lordship's presence ousted every consideration but the desperate need to avoid any sort of confrontation with him. He was looking as elegant as ever, in knee-breeches of cream and a smart blue coat, his neckcloth an intricate arrangement that baffled description. Serena longed for his smile, but knew if she was obliged to speak to him, she would inevitably say the wrong thing. Yet she could not help glancing in his direction—all too frequently.

She was addressed by any number of people, but she was sure she answered them quite at random. Her pulses ran chaotically, and she was obliged to dwell upon the lurid tales that had come from Cousin Laura's lips before she could bring her unruly yearnings under control.

In vain! She had succeeded in exchanging a couple of sensible words with the Honourable Mr Camelford, the son of the house. But just as he moved aside, she found herself face to face with Wyndham.

Serena could not utter a word. His eyes were cold steel, and a sensation of strong emotion emanated from him, washing over her in a wave. Serena shrivelled inside, and a hot flush of distress spread upwards through her veins. Her vision blurred a trifle, and she saw the Viscount's expression change as she quickly looked away.

'Excuse me, my lord.' A husky whisper only.

She whisked about, plunging swiftly among the knots of chattering guests. She thought she heard him call her name, but the tone was so low that she might have been mistaken.

Serena sought instinctively for Cousin Laura, who had, as was her invariable practice, effaced herself among the chaperones. But she emerged as soon as she saw her charge coming towards her, and Serena knew that this presence at her side must secure her from any attempt by Wyndham to accost her.

Not that he had any idea of accosting her! Indeed, Serena believed that he pointedly ignored her. Whenever she dared to look for him, he was certainly not looking her way. The evening became interminable, and Serena developed a headache.

She was glad to retire relatively early to bed, sped on by her duenna's recommendation to forget all about the Viscount. So far from doing so, Serena found herself beset by far too fond memories of the past. Yet each culminated in the horrid image of Wyndham's cold glance on Friday night. By Tuesday, Serena was ready to scream. She must do something to distract herself, or she would go mad.

Hitting upon the idea of finding herself an interesting novel to read, she ventured into Piccadilly with Cousin Laura, and entered Hatchards circulating library. After a pleasant quarter of an hour browsing along the shelves, she was rewarded at last by discovering a novel of which she had heard good report. It was by a new author, and had been published earlier that year.

Serena opened the first volume at random and ran her eyes down the page. She liked what she read, and looked up with the intention of picking up the other two volumes, only to find herself gazing directly into the face that had been haunting her thoughts.

'Well met, Miss Reeth,' said Wyndham drily.

Chapter Two

Serena promptly dropped the book she was holding. Wyndham bent to pick it up for her, noting as he handed it back that her fingers were trembling. She was evidently flustered, for she almost snatched the thing from him, and her eyes flew in every direction as if she sought to escape his gaze.

'Th-thank you, sir,' she uttered breathlessly, and relapsed into silence.

Wyndham tried in vain to suppress the anger he still felt at her perfidy. When he had run into her at the Camelford house, his rage had welled. It had been no surprise to find her conscious and confused. But the abrupt evidence of distress had jerked him out of his own emotions. Then she had turned away, giving him no opportunity to probe the oddity.

The remembrance of the altogether different reception which he had grown accustomed to receive from her had gnawed at him since. It had afforded him no small degree of satisfaction to see the pansy eyes light up at his approach, and the lovely features break into that enchanting smile. It had been the very look which had attracted him when he had first seen her among last Season's fresh crop of débutantes. She had been looking about her with frank enjoyment, and with none of the studied indifference which characterised so many of the young females drilled into conformity by their determined mamas.

When the Viscount had engineered an introduction, he had been obliged to coax her out of her initial shyness. But once Serena had begun to relax, she had astonished him by confiding to him her pleasure in having been singled out by so fashionable and important a member of the *beau monde*. If he had at first thought her guilty of a revolting display of sycophancy, he had been speedily brought to realise that Serena was far too naïve to have any thought of flattery. By the time she had blurted out a series of remarks of similar candour concerning others of his world—and not nearly as complimentary!—Wyndham was in a ripple of amusement.

Serena confided to him that she thought far too many matrons looked disgracefully fat in the fashionable high waists; that she had seen the Regent and thought him a roly-poly fellow; that the patronesses of Almacks were all proud ladies and it was very difficult to be obliged to conciliate them; and that although she knew Mr Brummell's approval was essential, she was in a quake lest he should speak to her, 'For I am bound to say something dreadful to him and disgrace myself.' She had then recollected that the Viscount was an acquaintance of Brummell, and had blushed adorably, saying in a conscience-stricken way, 'Oh, dear, what have I said? Am I already disgraced, sir? Will you betray me to him?'

Wyndham had reassured her, but had been unable to keep from laughing. His artless companion had demanded the reason, and he had readily informed her that so far from disgracing herself, she had succeeded in doing what no other female had done by chasing away the jaded boredom of his existence.

'Well, I cannot imagine how I should have done that,' she had said, looking at him with so much puzzlement as had instantly overset him again.

His acquaintance with her had blossomed, for he had sought her out with more frequency than he had intended until it had been borne in upon him that he was raising expectations which he did not know whether he was ready to fulfil. That had led him to shilly-shally in a fashion that appeared now to have lost her to him. He had not known how bitterly he must repent it when he was greeted by her in a manner so unlike that which had been his downfall.

She was looking delightful in a gown of jaconet with a neat blue spencer atop that enhanced the allure of her figure. And she was blushing furiously, her eyes now fixed upon the volume held tightly between her gloved fingers. On impulse, Wyndham reached out and took it from her, turning it over to find the title.

'So you have succumbed to the dictates of fashion,' he remarked coolly. 'An apt choice, I think.'

He looked up to find her eyes upon him, an expression in them compound of alarm and despondency. Wyndham could not withstand a feeling of compassion. 'Don't look so dismayed! If I have understood your honoured father, you have acted with both sense and sensibility.'

'I fear not, sir. I have too much of one, and not enough of the other.'

A slight smile accompanied the words, and in her eyes an echo of that shy sweetness of which he had grown all too fond. Hurt consumed him, and Wyndham was conscious of an urgent desire to demand of her what she meant by rejecting him.

'I believe you are not alone,' he said coldly, returning the book to her. 'Most females demonstrate sensibility above sense. Or did you mean it the other way about?'

The coolness of his tone struck Serena to the heart. Without thinking, she uttered the chaos of her mind. 'Oh, don't speak to me so, for I cannot bear it! Pray forgive me, sir. No, I don't mean that! But I would never…it was not by any will of mine that—but I must not say so!'

'But you have said so,' the Viscount put in swiftly. 'What does it mean, Serena?'

She felt herself grow hot. How in the world could she answer him? 'Oh, how very difficult this is!'

Wyndham saw her fingers tighten upon the book, and was seized with the conviction that Lord Reeth had fabricated his excuse. Serena was not behaving like a maiden confronted by a man whom she could no longer like! His voice softened.

'Come, Miss Reeth. You were not wont to be so tongue-tied with me.' He smiled teasingly. 'Quite the opposite.'

The smile was almost too much for Serena to bear. Her candid gaze searched his face, and she was no longer mistress of her tongue.

'Is it true that you own a hunting-lodge close to an Abbey? Steepwood, is it not?'

Considerably taken aback, Wyndham frowned. 'I do, yes. It is situated in a place called Steep Wood, and it is indeed a mile or two from Steepwood Abbey.'

Serena clutched the volume between her hands as if to draw support from it. 'Were you—were you there last summer? With Lord Buckworth and—and others?'

His frown deepened. 'I was. What of it? I invariably spend the summer months there.'

'You have done so for some years then,' she said in a blank tone, and drew back a step or two, away from him.

Astonished both by her manner and the line of questioning, Wyndham's tone became curt. 'Why do you ask, Miss Reeth?'

Had he but known it, the abrupt manner of his answer served only to convince Serena that he had something to hide. Her unruly tongue betrayed her.

'You must know why I ask it!' Recollecting herself, she looked away and back again, stammering in her haste to unsay the words. 'I b-beg your pardon, s-sir. I d-did not m-mean— I should not have— Oh, why did you speak to me at all?' she finished despairingly.

Wyndham was by now thoroughly bemused by the rapid contradictions of her attitude. But they could not be ignored!

'What the devil is amiss, Serena? I am at a loss to understand the significance of any of this.'

'But you understand the significance of the Marquis of Sywell, I make no doubt!' she flashed, the brown eyes alight with anger. 'And pray do not tell me that I should not have said anything about him, for that I know already.'

'Then I wonder at your bringing up the name at all! Sywell is scarcely a fit subject for the delicate ears of a female.'

'But fit enough for the indelicacy of males!'

There was a silence. The Viscount eyed her in no small degree of puzzlement, his natural anger dying away. He could make nothing of these remarks. But he was not going to enter into discussion about a man whose name should never have sullied the ears of a girl of eighteen years.

'Are you going to meet Miss Geary? May I escort you?' he asked, in a tone of chilly politeness.

Serena had been listening with horror to the echo in her mind of her own words. How could she have been so unguarded? She had as well have accused Wyndham outright! What had possessed her to mention the Marquis? Yet she was conscious of inordinate disappointment that the Viscount had ignored her comments. It seemed to Serena that this argued a guilty reticence that condemned him.

'No, I thank you,' she said, in an attempt to emulate the coolness of his tone. 'I can very well go by myself.'

Even to her own ears, this sounded more sulky than sophisticated. Forgetting to pick up the two other volumes of her chosen novel, she dropped a curtsey and swept past Wyndham to the counter.

To her dismay—and guilty triumph!—he followed her. But it was only to present her with the other volumes which he had collected on her behalf from the shelf.

'I think you may need these,' he said and, bowing, walked away from her and out of the shop.

He was seething, but determined not to let Serena see it. Her manner had convinced him that her father had spoken less than the truth. She might or might not have transferred her affections to another man, but he could be in no doubt that something had induced her to take himself in aversion. Had she coupled him in some way with the infamous Marquis of Sywell? Impossible! He knew his reputation to be well enough established that no one could accuse him of associating with a reprobate of that cut.

Before he could probe the matter further, he saw Serena come out of Hatchards, holding her package of books. She hesitated for a moment, looking towards the press of carriages down the street. Wyndham was within an ace of renewing his offer of escort when he saw a gentleman detach himself from a knot of men standing together upon the flagway and move to accost Miss Reeth.

He was a florid man, loose-limbed and somewhat careless in his dress, and one whom the Viscount recognised. And not with any degree of pleasure! He knew Hailcombe to be a landless lord, somewhere in his early thirties, who lived by his wits and gaming. He had been lately in His Majesty's naval service, and it was generally rumoured that he had been forced to sell out by the vociferous demands of his seniors.

Wyndham eyed this individual's approach to Serena with considerable disfavour. If this was the fellow whose affections had engaged hers in his stead, he must deem himself most cruelly insulted.

Serena viewed the coming of Hailcombe with no less disfavour. She did not like this bluff friend of her father's, and could have wished that Papa had not invited him to dine with them. He had an abrupt way with him, graceless and unrefined. Serena found him coarse. He had, as he phrased it, 'eaten his mutton' with them on no less than three occasions since they had returned to town. Each time he had devoted more of his attention to the daughter of the house, who had received his clumsy attempts to engage her in conversation with polite indifference.

'Ah, the lovely Miss Reeth!' he hailed her with heavy gallantry. 'Miss Geary awaits you. Allow me to escort you to your carriage. Nothing could afford me greater pleasure.'

It was otherwise with Serena, but she refrained

from saying so. Her attention was so concentrated upon her encounter with the Viscount that this interruption could be nothing but an irritant.

'It is but a step, sir, and I can very well go on my own.'

'What, and expose your prettiness for all the fools of London to gape at?' He doffed his hat and took from her the package of books.

Serena saw no recourse other than to take the arm he thrust upon her, and placed the veriest fingertip upon it, chafing at the dawdling pace.

'I must hurry, sir, for I have already kept my cousin waiting overlong.'

The carriage was standing some twenty-five yards from them, and Serena was relieved to arrive and allow her unwelcome escort to hand her up. But worse was to come.

'Lord Hailcombe, how kind!' said Cousin Laura in what Serena considered to be over-friendly tones. 'Are you walking? Can we take you up? We may easily pass by Half Moon Street on our way, if you should be returning to your lodging.'

To Serena's disgust, Lord Hailcombe accepted with alacrity, and jumped up into the barouche, taking his seat opposite her and ogling her quite dreadfully through his quizzing-glass.

It was really too bad that she should be subjected to such attention from a man nearly twice her age! It was not that his looks were odious, although his cheeks had a tendency to be high-coloured—weatherbeaten, Papa said, from his days at sea. But a pair

of full lips and two thick brows gave him an offen-
sively leering look, especially when he smiled.

He did so now, the lips lifting from his teeth in a
way that made Serena feel positively nauseous.

'Fortunate I should have chanced upon you, Miss
Reeth. Thought of the most delightful scheme.
There's a ridotto tomorrow evening. House of a friend
of mine. Mrs Henbury—you may have heard of her.'

Serena had not, and she looked instinctively to
Cousin Laura, knowing that Papa had strictly enjoined
her to permit his daughter to attend only Ton parties.
She was astonished, therefore, when her duenna
seemed inclined to look upon the invitation with a
favourable eye.

'Mrs Henbury? I do not think so. But a ridotto?
Such fun for the young folk!'

'My thought exactly. D'you suppose my friend
Reeth will allow our young innocent to attend? Under
your eye, of course, ma'am.'

Incensed, Serena heard Cousin Laura accepting the
invitation, subject only to Papa's agreement. Our
young innocent indeed! How dared he speak of her
in such terms? As if he had been an uncle, or something of the sort. She was slightly cheered by the reflection that Papa was bound to disapprove, but she
could manage only a vague smile when called upon
by her duenna to applaud the treat in store.

The house inhabited by Mrs Henbury proved to be
situated in an unfashionable quarter of Bloomsbury.
Which was just what Serena might have expected of

a lady whose name was quite unknown—even to Lissett, who knew everybody!

'No, Miss Serena, I have not heard the name. No doubt one of these hangers-on who live upon the fringes of society.'

There had been no relief afforded by Lord Reeth either. Serena had stood in stunned disbelief as Papa had not only agreed to the arrangement, but had enjoined his daughter to be sure and conduct herself towards Lord Hailcombe with proper deference.

'Let me not be put to the blush by hearing of your having spoken out in that pert manner of which you are sometimes guilty. His lordship is a particular friend of mine, and I desire you will treat him becomingly.'

Feeling betrayed, Serena had barely been able to bring herself to acknowledge this stern admonition. She had murmured what Papa might, if he chose, take for assent, and had dropped a curtsey. Then she had fled to her nursery parlour, there to indulge in a useless rodomontade against Wyndham for proving too unworthy to have rescued her with the betrothal she had so ardently desired.

But here she was, in a large house furnished with the tasteless opulence of gilded sofas in the Egyptian style, and ornate wallpaper of heavy brocade. The only consolation Serena could give herself was that she counted none of the guests among her acquaintance. Which was as well, for the lack of decorum and freedom of manners displayed by many members of the company quite shocked her. Worse was to follow.

Cousin Laura had melted away among the older females, leaving Serena no alternative but to accept Hailcombe's hand for the dance. The room set aside for the purpose was not large, and the press of persons under two massive chandeliers made Serena feel uncomfortably hot.

She had reason to be glad of the forethought that had caused her to choose a modest round gown—of a lemon yellow that suited little with her hair—which offered no real exposure of flesh. For her situation was horrid indeed when she discovered that the figures of the country dance gave her partner unlimited opportunities to touch and squeeze, and slip his arm about her waist. At one instant, Hailcombe contrived even to brush his fingers over the swell of her breast.

Unmindful of her father's warning, she burst out with, 'What are you doing, sir?'

'Doing, ma'am?' said he, wide-eyed with innocence under those heavy eyebrows. 'Why, dancing, m'dear.'

'You touched me!'

'But m'dear Miss Reeth, how am I to avoid it? The figure, ma'am, the figure. What d'you mean?'

'You know very well,' said Serena angrily.

'I don't, but let that pass. Sorry to have offended you. Assure you, it weren't by design. Such a crowd!'

Serena was obliged to accept this. One could not make a scene in public. But she made deliberate efforts to stand away from him for the remainder of the dance, and was at length forced to own that he made no further attempt to do more than take her hand for the requisite movements.

She was relieved, but could not help contrasting Hailcombe's conduct with that of Wyndham. Never, by so much as a look or a touch, had he taken the slightest liberty with her. She had felt so completely safe with him that it had not even occurred to her that he might do so.

It occurred to her forcibly now, however. A libertine, as he had been accused, would be expected to behave in just such a fashion. Or might he do so only with women of a certain class? Gentlemen, so Cousin Laura had instructed her, could keep a mistress among the demi-monde, yet never permit their wives and daughters even to speak of such women. It hurt Serena to think that Wyndham was just such a hypocrite.

To her shame, a sneaking regret came over Serena that Wyndham had not taken any liberties. She could not but admit that if it had been *his* fingers at her waist, she would not have been in the least revolted.

The evening could not have ended too soon, and Serena spent the remainder of it at as much distance from Hailcombe as she could conveniently manage without offence, fanning herself in a manner that hid her face from him for much of the time. She refused every request to dance again, and could not but be glad to see the growing discontent that overlaid the florid features of her escort. She only hoped that he would recognise how unwelcome were his attentions.

* * *

Serena's hope proved misplaced. On Friday, when she attended the play at Drury Lane escorted by Lord Reeth as well as Cousin Laura, she was immediately struck by Lord Hailcombe's appearance in a box opposite which she knew to be occupied by a notorious courtesan. Along with others of her stamp, the woman had been pointed out to her by her conscientious duenna, anxious to prevent her charge from making social gaffes through ignorance.

Serena had refrained from reporting the familiarities that had been taken with her to Cousin Laura. Not from any wish of saving Lord Hailcombe from censure, but because she felt a deep-seated fear that her duenna was capable of condoning even this licentious conduct. But she felt sure that Papa must be disgusted with his friend's public acknowledgement of the female in the box opposite. She knew that Lord Reeth saw it, for she had been within an ace of calling it to his attention when she saw that his eye was fixed upon Hailcombe—and in no very pleasant spirit.

Yet when he entered their box in the next interval, Serena was shocked to see Papa greet him with great affability. Indeed, the Baron went so far as to give up his seat, saying that no doubt Hailcombe wished to converse with his daughter.

Serena had barely got over this, and was with some difficulty parrying the ogling remarks addressed to her, when she saw that Viscount Wyndham was standing in the pit, his gaze trained upon their box. Since its situation was on the lowest level, he was at no great distance from them, and could not avoid recognising her company.

It was with mixed feelings that Serena noted the disapproval in his face. She was ashamed to be discovered by him with Hailcombe in attendance. Yet she could not but be angry at his daring to look censoriously, when by all accounts his own conduct left a great deal to be desired. Matters were not helped when Hailcombe chose to refer to it.

'See, Miss Reeth, what jealousy you inspire?'

Serena turned to look at him, feeling her colour mounting. 'I do not take your meaning, sir.'

Hailcombe tittered, his thick lips curling in something perilously close to a sneer. 'Why, I speak of your rejected suitor there. Almost sorry for the poor fellow, though I'm the richer for his discomfiture.'

A flame of anger lit Serena's breast. 'How did you know that Wyndham had been rejected?'

'Inference, Miss Reeth,' he responded, smiling with disgusting superiority. 'Just inference.' He leaned towards her in a pose distressingly intimate, lowering his voice to a murmur. 'Glad your tastes run on different lines. You're a sensible girl. You can see the advantage of maturity.'

Serena was struck dumb. She could not mistake the tenor of this speech. She knew not what to reply, for the thought of what must be in his mind made her sick to her stomach. She cast a wild glance around, as if in search of rescue, and her frantic eyes met those of Lord Wyndham.

He had shifted his position, and was standing

within a few feet of her. Without thought, Serena threw up her fan, plying it so that it hid her face momentarily from Hailcombe's sight.

Under cover of this temporary veil, she mouthed a desperate plea to Wyndham. 'Pray help me!'

Whether he caught it she could not tell, for at that instant the action began again upon the stage. Thankfully, Lord Reeth resumed his seat as Hailcombe vacated it and left the box. By the time Serena had leisure to look around once more for the Viscount, he was no longer there.

Saturday dawned grey and overcast, the drizzle at the window all too much in keeping with Serena's mood. She did not know whether she was more upset with Hailcombe for his untimely hints, or with Wyndham for ignoring her impulsive appeal.

Ringing for her maid, she requested her breakfast on a tray. 'I am feeling too weary to rise this early, Mary. I shall stay in bed and read my novel.'

'Oh, but his lordship asked me special if you was up, Miss Serena,' said Mary, 'for he wishes to speak to you as soon as ever you was ready to go down-stairs.'

These were most unwelcome tidings. What in the world could Papa want with her? Had he seen that look she had cast at the Viscount? Perhaps he'd had word from someone that she had been seen talking to him in Hatchards. Not that Papa could expect that she might avoid Wyndham altogether since he was bound to be at the same gatherings as she attended. But if he supposed her disobedient to his wishes, Papa could be unpleasantly severe.

All desire to take breakfast had disappeared. Instead, Serena bade Mary help her to dress. It felt as if it took an age to array herself in a white muslin gown, long-sleeved, with an overgown patterned in a simple sprig that added much needed warmth. Throughout, Serena's mind ran upon horrid visions of Papa's displeasure, and the probable reasons for it. By the time she was dressed, she had convinced herself that a scold awaited her, and anxiety had rendered her nauseous.

But when at last she entered the library, her father rose from behind his desk and greeted her in a perfectly affable way. Indeed, he was almost too full of bonhomie for his daughter's comfort.

'Serena, my dear child, very good of you to come to me so quickly. Have you eaten? No? Now what was Mary about to hurry you so? After breakfast would have done as well.'

'I—I was anxious to know what you could want with me, Papa,' Serena ventured.

Reeth laughed in a way that sounded false to Serena's ears. 'My dear girl, you are surely not in fear of your papa? You know I have always your interests at heart.'

Serena knew not how to reply to this. It had not been Papa's practice to seek her out merely for the pleasure of her company! It was not as if he doted upon her. If anyone was the object of Lord Reeth's caressing affection, it was her only surviving sibling.

Little Gerald, whose birth had been the occasion of their Mama's sad demise, was but five years of age and heir to the family estates in Suffolk, whither his fond father betook himself whenever he could spare time from his activities in government. Perhaps he was cosseted because his were the shoulders upon which the Reeth inheritance rested. But Serena knew that her own doting fondness for her brother did not exceed that of their papa.

'Sit down, Serena,' her father adjured her, flinging himself into one of the huge leather chairs placed either side of the fireplace.

Unaccountably nervous again, Serena sat down on the edge of the chair opposite, looking at her parent with a good deal of misgiving. She could not help but realise that Papa was most uncharacteristically ill-at-ease. He kept uncrossing and recrossing his legs, all the while with his eyes trained first upon the fire, and then upon the large timepiece that adorned the mantel. At length, he cleared his throat and turned his gaze upon his daughter. Serena held her breath.

'I have asked you here, my child, because I have made up my mind upon the subject of your future.'

A flutter disturbed the breath in Serena's bosom. Even had she thought of anything to say, she could not have opened her mouth to answer him.

'It was remiss of me not to have made some such arrangement at the outset,' Lord Reeth went on. 'Had your mama been alive, of course, none of this would have fallen upon my shoulders. And Laura, I am obliged to admit, has turned out to be unfitted to be a judge of these matters.'

Some inkling of where Papa was headed began to penetrate Serena's brain. It had all to do with Wyndham's turning out to have been unworthy. Was it Papa's intention to make her choice for her? A hideous premonition seized her.

'You have arranged a marriage for me!' she blurted out.

'No, not that,' said her father quickly. 'Not quite that. I hope I am not so Gothic in this day and age as to order you to give yourself to the man whom I would prefer you to choose.'

The Roman nose was thrust into the air, and that severity of countenance that Serena dreaded overlaid Papa's features.

'However,' he said heavily, 'I must say that I will be disappointed, Serena—most disappointed indeed!—if you should choose to thwart my wishes in this matter.'

Serena swallowed uncomfortably. Her voice felt thick and unwieldy in her throat. 'Who—may I ask who…?'

She faded out, unable to finish the question for the dread that rose up to choke her. An unwelcome image popped into her head. Papa could not have *him* in mind! Even the name in her head made her ill to think of it.

Lord Reeth cleared his throat again, and Serena saw, with a vague sense of disquiet under the dread, that he shifted once more in that fidgety way that was so unlike him.

'I have thought long and hard on the subject, my child, and I have decided that it will be safest for you to ally yourself with a man of mature years. One whom, I have reason to believe, is in a fair way to doting upon you. He has asked my permission to address you, and I have assured him of my support.'

Serena's tongue gave way. 'You cannot mean Lord Hailcombe! Oh, Papa, pray say it is not he!'

To her alarm, her father's cheeks became suffused with colour. 'Good God, girl, will you defy me so readily? I hope you are not going to tell me that you have taken Hailcombe in dislike. Have I not already given you to understand that he is a particular friend of mine? That alone should have secured your sympathy!'

She was on her feet. 'Pray, Papa, don't be angry with me! I am sorry for it, but I confess I cannot like him. As for marrying him—I could not!'

Reeth arose also, turning away to march across to his desk, in a hasty manner that told his daughter how much she had displeased him. He spoke without turning round.

'You must learn to like him, Serena. It is not only my wish, but my command.'

'But, Papa,' she uttered desperately, following him a little way and addressing herself to his unresponsive back, 'you said you would not force me! You said you were not so Gothic as to—'

Reeth swung round upon her, eyes blazing. 'Do

you dare to throw my words back in my face? Don't try me too far, Serena! I am well aware of the reason for your recalcitrance. You had not been averse to Hailcombe had it not been for this foolish fancy you have developed for Wyndham.'

Serena's voice trembled. 'Indeed, Papa, it is n-not so! Pray, pray b-believe that I would have disliked Lord Hailcombe even had I not f-formed a p-partiality for Lord Wyndham.'

'Poppycock! Do you think me a fool?'

'No, Papa, but—'

'Don't talk to me!' flared her father, striding away again to lash about the room, almost as if he could not bear to look at her. 'My own daughter to defy me to my face! How can you say you dislike him? You barely know him! And to refuse to accede to my request. Cannot you see that you will put me in an extremely awkward position? I have given my word to Hailcombe—' He broke off, stopping short and glaring at Serena. 'However, that is neither here nor there. But don't imagine that I will relent towards Wyndham, for I won't!'

Serena was shaking in her shoes, but she was quite as determined as her father. And she was fighting for her whole future! She must try what she might to placate him.

'I do not think of Lord Wyndham, Papa. Cousin Laura told me something of—of the Marquis of Sywell, and I quite see that he is not a fit person for me.'

'In that case, you should have no difficulty in turning your thoughts upon another.'

'Yes, if it were any other than Lord Hailcombe!' she burst out before she could stop herself.

Too late, she saw that her words had enraged Papa still further. Marching to the door, he dragged it open.

'Out of my sight! Until you can assure me of your obedience, I have no wish to see or speak to you again.'

Chapter Three

Stunned by this harsh ultimatum, Serena stared at Papa's unrelenting features. But there was no softening in them as they glared back at her. A vivid memory of Wyndham's face came into her mind—as hatefully cold. Her heart swept with a sensation of loneliness, Serena dropped her eyes and walked swiftly past her father, and out of the room.

She heard the door slam behind her, and flew upstairs to her nursery parlour, there to jerk up and down the little room, her thoughts all chaos. Dashing unregarded tears from her cheeks, she found herself raging as savagely as had Papa.

How could he treat her so? What possessed him to take this sudden decision? And to declare it to be unalterable! Never had he shown himself so unmindful of her preferences.

And to become obsessed with Hailcombe of all people! Why, he was not even eligible. The title into which he had told them he had recently come was neither an old nor a worthy one. His predecessor, he had said, had so wasted his inheritance as to lose the lands that had gone with the barony. He had even boasted of his luck at cards, which enabled him to support himself as a gentleman.

Why, he was a man whom Lord Reeth might have been depended upon to despise! Wyndham was worth a dozen of him. But Papa had taken against the Viscount, even without real proof of his guilt. Serena had not doubted Papa's wisdom in blighting her hopes. But in the face of his championing of Hailcombe, she dared to wonder.

Before she could pursue this thought, the door opened to admit Cousin Laura, who rustled into the room in her grey silk gown. Serena stiffened, fearing a lecture on her falling out with Papa. But it seemed that her duenna had not yet been made mistress of the occurrence.

'My dear Serena, what do you think?' she said excitedly, waving a letter. 'We have been invited to a house party at Lacey Court. It is to be for a week, and we are requested to go next Friday.'

Serena had never heard of Lacey Court, but the thought of removing from London at this time was only too welcome.

'Who lives at Lacey Court, cousin?'

'Why, it is the home of Sir Lucius Lacey. No, you are not acquainted with him, for I believe he rarely comes to London. You may have met his wife and his daughter, who came out last season. But I believe, dear child, that it must have been Lady Camelford who arranged it, for I have had the kindest note from her informing me that she is to be of the party, together with her son.' She frowned, removing her spectacles. 'I must say I cannot understand what motivates her. Her son has just become betrothed, so it cannot be that she thinks of him for you.'

Serena refrained from informing her that it would be in vain if Lady Camelford had any such notion, even had her son not been engaged. There was time enough for Cousin Laura to find out what her father had planned for her destiny.

But the lure of freedom gave Serena furiously to think. It was of the first importance to discover whether Lord Hailcombe was also to be at Lacey Court. Unlikely, for his acquaintance did not appear to be with people of the first consequence. Which made Papa's partiality the more incomprehensible. If Hailcombe was not to be present, it was probable that Papa would refuse his consent to the scheme. Particularly if he believed her to be still rebellious.

By Sunday morning, it was abundantly plain not only that Cousin Laura had been primed, but that her father was adamant. Breakfast on the Lord's day was always taken by the family together, prior to attending morning service at St George's in the square. This habit was adhered to, but Lord Reeth neither looked at his daughter throughout, nor addressed her by a single word. Cousin Laura, casting nervous glances at him from time to time, applied herself to her meal in between uttering a stream of inane remarks to Serena, accompanied by such facial contortions of warning as almost caused her charge to giggle—despite the severe discomfort brought about by Papa's attitude.

When Lord Reeth swept out of the room, with a general admonition to the ladies to hurry, the duenna seized the opportunity to whisper a frantic admonition.

'Do not anger him further, my child! We shall talk of it when we return from church, and I do hope I may persuade you to see reason.'

Which made Serena look forward to the coming discussion with strong misgiving. Cousin Laura had clearly been suborned by Papa into furthering his aim. Not that she had a choice. Her duenna was dependent upon Papa's good will. She had served him well in the capacity of surrogate mother to his children, but Serena knew her father was capable of parting company with Cousin Laura if she went against him. And then the only future she could hope for was to take up a post as companion or governess, just as she had done before being called upon by Papa when Mama had expired.

But merely because Cousin Laura had to support Papa was no reason why Serena should succumb to his tyrannical decree! A sentiment which she did not scruple to express when the promised tête-à-tête took place in the nursery parlour.

'But, my dear child,' protested Cousin Laura, 'you cannot wish to be at outs with your papa. Besides, it is most unfair to accuse him of tyranny.'

'What then do you call it?' demanded Serena rebelliously. 'Well, I am more his daughter than he knows! He will soon learn that I can be just as stubborn.'

Her duenna groaned. 'Serena, pray don't! It is so uncomfortable for us all. Won't you at least try to like Lord Hailcombe?'

At this, Serena was moved to condemn both his lordship's manners and morals, and to give her duenna a word picture of the liberties he had taken with her at Mrs Henbury's.

'Serena, why did you not tell me?' clucked Cousin Laura, shocked. 'Perhaps I should tell your papa of this.'

'It will make no difference,' Serena told her, dropping abruptly into despondency. 'Papa does not even like Hailcombe, I am persuaded. What drives him to this I do not know, but he is certainly determined upon this marriage.'

It occurred to her all at once that her duenna must have known of this several days ago.

'Papa told you to encourage Hailcombe, didn't he, Cousin Laura?' she accused. 'Else you could not have thought of inviting him into the carriage that day in Piccadilly. Nor would you have taken me to such a dreadful house as that Mrs Henbury inhabited!'

Looking extremely guilty, Miss Geary removed her spectacles and fiddled with them in her lap. 'Your papa told me he believes Lord Hailcombe to be a man of sense,' she said evasively. 'It is not his fault, your papa says, that his inheritance has been wasted, and Bernard thinks that a man who has known hardship may be depended on to develop a habit of providence.

He is truly thinking of your happiness, my dear child, for he has chosen for you a gentleman whose suitability does not depend upon worldly considerations.'

Serena's response was sceptical. 'If he was thinking of my happiness, cousin, he would not force me into marriage against my will.'

'But he is not forcing you to it, child. He has merely requested—'

'He has *commanded*, cousin, not requested. And he delivered an ultimatum that has hurt me very much.'

Cousin Laura tutted in a despairing way, shuffling her spectacles on and off her nose several times. Presently, she looked again to the chair by the fireplace where Serena was sitting.

'Do you know, Serena, I believe your poor papa was himself much hurt by your refusal to listen to his proposal. You are so impetuous, my dear. If only you would let him see that you are willing to be dutiful and obedient, perhaps he will listen to you with more patience.'

'But I am not willing,' Serena protested. 'Why should I pretend that I will consider Hailcombe when nothing in the world would induce me to accept him?'

Cousin Laura replaced her spectacles and through them gave her charge a straight look. 'I am much afraid that if you do not make your peace with your papa, my child, you will not be permitted to go to Lacey Court.'

Serena studied her duenna's eyes through the round panes. Was Cousin Laura beginning to come around to her side? Had she too realised that such a remove must offer a respite from this intolerable demand of Papa's?

Cousin Laura said no more, but excused herself and went away. More than ever, Serena determined to find out whether Hailcombe was to be at Lacey Court.

Her opportunity came upon the following day, when he arrived in Hanover Square to invite her for a drive in the park. Twenty-four hours earlier, Serena would have unhesitatingly refused. But with Cousin Laura's words in her mind, she decided to kill two birds with one stone.

'Thank you, sir, I will be very happy. Only give me a moment to put on my hat and pelisse.'

Wholly ignoring the astonishment in Cousin Laura's face, she ran upstairs to her bedchamber. Five minutes later, she was in the hall, clad in a charming bonnet with a dashing plume that admirably matched the green pelisse. Her escort bowed her out of the house, but in the doorway she halted.

'Oh, Lissett, pray inform my father that I am gone to the park with Lord Hailcombe,' she said airily to the butler.

'As you wish, Miss Serena.'

She was handed up into the curricle, which was drawn, most unfashionably, only by a pair of horses. Hailcombe, attired in a great-coat of yellow drab, took up the reins; his groom let go the greys' heads and leapt up nimbly behind.

During the drive, Serena adopted a cool manner towards Hailcombe, designed to give him no more encouragement than was contained in her apparent willingness to accompany him. She kept a rigid control over her tongue, and answered his every attempt to engage in dalliance with obvious detachment.

When they turned into the gates of Hyde Park, to Serena's dismay Hailcombe dispensed with the services of his groom. Aside from having no wish to be seen alone with him in a carriage, it opened the way for a tête-à-tête which was not at all to her taste. His first words confirmed this.

'By my faith, Miss Reeth, I believe your attention is otherwise,' he accused in a petulant tone.

Serena turned a limpid gaze upon him. 'No, indeed, sir. I would not be so impolite as to allow my attention to be distracted from my escort.'

Hailcombe was silent for a moment or two, evidently ruminating. Serena perforce bowed to an acquaintance in a passing barouche, feeling relieved that the cold must prevent many members of the Ton from taking the air.

When Hailcombe addressed her again, it was a trifle offhandedly. 'Wonder if your father has spoken to you.'

'Not recently.' Aware of the give-away flatness in her tone, she added quickly, 'I do not see a deal of Papa. He is seldom at home, and only occasionally accompanies us to parties.'

A hard note entered Hailcombe's voice. 'I meant, ma'am, has he spoken to you of me?'

Serena turned to look at him, widening her eyes. 'Why, yes, sir. He speaks of you with affection.'

'No, I don't mean—'

He broke off, pouting his heavy lips in a look of ill-humour. Serena hoped that she had led him to imagine that his way had not yet been smoothed. She waved to a young lady she knew in as nonchalant a fashion as she could manage, and decided she had best embark upon the subject that had brought her out on this excursion.

'I must tell you that I have received a most flattering invitation, my lord.'

'Yes?' It was grunted out, Hailcombe appearing abstracted.

'To a house party at Lacey Court. Do you know it?'

'Don't believe I do.'

'It is the home of Sir Lucius Lacey, and I think it was Lady Camelford who recommended me to his notice.'

There was discontent in Hailcombe's voice. 'Do you make a long stay there?'

'I hardly know,' Serena fibbed. 'A week or two, I dare say.'

'Reeth gives his permission, does he?'

A note of vague menace seemed to underlie this question. Serena felt impelled to prevaricate, for she was suddenly sure that Hailcombe would question her father on the matter.

'Papa would not wish me to offend Lady Camelford. She is the wife of one of his closest associates, you must know.'

'But he has no obligation to Sir Lucius Lacey.'

Serena was silent, conscious of a stirring of unease.

Hailcombe had lost his tone of bluff flirtation. His heavy brows were drawn together, and there was a harshness in his words that made her glad she had held out against Papa. Once again she felt that sense of question about her father's motives in supporting this man's application for her hand.

'You don't know of Lord Wyndham's relationship to Sir Lucius Lacey then?' asked Hailcombe, a sneer in his voice.

At the mention of his lordship's name, a flutter leapt into life in Serena's chest, and she was cast into immediate confusion.

'I d-didn't know,' she stuttered helplessly. 'What is—what relation is he?'

'Wyndham's uncle, as I'll warrant your father knows all too well.'

The implication was clear, as was the depth into which Hailcombe was in Lord Reeth's confidence. He already knew of the Viscount's rejection, and now it seemed he also knew the reason for it. A flame of anger leapt in her breast. It was not for Hailcombe to judge Wyndham's character! How dared he take it upon himself to warn her, even obliquely, that Papa was bound to refuse his consent? No doubt he would take care to inform Papa of the fatal relationship, should he not already be aware of it.

Despair lent her inspiration. 'If that is the case, I hardly think his lordship will be present. He cannot wish to endure the embarrassment of being at close quarters with a lady who has determined against him.'

Hailcombe gave her a straight look. 'But have you determined against him?'

'Since you are clearly master of what passed between my father and his lordship, sir,' Serena pointed out, betrayed into forgetting to guard her speech, 'I imagine you must know very well that I am so determined. I do not know why my father should choose to confide in you, my lord, but he plainly does, and I therefore do not scruple to mention the circumstances which have induced me to take against Lord Wyndham.'

'Such ugly circumstances, don't you think?'

Serena was obliged to bite down upon a heated retort. 'I am happy to say that I know nothing of the details.'

'But enough to turn you away from his lordship, eh?'

It was on the tip of her tongue to refute this. To her shame, she realised that even the worst of the excesses that had been related to her by Cousin Laura had failed to turn her thoughts from the Viscount. But it would not do to say so.

'I have put him quite out of my mind.'

A smile drew the full lips apart, but it was not pleasant. 'Like to believe you, m'dear, but it's a poor liar you are.'

It was too much. Serena lost her temper. 'I don't care whether you believe me or not, Lord Hailcombe. But this you may believe. However strong my dislike of Wyndham's way of life, it could not possibly be as deep as my dislike of you!'

There was a breathless pause. Time enough for Serena to regret her hasty words, and experience a flare of apprehension for the consequences.

'If that's the case,' Hailcombe growled at last, 'I'd best lose no time in returning you home.'

Serena made no answer, and the drive back to Hanover Square was accomplished in silence.

Entering the house in a mood of severe apprehension, Serena was guiltily aware of having spiked her own guns. She could not doubt that Hailcombe would speak to Papa. Even if her rudeness induced the man to draw off—which she dared not suppose to be likely—Papa was bound to forbid her to go to Lacey Court.

She had already set her foot on the stair when she became aware that Lissett, who had let her in, was hovering in a manner that indicated a wish for speech with her.

'You want me, Lissett?'

The butler bowed. 'His lordship requested that you should go directly to the saloon upon your return, Miss Serena.'

These ominous words struck Serena with instant dread. She gazed upon Lissett's kindly features, her heart jumping. 'He wishes to s-see me?'

'He does, Miss Serena. I gave him your message, like you asked.' A reassuring smile was bent upon her. 'His lordship seemed pleased.'

To what avail, when her subsequent conduct must inevitably infuriate him? Remembering, however, that he could not yet know of it, Serena took heart. Thanking the butler, she ran up the stairs and went directly to the saloon, forgetting in her haste that she was still clad for the outdoors.

The elegant first-floor saloon was done out in the discretion of straw and cream that gave it both light and a sensation of spaciousness. Entering in haste, Serena stopped short, startled to discover that Papa was not alone.

Lord Reeth was in a chair to one side of the fireplace, opposite a sofa upon which were seated Cousin Laura and a female of matronly aspect, fashionably dressed in imposing purple with a yellow turban all over feathers.

'Lady Camelford! I—I thought—'

'Good gracious, Serena!' broke in Cousin Laura, shocked. 'Why could you not have put off your pelisse and hat? Lady Camelford will think you a sad romp!'

'Nothing of the sort,' contradicted the lady, smiling graciously.

'I b-beg your p-pardon, ma'am,' stammered Serena, unbuttoning the offending garment. 'You see, I was told that Papa wished to see me at once, and I—'

'And you naturally hurried to obey the summons. I quite understand. But perhaps you should ring for your maid?'

'Thank you, yes.' Crossing hastily to the fireplace, and avoiding her father's eye, Serena tugged at the bell-pull. Turning back to the visitor, she recalled an omission, and dropped a curtsey. 'How do you do, ma'am?'

The matron looked amused. 'I am well, I thank you, Serena.' She held out a hand, and Serena put hers into it, feeling a warm clasp close over her fingers. Her ladyship spoke confidingly. 'I have been persuading your Papa to allow you to make one of the party at Lacey Court.'

Serena's eyes flew to her father's face. There was a relaxation in his features of the sternness to which she had hitherto been subjected. Reeth did not quite smile, but he nodded to his daughter.

'You are to go,' he said succinctly, rising. 'And now, if you will excuse me, ma'am, I have work to do.'

'Yes, yes, run along,' urged Lady Camelford, releasing Serena's hand. 'I am used to being abandoned for the demands of politics!'

To Serena's relief, Papa laughed out at this sally, and bowing briefly, withdrew. She slipped off her pelisse and threw it carelessly onto a chair, revealing beneath it a plain little gown of white spotted muslin.

Cousin Laura rose to help her off with the bonnet. 'Is it not kind of your dear papa, Serena? And so extremely generous of you, Lady Camelford, to take an interest in the child.'

'Yes, and I must thank you, ma'am,' agreed Serena, moving to take her father's vacated chair. She added involuntarily, 'Though I wonder that you should take me up in this fashion.'

'Serena!' hissed her duenna, who was busy tidying the discarded attire.

But Lady Camelford was laughing. 'I could prevaricate and say that I wish only to please your father, but the truth is that I had great difficulty in prevailing upon him to agree to the scheme. He was most unwilling to let you out of his sight, was he not, Miss Geary? I had no notion of his being so doting a father!'

Neither had Serena, but she refrained from saying so. She could only marvel at the good luck that had brought Lady Camelford upon this errand before Papa could have any inkling of her disgraceful rudeness to Hailcombe.

'It is fortunate,' said Cousin Laura, with a meaning look at Serena as she retook her seat, 'that his lordship was particularly pleased with his daughter's conduct just at the moment. He was brought to agree, my child, that you deserved this treat.'

Was this meant to convey that Papa had been induced to believe her to have had a change of heart because she had driven out with Hailcombe? How speedily he was going to be undeceived! Serena hardly dared hope that he would honour his decision to let her go to Lacey Court.

A knock at the door at this moment produced the butler, come in answer to the summons of the bell, and Cousin Laura requested him to send in Mary to her mistress.

The interlude served to deepen Serena's puzzle-

ment. Upon Lissett's leaving the saloon, she did not
hesitate to voice it.

'If Papa was so difficult to persuade, I understand
even less, ma'am, why you should go to so much
trouble on my behalf.'

She saw Cousin Laura's frown of admonishment,
but Lady Camelford forestalled any comment. A pe-
culiarly conscious look crossed her strong features.

'If you will have it, my dear, I hope you will not
be offended. Truthfully, I am acting not on your behalf, but on that of my prospective daughter-in-law.'

A recollection threw Serena into speech. 'Oh, your
son is to marry Miss Lacey! It had not until this moment struck me that she must be related to Sir
Lucius.'

Cousin Laura started. 'Good gracious, yes! She is
his daughter.'

And therefore Wyndham's cousin! But this Serena
kept to herself. A pattering started up in her pulses.
Could it be that this invitation had been issued at the
Viscount's intervention?

'But I do not—I do know Miss Lacey,' she faltered.
'At least, I have met her, only—'

'I see I shall have to confess it all,' sighed Lady
Camelford, her eyes dancing in the mock solemnity
of her face. 'Melanie is the liveliest creature. I am
already almost as fond of her as is my dear John. You
see, the Little Season has brought few of her own
friends to town. The dear child came herself only for
a short visit, just to see me. And she begged me to
think of one or two young persons who might be in-

duced to join the party, for according to Mel, it is to be composed of "the most dreadful collection of old fogies"!' Here Lady Camelford burst into laughter. 'Really, she is a shocking child! But one cannot help loving her.'

'And so you thought of Serena,' put in Cousin Laura.

'My mind naturally roved among the children of my political acquaintance,' agreed Lady Camelford. 'But it was Mel who selected you, my dear Serena. She had an impression, she said, that you would add spice to the occasion.'

Both the visitor and Cousin Laura looked as if they could not imagine why. Nor indeed, could the subject of this peculiar choice. But Serena was less concerned with this aspect of the matter, than with the clear implication that she had been chosen at random. Wyndham could have had nothing to do with it.

Lacey Court was a sprawling mansion, of no definite date. It looked as if its various inhabitants had impulsively added to its bulk with abandon, and no thought of fitting in with the architecture of the place. Which, as Miss Lacey informed Serena, had been precisely the case.

'The whole place is higgledy-piggledy,' said Melanie gaily. 'You may believe for a moment that you are in the Tudor wing, and instantly find yourself transported to Italy in the very next room! And the follies that have been committed upon the gardens have to be seen to be believed. I am sure Capability Brown must have been off his head!'

Serena was obliged to laugh, as she followed her young hostess through the bewildering corridors to find the chamber to which she had been assigned. She had taken an instant liking to the lively Melanie Lacey, and found it easy to understand why Lady Camelford had succumbed.

Miss Lacey had greeted her with a shriek of delight, and enfolded her in a stifling embrace. For Melanie was built on queenly lines, with a merry face and a quantity of chestnut hair which she wore piled in a topknot with ringlets falling down the back. She was engagingly breezy, and embarrassingly forthright.

'I have so wanted to meet you, Miss Reeth! Oh, no—how stupidly formal. You won't mind if I call you Serena? And you are so beautiful! How I shall scold George for letting you slip through his fingers, the silly fellow!'

Dazed by this eloquence, Serena had been able only to gaze at her, stuttering a confused greeting. 'Th-thank you, Miss Lacey. It is k-kind of you to—to—'

'Oh, stuff! Pray don't say that, for I am so grateful for your presence, I cannot tell you. I wish you will call me Mel. Everyone does. And we are going to be great friends, on that I am determined.'

'Are—are we?' had asked Serena doubtfully.

Melanie had burst out laughing. 'Don't look so dismayed! Of course we are.' She had tucked a confiding hand into Serena's arm and begun to lead her to the stairs, Cousin Laura trailing in their wake. 'I have heard so much about you, that I almost feel as if I know you already.'

Serena had been at a loss to know how her hostess could have heard anything about her, and had said so.

'But from George, of course,' Melanie had told her, looking amazed. 'He said that you were very shy—which I see is indeed the case—and also that you had a tendency to blurt out anything that was in your head. "Like me," I said. But George would have it that whereas I had cultivated a habit of saying just what I liked without caring what anyone thought of me—which I must tell you is perfectly true!—you, on the other hand, were apt to be regretful about having said it. Which, George says, is one of the most endearing things about you. As you may suppose, I immediately took him to task for not making up his mind months ago, while he still had an opportunity to attach you. For my part, I should think he must have windmills in his head, for anyone can see that you would have made him the perfect wife!'

By this time it had been borne in upon Serena that Melanie's 'George' was none other than her cousin, George Lyford, Viscount Wyndham. The freedom with which she had spoken of his suit had not unnaturally struck Serena to tense silence, and she had heard Cousin Laura faintly clucking behind her. Fortunately their hostess, whose tongue ran like a fiddlestick, had already moved on to discourse upon the ramifications of Lacey Court, and had been too much involved in her own diatribe to notice.

Serena found herself installed in a sunny bedchamber on the first floor, which gave onto some gardens to one side of the wing. The architect of Serena's new surroundings was obviously a follower of Adam, for a decorative pattern of vine-leaves ran over the mantel and created panels in the pastel shaded walls. The Sheraton furnishings were all of light woods with curving slim legs, and the four-poster was crowned with a circular tester from which billowed curtains of pink silk.

Her duenna was housed in an adjacent room of similar proportions, but with furnishings of so different a style that Serena could not but recognise the truth of Melanie's strictures. Dark wood panelling and hangings of red velvet gave a plush feel of luxury to the chamber, as well as a sense of having crossed into a different historical era. Cousin Laura looked upon it with distaste, but was moved—no doubt by the indiscreet chattering of Melanie Lacey!—to remind her charge of the injunction laid upon her by her father.

'I am not like to forget, cousin,' said Serena flatly, for the horrors of the last three days were not soon to be wiped from her memory.

The Baron, having received an account of the fateful carriage ride from Hailcombe, had stalked into his daughter's nursery parlour in order to deliver a tirade which had at first blasted all hope of Serena's attending the house party. Among a number of other threats, Serena had found herself in imminent danger of being

sent home to Suffolk in disgrace. Papa had not scrupled to warn her that she need not think herself too
much the young lady to receive a well-deserved chas-
tisement with the rod, and had promised that this
should be her fate if Hailcombe had any further cause
to complain of her impertinence.

Having reduced his daughter to mute dread, his
lordship had summarily forbidden the visit to Lacey
Court, and slammed out of the room. Cousin Laura,
an appalled spectator of this ugly scene, had amazed
Serena by embracing her and roundly condemning her
cousin, Hailcombe himself and men in general.

'It is the unfairness of it all that makes me so angry,' she had declared. 'One has so little choice as it
is when one is a female. But when these wretched
men must needs resort to bullying tactics—and upon
those who are necessarily weaker than themselves—
it is really too bad!'

This had been surprising enough. But it had been
entirely owing to Cousin Laura that Papa, in the end,
had been induced to withdraw his objections. Waiting
until his temper should have had time to cool, the
duenna had bravely bearded the lion in his den, and
come away triumphant.

'I was most unscrupulous,' she had told her charge
guiltily, 'for I am afraid I stooped to pretence. Now
if you will only do your part, my child, we may all
come about.'

Papa had been persuaded that a week away would
afford his daughter a period of quiet reflection, in
which Cousin Laura had undertaken to bring her to a

proper frame of mind—although she had no real expectation of Serena's paying the slightest attention to her. She had dared to suggest that Reeth's present methods had only awakened Serena's rebellious spirit, and had put it to him that a softer approach might produce the result he wanted. She had also pointed out that Lady Camelford might be seriously offended if Serena cried off.

Serena had been enjoined to feign gratitude for Papa's relenting, and to submit herself to the indignity of writing an apology to Hailcombe. She had hated the necessity, but she had done it. The result had been all that she dreaded. Her suitor had invited her and Cousin Laura to the theatre, where his assiduous attentions in public must, Serena felt certain, have advertised to the world at large the notion that she was preparing to receive his addresses.

Dreading the all too real possibility that she was going to be coerced into this hateful marriage, Serena had left for Middlesex with unalloyed relief. At least she had this one week of freedom. But any secret hope she might have cherished had been put to flight by Papa's final injunction.

'Should Wyndham happen to be present, Serena, you will oblige me by keeping a proper distance. Do you understand?'

The menace underlying that last had brought his earlier threat of violence forcibly to mind. Inwardly shuddering, she had consented, her tone subdued enough that her father had expressed himself satisfied of her being obedient.

It came therefore as a hideous shock to find herself seated at dinner that first night between an elderly cleric on the one side, and on the other, Viscount Wyndham.

Chapter Four

The immediate symptoms that beset Serena were dismayingly contrary to the behest of Papa. Her heart hammered in her chest, and she felt a touch faint. She could only be glad that she was already sitting down before she became aware of Wyndham's presence beside her. His attention was engaged by the lady on his other side, but it could not be long before he turned to Serena.

Gripping her fingers together in her lap, she strove for calm, glancing across to where her duenna was gazing narrowly at her. She caught Cousin Laura's eye, and a minatory frown was directed upon her. Serena gave a slight nod to show that she had understood. Although how she could 'keep a proper distance' in these circumstances, she was at a loss to imagine.

A plate appeared in front of her, containing a shell full of buttered crab, and several thin strips of toast. Serena stared at it as if she knew not what she must do with it.

'Do you dislike crab, Miss Reeth?'

Serena jumped, turning her head. The sight of the Viscount's warm smile quite melted her bones. Her tongue seemed to have deserted her. She had no idea how her eyes mirrored the disorder of her mind.

Wyndham had envisioned this moment in a spirit compound of mischief and pleasurable anticipation. He had known that Serena must be startled, and had half expected to be roundly taken to task—for he could not doubt that she would speedily fathom his hand in the unexpected invitation.

What he had not bargained for was the abrupt jolt at his chest occasioned by the disconcerted look in the lovely eyes. He was seized with a desire to catch her up and hold her in a comforting embrace—which was impossible. Instead he raised his brows in a teasing look, reached out for the appropriate fork, and gently placed it in her fingers.

Serena blushed and looked away from him, stabbing at the crab shell in a manner that threatened to jerk its contents in all directions. Wyndham sought his mind for a topic which might steady her.

'How did you enjoy *Sense and Sensibility*?' he asked in a carefully neutral tone.

'What? I mean—yes, thank you,' came the low-voiced answer. She appeared to realise that her response was inadequate. Throwing the briefest of glances in his direction, she faltered, 'No—that's not right. What should I say?'

'The novel you selected from Hatchards?' he prompted.

'Oh, yes. How silly! But I have not yet read it. At least, I began it, but...'

She faded out again, daunted by the impossibility of explaining the circumstances that had intervened to prevent her from finishing the book. Her pulse was calming a little, however, and she made an effort to begin upon her repast, digging with the utmost care into the crab shell and bringing forth a dainty portion.

Wyndham watched the quivering fingers lift the fork towards her mouth. It was poised there a moment, and then returned abruptly to the plate.

'I can't eat this!'

'Then don't,' he advised. 'I must say that I am not myself partial to shellfish.'

'It is not that,' Serena uttered, and immediately regretted it. In a rush of conscience, she turned to him, her voice an urgent whisper. 'It is intolerable to be so placed, my lord! Did you arrange it?'

He did not answer for a moment, but the grey eyes regarded her in a considering way. When he spoke, he did not respond directly to her question.

'Do you recall our last meeting—at Drury Lane? Perhaps I should not call it a meeting precisely, for we did not speak.'

Serena eyed him in some puzzlement. 'What are you at?'

A gleam entered his eyes. 'Why, Miss Reeth, can you have forgotten? How could I resist so poignant an appeal?'

All at once Serena remembered it. That look she

had cast him from behind her fan! She felt her cheeks grow warm, and looked quickly away.

'I had forgotten. So much has happened that—' The dreadful circumstances of her present situation came in on her, and she looked at him again. 'There is nothing you can do for me now. At the time, perhaps I... But it is too late!'

The tragic look of the brown eyes in their golden setting, the note of despair in her voice, were more than Wyndham could bear. He lowered his tone to a murmur, leaning towards her.

'Miss Reeth—Serena—don't look like that, I beg of you! Whatever it is, I pledge you my word that I will do anything I can to aid you.'

'Oh, no, you must not!' she uttered, in a frantic undertone. 'Pray do not speak of it. Do not speak to me, if you can avoid it. You will only make everything worse.'

Wyndham heard these words with deep concern. That Serena was in trouble he could not doubt. It put a completely different construction upon the situation from that which he had intended. He had enlisted his cousin's aid to ensure Serena's attendance at the house party in a bid to rescue her from Hailcombe's importunities. Not that he had supposed that the fellow posed any serious threat. He thought better of Serena than to suppose her capable of succumbing to such a man. But his underlying reason had been to find an opportunity to reinstate himself in Serena's favour. He had hoped to tease her into submission, and find out—and if possible eradicate—whatever it might be that had caused her to draw away from him.

But her present distress could not wholly be attributed to her finding herself in his company. That she was in a serious difficulty he could not doubt, and he determined there and then to extricate her from it.

'We will talk of it tomorrow,' he said quietly. 'I will arrange it without any harm to you, I promise.'

With which, he turned from her and devoted himself to the lady on his other side, leaving Serena to the attentions of the elderly cleric, who had by now discovered the presence of what he termed 'the lovely young thing' beside him.

It was with mixed feelings that Serena joined a riding party consisting of the younger guests and the daughter of the house. Melanie had invaded Serena's bedchamber at an early hour, with a giggling brunette in tow, to inform her of the projected ride and demand her attendance.

'You must hurry, for we must needs ride before breakfast, or it will be hours before we can do so without unsettling our stomachs. Now, Serena, do not say that you have not brought your habit, because—'

'Of course I have brought it,' broke in Serena, still heavy with sleep, 'but I have no horse, Mel!'

A trill of laughter gushed out of her hostess, and her companion broke into giggles. Serena had been introduced to her last night after dinner as Lady Fanny Gullane, a schoolfriend of Melanie's. Serena thought her pretty, if a trifle empty-headed, and judged her a devotee and follower of her more ebullient friend.

'You don't need a horse, silly,' chided Melanie. 'We shall mount you, of course. Do you ride well? Not that it matters. I am sure George will not sanction any other horse than will give you a safe ride.'

'Oh, yes,' chimed in Lady Fanny, 'gentlemen will never be brought to believe that one can perfectly well hold a strong horse. Felix is forever cosseting me about with restrictions, and insists upon my riding a *well-mannered* filly.'

'Felix' was Lord Horsmonden, the very young gentleman to whom Lady Fanny had recently become betrothed. He had only just attained his majority, and though their attachment was of long standing an engagement had been delayed until now.

Fanny's remarks provoked a lively discussion between the two young ladies on the subject of the ridiculous shibboleths with which they claimed that their respective husbands-to-be incessantly plagued them. But as the mists of sleep receded, Serena's attention became fixed upon the implications inherent in the proposed riding scheme.

According to Melanie, it was the Viscount who had the mounting of Serena. His cousin was ready to grant him the authority that could only be his if Serena had accepted him. An assumption that could not but raise a seed of resentment inside her. Unless it was Wyndham's plan? Had he chosen this method of ensuring that promised tête-à-tête, the thought of which had kept her awake for hours?

She had little opportunity to dwell upon this question, for Melanie and her friend proceeded to harry her to get dressed, both taking it upon themselves to act in the capacity of lady's maid, which hindered rather than speeded Serena's progress. But at last she emerged from the bedchamber, clad in a habit of sky-blue that so enhanced her beauty as to make two of the three gentlemen awaiting them at the stables goggle with blatant admiration.

The third, whose eyes Serena's involuntarily sought, gave her a smile of welcome that shot her through with ripples of guilty yearning.

'Allow me to help you to mount,' he said, adding softly, 'You look enchanting!'

'Th-thank you.' Delight set her cheeks aglow.

Wyndham took her gloved hand in his, and led her towards a neat grey in the charge of one of the many grooms. Too flustered to notice that the Honourable John Camelford and Lord Horsmonden were performing the same office for their respective fiancées, Serena accepted his aid in silence.

Under cover of the general chatter as the party mounted up, Wyndham murmured, 'Thank you for coming. We will find an opportunity to converse.'

She was reaching for the reins, but she paused and the pansy eyes flew to his, so vulnerable an expression in her face that he was hard put to it to refrain from kissing it away.

'Up with you!' he said quickly, and threw her into the saddle.

Automatically, Serena arranged her leg and settled

herself, slipping her foot comfortably into the stirrup as Wyndham guided it through, and gathering up the reins. She was obliged to take in calming draughts of air, for his nearness, the intimacy of his tone, and the pressure of his hands upon her waist had thrown her pulses into utter disarray.

Her resolution was in shreds. To be treated to just those attentions she wanted from the man to whom she must not give her heart, and from whom she had been ordered to remain aloof, was completely demoralising. His proffered help—no, his promise of it!—was that forbidden balm which she had been given no opportunity to refuse. She must refuse it! If he did take the chance to talk to her in some degree of privacy, she was in honour bound to reject his every attempt to win her confidence.

The thought of that necessity so wrought upon her that it was through a blur that she saw the Viscount swing himself into the saddle, to bestride a monstrous chestnut that he controlled with ease. The others were already trotting out of the stableyard. Winking away the momentary weakness, Serena nodded to the groom still holding her horse, and started off behind them.

Wyndham fell in beside her, but at a discreet distance that precluded conversation for the moment. No words were exchanged while the party made its way across the Lacey estates to a bridle path that ran adjacent, and which led, so Melanie had informed her, to a stretch of open country where they might enjoy a gallop.

Serena had ample opportunity to discover that so far from insulting her horsemanship with the dull ride deemed suitable to a lady, the Viscount had chosen a spirited filly with a number of sportive tricks that kept Serena pretty well occupied for some time in bringing her to heel. She could not but be aware of Wyndham riding nearby, and guessed that he was ready to intervene at need. Ahead, the two other young ladies, who were riding with their heads together behind their menfolk leading the way, had also been mounted on cattle of quality.

There was ample time for her nerves to settle, along with those of her mount. By the time they came to the bridle path—where necessity compelled the Viscount to ride at her side—Serena was able to answer him with scarcely a tremor. Though she could not prevent the blood from flittering down her veins.

'My uncle, I am happy to say, is a shrewd judge of horseflesh,' Wyndham began, innocuously enough.

'I can see that.' Serena threw him a glance. 'Did you select this mount for me?'

His brows went up. 'Do you object?'

A tremor ran through her, but she answered with an assumption of calm. 'On the contrary, I am very grateful. Particularly as your cousin assured me that you were bound to choose a *safe* ride for me.'

'Mel wants sense as well as conduct,' he said, mock-severe. 'I make you her apologies.'

'Oh, pray don't. I like her very much. Indeed, I do not see how anyone could not, for she is so very warm-hearted.'

'Yes, which is why she is forgiven the all too frequent indiscretions of her tongue.'

He was treated to Serena's shy smile, and a glow suffused his chest. She was relaxing at last.

'I am scarcely in a position to condemn her there.'

Wyndham grinned at her. 'But in you, Miss Reeth, such indiscretions are a refreshment and a delight—as I believe I have had occasion to tell you in the past.'

Her cheeks flew colour, and she looked quickly away. 'It is a—a past, sir, that had better be forgotten.'

The constriction in her voice warned him to tread with care. Yet there it was again! The inexplicable withdrawal that had at first so enraged him. It had been only the realisation that Serena was struggling against her instinct—which he would swear to be in his favour!—that had assuaged his wrath and caused him to question the origin of the change she had exhibited towards him.

He knew better than to mention the matter directly. Nor was he prepared to probe the meaning of her allusion to the Marquis of Sywell. Besides, his need to absolve himself had been superseded by the trouble he had perceived in Serena last night. His mission was not at this present to reinstate himself—beyond winning back her trust—but to investigate the mystery of her evident distress.

Serena's voice jerked him out of his thoughts. It contained a note of accusation. And a thread of anger?

'It was you who arranged for me to be invited, was it not? Pray will you tell me why?'

'Because I wanted an opportunity to recover our former ease of friendship,' Wyndham said without hesitation.

She was silent, looking directly ahead, but there was a telltale stiffness in her shoulders. Dared he pursue it? What had he got to lose? Even if she grew angry, it would at least break down this intolerable barrier. And it must be broken, or he would get nowhere.

'Your father told me that you had transferred your affections to another. Which led me to conclude that I had at one time the good fortune to be the object of your affections. Forgive my bluntness, Miss Reeth, but you must know that it is still my earnest desire to attach you.'

'Oh, don't!' came from his companion in a stifled tone. 'Pray don't! I am not permitted… I mean, you cannot wish—I think you cannot wish to—to distress me with…'

'That, never!' he declared. 'But it seems to me that you are already distressed, Serena—and not on my account.'

Unable to help herself, Serena looked round at him. The sincerity of compassion in his face was all too convincing. How could he be the monster that had been painted for her? He was waiting for some sort of reply. It did not occur to Serena to withhold herself from making it.

'I am at outs with Papa, that is all.'

But the Viscount was not to be satisfied with this dismissive response. 'Upon what occasion? Nothing, I do trust, to do with my offer?'

'Oh, no. At least—not directly.'

Realising that she was being drawn to reveal more than she wished—or indeed ought!—Serena tried to put a curb upon her tongue. It was so difficult to obey Papa, especially when everything in her cried out to her to do precisely the opposite to his commandments.

'He—he did not wish me to leave town at this present,' she said, improvising desperately in a bid to depart from the dangerous truth. 'He is desirous of my—my doing something that I—that I—' Hunting her mind, she came up with a compromise. 'I am afraid I have rebelled against his express command, and—and I do not know how it is to be resolved.'

She would have been appalled had she an inkling that Wyndham experienced no difficulty in interpreting this halting prevarication. But then Serena was not to know that her recent movements had been reported to him by his closest friend.

Sebastian Moore, Lord Buckworth, was a man of much larger proportion than his crony, but who shared with him both a sense of humour and a natural aptitude for the skill of fencing. They were remarkably well matched, which discovery had been, some years ago, the origin of their friendship. Buckworth was somewhat older than the Viscount, and apt to treat him with the lazy amusement that characterised him. But he had been serious enough when he had

deduced that the female of his best friend's choice—
having summarily rejected Wyndham, much to
Buckworth's astonishment—was the unwilling object
of the advances of a man whose reputation had led to
his being largely ostracised by the *beau monde*.

'If I am any judge, dear boy,' had said Buckworth,
in a light tone laced with sympathy, 'it is the parent
rather than the girl who favours that fellow's suit.'

Buckworth had seen Serena in Hailcombe's company, both in the park and at the theatre, and had been
unable to discern the slightest sign in her either of
attachment or enjoyment. The duenna, on the other
hand, had been encouraging in the extreme. Which
had been surprising, if Buckworth had not seen Lord
Reeth and Hailcombe together on two separate occasions.

It was thus clear to Wyndham that the dispute between Serena and her father must have to do with
Hailcombe's suit. The discovery both incensed and
disgusted him. That Reeth could reject himself, with
the flimsy excuse that Serena no longer favoured him,
was bad enough. And now he came to think of it, had
not the man floundered in embarrassment when asked
to give a reason for his refusal? But then instead to
determine to give his daughter to a man like
Hailcombe! It was beyond either belief or reason.

A hail from his cousin informed Wyndham that
they were approaching the open country. Another moment, and the opportunity for private speech would
be lost.

He looked at Serena, and found her studying his

face, a frown creasing her brow. Wyndham smiled at her.

'I thank you for your confidence, Miss Reeth. We will talk again later.'

Uneasily aware of having betrayed far more than she intended, Serena rode out into the open in a mood of silent anxiety. But the exhilaration of a gallop succeeded in driving away the cobwebs in her mind, if only temporarily.

The six horses flew across the turf, kicking up mud and grasses, their riders easy in the saddle, at one with the rhythmic rise and fall engendered by the speeding hooves. In a short space of time, Serena had reason to be grateful for the Viscount's choice, for the filly rapidly outstripped the mounts of the other two ladies, racing neck and neck with the big chestnut. Aware that Wyndham was holding in his horse in order to stay with her, Serena reined in to a canter.

'Give him his head! I will await you. Don't fear for me, for I will not gallop again when you are not by.'

A salute of his whip thanked her, and the chestnut streaked ahead. Serena heard a tally-ho behind her, and turned her head to see that the other two gentlemen were following this lead. Drawing her own mount in, she let them pass, and dropped to a walk, in which she was soon joined by the other two young ladies.

'Well, I wouldn't have thought it of George!' exclaimed Melanie crossly. 'Bad enough for Camel to have deserted me, but I never suspected Wyndham could be so selfish!'

'Oh, do not say so!' cried Serena, dismayed. 'I told him to go, for I could see his mount was itching for a proper run. And he is much stronger than this little lady.'

'Oh, well, I dare say there is no harm done then,' said Melanie merrily. 'To tell the truth, it is tedious to be forever subject to Camel's strictures and instruction.'

'Yes, and only see how comfortable a cose we may have without them all,' agreed Lady Fanny. 'We may abuse them to our heart's content.'

Serena had no wish to abuse the Viscount, but she had no need to say so, for the other two girls instantly embarked upon a laughing discussion of the faults of their hapless heroes, which proceeded without any assistance from her. Wistfully, she thought how little they both had real cause to complain. It was obvious that both John Camelford and Lord Horsmonden were gentlemen of amiable disposition. Serena could not suppose that either would turn out to have been corrupted by a horrible marquis! Nor did she think that either lady was filled with disgust at the thought of her coming marriage.

Her spirits dropped with the remembrance of Hailcombe. Somehow, while she permitted herself the guilty indulgence of partaking of Wyndham's company, it seemed to Serena the more inevitable that she would find herself forced to accede to Papa's demand.

All very well to stand out against her father, but for how long could she continue to do so?

She watched Wyndham riding back towards her. In an ideal world, she might have been awaiting the return of her betrothed, just as the other two females were doing. But the world—alas!—was far from ideal, and it was foolish to indulge in useless dreams.

Upon the thought, a swell of emotion rose within her, and she felt unequal to any further exchange with his lordship. Turning her mount before he could reach her, Serena encouraged the grey to break into a canter. She did not look round when Wyndham's chestnut appeared to one side, and deliberately ignored his call to her to wait.

But Serena reckoned without her host. Wyndham came in close and seized her rein, bringing both horses to a halt. A rush of sudden anger superseded Serena's distress.

'What the devil is amiss, Serena?' he demanded, a touch of irritation in his voice. 'But a few moments since I thought we had come to an understanding.'

Serena perforce turned her head and met his eyes. Her voice was pitched low and tense. 'Pray let go my rein!'

'I will do so when you answer me.'

Her breath caught in her chest and speech became painful. But there was no stopping the words from coming out.

'There can be no understanding between us, Wyndham. Every moment I allow you to draw me in, I am compounding my fault.'

'I am trying to help you, not to draw you in.'

'You cannot help me. You, of all people. I am not even supposed to talk to you!'

Wyndham's gaze narrowed. 'Is that your father's command?'

Serena looked him straight in the eyes. 'And my own determination.'

There was silence for a moment. He was holding her gaze, and pain gathered at her heart as she saw the grey eyes grow steely. His voice was no less chilling for its quiet.

'You mentioned once the name of a certain marquis. I do not know what you may have been told to my discredit in this connection. But it wounds me, Serena, that our acquaintance has resulted in you knowing me so little.'

With which he released his hold on her rein and, sharply turning his horse, rode a little away and stopped. With an ironic gesture he invited her to precede him towards the others who had ridden on ahead and were moving towards the entrance to the bridle path.

Having excused herself, on the score of an abdominal pain, from joining an excursion to a neighbouring estate for a morning assembly, Serena had watched the carriages depart, and then donned her green pelisse and taken her misery out of doors.

Cousin Laura was safely ensconced in a downstairs parlour, whither she had told her charge she would hide herself for the purpose of writing a long overdue letter to her friend, Miss Lucinda Beattie of Abbot Giles. The mention of that name, bringing to the fore the painful origin of Serena's unhappiness, had been enough to cause an escalation of her feelings that could not but result in a hearty bout of weeping.

A number of little summerhouses dotted the grounds of Lacey Court. Together with innumerable other grottoes, mazes and sunken gardens, these formed part of the extravagant landscaping and ornamentation created during the last century.

Concealed in one of these, Serena was finally able to release the dammed up well of emotion that had plagued her. How she had borne her part in the gaiety exhibited by the other young people, she did not know. She could only marvel that it was not apparent to others that my Lord Wyndham contrived to address only the merest commonplace to Miss Reeth, at moments when common courtesy demanded it.

There was a complete absence of the teasing look and the warm smile, and Serena knew she ought to have been grateful that it had been made easy for her to obey Papa's command. But she could only feel desperately hurt. If Wyndham had been wounded by her belief of his guilt, then he was wonderfully revenged!

Worse was the realisation forced upon Serena of the hope she had been secretly nursing. The Viscount had given her to understand that he still wanted to marry her; that he would help her if he could. In honour bound, she had rejected both sentiments. But their withdrawal seemed to seal her doom.

She would have to give in to Papa. What alternative
had she? She could not even think of one of the other
gentlemen who had admired her in the past. Lord
Reeth's determination was fixed upon Hailcombe.
And indeed, she decided dismally, if she could not
marry Wyndham, it mattered little whom she married,
for all hope of happiness was blighted for ever.

Upon this melancholy thought, a fresh deluge of
tears coursed down her cheeks. Serena dabbed inef-
fectually at them with her drenched pocket-
handkerchief, which had long since proved to be inadequate to the level of her woe.

'Take mine,' said a voice from nowhere, causing
Serena's heart to jerk with a violence that stopped the
flow of tears in its tracks.

Her startled gaze beheld Wyndham, hatless, one
booted foot upon the little step that led into the summerhouse, leaning towards her and holding out a pris-
tine white handkerchief.

'You made me nearly jump out of my skin!' she
cried involuntarily, seizing the handkerchief without
thought as a pounding started up in her chest.

He looked rueful. 'I beg your pardon. I have been
watching you for some little time, and there did not
seem to be a propitious moment for declaring my
presence.'

'You should have declared it!' returned Serena,
snapping uncontrollably as she attempted to repair the
ravages that her emotions had wrought upon her
countenance.

Hideously aware that her eyes must be swollen, her

nose red, her cheeks disgracefully patchy and her hair awry, she tried to turn in a bid to avoid his glance. But the round summerhouse, with its iron fretwork columns, was so tiny as to permit the half-circle that formed the little seat—built, one could not deny, for the comfort of two persons only—to offer no protection.

'Don't turn away from me!' begged Wyndham, stepping up so that he seemed to fill the restricted space.

She was dismayed. 'Oh, no—you must not! Pray go away again, sir!'

'By no means,' he said, placing himself beside her on the narrow seat, and possessing himself of one of her hands. 'I cannot leave you in such distress. Especially since I cannot rid myself of the conviction that I have contributed to it.'

In no small degree! But it would not do for him to know it. She tried to pull her fingers out of his hold, a trifle breathless for the chaos of her pulses.

'Pray l-let me go! It has—it is not—I am not crying for anything that you have done.'

Wyndham retained his hold on her hand. 'You might well, however. I am palpably to blame for taking unnecessary offence the other day. I gave you my word that I would help you, and then deserted you. I can only beg you to forgive me.'

These words, coupled with the disturbing touch of his fingers, could not but offer balm to Serena's bruised spirit. But a part of her rose up in obstinate defiance, and the words came unbidden from her mouth. She snatched her hand away.

'Why should I forgive you? You had me brought here for—for purposes of your own. You probed my secrets from me, though I told you I cannot accept your help. And then you must needs taunt me with— with judging you, when I have tried not to do so. And I cannot find out the truth, for I am not permitted to ask you about it, because females must not know of such things!'

Realising belatedly where her tongue was leading her, Serena stopped with a gasp, and made to leap from the seat. A strong hand prevented her, dragging her back again.

'Now you listen to me!' said Wyndham firmly, pulling her round to face him. 'I neither know nor care what stories may have been told to you, my girl, but I will not tolerate these insults. What I am or what I may have done in the past is not your concern! Had you accepted my suit, and found my conduct wanting in the future, you might have cause to complain. As things stand—'

This was not to be borne. Serena's temper flared. Seizing his wrists, she wrenched his hands off her shoulders.

'How dare you speak to me in this fashion? I had no idea how horrid you can be! I thought you kind and gentle, and now I see how mistaken I have been.'

'For the matter of that,' retorted Wyndham, 'I thought you a charming innocent. Little did I know

how shrewish a temper lurked inside that pretty fa-
çade!'

'Then you cannot be other than glad that Papa refused to allow me to marry you!'

Jumping up, Serena stepped quickly out of the
summerhouse. But she had hardly gone a few hasty
yards in the direction of the house, when Wyndham
was once more beside her, catching at her hand.

'Stop! Serena, don't run away!'

Before she knew what he would be at, he had
turned her to him, and his fingers were cupping her
face, while one hand snaked up to stroke her golden
hair. His eyes were alight with warmth and remorse.
Serena's furious resentment died, and her pulses pattered into life.

'Forgive me, for I did not mean it. I have been
unreasonable, have I not? If I am permitted an excuse,
let it be that my disappointment has made me subject
to unhappy changes of temperament.'

At these words, which contained the empty promise
of that fulfilment of her deepest desires, all Serena's
earlier misery welled up again, and she spoke her
heart aloud.

'If you are disappointed, how much greater must
be my unhappiness in the choice that has been made
for me.'

Her voice failed, and she saw Wyndham's expression change.

'Oh, don't weep!'

His fingers left her face, and Serena found herself
caught into an alarming embrace, his encircling arms

bringing her so close that she could feel his limbs against her own. A trembling started up inside her, and a sensation of lightness invaded her head.

Wyndham held her so for a moment, looking down into her face. In some dim corner of Serena's brain, she knew she ought to release herself. But she could not have moved if she had wanted to. Mesmerised, her eyes locked with his.

'My sweet Serena,' he murmured. 'So very beautiful. And so innocent, God help me!'

And then his lips came down on hers, his eyes closing. The touch was featherlight. Serena felt her knees go weak and the feeling of light-headedness increased. Into her mind floated a random thought. This was how it ought to have been—after her betrothal. Only she was not betrothed to Wyndham.

Her eyes flew open, and she pulled back in instinctive reaction, staggering as the support of his arms gave way.

'You kissed me!' she accused stupidly.

Wyndham was unable to help a shaky laugh. 'Yes, I'm afraid I did.'

'You had no right to kiss me.'

A vision leapt into her mind. Wyndham—kissing other females. Women whose class permitted such licence.

'No right—save that of my need of you,' he said. 'And that is very real!'

The next instant, Serena found herself locked in an embrace more powerful than the first. Wyndham's mouth sought hers again. Not gently at all, but roughly, with a pressure that forced her lips apart. Instinctively, Serena knew that this second kiss was dictated by passion.

But the thought was swiftly drowned by an impression that she was bursting into flame as the power of his assault upon her mouth intensified. Her own violent reaction sent her into panic. Struggling, she fought to be free.

Recollecting himself suddenly, Wyndham let her go. She reeled back, the brown eyes gazing at him in mute horror. He put out an unsteady hand.

'Serena—I beg your pardon! I forgot myself.'

But the apology came too late. She put her fingers to her mouth, touching her lips as if to assure herself they were not injured. She was shaking uncontrollably, her voice hoarse.

'How could you, Wyndham? Oh, how *could* you!'

Turning, she fled from him, her faith in him shattered.

Chapter Five

The Reeth coach drew slowly away from the environs of the Lacey estate. Cousin Laura, who had been leaning forward to look out of the window, now sank back against the squabs, turning with a sigh towards Serena.

'I have so enjoyed this little trip. What a pity you chose to come away a day early, my dear. Now you will have no young companions for your outings.'

'It makes no matter,' said Serena listlessly, for she no longer cared whether or not she had company. She anticipated no pleasure in any outing, and would as lief stay at home.

'I cannot conceive why you wished to leave,' pursued her duenna, fiddling with the dull grey cloak she wore. A trifle of peevishness crept into her voice. 'There was plenty of amusement, and you have learned to hold Wyndham at arm's length, so that—'

'I beg you will not mention that name to me again, cousin!' flared Serena. 'If at one time I thought well of his lordship, that is all at an end.'

She was dismayed to see that Cousin Laura peered closely at her in the relative gloom of the carriage, and hastily turned her face towards the window. For no consideration would she discuss the circumstances that had led to the realisation that Papa had spoken nothing but the truth. Else Wyndham would not have treated her to a smouldering embrace that ought better have been reserved for the women of that class whose business it was to receive such caresses.

That her memory of the dreadful event had a curious power to make her go weak at the knees was but a blacker mark against him. He had no right to make her feel as if her bones had been filleted! But that was not the worst. Until he had kissed her in that deplorable fashion, Serena had thought him too gentlemanlike to have been guilty of the sort of conduct of which Cousin Laura accused him. Now she knew her partiality had been mistaken.

Worse yet, Wyndham had categorically stated that his way of life before he met her was no concern of hers. Which served only to convince her that, in his eyes, those shocking activities indulged in with the Marquis of Sywell were merely the peccadilloes which Cousin Laura had said might be forgiven.

Recalling how the Viscount had told her he was wounded by her judgement of him, Serena could only marvel. Could he not see how his licentious conduct must give her a disgust of him? He had so often spoken of her as innocent, yet he believed that she ought to condone it. Or, at the least, ignore it.

Serena had been made to understand that, despite

her misplaced feeling for Wyndham, they were poles apart. Papa had been right all along. All hope of happiness was thus at an end, and love was dead.

She realised that Cousin Laura was speaking, and tried to concentrate. She could understand her duenna's disappointment in leaving Lacey Court, for she'd had little need of chaperonage and Cousin Laura had been free, for once in her life, to pursue her own interests.

'I believe I have read as many as three novels, for Lady Lacey has an excellent collection. And I have discovered that Lady Camelford enjoys a game of chess, which as you know is one of my accomplishments, thanks to my Reverend Papa's teaching. We had several bouts, and I must confess myself to have been delighted to beat Lady Camelford twice more than she beat me.'

Serena wished she might share Cousin Laura's enthusiasm. But the truth was that, although she had played her part in the various entertainments got up amongst the younger set, and had tried to emulate Mel's enthusiasm—more for the purpose of showing Lord Wyndham that she could very well get on without him than anything else!—Serena had been too sick at heart to enjoy anything. After two days, she had grown weary of feigning, and found an excuse to take her departure on Wednesday, a day earlier than the rest of the party.

Not that Melanie had believed her fabrication! Serena had complained of increasing pain and nausea at her stomach, and refused all offers to send for the local doctor.

'I do not wish him—that is, *people*—' correcting herself hastily '—to suppose that I am unwell. It will only spoil the party.'

'But if you go early, Serena,' Melanie had pointed out with alarming candour, 'these "people" are bound to think that something is amiss. What am I supposed to tell *them*?'

The stress laid on the final word had warned Serena that her subterfuge had been detected. Refusing to acknowledge it, she had persisted in her determination.

'Once I am gone, you may say what you please.'

'And what reason do you propose to give before you are gone?' had demanded Melanie.

Serena had sighed. 'Oh, we shall say that I have a recurrent disorder that forces me to return to London to consult my physician. He is familiar with my case, you see.'

'Yes, and if you ask me, there is a great deal more to your "case" than a pain at the stomach!'

Which percipient remark had almost been Serena's undoing. But Melanie was as warm-hearted as she was loose-tongued, and had given her guest a quick hug.

'There, don't cry! You shall go if you choose. Only pray don't try to bamboozle me into believing that George has not upset you, for you will not succeed. If I could think it might do some good, I would take him roundly to task!'

'Oh, pray do not!' had begged Serena, alarmed.

'No, I shan't, for he wouldn't listen to me if I did,' had said Melanie frankly. 'I should think Buckworth is the only person who has influence with George, and his advice is unlikely to be of the least use.'

With which sentiment Serena found herself to be in full agreement. Indeed, she must suppose that a rake, as Buckworth had been described to her, could only encourage that side of Wyndham to which she fervently wished she had herself remained a stranger. An uncomfortable reflection that had sunk her below melancholy into the apathy that now engulfed her. For there was only one future for her, and she had determined to school herself to endure it.

The Viscount's attention was so distracted that, for the second time at practice, he foolishly allowed a simple pass to break through his guard. Buckworth leaped back out of range and dropped his point.

'A child's trick, Wyndham, and you let me through! You are not concentrating. *En garde!*'

The mock fight resumed, and Wyndham, always on the defensive, parried almost mechanically, for his mind continued to run on the difficulties of his situation.

Once Serena had left the Lacey Court party, it had proved abominably insipid—despite the fact that she had virtually ignored him for the last two days. He had tried to convince himself that he had been wasting his time. It was not his business to sort out Miss

Reeth's life. He was out of the running, and she could well manage her affairs for herself.

But he'd had glimpses of her during this past week since his return to town, and had caught himself out in a high tide of jealousy on seeing Hailcombe assiduously at her elbow. He had forced his attention on to his own plans, for he was due to go to Brighton in a day or so. Custom dictated that gentlemen of the Ton followed the Prince, who had already left the metropolis to spend time there with his particular cronies.

Wyndham was just reflecting that Brighton held no lure for him at this present, when it was borne in upon him that Buckworth was attempting a lunge *in quarte*, high to the shoulder. Too late, he fumbled a parry, and his friend's buttoned point came to rest upon his left breast.

'*Touché*,' he acknowledged, and stepped back.

'No credit to me,' Buckworth pointed out, putting up a hand to remove the mask from his face. 'Your guard was weak, and you know it.'

'True.' With a sigh, Wyndham removed his own mask. 'I have had enough, in any event.'

'What's amiss, dear boy?' asked Buckworth, taking his friend's foil and placing both back in the rack.

Wyndham answered only with a grunt, handed his mask to one of the attendants, and headed for the washroom. Buckworth had better have asked what was not amiss! How could one begin to tell him? That he had been a fool? But that went without saying. He had been precipitate, ungentlemanly, and above all, he had lost control. And it had cost him dear.

A large arm was placed about his shoulders, and he found Buckworth at his side.

'Come on, man, out with it! It's the little Reeth creature, I take it?'

Wyndham looked quickly about, but the washroom was deserted. Most of the fellows who frequented Angelo's academy must be still at practice in the long room set aside for the purpose.

'As you say,' he said lightly.

Moving out of his friend's embrace, he went to a stand and, lifting the ewer, poured water into the basin.

'I'm not going to leave it, my friend,' said Buckworth, following suit at another stand, 'so you may as well cut line.'

'The thing is,' confessed Wyndham, taking off his shirt and throwing water over himself, 'that I don't know where to start. I've made a mull of it, I can tell you that.'

'That much I had already deduced,' said his friend. 'I've never yet met a man who was blue-devilled in affairs of the heart who hadn't done his best to shoot himself in the foot!'

Wyndham gave a short laugh, and picked up the soap. In a few pithy words, he put his friend in possession of the salient facts. He did not spare himself, for it was much needed balm to be able to throw off the social mask with this friend whom he trusted above all others.

'I should have known better,' he said bitterly at the end of his recital. 'She's only eighteen.'

'That means nothing at all, George. I've known girls of eighteen who wouldn't turn a hair. It all depends on the upbringing.'

'Reeth is very strict, I believe. And she is childishly innocent. Her conversation is enough to tell one that. Lord knows what sort of a fairytale he concocted for her benefit! And just when I thought I had succeeded in convincing her otherwise—'

Breaking off, Wyndham ground his teeth, feeling a resurgence of all the useless fury he had expended against himself. That Serena had been frightened by his kiss into withdrawal, he knew. That she now regarded him with revulsion, he could not doubt. And he was almost certain that she had decided to believe whatever tales had been told of him to put her against him. Couple that with the prohibitions that her father had evidently laid upon her, and the Viscount must conceive his case to be hopeless.

He looked at Buckworth, who was vigorously rubbing himself with a towel, and found an amused gaze upon him.

'And what, may I ask, do you find so devilishly funny?' he demanded. 'My life is in ruins, and all you can do is laugh!'

Buckworth grinned at him, and threw him one of the towels that hung on a convenient rail. 'I always thought you would take it badly when it hit.'

'When what hit?'

'Love.'

Arrested, Wyndham paused with the towel draped about his bare shoulders. He regarded the twinkling eyes of his friend without annoyance, for the significance in that one word took all his attention. It struck him that in all his dealings on this matter, he had never admitted the truth.

Having been dismissed by Reeth, he had wanted to wash his hands of the whole affair. But that had proved impossible. For there had been Serena—distressed from the outset!—and he had been unable to leave it alone. He had thought it was her difficulties and tribulations that had been driving him. Had he been deceiving himself all this while?

'Lord, Buckworth!' he uttered dazedly. 'I am so very deeply in love with her. What the devil am I to do?'

October was almost at an end, and the lonely week since Serena had departed from the house party at Lacey Court felt like a lifetime. Hailcombe had been her escort at almost every engagement she had attended, and she had been made aware—by Cousin Laura, who spoke of it with satisfaction—that the announcement of her betrothal was daily expected.

Serena had not herself noticed the whispers, for she had been living in a hazy world where nothing seemed any longer to be real. Her speech and actions were mechanical, and she could not remember what had been said to her five minutes after a conversation.

Only one thing penetrated the cloud of abstraction in which she had enwrapped herself. Despite every determination to cut a certain unmentionable gentleman out of her life and memory, it was upon the three separate occasions when she discovered him to be present at the same event she was attending that a piercing pang shot her into a state of mental alertness.

Serena's remembrance of the week behind her jumped from one to the other of these unfortunate encounters. The difficulty, she discovered, was that Wyndham was as personable as ever, and had yet the smile and warmth that characterised him—if not towards herself. He should, she felt, have grown horns and a tail, and shown his evil propensities in some harsh transformation of his countenance! It was really too bad of him to hide his true identity under that engaging personality which had captured her fancy. It was all of a piece, and just the hypocritical conduct one might have expected.

These damaging reflections, however, failed to cure Serena of her depressed spirits. Indeed, they had an opposite effect, and her wan looks at length drew her duenna's expostulation.

'My dear child, anyone would suppose you to be at death's door! Do try to show a little animation. It is of particular importance this morning, for Hailcombe is coming to see your Papa and I have no doubt you will be expected to attend him.'

Serena was vaguely aware that there was significance in this announcement. 'I thought we were with him last night at the Opera. Am I engaged to drive out with him?'

Cousin Laura was moved to click her tongue, shuffling her spectacles on and off again. 'I do wish you will come out of this stupid dullness, Serena! Surely you heard him say last night that he would call upon your Papa this morning? You must have done so, for you readily agreed that it was convenient.'

No recollection of having said any such thing came into Serena's head. But then last night had been a severe trial to her, for the Viscount had been in a box on the other side of the opera house. Had it been his aunt, Lady Lacey, with him? She rather thought it had, but she could not be sure, for her gaze had been strictly confined to the stage. Not that it had helped. She'd had no notion how large an arc was encompassed in the periphery of one's vision! Nor how obtrusive upon it could be a single figure at a distance.

A knock at the nursery parlour door produced Lissett. 'His lordship requests you to join him in the library, Miss Serena.'

Serena looked at him blankly. 'Do you mean Lord Hailcombe?'

'Lord Hailcombe is in the first-floor saloon. It is my Lord Reeth who wishes your presence in the book-room.'

'Very well, I will come.'

The butler withdrew, and Serena rose from her chair, only to be checked by Cousin Laura.

'One moment, child.' Her duenna twitched at the demure muslin gown, and prinked the golden curls. 'There, that will suffice. Now, Serena, you are going to do your duty, are you not? It will not do to turn tail at this juncture.'

Serena fought down a sudden disquieting nausea. 'I am quite ready, cousin.'

Her duenna gave her a doubtful look, but turned to escort her along the corridor and downstairs to the library. Opening the door, she gave her charge a little push that precipitated her into the room.

Lord Reeth was standing before the fireplace, gripping the mantel. The bronzed head turned, and the Roman nose was directed towards his daughter. There was question in his lordship's gaze, and a riffle of feeling disturbed Serena's comforting blanket of unreality.

'You wanted to see me, Papa?'

For a moment, her father continued to regard her silently, as if he sought to satisfy himself upon certain points in his mind. The appraisal proved disconcerting, and Serena dropped her eyes.

'I do not know, Serena,' began Reeth at length, in that heavy tone which caused an uncomfortable sinking within his daughter's stomach, 'what may have occurred at Lacey Court to effect this change in you. Laura assures me that you are now schooled to obedience. I can only trust that this will be found to be the case.'

Serena's head continued downcast. Like a schoolgirl, she clasped her hands together behind her back, and closed her lips upon utterance. There was nothing to be said.

'Lord Hailcombe,' continued her father after a pause, 'has chosen to be magnanimous, and forgive the insulting nature of your earlier dealings with him.

He tells me that he has received nothing from you lately but that docility which must, he is persuaded, form the foundation of the sort of alliance that he desires.' The voice sharpened. 'In other words, Serena, he wishes for a wife who knows her duty and from whom he may expect obedience.'

There was a further dilution of the grey clouds about Serena's mind. With it arose a growth of sensation which was faintly reminiscent of the first occasion when she had been told of Hailcombe's offer. Serena kept her gaze lowered, apprehensive lest Papa's discerning eye should penetrate into the secret hollows of her bosom.

'You have nothing to say?'

There was scepticism in the voice. Serena drew a breath against the slight rise of panic, and looked up.

'What do you want me to say, Papa?'

'Good God, girl, don't you know? Don't think I have not observed you closely. I see you apparently cowed, but I am forced to wonder. I know you, Serena, and this conduct is not in your nature. What are you playing at?'

Hurt surprise jerked Serena into speech. 'Indeed, Papa, I do not know what you mean! I am ready to do as you ask. I made up my mind to it some time ago.'

Reeth frowned doubtfully. 'You will accept Hailcombe?'

'If that is your wish,' she agreed.

Papa seemed not to be satisfied. 'I warn you,

Serena, that if you again give me cause for embarrassment in this matter, I will not spare you!'

The meaning of this was plain. The remnants of the protective shroud in Serena's mind shredded away. Fully aware, she felt her heart knock against her ribs. A recognition that the fate outlined need not overtake her crept into her thoughts. She had every intention of obeying him. There was nothing to fear in Papa's veiled threat.

'You need not have said as much,' she said reproachfully. 'I have given you my word.'

Lord Reeth was unimpressed. 'Then see that you keep it!'

He strode past her to the door, and flung it open. Turning, Serena saw that her duenna was waiting in the corridor.

'Take her to the saloon, Laura. But wait outside. You had better let her face him alone.'

Hailcombe was standing behind one of the straw-covered sofas, his attention absorbed by something in the square below. Serena felt an upsurge of nausea. But her resolution, she reminded herself, was fixed. She trod silently to the centre of the saloon. The door clicked shut behind her.

His lordship turned his head, and Serena saw a frown in his eyes. His full mouth was tight-lipped in the florid features. It was not, Serena told herself, a bad-looking countenance. Well-proportioned with a strong jaw. If only the brows were not so heavy, and his smile had been engaging.

Was it a smile? He was showing his teeth, but there
was no gleam of warmth at his eyes. They were grey,
like Wyndham's. Only so unlike!

Serena's breath caught. Why had she thought of
him? That was just the sort of comparison that must
not enter her head. Feeling her control slipping,
Serena dropped her gaze from his, and made her curtsey.

'You wished to see me, sir?'

Hailcombe came around the sofa and strolled to
stand before the fireplace, at a little distance from her.

'Look at me, girl!'

It was a command. Something jolted in Serena's
breast, but she obeyed, lifting her eyes again. She
could not but note an arrogance in Hailcombe's pose,
and with the lifted chin, the smile became a mocking
sneer.

'Are you done rebelling?'

Serena knew not how to answer. Was he seeking
to know if his way was clear, or was this to taunt her?
It struck her that, for all the flaccidity of his frame,
there was power in its very largeness. At her silence,
the mockery intensified.

'Don't think me jealous. You're very young, and
the young are wayward. Given time, I thought you'd
come round.'

No longer sheltered by the numbness that had kept
her docile, Serena was provoked into retort.

'My alteration, sir, had nothing to do with you!'

Hailcombe laughed. 'D'you think I care for that, if
the prize be mine?'

Had she not schooled herself to accept this fate, Serena would have repudiated this assumption. She clamped her lips upon a rise of revulsion. But was there no ardour here? Had it been all pretence? Then why did he wish to marry her? She found a compromise of words.

'You presume it to be so, sir.'

'I think I may, don't you? You've behaved well to me these last days. Caused me to hope.'

Had she not intended this result? Then why should she feel so ill? Unable to answer, she dropped another curtsey, as if in acquiescence.

'Oh, that's submissive!' A smug satisfaction in his voice added nothing to Serena's comfort. 'Augurs well for our future together, Miss Reeth. Or might I use your pretty name now—eh, Serena?'

He came away from the mantel, and took a couple of paces towards her. 'I'm running before the horse, though. Let's do the thing in form.'

He made an elaborate, if clumsy, leg, and Serena could not tell whether he meant it in seriousness or mockery.

'Miss Reeth, will you honour me with your hand in marriage?'

A hard weight of denial settled squarely in Serena's chest. She knew it behoved her to speak, but her tongue refused to utter the necessary words. She swallowed hard, taking refuge in a further curtsey. Let him take that for his answer, for she could give him no other!

It appeared that Lord Hailcombe was all too willing

to take her answer as read. He came forward until he
towered over her. Serena shrank into herself, and the
sensation of sickness grew stronger. Under the thick
brows his eyes looked down into her face with hard-
ness in them, though his mouth smiled.

'By my faith, you're as pretty as a picture!' He
chucked her under the chin. 'Made my path prover-
bially rough, but I won't repine. You can call me a
happy man!'

Above her, the full lips protruded, the skin about
them glistening. Before Serena had time to take in
what he would be at, Hailcombe's hands were grasping her shoulders, and his face came down to the level
of her own.

The next instant, a moist slab of rubbery flesh was
fastened to her mouth, and a thrusting invader came
oiling between her lips.

For several hideous seconds, the stark horror of the
attack held Serena motionless, her limbs turning rigid.
Then her stomach heaved, and an urgent need gave
her strength. Recoiling, she tugged herself free.

With the back of her hand she wiped away the
obscenity of his kiss, and her tongue gave utterance
to the sensations consuming her.

'It is of no use! How can I marry you? *You repel
me.*'

Turning from him, Serena ran for the door, brushing past her startled duenna. Clapping her hand over
her mouth, she lifted her skirts, and flew up the stairs,
racing for her bedchamber, convinced that at any mo-

ment she would regurgitate the churning contents of her stomach.

The furious banging on the door had abated. Papa's irate demands to Serena to come out had given way to a low-toned conversation in the corridor. Since she had—not without considerable difficulty—dragged the heavy oak chest across the locked door, and placed upon it a further barricade consisting of her bedside table and two straight-backed chairs, Serena was unable to approach close enough to place her ear to the woodwork—even had her trembling limbs permitted it. She could not therefore hear what was being said, but she knew that the participants consisted of her father, her duenna and the object of her violent rejection.

She was quivering still from the tirade that had been unleashed from the other side of the door. Papa's fury had known no bounds, and Serena had reason to congratulate herself on the quaking forethought that had led her to turn the key upon his inevitable revenge. In the appalling state of her nerves as she had fled for this refuge, it had been all she could do to slam the door and lock it before running for the washstand. In her frantic haste, she had dropped the ewer—mercifully empty!—and seized the basin in both hands.

She had not been sick, but the nausea continued to rise up from time to time. The basin was now on the bed where she had sat for several earth-shattering minutes, holding it ready, while her heaving interior made her retch over and over again.

And then had come the heavy footsteps of pursuit. At the first knock, and the demanding shout, Serena had staggered from the bed and stood, shivering with fright.

'Serena, open this door!'

The command was repeated several times. But so far from doing anything of the kind, Papa's erring daughter, driven to desperate measures by the vivid memory of his earlier promise, had well nigh exhausted herself in piling up her barrier.

'Call someone to break it down, Laura!'

But her duenna, to Serena's thankful ears, had vetoed this suggestion in no uncertain terms.

'Pray do not resort to ridiculous extremes, Bernard! She cannot remain in there for ever. You have only to have patience.'

'*Patience?* I'll show her patience!'

This outrage had been the prelude to a burst of invective and threatening language, accompanied by a thundering battery of fists upon the door. By the time Papa had run out of steam, Serena found herself backed into the opposite wall, with the bed between herself and the door, almost as if she would climb inside the stonework for protection.

She was able now to discern Hailcombe's voice as well as Cousin Laura's, in between the growling mutterings of Papa. But the words were indistinct. Eventually, the voices trailed away, and footsteps indicated that the party was moving off.

Serena's legs gave way and she sank into a huddle at the base of the wall, feeling numbed. For what felt like an age, she was unable to move from the spot, as the realisation of what had happened began to seep into her brain. With it, came a riot of conjecture.

How had she ever supposed she could ally herself with that creature? Yet how was she to escape him? What was she to do? Cousin Laura had spoken nothing but the truth. She could not stay here for ever. Would Papa's wrath be any more lenient for having grown cold? Retribution must await her, however long she held out. Hold out she must, for she would rather die than marry Hailcombe! How loathsome had been that kiss! Was she to endure a lifetime of revulsion? Better by far that she threw herself from the window of this room!

But the absurdity of this notion caught at her reason. No, that was foolish. Death was no solution. She must not fall into a distempered freak. Better to think how she could placate Papa, how to prevail upon him to realise the sheer impossibility of acceding to his wish.

A mountain loomed ahead of her. Involuntarily, she sighed aloud the root of the evil.

'Oh, Wyndham! If only you had not been a libertine!'

A memory shot into her mind. That kiss of his! It had shocked and alarmed her. But how unlike it had been to the hateful unpleasantness of Hailcombe's mouth upon her own. No such flame of heat had coursed through her as it had done upon the touch of

Wyndham's lips to hers. Had she to face again *his* arms about her, *his* assault upon her innocence, she had rather that a thousand times than to endure a single instant in the embrace of Hailcombe!

But that choice was not open to her, Serena reflected dismally, and dragging herself up from the floor, she drooped on to the bed. Faintness overcame her, and she lay down upon the coverlet, closing her eyes.

Exhaustion presently claimed her, and she knew no more until a gentle tapping on the door jerked her into wakefulness again. Starting up, and forgetful at first of the circumstances which had led to her being closeted in her bedchamber, Serena called out to know who was there.

'It is Mel. Dear Serena, do pray open the door!'

Bewildered, Serena stared blankly at the barricade. What in the world was Melanie doing here? And why was she lying upon her bed in the middle of the day?

It was a moment or two before remembrance came to her, and she recalled why the chest and other items were barring the doorway. By the time she had risen unsteadily to her feet and begun to cross the room, Melanie was again speaking.

'Serena, do you hear me? Pray come out! I have Miss Geary here, and she thinks you should come home with me for the night.'

Reaching the door, Serena took in the sense of these words with an abrupt rise of hope. But she was all too wary. Was this a trap?

'Mel? Is it indeed you?'

'Of course it is! Mama and I are in town for a few days for the purpose of ordering my bride clothes. But no matter for that. Pray let me help you, dearest Serena. You cannot remain in there indefinitely. Besides, you will soon be starving, and there is no bearing that.'

This aspect of the matter had not before occurred to Serena. But she now became aware that the nausea with which she had gone to sleep had given way to the pangs of hunger. Nevertheless, it was essential to proceed with caution.

'Cousin Laura?'

'My poor dear child,' came her duenna's anxious voice. 'You need have no fear. Your papa is out of the house. Come, Serena, open the door.'

'And Hailcombe? Is he here?'

'Dear me, no. He retreated in no small degree of umbrage several hours ago.'

Melanie took up the plea again. 'Serena, I do not know what has been happening here, but you will be safe at my home, I promise you.'

It took some further argument, but at length Serena allowed herself to be persuaded. Struggling, she undid her barricade, heaving the chest to one side. Unlocking the door, she opened it with a degree of stealth.

But the faces revealed proved to be none other than the two ladies to whose pleadings she had succumbed. Serena fell into Melanie's ready arms in a fit of over-whelming relief, shedding a few unheeded tears.

Cousin Laura's eyes were also moist, she discovered, when she turned to her. But the duenna urged speed.

'You must be gone from here swiftly, before your papa returns. I will lock the door from this side, and Lissett and I will pretend that you have refused either to open it or to answer us.'

'But what will happen in the morning?' Melanie wanted to know, straightening her pink beribboned bonnet as the three ladies went back into the bed-chamber and began a swift selection of suitable garments. 'You cannot pretend for ever that Serena is in her room.'

Cousin Laura drew herself up. 'Tomorrow, I will confess the truth—and say a good deal more besides. I trust that Bernard may be suitably chastened.'

If Serena doubted it, she did not say so. But she trembled for her duenna, and begged her not to court any risk. 'For I have taxed Papa's temper to its limit, and I do not wish his wrath to fall upon you instead, cousin.'

'You do not know your father, child. Even by this time, his temper will have cooled. If he is not already writhing in his conscience, you may call me a sim-pleton. Believe me, Serena, by the time he has passed a night in the belief that you are cowering in your room in fear of him, he will be a different man.'

Spurred by Cousin Laura to hasten, the two young ladies were soon creeping down the stairs, the butler in the hall below having signalled that all was clear. Clutching a cloak bag containing the most necessary items, and clad in a dark green pelisse with a fur collar, her free hand tucked into a matching muff, Serena bid her duenna a grateful farewell, and hurried out of the house and into the waiting coach.

The Lacey town house was located in Hay Hill, and the drive from Hanover Square did not occupy many minutes. But Melanie nevertheless contrived to extract a brief outline of the day's events from her friend, promising that they should enjoy a comfortable cose when once she had shaken off the inevitable questions of her parent.

'For Mama is bound to wonder why I have invited you to stay with me when you have a perfectly good house of your own. Especially at a time that is supposed to be devoted to the selection of my bride clothes.'

Severely conscious, Serena asked what was to be done. 'Had I better return home again, Mel?'

'Upon no account!' declared Melanie. 'Have you forgot that you are escaping from persecution? Lord, here we are at Berkeley Square already! We shall be at home in a trice. Never fear, Serena. I will concoct a tale that will satisfy Mama, you may be sure.'

Serena did not know Melanie very well, but a week in her company had been enough to reassure her on this point. Besides, she was so grateful for the offered respite that she made no further demur. Though she was far from sanguine about the outcome of Cousin Laura's determination to bring Papa to a more malleable frame of mind.

The carriage drew up outside a pretty establishment, by no means as large as the Reeth house in

Hanover Square, but a perfectly adequate town residence. The ladies descended, and the doors were flung open to welcome the daughter of the house.

Not without some qualms, Serena allowed the footman to take possession of her cloak bag and pelisse—'Take them up with my things, Bordon, and ask Mrs Pawley to make up the room next to mine for my guest' —and followed her rescuer towards a door on the ground floor to the right of the hall.

'For we may as well beard Mama at once,' whispered Melanie as she led the way.

Serena entered behind her hostess into a large drawing-room, done out in a striped paper of pale blue and cream, laced with gold. The theme was repeated in the cushioning to a set of chairs and two wide sofas, upon one of which Lady Lacey was seen to be seated. But no further impression was created upon Serena, for it was to be seen that the lady of the house was not alone.

In a chair by the fire sat the Honourable Mr Camelford, who leaped up to greet his betrothed with becoming enthusiasm. Another gentleman had been standing by a window, so that his profile only was exposed to the door. Serena had taken but a few paces into the room when he turned, and she discovered him to be none other than Wyndham.

Chapter Six

So concentrated had Serena been on her flight from Hanover Square that it had not occurred to her that in this house, the presence of Melanie's cousin was only to be expected. The effect upon her was not one which either duty or common sense dictated. She was overtaken by an overwhelming desire to run across the room and throw herself into Wyndham's arms, pleading for his protection.

It was perhaps fortunate that her attention was captured by Lady Lacey addressing her in greeting. Melanie's mother was a youthful-looking matron, who had retained a good figure and some degree of that warm insouciance that characterised her daughter.

'How charming to see you, Miss Reeth! Have you come to dine with us? Such a pity that you left us the other week. You were sadly missed.'

'Yes, and that is why,' chimed in Melanie, turning swiftly from her betrothed, 'I have invited Serena to stay for a day or two, Mama.'

'To stay? But your bride clothes, my love. Not that I mean to say you are not welcome, Serena, but—'

'Ah, but you see, Mama, Serena is to help me choose. It is so dull to be shopping without a companion! I know you will be with me, Mama, but it will be so much more fun to have my new friend as well.' Sailing across the room again, Melanie put both arms about an extremely embarrassed Serena. 'Now you must not be difficult, Mama, for I positively insist upon having my own way in this.'

'You nearly always do have your own way,' remarked Wyndham, taking a step or two towards Serena and making a slight bow. He spoke with deliberate amiability, as if nothing had occurred to mar the good relations between them.

'How do you do, Miss Reeth? I beg you will not allow Mel's chatter to dismay you. If I know my Aunt Lacey, she will not be so unkind as to turn you out of doors.'

'Heavens, no!' echoed Lady Lacey, laughing. 'Indeed, my dear, I am very happy to have you with us. John, pray ring the bell.'

'If it is for Bordon, Mama, he need not trouble, for I have already arranged everything. Serena is to have the chamber next door to mine.'

Serena found herself herded to a seat beside Lady Lacey, who immediately drew her into the conversation she had been having with her prospective son-in-law before the young ladies had entered the saloon. Serena bore little part in it, for she could not help noticing that the Viscount took his cousin aside where they became engaged in earnest conversation. She could only trust that Melanie would not betray her. To have Wyndham master of the horrible circumstances that had driven her out of her home must sink her into the ground!

'For pity's sake, Mel, what has been happening?' Wyndham was demanding urgently, in a low tone. 'She looks like death! And don't try to fob me off with this taradiddle about your bride clothes. It may do very well for my aunt, but it will not serve for me!'

'Yes, but the thing is,' confided Melanie frankly, 'that I can't tell you. I have not learned much myself. I only know that I found poor Serena hiding in her room in a state of great distress and fear.'

Wyndham felt his chest go hollow. 'Upon what occasion? Has it anything to do with that wretched fellow, Hailcombe?'

'It is no use asking me, George. You had best enquire of Serena herself.'

'How can I possibly do so?' he asked irritably, horribly conscious of that fateful last encounter. 'As things stand between us…'

He was disconcerted to receive a straight look from his cousin, a trifle of unusual seriousness in her face. 'How do they stand, George?'

Wyndham eyed her with suspicion. 'I imagine you must know that very well.'

'I am not in her confidence, if that is what you think.'

'Then you need not look censorious.'

'Do I?' A gurgle of mirth escaped Melanie. 'I wish you will tell Camel so. He can never be brought to believe that I have any notion of censure.'

'I don't wonder!' Wyndham clicked his tongue. 'Keep to the point, Mel. And stop trying to hoax me that you don't know perfectly well what ails Serena.'

Melanie threw up her eyes. 'If you must know, I think it was her papa from whom Serena was hiding. From the little I was able to find out, I believe he is constraining her to marry that dreadful man.'

Not without misgiving, Wyndham noted the mischief that entered her face. 'But if you are bent upon playing knight errant, George, I have a splendid scheme to help you.'

The rose parlour was a cosy room, with pretty pink walls and a neat marbled fireplace, from which a cheerful blaze gave off much needed warmth. It was not merely the bleak imminence of November that chilled Serena. She was haunted by the fear that today Papa would come to fetch her back.

Melanie had averred that she would be safe, here in this little family chamber, to which few guests were ever invited.

'And, in any event, I shall tell Bordon to deny you should your papa arrive.'

With which assurance Serena had to be content. It was dreadful to be scheming against Papa, but what else could she do? Her conscience was sorely troubled, for she seemed to have become caught up in a multitude of prevarications. The excuse that Melanie had concocted for her presence to Lady Lacey had to be overlaid with yet another fabrication.

'It is obvious that you are in no fit state to come out with me, dear Serena. Besides, I am sure you cannot want to be gadding about the shops. I shall tell Mama that you have a headache.'

Since Serena had in fact been dreading the necessity to go out at all—who knew but what she might meet Hailcombe or Papa in the streets?—she was only too happy to agree to this subterfuge. On the other hand, her spirits were too restless for the confines of the little parlour.

She shifted from a chair that gave onto the fire's warmth and went to the window. From there she began to tread a path between the two sets of straight-backed chairs with brocaded seats, which were the only furnishings the parlour afforded, besides a small writing desk and a couple of little tables.

It was all very well to have run away from Hanover Square, but she would have to go back sooner or later. If Cousin Laura failed to turn Papa from his purpose—it could scarcely be otherwise, for her poor duenna could have no influence over him!—what was to be the outcome? But beyond the dread punishment that was meant to bring her to heel, Serena could not think. She knew only that her revulsion towards Hailcombe precluded any possibility of becoming his wife. If Papa proved adamant, she had rather throw herself upon Wyndham's mercy!

Upon which thought, the door opened. Serena happened to be at the window and, turning swiftly, discovered the Viscount himself standing in the aperture.

'Pray don't be angry!' Wyndham said quickly, seeing the startled frown that leaped into her pale features.

'You should not be here!'

He entered the room and closed the door. 'It is most improper, I'm afraid. But there is no help for it, Serena. I cannot stand aside, when I see you looking so white and ill.'

A rush of heat struck at Serena's bosom. Without knowing what she did, she crossed to the nearest chair and grasped its back tightly, as if without its support she must inevitably fall.

Wyndham watched her with a twist at his heart for the further evidence of her distress of mind. Her hair was loose, falling about her face and shoulders, and the figured gown clung, cupping her breasts into tantalising mounds that caused the air to dry in his throat. He dragged his eyes back to her face, and moved to the fireplace, resting one hand upon the mantel.

'What has happened? Or should I first tell you what I suspect?'

Serena shook her head dumbly. Last night she had dreamed of his coming! But the actuality of his presence forced her to confront the impossibility of her misplaced hopes. All the horrid circumstances of their last meeting at Lacey Court flooded back. She had as well court unhappiness in marrying Hailcombe as sue to Wyndham for aid!

'I do not know why you have come here,' she ventured without looking at him, 'nor why you should take it upon yourself to—to—'

'To help you? Have you forgot that I pledged you my word that I would do so?' And then broke it, he might have added. 'Rest assured that I have not come to importune you in any way. I hope you can bring yourself at least to accept my apologies for conduct which was, I admit, unforgivable. I will not repeat it.'

Serena found herself with nothing to say. The remembrance of his passionate caress filled her with warmth—not entirely due to embarrassment. And this last promise left her prey to a stupid disappointment. Without realising it, she took in the strength of muscle outlined by the buckskins and topboots, and found herself fighting against the tug of attraction. Her gaze rose upward, to the smooth-fitting broadcloth coat, the deliberately unruly style of the dark hair. Then she met the grey eyes, and the concern in them quite crushed her.

'Pray do not think of it again,' she said rapidly, as if impelled. 'I assure you I have forgotten it.' May God forgive her for a further lie!

'Thank you.'

It was said in a low tone, accompanied by a diminution of cordiality in his countenance. A frown creased his brow. He gestured to the chair she was holding.

'Won't you sit down?'

Serena complied, folding her hands tightly in her lap and turning her gaze upon the fire, in a bid to diffuse the disturbance of his presence.

Seating himself in the chair opposite, Wyndham let his eyes rove over her features. She was pallid, and shadows hung about the brown eyes. It occurred to him that the eager freshness that had won his interest was conspicuously absent. She was but eighteen, and already the harsh blows of fate had succeeded in damping her spirit. A bitter irony, that the only female who had touched him should have been pushed beyond his reach. But at least he could do what he might in friendship. To leave her to her fate would be intolerable.

'Serena, if you will not confide in me, at least let me give you fair warning.'

The pansy eyes flew up, a startled expression within them. 'Warning! What can you mean?'

Wyndham threw up a hand. 'No threat, I promise you. It is only that I have made it my business to set certain enquiries in train. Forgive me, but I had guessed—when we were at Lacey Court and you told me that you had some quarrel with your father—that the matter concerned Lord Hailcombe.'

A rush of anger spurted out of Serena. 'Mel told you!'

'Not at all. It was my friend Buckworth who had observed you to be often in his company. He had also seen Hailcombe and your father together, and had deduced that he and Miss Geary were encouraging that gentleman.'

'Lord Buckworth has not been the only one to see it!' she blurted out bitterly. 'My cousin says that everyone is daily expecting the announcement of our betrothal.'

Wyndham leaned forward a little. 'Then I most earnestly beg of you to consider well before you engage yourself to a man of whom I have been able to ascertain only the most disquieting of facts.'

It was on the tip of Serena's tongue to refute any intention of engaging herself to Hailcombe, but the words were stayed. With a flicker of something like hope, she recalled that he had earlier spoken of making enquiries.

'You have discovered something to his discredit?'

'And nothing to his credit,' agreed the Viscount grimly. 'Forgive me for asking this, but is your portion of sufficient value to prove a temptation to a needy gentleman?'

'Don't you know?' Serena asked, surprised.

Wyndham emitted a short laugh. 'My offer did not reach the point of enquiring into your circumstances.' He saw the colour creep into her cheeks, and added gently, 'It could be of no interest to me, in any event.'

Because he was himself so wealthy? Or because he no longer cared to marry her? Serena was depressingly aware that her rejection of him might well have caused him to suffer a reversal of feeling. After all, he had said that his shocking conduct would not be repeated. Perhaps he had no wish to repeat it. She dragged her mind back to the point at issue.

'My portion is respectable, but it is not a fortune. Enough to secure a good marriage, Papa has always said.'

And he had seen fit to reject a brilliant one! Which was all at once incomprehensible to Serena. If he was prepared to see her married to a man like Hailcombe, why in the world should he force her to throw away a coronet merely because its wearer led an immoral life?

'Then there must be some other incentive,' Wyndham was saying in a musing tone.

Serena was conscious of a spurt of indignation, and the question was out before she could stop it. 'I presume you mean to imply that he cannot have fallen in love with me?'

'I must be the last man to claim that!'

Her breath caught. Then he did still care for her! Her fingers quivered and she was obliged to clasp her hands tightly together to prevent him from seeing it.

But Wyndham was already regretting his hasty response. It had come perilously close to a declaration. One which he could not make when he knew her father—and Serena herself—to be against him. Pulling himself together, he quickly resumed.

'I am persuaded Hailcombe cannot afford the luxury of a mere attachment. He has no place in the highest circles, as you must know well. It may be that he hopes to improve his acceptance by such an alliance. He is an adventurer, and his career has been a chequered one. That need not condemn him, but you are mistaken if you suppose him to be an honest man.'

'It is Papa who supposes it,' she answered flatly,

out of an unacknowledged disappointment. 'I am led to believe that he is at least respectable.'

'Far from it. I will not distress you with a tale of those exploits of which I have been informed. But you should at least know that he is a man who lives by his wits as well as gaming. Which means, you must know, that he uses dubious methods to gain favours.'

Serena became victim to a curious sensation of *déjà vu*, as if she had heard it all before. Just so had Papa warned her against my lord Wyndham. And now here his lordship was, speaking in much the same fashion against Hailcombe. And with no more explicitness than Papa had used!

Her temper flared, and she jumped up from the chair. 'How am I to know? What are these methods? Are they any more to be deprecated than—than the licentious behaviour to be expected of a—of a libertine?'

Wyndham had risen when she did, but he had stiffened and his voice was ice. 'Is that to my address?'

'Take it as you will!' Serena threw at him, swinging away towards the window, and turning there. 'I must thank you, sir, for your warnings against Lord Hailcombe. It is a pity that you did not think to warn me against yourself!'

'There it is again!' exploded Wyndham, shifting to the centre of the little room to face her. 'What have you been told? Who has dared to throw these slurs upon my name? Of what licentious behaviour am I accused? And what have I done that you should take me for a libertine?'

'You kissed me!' Serena flung at him hotly. 'You used me in a way that—in a way that you might use a—'

'Don't say it!' struck in Wyndham. 'I can guess what you mean, and I have no wish to hear such words upon your lips. But I protest you know nothing of passion, Serena, if that is what you believe!'

'How should I know anything of passion?' she raged. 'I am not a whore!'

With which Serena gasped at her own daring, and fell deathly silent. There was such a blaze of anger in the Viscount's eyes as caused her to quake in her shoes. When he spoke, the deliberate calm in his voice was more alarming than a shout.

'It is as well that you refused me. If we were betrothed, such a remark would certainly tempt me to slap you.'

It had needed only that! Serena crumpled where she stood, half falling to slump upon the window ledge, and covering her face with her hands.

'Go away,' she whimpered. 'It is all of a piece. I had as well submit myself to Papa. You men are bullies all! I do not know why I should have thought you could be any different.'

Wyndham was already cursing himself. What had possessed him to carp at her? As if he would truly dream of offering her the slightest hurt! It was with pain that he saw the fight go out of her. He had meant to bring balm and aid, not push her further into the mire. And what was the implication in her reference to her father? But that could wait.

He came to her and slipped his arm about her where she sagged against the window ledge. She made a feeble effort to push him away, but he ignored it, drawing her forward and guiding her towards the chair in silence. Pulling up the other chair, he placed it close enough that he might take one hand in a comforting hold. Obeying his instinct, he infused command into his tone instead of gentleness.

'Tell me what happened.'

Serena's fingers trembled in his grasp. She was beyond thinking of anything but the deep despair of her situation. The words came haltingly, but she could not withhold them.

'Papa is—is set upon my accepting Hailcombe. He—he does not care that I detest the man. I have b-begged him not to f-force me into this m-marriage, but he is adamant. He threatens to b-beat me into submission, if I will n-not accede.'

She drew a shuddering breath, and Wyndham was obliged to clamp down upon the hot protests that rose to his tongue. Serena was not looking at him, and her free hand plucked aimlessly at the muslin folds of her gown.

'I meant to obey,' she said, suddenly turning the brown eyes upon him. 'After Lacey Court, I made up my mind that I should do so. But when it came to the point—when he...' Her voice faded out, and she shuddered, dragging her fingers free. 'I ran away from him! I hid in my chamber, and Papa banged on the door. I was too frightened even to answer him. Then—then Mel came, and Cousin Laura said I should come away with her.' A huge sigh escaped her. 'But I do not see what is to be done. Papa is bound to come here looking for me.'

'Then he must not find you!' said Wyndham with decision, rising to his feet.

Serena looked up at him, a tattoo starting up in her pulses. 'Why, do you think to hide me?'

He seized her hands and pulled her up. 'No, Serena. I think to marry you! Out of hand, if need be.'

Serena's heart took a leap that deprived her of her senses, and for an instant, the world spun. Had Wyndham not caught her, she knew she must have fallen. But the spurt of joy was swiftly over, and she found herself shaking.

'Pray let me go,' she managed to say. 'Give me a moment, if you please.'

'As many as you like,' replied Wyndham, himself prey to a discomfiting apprehension. He did not release her instantly, for she looked distinctly unsteady, but he relaxed his grip enough for her to slide out. Watching her shift slowly away towards the window, he found himself holding in abeyance a resurgence of the wounding sensations that had attacked him upon first hearing of her rejection.

But this was Serena in person—and the conviction grew upon him that she was going to refuse him, even in this extremity. He fought it down, for at this present he could think of no better method of rescue.

Serena was in turmoil. She was torn between a rash

impulse to give in to him, and an obstinate conviction that if she did so, she would be throwing away all hope of that rosy future she had once dreamed of, envisaging herself as his wife. She turned to look at him, and found his eyes intense with some emotion she did not recognise.

'You are proposing a flight to the border? I am under age. Do you wish for such a scandal?'

'It can't be helped,' said Wyndham brusquely. 'Your situation is desperate, and it calls for desperate measures.'

Overwhelming grief gushed into Serena's bosom, and she turned away. This was not how it should have been! She had never been a languishing miss, cherishing thoughts of romance. A marriage of mutual respect and liking had been all she had hoped to achieve. Nothing had been further from her mind than to discover in herself an obsessive *tendre* for a man to whom she longed to be betrothed.

But the Viscount had drawn her into a fatal attachment, making her foolish with dreams. And now, instead of a marriage that had the approval of all, she was offered a hasty scramble of a wedding that must subject her to the censure of her acquaintance—and the certain disapproval of her parent.

Wyndham moved into the room, driven by more than the desire to extract her from an unhappy fate. 'Serena, why do you hesitate?'

She did not look at him. 'It is not what I want.'

'Nor I, if there were any easier way, but—'

'Pray try to understand!' Serena burst out, moving

to face him. 'Don't think I am ungrateful, Wyndham. It is noble of you to offer it, but—'

'For pity's sake, don't talk such fustian, Serena!'

'—it is a solution,' she rushed on, as if she had not heard him, 'that could never bring contentment. To be forced into it, to take it for an alternative to a worse fate—and the dreadful scandal that must ensue. I could not do it! Nor should you, my lord. It is a recipe for disaster.'

He was frowning now, suspicion in his eyes. 'Not if there is a strong enough bond of attachment.'

The brown gaze met his own boldly. 'There cannot be that—where there is not also mutual trust.'

So she was at that again? Hurt welled up. 'I might have known it! Very well, take your chances with Hailcombe.'

Striding to the door, Wyndham set his fingers around the handle. But without turning it, he looked back.

'One day you will learn how you have misjudged me. I can only hope that you will not too bitterly regret it!'

November, 1811

After a restless night, Friday found the Viscount no nearer an acceptance of his own decision than he had been the day before. Having left Serena, he had put himself through an all too lengthy sojourn at White's, where he had imbibed freely of an excellent claret while animadverting with some degree of acidity on the general recalcitrance and waywardness of the female heart.

Lord Buckworth, who was upon the point of leaving for Brighton, had delayed his departure long enough to advise his friend to go home and put his head in a bucket. Wyndham having bitterly stated his preference for a noose, Buckworth had laughed at him and bid him instead accompany him to the coast.

'No, I thank you,' had growled the Viscount. 'I am in no humour to endure Prinny's excesses. Besides, she need not think that I will leave her to fall like a ripe plum into the hands of that blackguard!'

'Well said!' applauded Buckworth, a teasing glint in his eye. 'I am tempted to remain to pull you out of whatever undoubted scrape you are bound to throw yourself into, but I shall refrain. If a man can't win himself a doting wife without the assistance of his friends, he had better not have one at all!'

Wyndham had toasted this sentiment, tipping the remainder of the contents of his glass down his throat. But with his friend's departure the resurgence of bravado proved brief. If Serena would not marry him in this extreme, she must be wholly set against him. He had as well abandon the game and turn his thoughts otherwhere.

But the obstinate pull of his emotions would not let him. In the long night hours, he kept seeing Serena's face. As she had been in those early days last season, which was in stark contrast to the wan features lately imprinted upon his memory. She might say what she pleased, but she could not deny that she was deeply unhappy. And somewhere in the distant reaches of his mind lurked the conviction that she still cared for him.

It might have been that which sent him riding in the direction of Hay Hill after a vigorous half-hour of early exercise in the Park. Dismounting by the back garden gate, Wyndham called to one of the boys at work within the grounds of the Lacey house, and flicked him a coin to hold his horse. Trading on his close relationship to the family, he then walked up to the house and entered by the conservatory.

About to go through into the hall, he heard Serena's voice close at hand. Checking, he listened for its source, and had just decided that she must be in the room adjacent when he was alerted by the deeper tones of a man. For an instant, he thought it must be Hailcombe, and he strode forward a couple of paces towards an aperture. He knew this connected the conservatory with a summer saloon beyond, where the Laceys generally received visitors in warmer weather in order to enjoy the greenery.

Just as he reached it, he recognised the man's voice to be that of Lord Reeth. Halting before he could be seen, the Viscount unashamedly placed himself in a position outside the opening from which he might eavesdrop. The result was distinctly rewarding, if a trifle wounding to his pride.

To Serena's intense relief, her father's anger appeared to have spent itself. Cousin Laura had done her work well. There was a different air about him, and his manner towards her was a good deal less frightening.

'Laura tells me that you went off with Miss Lacey because you were afraid of me. Is that true, Serena?'

She was sitting in an alcove that gave onto the back gardens, in one of a suite of white-painted ironwork chairs. Together with the potted palms that graced the walls, and a number of exotic plants, the saloon had all the appearance of an indoor garden. It was little used at this season, so Melanie had said, deeming it a sufficiently private spot for this much dreaded visit. The winter sun made it a virtual hothouse, which perhaps contributed to Serena's feeling a trifle overwarm. However that might have been, she could not confront her parent without a degree of trepidation.

'Yes, Papa,' she answered breathlessly, watching him shift with apparent aimlessness in the free spaces of the saloon.

Reeth sighed heavily. 'I am sorry for it. I have been guilty of harshness towards you.' To Serena's mingled astonishment and dismay, he covered his eyes with one hand, and a note of anguish entered his voice. 'My only daughter! It is hard to bear!'

Serena stared at him, unable to think of anything to say. It was such an odd way for him to behave. And what in the world could he mean? What had he to bear? But in a moment or two he had collected himself. Emitting another sigh, he sought for a nearby chair and sat down. When he turned his eyes once more upon her, it struck Serena that he looked older, and careworn.

Impulsively, she leaned forward. 'Papa, are you ill?'

Her father shook his head, seeming to brush off this unaccustomed mood. 'Nothing of the sort. But we must needs be done with this matter, Serena. It is unbecoming in you to fly from your own father's protection. You must come home.'

Fearing to put him out again, Serena checked the protest that rose to her lips. It would not do to point out that she had flown because she needed protecting from him! But she was unable tamely to abide by his wish.

'I beg your pardon, Papa. I was too upset to be thinking of what was right. I want to come home, but I am afraid that you will not listen to my excuses.'

Her father's hands clenched where they were resting on the arms of his chair. 'Your words reproach me!'

'I did not mean it so.'

'I know. You need not explain further. You wish to give me your reasons for rejecting Hailcombe.' His voice became heavy, and he sagged where he sat. 'I would I might accept them, for I know them all. My child, I understand your dislike of the man, believe me!'

A rush of indignation beset Serena. 'But if you understood it, Papa, why—'

He threw up a hand. 'Do not ask me. I cannot tell you. Suffice it that I have a particular reason for this determination. You must wed him, Serena!'

This was utterly incomprehensible. He understood

her dislike, and he was sorry for having driven her to run away. Yet he could not release her from this intolerable future? She was to be given no reason, but she must marry a man she hated? She had as well have eloped with Wyndham after all!

The thought of the Viscount threw her into rapid speech. 'Papa, I have obeyed you in one matter which has caused me no small degree of heartache. Cannot you see your way to relieve me of obeying you in this?'

Reeth frowned. 'You are referring to Wyndham, I take it.'

A crushing at her breast made Serena's voice shake. 'You t-told me that you would have k-kept me at a distance from him had you known earlier of his true character. But it was too late, Papa! And yet I have given him up. You do not know what temptation has been put in my way to disobey you in this.'

'What are you saying?' demanded her father, a slight bark in his voice.

Serena shrank a little, and moderated her tone. 'I only mean to make you realise that I have not lightly disobeyed you in refusing to marry Hailcombe.'

'Yes, but what has occurred between you and Wyndham?'

'Nothing, upon my honour!' Serena assured him, horribly aware of perjuring her soul. Seeing that her parent looked far from satisfied, she sought her mind for some way of deflecting his question. 'I found it difficult to believe that what you told me about him is true. I have tried to ask Melanie—his cousin, you must know—but in a roundabout way. And she has nothing but good to say of Lord Wyndham.'

The Baron snorted. 'Of course she speaks well of him. Do you suppose she would tell you, even if she knew, which I'll wager she does not. No one is likely to have informed a young girl of her years that her cousin was one of the dissolute young men who hung about the Marquis of Sywell and emulated his vicious immorality.'

Despite all her own doubts, Serena experienced a rise of unprecedented fury at hearing the Viscount so described. She curbed it, for any attempt to defend him would inevitably draw Papa's fire. But she could not withhold a little protest.

'Yet it does not appear to be generally known.'

'How do you know? No one would speak of it to you either.'

'Perhaps the tales have been exaggerated,' she cried on a note of desperation.

'Your desire that it should be so, Serena, will not, I fear, make it so,' said Reeth heavily.

A fact of which she was only too well aware. But Wyndham had shown himself again injured by the accusation. If she had not experienced at first hand an instance of his depravity, Serena would have been much inclined to believe him innocent. How little Papa knew her, she realised, not to recognise that it was the very urgency of her desire for the stories to be proved to be without foundation that caused her rather to believe in them.

'Yet have you not seen, Papa, in my willingness to

give up all thought of Lord Wyndham that, despite all tender feeling towards him, I cannot marry a man whose way of life must disgust me? And still you would force me into wedlock with a man whom I can neither like nor respect!'

Her father sprung out of the chair, throwing his hands to his head. 'Heaven defend me, Serena! Cannot you see that I have no choice?'

Serena stared at him, bewildered. 'No choice! No choice but to give me up to such a man?'

Lord Reeth paced for a moment, running fingers through his hair in a way that disarranged the order of his bronze locks. It dawned on Serena that he was distraught. Her heart dropped, and a chill swept through her. Could it be true?

He turned to confront her, and there was a—yes, haunted!—look in his eyes. 'Serena, I regret it almost as much as you do. Perhaps more. It may have been wrong of me not to tell you this before. My child, I cannot save you from this marriage. There is a matter of honour at stake.'

The word struck Serena like a blow in the face. A feeling of deadness crept over her. Honour among gentlemen was sacred. It was the single quality that determined acceptance. To lose honour was worse than loss of life. Everything must fall before it.

She looked at her father, and saw a stranger. With a corroding sense of disillusionment, Serena realised that she was no longer afraid of him.

'I see. You must forgive my ignorance, sir. I had not realised that honour could demand that a man must sacrifice his daughter.'

Chapter Seven

Cousin Laura fidgeted with her spectacles, but it had no effect upon Serena. Disposing herself upon the day-bed in the nursery parlour, she had refused all attempts to dislodge her for any reason whatsoever. She lay back against the cushions she had piled behind her, and fanned herself gently, watching her duenna whip off the spectacles and pace to the door and back again to the fireplace. Then she directed a reproachful look upon her charge, replacing her spectacles for the purpose.

'I suppose you realise that you are in disgrace with your papa, child? I have done my best, but there is no moving him.'

Serena remained unchastened. 'I told you he would not budge.'

'Then I am at a loss to understand why you allowed him to persuade you to come home.'

Serena turned her gaze to the window. 'There was little point in withstanding him on that score.'

Her duenna rustled to the day-bed. 'Yet you persist in refusing to marry Hailcombe!'

'Yes,' agreed Serena, looking round. 'And I will persist despite anything Papa may say or do.'

Cousin Laura sighed, plonking down onto the end of the day-bed. Serena shifted her feet a little, and produced a weary smile. The fan stilled, held so between her fingers.

'It is of no use to try to persuade me, cousin. My mind is made up.'

'And Bernard's no less so!' Leaning forward, she reached for one of her charge's hands. 'I wish you will consider, Serena. Though he exhibits no anger now, I cannot answer for his temper. If it should overtake him again, I am much afraid that he will carry out his earlier threats. You cannot for ever lock yourself in your chamber.'

'I have no intention of locking myself in. Let him beat me if he chooses. I will not yield.'

Cousin Laura's astonished stare would have been amusing if Serena had been capable of laughter. Her duenna let go her hand and sat back, ripping off her spectacles.

'I have never heard you speak so. Are you not afraid?'

Serena's fingers tightened briefly on the fan. 'Of the pain of it? Certainly I am. But I had rather endure that than marriage with that hateful creature!'

'My poor girl, do you not understand? Your father can compel your obedience.'

'By what means, cousin? Unless he intends to dis-own me and show me the door, I do not see how—'

'He will scarcely proceed to such an extreme,' cut in Cousin Laura. 'But there is nothing to stop him forcing you to the altar. He has even spoken of bring-ing a priest here to perform the ceremony.'

Serena did not flinch. It was plain that her duenna had no notion how coldly determined she had be-come. As a means of avoiding Hailcombe, in the last three days she had denied herself when he called, sending a message that she was ill and keeping her room. She had backed this up with written excuses to every hostess to whom she was promised through the following week. And as if that were not enough, she had ordered that all her meals should be sent to her on a tray, either in her room or in this parlour. Cousin Laura came and went, but the only visitor admitted to her presence had been Melanie, who had come yes-terday to see how she did.

She had seen nothing of Papa. After their last in-terview, Serena felt no wish to speak to him. The worth of his regard had been tested, and found want-ing. Why should she have any scruple about failing in her duty? She could owe no duty to a father who would throw her life away to save himself. That Papa was conscious of the enormity of his demand had been made abundantly plain, and Serena felt confident that he would not seek her out. The more she took matters into her own hands, the stronger became her will to stand firm. But she had never felt so alone in her life.

'Cousin, it is you who does not understand,' she said patiently, feeling for all her youth as if she were the elder. 'Papa may do his worst, but a marriage ceremony cannot take place without my co-operation. If I refuse to say the vows, I cannot be married. And I will never vow myself to Hailcombe.'

Deep in his cousin's confidence, Wyndham's anxieties had been a trifle laid to rest by the report Melanie had given him. It was Thursday, and November was a week old—a week since Serena had left the Lacey house. His worry had been acute. Much as he applauded Serena's determination—as related to him by Mel—he could not feel sanguine about the outcome. Though her decision to keep her room must afford her protection, the Viscount felt it would prove temporary. From what he had discovered of Hailcombe, he could not but fear that the man would stop at nothing to gain his ends. While as for Reeth—! Here, Wyndham had recourse to a pull at the tankard from which he was refreshing himself in the Long Room at the Castle Tavern.

He had chosen this haunt of the boxing fraternity rather than the austere precincts of White's, in hopes of running into someone who might be acquainted with Hailcombe. All sorts and conditions of men frequented the Daffy Club, and his valet Streatley, who had been set to probe his rival's history, had told him that the fellow was a keen follower of the ring.

But though his eye might probe for someone he knew among those imbibing under the portraits, elegantly framed and glazed, of Mendoza and Belcher, along with others of their ilk who had distinguished themselves with their fists in past battles, Wyndham's mind was elsewhere.

Having been privileged to hear the disclosure that Reeth had made to his daughter, the Viscount had a strong desire to find out just how that gentleman's honour had come to be involved in the matter of Serena's marriage. Passing over the insulting nature of the fellow's remarks upon himself, it had become apparent that his own suit had foundered upon this obstruction.

It was just as he had several times suspected. Reeth had lied when he had said that Serena no longer favoured him. His heart had warmed to the evidence of her regard—culled from her own lips! She had not wanted to believe ill of him. Wyndham knew he had only himself to blame that she had ended by doing so. But the task of proving himself could not be undertaken until all danger to her was past.

The Baron's approval was no longer relevant. The man who could—in Serena's own words!—sacrifice his daughter to his own honour had forfeited any right to a say in her future. Even less could he be permitted to keep her from a man who truly loved her, and who would cherish her to the limit of his own disgrace or death.

But that was for the future. At this present, it behoved him to discover, if he could, what Hailcombe might intend. What incentive drove him, Wyndham could not tell. But if he had failed by fair means to win Serena, would he resort to foul? And what hold had he over her father?

This last was puzzling in the extreme. One would surmise that he owed the fellow money, except that Reeth was no gamester. Besides, the implication of dishonour hinted at something disreputable. Certainly the Baron's political standing could readily be placed in jeopardy.

He was no further forward in trying to think of a scandalous proceeding that might be laid at Reeth's door, when he was hailed by a couple of acquaintances whom he knew from his visits to Bredington.

'I didn't think to see you here, Wyndham,' said one. 'I thought your taste ran rather to swords than fisticuffs.'

Giles Rushford was a man for whom Wyndham had some sympathy. His father having dissipated his inheritance, Rushford was in much the same position as Hailcombe. But Giles was a man of honour, and his position in society was fixed.

Besides, his cousinship to Hugo Perceval, a handsome fellow of excellent family, cast an umbrella of respectability over Giles. For Hugo was nothing if not respectable. The Viscount knew him well, and must admire his uniform prowess at all forms of sport. But he found Hugo too apt to stand upon his dignity. Still, they had enjoyed good hunting together many a time, and he was glad enough to see him.

'How do you do, Perceval? No, Rushford, I am not generally a fan of boxing. I came looking for someone here, that is all.'

'You do not follow the Prince to Brighton?' asked Hugo. 'I had heard that Buckworth has gone there.'

'I have business in town.'

'Then you won't have heard the news?' Giles said thoughtfully.

'Giles, I hardly think—'

'Wyndham is as much our neighbour as anyone, Hugo. He is bound to hear of it sooner or later.'

The Viscount frowned in some degree of puzzlement. 'What are you talking of?'

It was Hugo who answered, his disapproval patent. 'It is only what was to be expected. Yet another scandal emanating from the Abbey. I wish that fellow Sywell might take a fall and break his neck!'

Wyndham began to see daylight. The cousins lived at Abbot Quincey, one of the villages that surrounded the infamous Steepwood Abbey in the vicinity of which Wyndham's own hunting lodge was situated. It was no pleasant thing at this juncture to be reminded of the iniquitous Marquis with whose name Reeth had seen fit to couple his own.

'What has he done now?'

'Driven his poor wife into running away from him,' Giles told him.

'What, the lodgekeeper's daughter he married last year?'

'Bailiff's daughter,' corrected Hugo. 'And it is less than a year since he scandalized the community with that piece of foolishness. The girl was barely one-and-twenty at the time.'

'The more reason for her to run away from the old

lecher,' put in Giles. 'Not but what it is by no means certain that she has run away.'

Hugo Perceval threw his cousin an austere look. 'If you set store by the ridiculous theory that Sywell has murdered her, Giles, I can only say that I do not.'

'Local gossip will have it so, I dare say?' suggested Wyndham, faintly amused.

'Lord, you know what country folk are like! Besides, it hardly accords with that part of the tale which declares there to be gold missing as well.'

'There is that,' Giles conceded. 'The one thing that is certain, Wyndham, is that the girl has disappeared. No one actually knows how long she has been gone, for to tell the truth, very few people have seen her since she married Sywell.'

'Very true,' said Hugo. 'She might have been gone for months for all anyone knew.'

Wyndham was more disgusted by these details when his own integrity had been called in question, than he might have been at any other time. To think that Serena could suppose him capable of the sort of conduct that might drive a young bride from her legitimate home!

'How is it that her disappearance has been discovered, if no one knows when she left the place?' he asked, although his interest in the subject was but tepid. For his part, Sywell was deserving of being abandoned.

'By the usual route, I imagine,' said Hugo, scorn in his voice. 'That fellow Burneck likely told it to the washerwoman.'

'Yes, Aggie Binns is about the only female who will venture near the Abbey these days,' assented Giles. 'As for Solomon Burneck, I have it from my sisters that he has been going about quoting from the Bible again. A habit of his whenever Sywell does anything particularly scandalous.'

The fellow Burneck, an unprepossessing individual with a hooked nose, was valet-cum-general factotum to the Marquis. The Viscount had met him once or twice, and found him a dour character, whose strange loyalty to Sywell had ever been a cause of question. Wyndham felt resentment boil up that Serena should believe him so lacking in taste as to frequent a hell-hole that contained this creature Burneck as well as the Marquis himself.

The cousins continued to speculate, but the Viscount was hardly attending. An unsettling notion had been borne in upon him. How could a girl of Serena's undoubted innocence know anything of that sort of licentious conduct indulged in by Sywell? Even *in extremis*, she had been steadfast in her refusal to marry him. She must have been severely shocked by what she had been told. Had her father or Miss Geary given her some of the gruesome details? Had either of them access to one of the residents around Steepwood? Who there might have chosen to vilify his character?

He was no nearer solving this problem by the time he returned to his lodgings in Ryder Street. He had long since removed from the Lyford family house in Berkeley Square, preferring the informality of this smaller apartment. It had a severely masculine parlour, containing little beyond a couple of red leather sofas, and a writing table upon the surface of which lay the paraphernalia of a bachelor existence. Magazines, discarded gloves, a dice-box and several silver containers used as a catch-all for visiting cards, buttons and other debris. The adjacent bedchamber, for which Wyndham headed, had only a comfortable bed, a press and a shaving-stand which serviced the needs of his toilette. The place was agreeably simple, in contrast to the cluttered furnishings of his allotted chamber at home.

Wyndham enjoyed the freedom of it, and nothing but his marriage would serve to alter the arrangement. Which brought him to the disagreeable recollection that at this present his marriage was not in question.

He was greeted by his valet with the depressing information that Hailcombe continued to haunt the Reeth house in Hanover Square.

'And in the foulest of moods from all accounts, m'lord,' reported Streatley, receiving the Viscount's coat and tenderly smoothing its folds. 'Seems he don't scruple to show his displeasure, for his man's been sporting a painted peeper these two days. And for all he says he had an argy-bargy with a misplaced door, I take leave to say it was his master's work.'

'You mean Hailcombe gave his own valet a black eye?' asked Wyndham incredulously, unfastening his waistcoat.

Streatley laid the folded coat carefully into one of the drawers of the press. 'If he didn't, there's no call for Togworth to speak surly of his nibs, which he does, m'lord, make no mistake.'

Wyndham handed him the waistcoat in silence, disquieted by the inevitable reflections that must beset him on discovering that Hailcombe was capable of this sort of petty violence. If the man could lay vengeful hands upon a blameless manservant, what price the safety of a recalcitrant wife? Put in mind of his own foolish threat of slapping Serena, Wyndham's conscience writhed. If he had not done so, would she have flown with him? No, for it had not been that which had stayed her. It was his alleged moral turpitude that had effectively barred him from that form of rescue.

He became aware that his valet was coughing in a meaningful way. He stripped off his shirt.

'What is it, Streatley?'

The valet went to pour hot water from the ewer into the basin. 'There's another matter as might warrant your lordship's attention.'

'Well?'

'Certain company as Togworth has been keeping, m'lord.' Holding a warm towel at the ready, Streatley waited for his master's face to emerge from the basin. 'When I went to meet him at The Feathers, m'lord, he was sitting close and murmuring with a set of fellows as one might expect to meet in a dark alleyway.'

Wyndham lowered the towel. 'Unsavoury?'

'Distinctly so, m'lord.'

A riffle of unease crept into the Viscount's chest. Hailcombe must be hatching something. If his valet was in a string with disreputable characters, the fellow could be up to no good. Had he not suspected as much?

'Keep your eyes peeled and your ears open, Streatley. Try if you can to get the measure of what may be in the wind.'

'I will do my best, m'lord.'

Wyndham passed a fretful night. Early on the following morning he sent a note round to his cousin, asking her to pay a visit to Hanover Square to find out how Serena did. He spent some hours at White's in a bid to prevent himself from brooding. But in the late afternoon, when no reply had been forthcoming, he set out on foot for Hay Hill to find that his cousin had only just returned.

Melanie, fresh as a rose in pink muslin, whisked him into the summer saloon. 'For Mama is bound to want to know the reason if she thinks we are talking secrets.'

'Have you seen Serena?' demanded the Viscount, brushing this aside. 'Is she well? Pray don't tell me that she has given in to Hailcombe, for I know he means mischief!'

'Given in?' echoed Melanie scornfully. 'Of course she has not given in! I told you she was utterly determined, even if her Papa should end by beating her.'

'He won't do that, I am persuaded. But how is she?'

'How do you know he won't? When he has threatened poor Serena I don't know how many times and—'

'Mel, I'll shake you in a minute! How—is—Serena?'

'There is no need to—'

'*Mel!*'

'Dear me, George, you must be in love!' His cousin giggled, as he made a purposeful move in her direction. 'No, don't! She is perfectly well, I assure you. At least—'

'What do you mean, "at least"?'

Melanie threw up her hands, dropping into one of the ironwork chairs. 'Lord, Wyndham, will you let me speak?'

The Viscount took a hasty turn about the room, setting the tassels on his hessians swinging. Then he, too, seated himself, sighing a little. 'Forgive me, Mel. If you knew what I have been through! But never mind that. Only tell me the truth, if you please.'

He was obliged to contain his impatience, for his cousin could not tell her tale without a good deal of embroidering comment. His air of calm was severely tested by an account—which he devoutly trusted Melanie was exaggerating—of Serena's state of mind.

'It seems to me, George, that she is dreadfully unhappy still, despite the strength of mind that compels her to stand out against them all. There is a look in her eyes—I cannot describe it, but—'

'Try, Mel!'

'Well,' pondered Melanie, frowning portentously, 'since you press me, I will say that it was as if the light had gone out of them.'

A shaft of something very like grief struck

Wyndham in the chest. That precious innocence—and it had been destroyed. He would give all he owned to bring it back!

With difficulty, he dragged his attention on to what his cousin was saying, and was conscious of a small degree of relief on learning that Serena was to leave the metropolis on the coming Tuesday.

'Then she will be out of harm's way.'

'Yes, but it is not comfortable for her, poor Serena,' said Mel distressfully. 'She says that her papa is disgusted with her, and that she is being sent home in disgrace.'

'No one is to know that outside of the family,' Wyndham said. 'On Tuesday, you say?'

'The twelfth. Is Tuesday the twelfth?'

Wyndham nodded. 'Four days. Then if she continues to keep her room, I do not see what either Hailcombe or Reeth can do in that time. And it will take her to safety, which is all that matters at this present.'

From this heartening belief he was rudely awakened on Sunday the tenth of November.

Having taken dinner at Limmer's with some of the few friends who had not been lured to Brighton by the presence there of the Prince Regent, Wyndham was enjoying a rare cigarillo, and—at this touchy point in his career—an even rarer moment of conviviality. This was rudely shattered upon receipt of a note from his valet urging his return home at his earliest convenience.

'I know your lordship will wish no delay in receiving the intelligence with which I am regretfully obliged to burden you,' ran this unwelcome missive.

His mind afire with a number of hair-raising possibilities, Wyndham excused himself to his friends and hurried back to his lodgings.

'Out with it!' he demanded of his grim-faced valet, who was waiting in the parlour. 'What have you discovered?'

'Does your lordship recall me speaking of Togworth taking up with some fellows I wouldn't care to run into after dark?'

'The devil! What about them, Streatley? Speak, man!'

The valet relieved him of his greatcoat and hat, and laid both aside, on the back of one of the leather sofas. 'I've been on the watch, so to speak, m'lord, and tonight I saw them again. Togworth wasn't with them at first, so I was able to park myself in a settle just behind so as he wouldn't see me when he did come in. And though they talked quiet, I was able to hear something of what was said.'

Even in his anxiety, Wyndham managed a short laugh. 'Well done, Streatley! I had no idea how excellent a conspirator you could be.'

The valet bowed. 'I am glad to be giving satisfaction, m'lord.' His face became grim again. 'Though I don't see as even the little intelligence I've gleaned is likely to satisfy you in the least.'

With mounting dismay, the Viscount learned that Streatley had gathered an impression of a scheme afoot. But although he could not say where or how, nor precisely what was planned, the Viscount was particularly alarmed by the fact that he was able to confirm mention of a date. The valet Togworth had specified Tuesday the twelfth of November—the very day fixed for Serena's journey to the Reeth estates in Suffolk.

That his visit was unwelcome came as no surprise. Wyndham watched Lord Reeth cross the library to the mantel and grasp it, turning there to confront him.

'If you are come to renew your offer, my lord, I must tell you at once that I have not changed my mind.'

Wyndham's smile was not pleasant. 'Is that why you refused at first to see me?'

He had sent back a message via the butler that he would remain outside the Hanover Square residence until Reeth saw fit to admit him. It had done the trick, as he had known it would. The last thing a politician needed was to arouse speculation in anyone who might chance by to see a prominent member of society parked upon his doorstep.

Reeth's roman nose went up. 'What is it you want, Wyndham?'

'To alert you to the fact that your daughter stands in danger from a set of ruffians whom I believe to be employed by Hailcombe,' said Wyndham without preamble.

A bark of laughter escaped his host. 'Poppycock!'

'Hear me out, sir. These fellows have been heard by my valet to speak of a plot due to be perpetrated tomorrow. Miss Reeth travels to Suffolk tomorrow, I believe.'

'What of it?' scoffed Reeth. 'Was her name mentioned?'

'Not specifically, but the man interviewing these rogues happens to be Hailcombe's valet.'

'And that makes Hailcombe suspect? Your imagination has been playing you false, Wyndham. I say again, poppycock!'

The Viscount regarded him through narrowed eyes. 'Is it? You will scarcely deny that the fellow is a suitor to Serena's hand. Nor that she is resolute in refusing him.'

Reeth's cheeks suffused with colour. 'Not that it is any of your affair, sir, but I deny neither of these facts. I would add, moreover, that you are in no small way to blame for the latter!'

It was Wyndham's turn to laugh. 'I wish it might be found to be so. But I believe Serena to have more commonsense—not to say taste—than to ally herself with such a man. My task, however, is not to bandy words with you on my own account, but to warn you that—'

'Enough!' roared Reeth suddenly, banging his fist upon the mantelpiece. 'I will hear no more of this! If you have barged your way in here to insult my friend—'

'I am amazed that you have the gall to call him friend!'

'*Will you have done, sir?*'

Wyndham checked a violent retort, reminding himself that his purpose would not be served by quarrelling with the man.

'Let us discuss the matter without heat,' he suggested coolly.

'Don't talk to me!' returned the other, rejecting this advice and pacing away from the fireplace. 'Who the devil are you to lord it over me as if you were betrothed to the girl? I refused you, damn it! By what right do you dare to come here?'

'If I had no other right,' Wyndham snapped back, unable to help himself, 'I could throw my honour in your face! Only it is evident that such an argument would scarcely weigh with you, my lord Reeth.'

'How dare you, sir?' raged Reeth, turning on him.

'I am sure you know well enough! Leaving that aside, this alone should suffice. You chose to vilify my character in a way that—'

'Impugning my honour, are you? Not content with insulting my friends, you now choose to insult me, damn your eyes! We'll see, my young buck! We'll see!'

Crossing to the fireplace again, Lord Reeth tugged upon the bell-pull. Turning there, he glared at his visitor, breathing heavily.

Wyndham surveyed him frowningly. This fury was out of all proportion. Was it bluster? Was there a degree of fear beneath the fierceness of those eyes? One thing was certain. Reeth was bent upon giving him no further opportunity to speak his piece. Should he reveal that he knew a good deal more than he ought? No, for that must involve him in admitting to having eavesdropped upon his host's conversation with Serena.

'Before you have me shown out,' he said quickly, for the man's intention was obvious, 'will you at least tell me what merit you see in Hailcombe that you can favour his suit?'

To Wyndham's surprise, a look of revulsion crossed Reeth's features. 'Merit? I wish he had any!'

'Then for pity's sake, what the devil possesses you to foist him upon your daughter?'

The look blanked out, to be replaced with a cold stare. 'I have nothing further to say to you, my lord.'

Wyndham might have argued, but he had heard the door open behind him, and turned to find the butler standing in the aperture.

'Lord Wyndham is leaving,' said Reeth.

Thoroughly disgusted, the Viscount favoured him with a look that he trusted advertised his feelings. 'One last word. I give you fair warning, sir, that I fully intend to frustrate whatever design may have been formed by the person about whom we have been speaking. As for my rights in the matter, I leave that to your own judgement.'

Lord Reeth replied only with a lift of that arrogant nose, addressing himself to the butler. 'Lissett!'

The butler moved into the room, but Wyndham had already turned for the door. His tone became ironic. 'Have no fear! It will not be necessary for you to lay violent hands upon me.'

The man bowed, and passing him, Wyndham withdrew.

* * *

'But why did he come, if it was only to see Papa?' asked Serena distractedly.

'It is no use asking me,' said her duenna, shuffling her spectacles on and off her nose. 'All I know is that he has put Bernard in a towering rage.'

Serena swished back and forth in the narrow confines of the nursery parlour, a prey to confusion. From her station on the day-bed—which had been moved so as to give on to a view of the square below—she had caught sight of the Viscount driving around the far corner. Due to the height of her second-floor window, he had been lost to sight immediately upon reaching their side of Hanover Square. But Serena had leapt up and had her nose to the pane in a moment.

Her heart pattering, she had seen Wyndham stand for some time upon the doorstep, while her mind had run crazily on what it might mean. Since that day when she had repulsed his scheme to save her from Papa's wrath, she had heard of his lordship only through Melanie. His cousin had declared him to be still devoted to her, but Serena had refused to listen. Especially since, along with that affirmation, Melanie had brought tidings of gossip concerning the Marquis of Sywell. A reminder of Wyndham's depravity that could only give her pain.

But today he had come in person, and the disappointment was acute when he failed to request an audience with Serena.

'Could he have gone to Papa to renew his suit?' she suggested, not without a guilty surge of hope.

'Not unless he is a fool,' declared Cousin Laura, seating herself upon the vacated day-bed.

'Why do you say that?' demanded Serena, conscious of an inappropriate annoyance.

'Why, my dear, because he must surely be aware that with all this talk of the Marchioness having run away from Steepwood, your papa is unlikely to have forgotten his involvement with her wretch of a husband.'

Serena halted in her perambulations about the room. She had forgotten that Cousin Laura's friend had also seen fit to burden them with this odious story. It was excessively difficult to stifle an unwarrantable urge to defend the Viscount. Yet she could not keep from speaking her mind.

'You can scarcely lay that at Wyndham's door.'

'Gracious, no,' agreed Cousin Laura, her eyes glinting through the spectacles. 'I am sure Sywell cannot have needed any assistance in driving the poor girl away. Though no one could have blamed her, Lucinda says, if she had gone off with some man.'

'Wyndham perhaps?' suggested Serena scathingly.

'Oh, no, for we would have been bound to hear of it, if that had been the case.'

It could not be, thought Serena resentfully, that the Viscount was too honourable a man to run off with the wife of another!

'Besides,' pursued the elder woman thoughtfully, 'it is not at all certain that Lady Sywell has indeed run away. Lucinda maintains that a number of persons believe that Sywell has murdered her.'

'You don't mean it!' exclaimed Serena, startled.

Cousin Laura nodded emphatically. 'The Roade girls—who live in the same village, you must know—are even said to have spent some time searching for the body.'

Serena shuddered. 'What a horrid place Steepwood must be! I hope I may never go there.'

The spectacles came off. 'There is only one place you are going, my child, and I must say that I am heartily glad of it!'

So indeed was Serena. She had scarcely been able to believe her good fortune when her father had announced that she was to return to Suffolk.

'I own I am astonished that Papa has given up,' she said, coming to sit beside her duenna upon the day-bed. 'I know he has said that he is sending me home in disgrace, but I care nothing for it. I will be out of Hailcombe's reach, and that is all that matters to me.'

Cousin Laura replaced her spectacles, sighing. 'I wish I might believe that our departure signals the end of that man's chances, but I am not sanguine. I think your papa is hopeful that you may come around to his way of thinking.'

'Well, I shan't,' said Serena, not mincing her words. 'I had rather hire myself out as a cookmaid!'

Her duenna was not inclined to give this declaration any credence. 'I fear you know nothing of the life of a servant, child. One week of domestic service, and even Hailcombe would seem a godsend. You had best consider the alternative before you flout Bernard when he next proposes this match to you.'

Serena shrugged. 'Very well, what is the alternative?'

Cousin Laura took off her spectacles, and a sad little smile crossed her mouth. 'I am, Serena. Look at me. Look at my life.'

With which, the duenna rose up and quietly left the room. Serena stared after her, a bleak sense of emptiness pervading her bosom. A despairing protest rose up. That could not be her future! *He* would not leave her to that. He might have gone just now without seeing her—how could he see her, when Papa was so much against him?—but Serena was sure he would marry her in the teeth of them all, if he thought she was to suffer that fate.

Then Serena remembered the Marquis of Sywell, and came down to earth with a bump. Between the devil and the deep blue sea! How in the world was she to decide?

There being no immediate solution forthcoming, Serena sought relief in going to her bedchamber to supervise Mary in the packing of her garments. The task served to distract her mind from the problem of her destiny, and by the time it was finished, Serena was so tired that she dropped readily into bed after consuming the repast brought to her room, and was soon asleep.

The morning brought all the bustle of preparing for departure. When the footmen arrived at her bedchamber to carry her belongings down to the coach, Serena went to her nursery parlour to partake of breakfast. She was writing a hasty note of farewell to Melanie when Cousin Laura burst into the room in a state of unaccustomed dismay.

'Oh, Serena!'

'Why, what is it, cousin? You look as pale as death!'

The duenna's spectacles came rapidly on and off upon each bursting phrase. 'The most dreadful thing—and I do not know what to do! He will not listen to me. I have begged and pleaded—but to no avail. I cannot move him!'

Serena grabbed her arm with one hand, and removed the spectacles from her cousin's wild grasp. 'What in the world is the matter? Tell me, pray. Is it Papa?'

Tears stood in Cousin Laura's frenzied eyes, as she nodded. 'He has had all my trunks removed from the carriage. I think he has run mad!'

'Had all your trunks removed?' echoed Serena blankly. 'But, why, cousin?'

'Because he refuses to allow me to go with you. He says you must travel alone.'

Chapter Eight

Serena fairly gaped. 'But—but you must go with me. How can I possibly travel unchaperoned?'

'Bernard says you will have Mary, and—and that must suffice you. Nothing will move him! I have tried every argument I can think of, Serena.'

'Why? I don't understand, cousin.'

'No more do I. Do you think I have not asked him?' Seizing her spectacles from Serena's slack grasp, she rammed them into her face. 'I declare, I have never been so cross with Bernard! All he will say is that you must be punished, and to go alone will serve his purpose.'

A pulse began to throb in Serena's veins. Why should she be surprised? A father who could prefer his own honour to his daughter's happiness might as easily be as careless of her safety. Not that it was a great distance to the Reeth estates, but she would certainly be travelling all day.

'At least you will not be spending a night on the road,' said Cousin Laura worriedly. 'Although I told

Bernard that an accident might put you to the necessity. What with the weather turning, and the roads so bad, who is to know what might not happen?'

But Serena was too angry to put her mind to probabilities. 'There is always the coachman. I suppose Papa is not minded to let me go without him!'

'Don't be silly, Serena, how could you do so?' chided her duenna, too upset to be susceptible to sarcasm. 'Oh, dear, whoever would have suspected that Bernard could be so careless of your reputation? Setting aside the danger, it is most improper. And you will have to stop to eat. Gracious, you will be alone in a public inn! You must demand a private parlour, Serena, and make sure Mary remains with you. Oh, dear, I only hope you are not seen by anyone who knows you.'

'Well, if I am, it will serve Papa out,' said Serena snappily. 'It is all of a piece. Not that I anticipate any danger, but it just shows how little he cares for me.'

Cousin Laura readily agreed, adding that she had not thought it of him. 'It was bad enough to be forcing you into wedlock—and in so brutal a fashion!—but this goes beyond the line of what may be tolerated.'

Yet there was nothing she could do, as Serena pointedly reminded her. 'Don't fret, cousin. I cannot think that any ill will befall me. Why do you not ask Lissett to make certain to send a groom along with a blunderbuss, if you are so concerned? Papa cannot object to that.'

'He may object if he likes,' said Cousin Laura with

decision, 'but it will be after the event, for I shall not tell him!'

Filled with a new determination, she departed, leaving Serena to her uncomfortable reflections. It was all very well to have buoyed up Cousin Laura with a show of bravado, but the further evidence of Papa's lack of affection could not do other than sink her spirits. No father who truly cared for his daughter could subject her to the indignity and discomfort of travelling for such a distance with only her maid for company. And for a punishment! Was he so lost to all sense of what was due to her? Had his obsession with this arrangement he had made to marry her to Hailcombe completely deprived him of that level of responsibility which she had believed him to possess? And he a politician. What his colleagues might say to such conduct, Serena dared not think.

She had been looking forward to going—not least for the imminent prospect of seeing little Gerald—but now her feet dragged as she went upstairs to fetch her pelisse and tie on her bonnet.

Mary had laid out a thick travelling cloak as well, for the weather had worsened, and the November fogs had started. A weak sun was at present in evidence, but it could hardly be relied upon. And though a hot brick would undoubtedly have been provided, it was bound to be cold in the coach.

Serena had not thought that anything could make her feel worse than she did already. She was in the hall, clad in the furred woollen cloak that covered her shoulders and enveloped the green pelisse, adding extra warmth to just below the knee. The moment had come to say farewell, and she became aware that Lord Reeth was nowhere to be seen.

'Where is my father, Lissett?'

The butler appeared apologetic. 'He is in the book-room, Miss Serena.'

'Does he know that I am about to leave? Shall I go up to him there?'

Lissett coughed delicately. 'His lordship asked me to convey his good wishes for your journey.'

Serena stared hard at the butler, feeling as if a stone were lodging in her chest. 'You mean that he does not wish to see me to say goodbye in person?'

The butler maintained a prudent silence, but the answer was evident in his concerned features.

Serena drew a painful breath. 'I see.'

'Oh, Serena!' wailed the duenna.

If only Cousin Laura had not burst into sobs, and hugged her charge so tightly. If Lissett had not chosen to produce a little flask before handing her up into the coach, urging her to drink.

'A nip will warm you, Miss Serena.'

She obligingly sipped a little of the brandy, and returned the flask, her smile a trifle uncertain. Then Mary must needs weep copiously as she climbed in beside her mistress, clutching a basket of choice sweetmeats sent up by the cook for Serena's refresh-ment upon the way.

The sympathetic kindness of her well-wishers only served to drive in deeper the hurt inflicted by the one person who ought to have made her comfort his first concern. And Serena saw the waving hands and bravely smiling faces only through a blur as the coach moved off.

Wyndham was only half-aware of the desultory chatter at a slight remove from where he sat. There were few gentlemen gathered thus early in the coffee-room at White's, for it was not yet eleven. And the one he had hoped to see was not among them.

He was deeply troubled, for he found himself at a stand. It was one thing to assert his determination to protect Serena at all costs from Hailcombe's machinations, but when it came to the point, he knew not how to proceed.

He had little enough to go on. He knew that Serena was travelling to Suffolk today, and he had every reason to suppose that Hailcombe intended some mischief. But the rest remained a mystery. It was a great pity that Streatley had not managed to glean anything more useful.

The Viscount had toyed with the notion of confronting Hailcombe with an outright demand to know what he would be at. But the fellow was certain to prove even more obdurate than Reeth. And the devil of it was that, with a ready welcome in Hanover Square, Hailcombe had the advantage of him. He had himself no means of discovering what time Serena and her chaperone meant to set out, although he must guess that they would make an early start. Unless they intended to spend a night on the road, which he could not think to be likely. The journey was lengthy, but in a well-sprung coach, it could certainly be accomplished in one day.

But the coach would make slower progress than his own curricle and four. He felt confident of overtaking it within a very few hours, should it prove expedient to chase after Serena. Indeed, he was rapidly inclining to the view that this would be his best course. In the meanwhile, the presence of Miss Geary must afford Serena protection. But he had already alerted his servants to make certain preparations, and had dropped in at White's in a last-ditch hope that Buckworth might have returned from Brighton, for the Prince, so he had heard, had left there on the ninth, some three days since.

There was no sign of his friend, however, and Wyndham had to abandon a half-formed idea of asking his aid and advice. He uncrossed his legs, which were encased in fashionable yellow pantaloons, and laid down the paper he had taken up. A pretence of reading had enabled him to avoid participation in the prevailing discussion. Just as he did so, he caught the name of his arch-rival on the lips of one of the gentlemen involved, a man by the name of Ingleborough.

'I must say, I never thought that fellow Hailcombe might succeed. Yet I had it from Boulby, who met him last night at the Daffy Club, that he was boasting of his conquest.'

A disbelieving laugh came from one of his companions. 'Her fond father has never consented?'

Wyndham stiffened. There could be no doubt of whom they were speaking. Let one of them but mention her name, and he would know what to do about it!

'I suppose he must have done,' Ingleborough was responding. 'Though I must say, Millhouse, it seems most odd.'

'What's odd?'

'Well, Boulby said Hailcombe claimed that he would have a certain young miss—who shall, of course, be nameless—for his wife within the day.'

'Within the day! What, is it an elopement?'

There was a general laugh, and a sensation of disgust warred in Wyndham with a surge of fury. How dared they bandy her affairs about the club!

'Boulby thinks it's a hum. We all know how arrogant Hailcombe is.'

'Yes, but his quarry is leaving town today,' argued Millhouse, 'or so I heard.'

'If you ask me,' chimed in another voice, whose identity was hidden from the Viscount for his chair backed towards him, 'that golden-haired chit don't like him above half.'

'What's that to say to anything?' returned Millhouse. 'Anyone can see that Reeth is thick as thieves with the fellow. Lay you any money she takes Hailcombe.'

Two of his companions immediately closed with the wager, adding to Wyndham's discomfort. Instinct urged him to call them all to account. But he knew that to do so would serve only to precipitate further talk. He stood up, intending at least to make his presence felt, for he knew well that his own pursuit of Serena was widely known.

Just then the fellow he could not see piped up. 'I wonder what Wyndham will have to say to it?'

There was a flurry of determined coughing from those who were facing Wyndham and had seen him rise. The speaker turned his head, and his eyes popped.

'Wyndham, sir,' said the Viscount in a voice of ice, 'will say that he had always supposed White's to be inhabited by gentlemen—and not by gossiping hens!'

He executed an ironic bow into the embarrassed silence, and walked out of the coffee-room. He was seething, not least at Hailcombe for the possession of a careless and arrogant tongue. Or had it been carelessness? A cold feeling drove through the anger. Had it been part of Hailcombe's scheme to set in train a babble of talk that must inevitably damage Serena's reputation? Was he attempting to make it impossible for her to do other than marry him in order to save her face?

One of the footmen assisted him on with his greatcoat and beaver, and Wyndham, lost in a brown study, almost collided in the doorway with a fellow who was just entering the building. He fell back with a word of apology.

'It makes no matter,' began the other man, and stopped with a look of surprise. 'George Lyford, is it not? Or rather, Viscount Wyndham?'

Wyndham looked more closely, and thought he discerned a vague familiarity in the features of the fellow who was accosting him. He was a man something of Wyndham's own height, but loose-limbed, and perhaps a few years older. He was removing his hat to reveal a head of fair hair, and a pair of grey eyes smiled at Wyndham out of features strongly tanned.

'Lewis Brabant,' said the gentleman encouragingly. 'We used to hunt together some years back. When you stayed at Bredington, remember?'

Wyndham's puzzlement cleared. This was another of the inhabitants of the area around Steepwood Abbey. It crossed the Viscount's mind that the place seemed to have an insistence at the moment on forcing itself upon his notice. Nevertheless, he greeted the newcomer with cordiality.

'You are Admiral Brabant's son. You went to sea, did you not? How do you do?'

Shaking hands, Brabant said that he did very well, but that he had sold out and was in fact just returning home. Dredging his memory, Wyndham recalled that his brother had died a couple of years back.

'Are you leaving? Come back in and have a glass with me,' suggested Brabant.

Wyndham hesitated. While he did not wish to appear discourteous, he was in something of a hurry. Brabant's look became questioning.

'You are pressed for time, perhaps? Don't let me keep you, if that is the case.'

But the Viscount thought he detected a shade of disappointment in his tone, and was conscious of regret. He had warm memories of Lewis Brabant, a less dashing fellow than his brother, but Wyndham had preferred the quieter and more intelligent of the two. Nevertheless, he could hardly afford to delay. His horses were swift, but Serena had all too likely set off already.

He felt obliged to refuse. 'I wish I might, Lewis, but I'm in the devil of a hurry. There's a matter demanding my urgent attention, and—'

Struck by a new thought, Wyndham broke off. Hailcombe had served in His Majesty's naval forces! It might well be that Brabant had known him—or heard of him at least. He might learn something of the man that could be turned to advantage.

Smiling suddenly, he gave his hat up to the footman again. 'But why not, after all? I'll take a glass with you, by all means, Brabant. Though it must be a swift one.'

'As swift as you please,' agreed the other.

Having divested himself again of his greatcoat, Wyndham bade a waiter bring them some wine and led the way into one of the parlours, preferring not to encounter the frozen faces of his earlier companions in the coffee-room.

Several moments were taken up with relating what had happened to various mutual acquaintances, and the discovery that Lewis had advanced to the rank of Captain. Wyndham was searching his mind for a casual way to bring Hailcombe into the conversation, when Lewis disconcerted him by touching on the question of his matrimonial prospects.

'I had heard from some source or other that you were on the point of offering for the prettiest débutante of the season, George. Am I to wish you happy?'

Wyndham fairly winced. 'Sadly, no.'

'I am sorry to hear it, if it was what you wished for. I never heard her name.' He seemed to note the Viscount's unease, for he added quickly, 'But don't mention it, if you would rather not.'

'I have no objection to telling you her name,' said Wyndham, an edge to his voice. 'It is Reeth. Miss Serena Reeth.'

'Reeth?' echoed Lewis. 'She wouldn't be related to the Reeth who is involved in politics?'

Wyndham frowned. 'His daughter. Why, do you know him?'

Brabant shook his head. 'Not him, but his brother. Lieutenant Reeth. We served together on *Neptune* at Trafalgar. Under Captain Fremantle it was then. He was a devil of a fellow, Gerald! Utterly fearless. Too much so, in fact, for it cost him his life.'

'How was that?' It was interesting, if not yet useful.

Lewis related briefly the circumstances of Lieutenant Reeth's death. In the heat of battle, a youthful midshipman had been hit, falling overboard.

'When Gerald saw that he was still alive, he first attempted to throw the boy a rope. But the poor fellow couldn't seem to grasp it. And the sea was aflame below with debris from a burning vessel. But Gerald wouldn't leave him. He stripped off his coat and handed me his sword. Then, before anyone could stop him, he had leaped over the side.'

'The devil he did! Did he succeed in rescuing the boy?'

Brabant nodded. 'No one really knows what happened next. And the boy was too dazed. We pulled him up with the rope strapped about his chest. But Gerald went under—and he didn't come up again. His body was never found.'

It was a shocking tale, distracting the Viscount from his mission as he listened to a recital of the speculation that had attended the death of Lieutenant Reeth. The best guess seemed to be that he had got caught on hidden debris under water, and been burned along with it. The *Neptune* had been obliged to change position in the battle soon after, and no one had therefore been able to determine the precise circumstances.

'He was a good fellow,' Lewis finished. 'He'd have had a Captaincy by now.'

Wyndham made an appropriate response, but he could see nothing in this story to help him. These events had occurred six years ago, and could have no bearing on the present. But it had given him the opening he needed.

'Tell me, Lewis. Did you ever come across a fellow named Hailcombe?'

Captain Brabant happened to be taking a sip of wine just at that moment, and the name appeared to affect him powerfully. He sputtered, choked over the claret and fell into a fit of coughing. Wyndham got up and gave him a buffet on the back. In a moment or two, he had recovered himself, and the Viscount returned to his own chair in frowning question.

'I take it you've heard the name,' he suggested drily.

'Heard it? I've cursed it—and with frequency!'

A rush of triumph engulfed Wyndham, and he reached for the bottle of claret. 'Another glass, my friend? You interest me very much indeed.'

Fifteen minutes later, the Viscount left White's, feeling that his time had been well spent, even if it meant that he would now be further behind in the chase than he could wish. He had occasion, however, to revise this opinion. Awaiting him at his lodgings, he discovered his cousin Melanie, in company with an extremely agitated Miss Laura Geary.

The oppression of spirits that had attacked Serena at the beginning of her journey had lifted a trifle, though it had left her with the sensation of having a dead weight in her chest. Which could not in all honesty be attributed wholly to Papa's unkind conduct. For her obstinate thoughts, refusing to obey her own commands, insisted upon presenting her with a collage of images—all on the same theme. Since there was no point in thinking of Lord Wyndham, it was distressing to discover that she could not get him out of her head. Even more so to find that instead of being thankful to be getting out of London and away from Hailcombe, she was counting the miles that were taking her further and further away from the Viscount. And depressing herself thereby.

For ever since Wyndham's visit to Hanover Square yesterday, Serena realised, she had been foolishly cherishing a hope that his lordship might be proved innocent of the charges laid against him. Had he not said that she was misjudging him? Were it not for Cousin Laura's horrid friend, whose information must be counted impartial, Serena would believe Wyndham. For Papa she could no longer trust.

How dreadful to be obliged to say so! A faint sigh escaped her, drawing her maid's attention. The girl proffered the basket she held, uncovering the napkin in which the various items from Cook had been wrapped.

'Have another sweetmeat, Miss Serena.'

Serena selected a sugared almond, and chewed in silence for a moment, tucking her hands back inside her muff. 'How long have we been upon the road, Mary?'

'Near two hours, Miss Serena. We're just past The Bald-Faced Stag, and will be within the forest in a moment.' The girl apparently felt Serena's tension. 'You've no call to be afraid, Miss Serena. Mr Lissett give orders as Harbottle was to ride on the box with the blunderbuss.'

Epping Forest was certainly one of the danger spots, but Serena knew that there was nothing to fear in the daylight hours. Besides, it was a mere matter of six miles or so to Epping Place, and there were bound to be people abroad.

'I am not afraid, Mary. We are in no danger from highwaymen at this hour.'

Serena saw that her maid was peering at her in the gloomy interior, for the day was dull and heavy with cloud, affording little light to the travellers. The gathering denseness of the encroaching trees as they entered the forest did nothing to improve matters.

'What is it, Mary?'

The maid laid a hand upon her arm. 'I don't like to say nothing, Miss Serena, only you don't seem nowise happier.'

'Don't I? Well, I am finding it a trifle difficult to be happy just now.'

'Oh, Miss Serena, I'm that sorry,' uttered Mary, squeezing her arm. 'But nothing ain't nowise so bad as it can't be cured, you'll see.'

'Will I?' said Serena doubtfully. If so, that cure seemed a long way off.

'I was thinking as how it might be good for you to go home,' pursued the maid. 'I mean, seeing Master Gerald and all. He must miss you something terrible.'

'Thank you, Mary,' Serena said, patting her hand and laying it gently aside. 'I am not unmindful of your care of me. And yes, I am looking forward to seeing Gerald. Only—'

A sudden and deafening report interrupted her, accompanied by a medley of shouts. From without came a confusion of stamping hooves and cursing. The coach lurched, throwing both startled occupants forward. There was a piercing cry, a flurry of hoofbeats, and the vehicle came to a halt.

Serena, her heart in her mouth, righted herself in the seat. Hearing a whimper beside her, she turned to find Mary in a heap on the floor of the coach. A swift decision was dictated by common sense.

'Stay there, Mary!' she ordered in an urgent whisper. 'It will be safer.'

Holding her breath, Serena waited within the dark interior, as shadows passed the window, and a rumble of deep voices indicated the presence of several men. Seconds crawled by while nothing happened. Then the door was wrenched open, and a figure in a mask leaned into the aperture, blocking out the light.

Serena could not forbear a frightened gasp, but she sat still, staring at the monstrous dark shape that observed her in silence for a space. Her heart thumped painfully in her bosom, and all thought was suspended.

Then the figure shifted out of the doorway, and a large gloved hand gestured towards her with a pistol.

'Come on out, missie!'

'Don't, Miss Serena!' quavered Mary from the floor.

'Quiet!'

Let them not realise that there were two females in the coach! Pushing herself up, Serena reached towards the door. She was immediately obliged to grasp at the jamb, for she discovered that her knees were shaking.

Her hesitation caused the masked man to mutter an impatient exclamation. She was roughly seized by the waist, and dragged from the coach. Landing somewhat abruptly, Serena had all to do to keep herself from falling. But in a moment, she had regained her balance, and was able to look about her.

After the gloom of the carriage, there was a surprising amount of light coming through the trees, despite the dullness of the day. The fellow who had ordered her from the coach still stood by its door, surveying her. Upon the box, both groom and coachman were held at pistol point by two masked riders. So much for the precaution of Harbottle and his blunderbuss! The poor man could have had no time to fire it. Another rider, also masked and armed, had reined in at the side of the coach, and was holding a fourth horse, presumably that of her captor.

Serena's glance went from one to the other. All were in frieze coats and slouch hats pulled low over their eyes, lending each a sinister aspect. She felt as if she were trembling all over, and involuntarily clutched her cloak tightly about her. But the only thought in her head was to prevent these undoubted highwaymen from seeing the depth of her fear.

'Is it the one?' came gruffly from the mounted man. 'Can't properly see her face.'

'Nor me,' growled the fellow on the ground. He approached Serena, and she flinched back. 'Now then, me beauty. I ain't going to harm yer. Just want a glimpse of yer hair.'

With which, he reached out and flipped the low-brimmed bonnet, which fell back on to Serena's shoulders, revealing her golden locks.

'Aye, that's she,' confirmed the man on the horse.

'She it is,' agreed his companion, peering closely into Serena's face. 'Yaller hair, brown eyes.'

It was as much as Serena could do to refrain from wrenching away. She was obliged to clench her teeth together, glaring into the fearsome eyes that examined her from above the black handkerchief that hung over the rest of the man's face.

A coarse laugh escaped him as she stood back. 'She ain't short of spunk.'

He shifted away to the other horse and entered into a low-voiced conversation with the rider. Serena breathed more easily, and it occurred to her to wonder why they had not yet demanded any money or jewels. Her mind ran rapidly over the belongings reposing in her trunks, trying to recall which of the more valuable trinkets she had selected to bring with her out of the collection inherited from her mother.

She saw Mary peeking from the open doorway of the coach, and gestured her back with a minute wafture of her fingers. Thankfully, the maid's features disappeared. Serena was only too well aware that while her gentility provided her with some measure of protection—for it was unlikely that these men would do more than take her valuables—her maid's class made her vulnerable. There was no saying what they might not do upon discovering Mary hiding there.

It seemed an age that she waited, while the men conferred together in low tones. Serena had just begun to wonder whether some chance wayfarer might not come to their rescue, when a distant rumble coming from behind signalled the approach of another carriage.

There was a concerted shift from all the highwaymen. Those covering the servants on the box shunted their mounts back a pace. The one on foot took a few hasty steps towards the rear of the coach, and the rider sidled his horse on to the verge.

Serena thought they were poised for flight, and toyed for a moment with the idea of running for the doorway of the coach. But it was obvious that the man afoot was close enough to catch her before she could reach it.

For several moments there was no sound but the growing rumble of the approaching carriage, and the distinct pounding of hooves upon the ground.

Then they ceased, as if the vehicle had come to an abrupt halt. The second rider shifted back to the other mounted men, and handed the rein of the led horse to one of them. Then he broke away. But instead of fleeing, he sped off in the direction from which the sounds had come. Serena had no time to speculate, for the first man took several hasty steps towards her. Instinct made her attempt an escape, but an iron grip caught at her.

'No, you don't! This is where we gets what's coming to us, and I ain't a-losing of it now.'

Her arms were pinioned behind her. A recognition of the oddity of this whole proceeding sprang into her mind. If she had before been frightened, terror now rooted her to the spot. She could not have struggled had she wanted to, for the horridest suspicion dominated her thoughts.

Highwaymen they might be, but these men had a darker purpose. They knew her. They must have been lying in wait for her. She was a prize worth some sort of ransom, and someone would pay them well. And that someone, she felt certain, was in the coach behind.

Sitting bolt upright, her face turned determinedly away from the loathsome creature beside her, Serena strove against an overwhelming desire to scream. With one hand she was grasping the strap, in a grip far stronger than was required by the swaying progress of the hired chaise, which rumbled along behind only one pair of horses. The other hand, tucked under her cloak out of sight—for her muff had been lost in the scuffle—was clenched so tightly that the nails dug into her palms.

She had long abandoned speech. Having vent her outrage in no uncertain terms, she now sat mumchance, refusing to respond to anything her abductor chose to say.

He had not even had the courage to do his dirty work himself. Instead, he'd had ruffians do it for him, exposing her to the roughness of a brutish highwayman.

For upon a signal from his companion who had ridden ahead, the man had dragged her to his horse and flung her across his saddle bow. Serena had heard Mary's shrill protests, which had been summarily stopped—leaving Serena to wonder later what horrid measures had been taken to ensure her silence. She devoutly trusted that they could not have been worse than what had befallen her mistress. Winded, Serena had been jolted for an excessively uncomfortable space—mercifully not far—and had then been dumped unceremoniously to the ground.

Her legs had been trembling, and her breath too short for protest when she saw Hailcombe waiting by the chaise. For several hideous seconds she had remained mute and resistless. But the instant her captor had begun to move, pulling her towards her hateful suitor, Serena had given way to panic. Losing all control, she had struggled madly, shrieking at the unresponsive post-boy for aid until the villain who had her captive had clapped a hand over her mouth.

He had manhandled her into the clutches of the vile beast who now had her at his mercy, and who had not scrupled to show his power. The smart at her cheek had dulled, but she felt battered, and was certain that both her upper arms and wrists would be found to be bruised.

Oddly, the pain of the blow had made Serena more angry than afraid. Her struggles had ceased, but she had poured venom upon Hailcombe's head with words that she had not even known were at the command of her tongue. It was only now, with leisure to recognise the invidious nature of her situation, that the fear had returned. But this time she was determined not to show it.

Outside, the dense trees began to give way to open

country, and it was borne in upon Serena that they were emerging from the forest. With a jolt at her stomach, she discovered that the terrain was unfamiliar, and realised that until this moment she had given no thought to the direction of travel. She remembered that shortly after Hailcombe's chaise had started off, it had passed her own coach and continued upon the same route. But had it then changed direction? Or had she not noticed Epping Place and missed the turn off to Duck Lane at the North Weald turnpike?

Forgetting her resolve not to exchange another word with the wretch who had served her so ill a turn, she turned her head to look at him.

'Where are we?'

Even in the gloom Hailcombe's eyes lowered at her under the heavy brows. A voluminous greatcoat and a hat cocked in the naval style made him appear monstrously large.

'Got your temper back, eh? Trust you've realised that it's dangerous to cross me?'

Serena felt her muscles tighten. 'I said, where are we?'

A coarse laugh came at her. 'You've a deal of courage, I'll give you that. We're past Woolreden, and heading for Waltham Abbey.'

Waltham Abbey? 'Then we are driving cross-country.' A throb began in her chest as an inkling of his purpose seeped into her mind. 'And after Waltham Abbey?'

'Hatfield.' A note of smugness was in his voice.

'On the Great North Road, Serena. I'm sure you know that.'

She did indeed know it. Her stomach lurched. 'Scotland!'

'Bright, aren't you? Yes, we are going to Scotland.'

Serena was so much shocked by this disclosure that she closed her lips upon any further utterance, turning despairing and unseeing eyes first upon the post-boy—heavily bribed, no doubt, since he had been blind and deaf to her sufferings!—and then upon the view beyond the window. It was some time before she was able to control a desire to weep. She would not give Hailcombe the satisfaction of seeing her so reduced.

This resolve was sorely tried as they passed through Waltham Abbey, and when the coach stopped for a change two miles further on at Waltham Cross, Serena even toyed with the idea of leaping out. If she could get away, she might hide herself out in the fields. But it was certain that Hailcombe would catch her before she could reach any sort of haven.

When the carriage turned on to the road to Hatfield, Serena could barely repress a cry of protest. But presently, the pangs of despair gave way to hunger, and she recalled that she'd had nothing but sweetmeats to eat since breakfast.

'What time is it?' she asked, forgetting that she was not speaking to Hailcombe.

Her companion fished out his fob watch and consulted it in the light from the window. 'Going on for two and thirty.'

'No wonder I am hungry! Can we not stop to eat?'

'We'll dine at Welwyn for the change.'

'How far is that?'

'Ten miles from Hatfield, I'd say.'

And for Hatfield, upon enquiry, Serena discovered they had to go another seven or so miles. Oh, it was too bad! Not content with employing those horrid men to drag her to him, he must needs starve her too. She gazed miserably out at the dull day, which only added to her discomfort.

'I'll get you cakes at Hatfield,' Hailcombe offered.

Serena was too sunk in gloom to answer. The time dragged, and her stomach gnawed. When she tried to think how to extricate herself from this intolerable fate, she found her mind as dull as the weather, devoid of ideas.

Hailcombe alighted at Hatfield, and returned with a plate of cakes and a glass of wine. Serena would have liked to spurn them, but her hunger quickened at the sight and she took them gratefully, seizing upon a cake and stuffing it into her mouth. Her escort seemed not to be impatient, but made the post-boy keep the fresh pair waiting for several moments while Serena ate another two cakes and downed the wine.

When they again set off, she felt so much revived that she began to cast about in her mind for some means of escape. But by the time she had discarded at least five promising ideas on the score of their likelihood of casting her into worse trouble, she found herself once again aroused to wrath.

'Why in the world has it to come to this?' she

demanded. 'And pray do not say it is my fault for refusing to marry you.'

'I won't say that,' Hailcombe agreed readily. 'It was your father thought you'd reconsider. I had no such illusion.'

'You cannot mean that you have had this scheme in mind from the outset?' asked Serena, aghast. Had her rebellion been altogether futile?

Hailcombe laughed out. 'What, toil all the way to Scotland? No, m'dear. A forced flight, though, would mean you'd have to marry—or face ruin.'

Serena could not answer him. It had not until now occurred to her that escape could avail her nothing, if once the story came to society's ears. She would be ruined, and would have no choice but to marry the fiend.

But Hailcombe had not completed his disclosures. 'I should have preferred to have married you in a quiet hamlet, somewhere a good deal closer, but your fond father could not bring himself to assist me to a special licence.'

Serena felt sick. 'Are you telling me that Papa connived at this—this—?'

'Elopement,' supplied Hailcombe comfortably.

'Abduction!'

'Reeth won't call it that. He didn't want to know my plans, but I'll warrant he guessed I'd pick Gretna.'

Serena turned quickly away from his mocking gaze, lest the horror she was feeling should be visible in her face. That was why Papa had refused to allow Cousin Laura to accompany her. That had been bad enough. But now to know that he had done it on purpose, so that she might be made captive to a despicable plot—oh, she was lost indeed!

'Why has he done this?' She muttered it half to herself, hardly recognising that she must be overheard. Hailcombe's response almost startled her.

'Why, to oblige me, m'dear. What else? Thought you knew how fondly your father regards me.'

The mockery in his tone was unmistakable. Serena found herself looking round at him again, impelled by an urge to uncover the reason for her sacrifice.

'I know that he regards himself indebted. A matter of honour, he said, but I believe there is more to it than that.'

'Clever of you.'

'Papa must have promised you more than my dowry. Your suit has been too determined for it to be otherwise.'

Hailcombe gave a caustic laugh. 'You're a bright girl, Serena. By my faith, I could value you just for yourself! Come on, then. Tell me what else ''Papa'' offered me—and why?'

'If I knew why,' returned Serena, 'I might have judged of its validity—and spared Papa the humiliation of selling his only daughter for the sake of his honour.'

'And come a willing sacrifice to the altar? I doubt it.'

So also did Serena, but she held her tongue upon the natural retort. Ignoring the taunt, she continued, 'As for what he has offered you, I cannot guess.'

'And you so all-alive! You can't think of the advantage of being the son-in-law of a noted politician and respected member of the *Haut Ton*? You don't foresee that of Reeth's estates, at least one may go to this new member of his family? Young Gerald won't notice a piece missing from his inheritance. Then there's the matter of a regular allowance, which must, from time to time, be enlarged to keep pace with the times. And the expense of keeping Lady Hailcombe in the style to which she is accustomed. And more than that—'

'Pray say no more!' uttered Serena in a stifled tone. She could not bear to hear it. If Papa was prepared to go to these lengths for the security of his honour, the circumstances which demanded it must be dreadful indeed. And this was a man who had spurned Viscount Wyndham on account of his moral excesses!

The thought of his lordship gave her a pang. At this moment, Serena felt she would willingly compound for the man of immoral excesses could she but escape the future mapped out for her by Hailcombe.

The thought had barely crossed her mind when there was a loud protesting shout from the post-boy out in front, and the chaise slowed down and came to a stop. Hailcombe cursed, and opened the hatch to shout at his hireling. Letting down the window, Serena looked out.

Astonishingly, a curricle had been drawn across the road, blocking the way. A groom was at the horse's heads, and a gentleman in a many-caped driving-coat was jumping down into the road. To her intense joy, Serena recognised the features of Wyndham himself.

Chapter Nine

Her heart leaping, Serena fumbled for the doorhandle. How or why Wyndham came to be here were matters which did no more than flit through her head. It seemed to her no less than a miracle, and her only tangible thought was to hurl herself out of the chaise and into his arms.

'No, you don't!' came from behind her, and a strong arm forced her back, holding her hard against the solidity of Hailcombe's person behind her.

'Let me go!'

'Quiet!' he ordered, and with starting eyes, Serena saw that in his hand reposed a silver-mounted pistol, pointed towards the door.

It was wrenched open. Wyndham's countenance appeared in the aperture, fury in his eyes.

'Unhand her, you blackguard!'

Hailcombe's laugh was ugly. 'So easy? Keep back!'

'Wyndham, he has a pistol! Don't you see it?'

Then Serena saw that the Viscount also had a gun

in his hand. But although it should have been trained upon Hailcombe, he was shielded by her own body. Her heart seemed to stop.

Hailcombe's voice mocked. 'My trick, eh?'

To Serena's bewilderment, Wyndham smiled. It was not at all a pleasant smile, but it held a quiet triumph.

'Too previous, Hailcombe. Pray look again.'

Serena blinked uncomprehendingly. But her captor's movement behind her caused her to glance round. In the bustle, neither had noticed that the opposite door had been opened. Through it gleamed the barrel of a musket.

'One move, and my groom will blow your head off,' promised the Viscount. 'Now release Miss Reeth, if you know what's good for you!'

But Hailcombe did nothing. Serena held her breath while he looked first at the musket, and again at Wyndham.

'Think you have me at *point non plus*, eh? And all to be decided upon who fires first.'

'Don't be a fool!' snapped Wyndham, lowering his own weapon a trifle.

'You won't harm Serena, I know that,' observed her captor calmly. 'On the other hand, is your groom going to risk his own neck if I shoot you dead?'

At this point, the groom was heard to mutter words to the effect that he was ready to murder Hailcombe immediately. Wyndham ignored this, and stepped back.

'Since you will have it so, let us agree that at this

present we are even. But that can soon be remedied.' With an ostentatious gesture, he raised his pistol, uncocked it carefully, and slipped it into his pocket. 'There. Now only come out of that carriage, and I will fight you for her, fair and square.'

There was a silence. Serena stared in a bemused way upon her would-be rescuer, hardly able to take in the rapid turn of events. Hailcombe's voice was measured, but the mockery held.

'Are you proposing swords or pistols?'

'Swords. I have no wish to make this a killing matter.'

Her captor's mouth crept close to Serena's ear. 'He thinks me a fool.'

She shivered, and shifted her head, her eyes on Wyndham's. 'I don't understand you.'

'What, Serena? You don't know how expert with the foil is my rival to your hand?'

Serena had not known, but her mind fastened upon that point which most provoked her disgust. 'Wyndham was never your rival! And I will not be fought over by you!'

The leer was back in his tone. 'I don't think you've a choice, m'dear.' Then Hailcombe's grip about her slackened. 'But I do. And the odds are against me.'

Was this defeat? Wyndham knew he had taken a dangerous gamble in disarming himself. But with Serena in the way, his weapon was useless. He could not have risked firing. His reliance was not upon Hailcombe's honour, for he had none. But unless Wyndham missed his bet, the villain had a lively sense of his own safety—and the musket was aimed at his head.

Shifting another pace backwards, Wyndham prepared himself for any trick. If the blackguard would only let Serena come down out of the coach! She was so pale that he hardly dared to look at her, for fear that the sight would distract him. The pistol in Hailcombe's hand was still trained upon him, but the moment the man chose to move he must lose his aim.

Distraction came from an unexpected quarter. The post-boy, until now a pop-eyed spectator of events as he sat the lead horse, chose this moment to object to these unorthodox proceedings. In an eloquent speech, he gave the newcomers to understand that they were no better than the highwaymen who had earlier been involved, and certainly worse than the fellow inside who had hired his chaise, who was a rum touch if ever he had seen one.

'Highwaymen?' echoed Wyndham, his startled eyes flying to Serena's face. Curse the villain if that were true!

'Fine doings on the King's highway!' grumbled the post-boy.

Wyndham turned to him, acid in his tongue. 'There have been worse doings before this. And since you have yourself spoken of highwaymen, I am sure you may usefully be had up as an accessory to kidnapping.'

'T'weren't any of my doing,' said the post-boy, his tone both aggrieved and fearful. He pointed towards the coach. 'He's the one as put them to it, not me!'

'Then if you continue to keep your mouth shut, there will be no harm done.'

'Close as an oyster, yer honour!' said the boy promptly.

Hailcombe snorted his disgust. 'Yes, on my money, curse you!'

Of a sudden, he seized Serena and thrust her bodily from the coach. Too stunned even to shriek, she felt herself falling and knew she could do nothing to save herself.

Wyndham leapt on instinct, catching her as she tumbled through the door. The impact made him stagger and his hat fell off. In the few seconds it took to right them both, he was aware that Hailcombe had acted.

Crouching low, well under the aim of the musket, he had jumped into the road and backed himself against the side of the coach.

Turning with his arms about Serena, the Viscount found himself again facing the man's pistol. Without thought, he put Serena behind him. Where the devil was Bosham with that musket? He met Hailcombe's eyes. The fellow was grinning with an unpleasant show of teeth.

'Thought you'd bested me, eh? Now we'll see who wins!'

Wyndham wasted no words. With an unexpected spring, he closed with the man and, seizing his arm above the wrist, forced the pistol down.

'Let go, you fool, it's cocked!' cried his victim, struggling to withstand the pressure on his arm.

Serena hardly took in what happened. One moment, there were Wyndham and Hailcombe locked in close combat. The next, Hailcombe was sprawling in the road, felled by the butt end of the groom's musket, and Wyndham had possession of his pistol.

'Keep him there, Bosham!'

The groom stood over the inert body, and Wyndham uncocked the pistol and pocketed it along with his own. Then he turned back to Serena.

'Come! He will wake up soon enough, and we must be away.'

She reached out automatically and Wyndham, acting on impulse, pulled her to him, catching her into a convulsive embrace. He had her safe!

She moved a little and the pansy eyes looked up into his. A tremulous smile curved her mouth. 'Thank you!'

Wyndham's heart warmed. 'Did he hurt you?'

'Yes, but no matter for that.'

'Villain!' He released her, and found one of her hands, bringing her fingers to his lips. 'But come now. We will have time enough to discuss it all.'

The next few moments passed like a dream. Serena found herself handed up into the curricle, a rug was tucked securely about her, and soon she was bowling back along the way she had come. She could scarcely believe that her ordeal was at an end. In bemused silence, she looked behind, unable to comprehend that she was not still in Hailcombe's chaise being driven to Gretna Green. She shivered within the woollen cloak, hugging it close about her.

'Are you cold?'

Serena's gaze came back to Wyndham. 'No, I thank you.'

His eyes were on the road. She regarded his profile under the beaver hat, wondering if she were dreaming. Perhaps she would wake up soon, and discover that she had not been rescued. Had it been anyone other than the Viscount, she might not have doubted herself. But that he should have come after her—that he should have known…

'How did you know?'

He turned his head briefly, and the grey eyes were somehow alight. 'Miss Geary went to Melanie, who brought her to me. But I had already a notion that something was in the wind.'

Serena caught her breath. 'Was that why you came to our house yesterday?'

He nodded. 'I could not get your father to listen to me, however. I have had my own valet watching Hailcombe's. The fellow had dealings with the ruffians I take to have kidnapped you. But I had no inkling of that intention.'

'Then how could you have known that you might catch us up on the Great North Road?'

'Logic,' answered Wyndham, with a passing smile. 'It was not difficult to work it out, once I knew you had been sent off alone. I must say that it has been relatively easy to secure your release.'

'Easy!'

'Decidedly.' He laughed. 'I have been driving for no more than two and a half hours, though at a pace that has demanded all my skill, I admit. My own team took me through the first twenty miles, and I was fortunate enough to pick up this one—not of as high a calibre, but they are four good horses. To tell the truth, I had not expected to overtake you before Welwyn, but enquiries at Hatfield rewarded me, and I managed to get ahead of you quite readily.'

'Then you passed us!' marvelled Serena. 'I did not even think to look.'

'Why should you? Unlike me, you had no reason to be studying the occupants of every vehicle.'

'Did you?'

'I had to. But even at the last I was uncertain whether I had calculated aright. The sight of you looking out was decidedly relieving, I can tell you.'

Serena was silent for several moments. It was in an odd tone that she spoke again. 'So Cousin Laura went to Melanie. Because Papa would not let her accompany me, I suppose.'

'I believe she became suspicious of your father's motives,' Wyndham said carefully. 'It seemed to her a bizarre thing to do. She began to think—as I do, Serena—that Hailcombe has some sort of hold over Lord Reeth.'

'I don't know what it is,' she said tensely. 'He would not tell me. Only that he expected to gain an estate and—and money. An allowance that would increase every year, he said.'

Wyndham looked worriedly at her, and discovered that her features were taut. He could readily curse Reeth! Miss Geary had told him—in among the desperate and tearful agitations—how hurt Serena had been by her father's behaviour. If she had now proof of his perfidy, how painful must it be! Let him distract her from that, at all events.

'Do you feel up to telling me just what occurred?'

Serena shivered. 'Hailcombe had four masked men stop the coach. I thought they meant to rob us, but instead they did nothing but wait—except that one pushed off my bonnet to see the colour of my hair. Even then I had no suspicion.' Her voice tightened. 'But when I saw how they reacted to the sound of another coach behind us… I guessed it all then.'

Admiration filled him. 'You seem to have confronted these horrors with a good deal of courage.'

A faint laugh escaped her, and he caught a rueful look in her countenance as he glanced briefly at her. 'On the contrary. When I saw Hailcombe, and that creature made to drag me to him, I erupted into the most cowardly hysterics!'

'But you were far from hysterical when I caught you up,' he pointed out.

Her features became taut again, her tone steely. 'No, for though he used me abominably, I had determined that he should not have the satisfaction of seeing me afraid a second time.'

Wyndham was conscious of a surge of pride. Lord, but she had spirit! Which put him in mind of the tricky task ahead of him. How soon would it be before she abandoned gratitude in favour of war? He had no choice in what he must do, but he doubted if that was going to weigh with Serena.

What complexities awaited him! Was his reward to be just that one glowing look?

The private parlour designated by the landlady for Wyndham's use at the Cross Keys was a small apartment. There was only one casement window and the atmosphere was stuffy, for the fire in the grate smoked a little. There were several chairs set about a square table, which took up the centre of the room, and a couple of wall-sconces gave off so little light as to leave the place in relative darkness.

Wyndham ushered Serena inside, but himself paused upon the threshold, fastidiously surveying the interior. He turned to the woman behind him, about to demand a change. He should have been well enough known at this hostelry not to have been fobbed off with an inferior apartment. But before he could speak, he caught a certain gleam in the landlady's eye, and realised that he had never before baited at St Albans alone with a young lady, and one of obvious gentility.

The recollection that he had laid himself open to this sort of censure could not but annoy him. Yet if a mere landlady presumed him to be upon illegitimate business—and proffered a room suitable to the occasion!—how much more censorious must be the members of his own circle? For Serena's sake, he shut his mouth upon complaint, reflecting that at any rate they would be less likely to encounter anyone they knew in this out of the way parlour.

'Bring some more candles, if you please,' he requested instead, infusing deliberate hauteur into his tone. 'And I should be obliged if you will rustle up some dinner that may be acceptable to the lady.'

Doubt flickered for an instant in the landlady's eyes, and she cast a glance at Serena, who had thrown off her cloak and was standing before the fire, spreading her hands to the blaze. Her voice took on a hint of apology.

'Well, sir, I don't know what you'd call acceptable. But there's pork olives or a raised pigeon pie. Or, if the young lady should happen to fancy it, we've sole as can be baked.'

Serena's head had turned, and Wyndham went into the room towards her. 'This woman has a choice for you, ma'am. Have you any preference?'

Hunger had been gnawing at Serena again for the last several miles of the journey. So much so that she'd been unable either to converse with any degree of ease or to pay much attention to the route. It was past four and thirty, and darkness had already set in by the time they arrived at this place. She had been travelling for some six hours, and she was desperate for food. Yet the thought of eating made her feel nauseous. Or was that because she was so very hungry?

'Nothing heavy,' she said, a shade of anxiety in her voice. 'I don't think I could swallow either pork or fish.'

'Then you shan't try,' soothed Wyndham. He turned again to the landlady. 'Some broth or pottage, if you please, and perhaps a little ham. You may bring the pigeon pie for me.' He smiled blindingly, and saw with satisfaction that it had a visible effect upon the stiffness of the landlady. 'Wine, of course, and any other suitable delicacy, which I leave to your judgement.'

'You may safely do so, sir,' said the woman, thawing considerably. 'Likely the lady is fatigued, and will find eating a chore. I'm sure we'll find something she'll fancy.'

She then bobbed a curtsey and withdrew. Wyndham could not forbear a faint laugh. He went to Serena, who was struggling with a knot that had tangled the strings of her bonnet.

'Allow me.'

She stood still. As he wrestled with the knot, her gaze roved his face, shadowed in the half-light of the room. It struck her that it was already night, and she was alone with the Viscount in a private room in a strange inn at an unknown town. A vein pulsed into life.

Wyndham worked in silence, acutely aware of the pansy eyes. A tiny quiver at her throat disturbed her stillness as his fingers brushed her neck without intent. This was impossible! How the devil was he to survive the next few days without abandoning every principle of honour?

The strings came apart, and he sighed out his relief. He removed the bonnet, and found the golden curls sadly crushed. Without thinking, he threw the bonnet aside, uncaring where it went. His fingers shifted to her hair, and he prinked at the unresponsive locks.

His eyes moved to hers, and found them staring up at him.

His fingers stilled. In the brown depths was a look unfathomable, but one that caught at his heartstrings. He cupped her head between his hands.

'What is it?'

The words were a whisper. Serena responded to its warmth, and spoke the thought in her mind.

'You have taken his place.'

His brows snapped together. 'Hailcombe?'

Serena nodded, with that uncomprehended look yet in her eyes. Wyndham felt accused. Dropping his hands, he stepped smartly back, and turned away from her. Well, it was true! In a way, it was true, he thought savagely.

With hands that shook slightly, he ripped off his driving-coat and, drawing forth one of the chairs, threw it over the back. The beaver hat followed it. Without knowing what he did, Wyndham began to pace the small room, unable to look towards Serena.

She watched him in silence for a moment or two. Why had she said that? It had come from nowhere, as of instinct. But now she did not understand the portent of her own words. She swallowed on a throat grown inexplicably dry, and cast about for her discarded bonnet. Finding it, she placed it on a chair where she had thrown her cloak, and unbuttoned her pelisse. Then she sat down at the table and rested her forehead in her hands, staring down at the white cloth. A suspicion of a headache had begun to nag at her, adding to the nausea that churned along with her hunger.

'I did not mean to compare you to him,' she murmured, half to herself.

'But you consider your situation to be no better!'

The harsh tone sank her spirits. She did not feel equal to answering him. She felt confused, and disorientated. And too ill to enter into this discussion. With an effort, she took her hands from her face and pulled herself upright.

'When do you think we will get to London?'

Wyndham was startled into blurting it out. 'We are not going to London, Serena.'

She looked at him, and he could see the puzzlement, for his eyes had grown accustomed to the poor light. He had thought she had realised that they had turned off the road to London. Perhaps he had misunderstood her earlier words.

'You are not then taking me home?'

'To your father's estates? It would be useless.'

Serena began to feel lightheaded. The conversation seemed to be utterly at cross-purposes. 'No, I meant to Hanover Square. I know we are not upon the road to Suffolk.'

'We are upon the road to Northampton,' he said.

She stared at him. Why was he gripping the chairback in that odd way? Northampton? Bewildered, she put her fingers to her head and rubbed her temples.

'You are tired, Serena.'

'I feel quite sick.'

'Then let us postpone this discussion until you have

eaten. You may not think so, but with some food inside you, you will feel much more the thing.'

His tone had changed again. Serena felt as if she were living in a dream. She watched the Viscount draw out a chair and take a seat to her left. He clasped his fingers together, sighed a little, and rested his chin upon them, staring before him in an abstracted way.

The sensation of unreality persisted. Serena regarded the Viscount with a rising glow at her breast. The months rolled away. In her dreamlike trance, she hardly knew that she spoke aloud.

'When we met, I remember that I said such foolish things to you.' His head turned, and she smiled at him. 'You must have thought me so silly. Only I was silly when you were by. You robbed me of all power of thinking.'

Wyndham did not speak. It hurt him to be reminded of those early days. There was a hush about her as she spoke, a faint echo in her face of that lost innocence that he had so often mourned. And she said it as if it was in the past—as if he were in her past. The suspicion that he had already lost her crept into his heart. Now, when he had her at last, and could not let her go—for her own sake.

'But then you were so kind to me,' she pursued, and her eyes misted. But the smile remained on her lips, and he found it unbearably sweet. 'You were excessively teasing, Wyndham. But you were always kind.'

'Serena—'

He broke off as the door opened behind him.

Turning, he beheld a blaze of light from two candelabra. A waiter brought them in and set them upon
the table. Wyndham blinked in the glare, and glancing
at Serena, saw her briefly cover her eyes with one
hand.

The intimacy was shattered. By the time the meal,
brought in by several pairs of hands, had been placed
before them, Wyndham saw that Serena's strange
mood had given way to growing interest. If he was
himself extremely hungry, then Serena must be fam-
ished.

There was no further conversation exchanged beyond the strictly necessary for some fifteen minutes,
while both took the first edge off their hunger. Serena
at length sat back, setting down her spoon and sighing
out her satisfaction, for the broth had been wholesome
and tasty.

'I find that you were right, sir. I feel much better.'

'You had better eat your fill,' he advised, helping
himself to another slice of the pigeon pie. 'We have
some way to go yet.'

Which statement effectually killed Serena's appe-
tite, as the unsettling realisation of her uncertain future flooded back. She made no demur when the
Viscount served her with several slices of ham and
placed the fresh baked rolls within her reach. She ate
a little of the ham, but absently. No longer troubled
by the confusing state of mind induced by hunger and
tiredness, she broached the question without hesitation.

'Why are you not taking me back to London?'

It had come. Wyndham's fork paused halfway to his mouth, and he drew a steadying breath. But it had to be said.

'It would be useless, Serena. Even Miss Geary advised against it. Nor did she suppose it would help matters if I were to take you to Suffolk—though that I did suggest. For I imagine Hailcombe will certainly return to London where he can beard your father. Once they put their heads together, there is no saying what course they might pursue.'

Serena laid down her knife and fork. 'Hailcombe said that Papa did not wish to know his plans.'

'But that did not stop him from making it easy for Hailcombe to have you abducted,' Wyndham pointed out deliberately.

She looked away. After a moment, she put out a hand for her glass and sipped a little of the wine it contained.

'It is no pleasant thing for you to know that your father is in cahoots with that man, Serena, but the fact remains that he is. Your cousin believes that Lord Reeth will continue to assist him.'

What Miss Geary had in fact said to him was, 'It is no good bringing her back here, Lord Wyndham. That man means mischief! He will try again, and you may depend upon it that my cousin Reeth will aid and abet him.'

It had been due to Miss Geary that he had abandoned his first intention of following Serena to Suffolk. He had told her about his warning to Reeth, and she had exclaimed her immediate conviction that there was villainy afoot. A hurried consultation had resulted in his opting for the Great North Road, believing that sooner or later he must find himself either before or after Hailcombe on that route. So indeed it had proved. But in rescuing Serena, he had been obliged to place her in a situation that was even more potentially scandalous.

He had no wish to distress Serena by informing her of the other reason why a return to London was ineligible. What he had heard that morning at White's must have been airing all day through the capital. He could not doubt but that Serena's reputation was already blasted. It was less a case of rescue than one of repair.

'What then do you propose to do with me?'

The question took him unawares. Unprepared, he brought it out flat, with no mitigating preliminaries.

'I am taking you to my hunting-lodge at Bredington.'

Serena awoke in a panelled room that she did not recognise. She was in a plain wooden four-poster, from the corners of which hung curtains of faded yellow brocade which had been left open around her. From a wide sash window to one side, light streamed between the half-open drapes.

She started up on her elbow, and her eyes fell first upon a small press opposite the bed, and a stand upon which were set a basin and ewer. Shifting her gaze, she discovered the gown in which she had travelled, discarded upon a chair near the bed. Instinctively, she looked down at her own person and found that she was wearing a garment that felt strange in feel and size.

Serena threw aside the covers. A man's nightshirt! She stared at the folds of the voluminous garment, unable to imagine how she came to be wearing such a thing. Where was she? What was this place?

A knock at the door startled her, and she dived hastily back under the bedclothes, pulling them up to her chin. The door opened, and the round plump features of a middle-aged woman peeked around it.

'Ah, you're awake, ma'am. His lordship's compliments, and there'll be food awaiting you as soon as ever you're ready. I've brought Joyce here with some fresh hot water, and she'll stay to help you dress.'

His lordship? Serena blinked away the remnant mists of sleep. And then it hit her. *Wyndham!* He had brought her here last night. Bredington. She was at his hunting-lodge at Bredington.

All the evils of her situation came back to her with stunning force, and she fell back upon the pillows with a groan. She was ruined! The man in whom she had foolishly reposed her trust had betrayed her.

'Shall you get up now, miss?'

It was the girl Joyce, bobbing a curtsey and gently peeling away the protective covers. Serena felt herself grow hot with embarrassment. What must she think? Well, it was obvious what she must think. It was what anyone would think, finding her here. The only wonder was that Wyndham had not had the effrontery to have entered the room himself!

Allowing herself to be helped from the bed, Serena blushed again at the shocking nature of her attire. But it did not apparently trouble the maid, who was pouring hot water into the basin. Why should it affect her? Serena cannot have been the only female to have been found in so compromising a situation in this dreadful place.

The events of the previous night began to piece together in her mind as she dealt automatically with the business of preparing herself for the day. It was soon clear why she had been dressed in a man's nightshirt—was it Wyndham's? She had no clothes with her other than those she had been wearing when Hailcombe's bullies had taken her from her own chaise. She wondered how he had proposed to clothe her for the few days it would have taken to reach to Gretna Green and back again.

But that was scarcely relevant. For the Viscount, who had rescued her from a hideous marriage, had instead brought her to the very establishment that had been the hotbed of his horrid lusts. True, he had said that there was no other course open to him. But Serena had refused to be persuaded of this. The moment he had mentioned Bredington, she had been unable to withstand a violent wave of hideous suspicion.

She had been hushed and anxious for the rest of the way—near three hours in an open carriage which had left her well nigh exhausted. Indeed, she thought she must have fallen asleep towards the end, for she had little memory of their arrival here. And none of being put to bed. A dreadful thought assailed her.

'Who undressed me last night?' she asked abruptly of the maid.

The girl was doing up the buttons of her gown, but she paused in her work. 'It were me and Mrs Pitchcott, miss, his lordship having carried you in. We tried to wake you, but you was that tired. His lordship says as how you'd been on the road for ten hours or more.'

There was shocked awe in Joyce's tone, but Serena's attention had caught upon the intelligence that she had been borne into the place in Wyndham's arms. A betraying pulse pattered for a minute or two. She suppressed it, and put another question.

'What time is it, if you please?'

'Past noon, miss. His lordship said as how you weren't to be disturbed.'

His lordship said! With a little spurt of rage, Serena wondered just what else his lordship may have said. What reason had he given for his scandalous arrival with a genteel female in his company? Or were these people too used to such doings even to be concerned at the impropriety of it?

By the time she had donned her only gown, the green kerseymere in which she had chosen to travel, and was ready to follow the maid through a lengthy passageway and down some stairs, Serena was in a state of nervous expectancy that caused flurries of butterflies to leap about her insides. She came down into a modest hall, with rooms going off in several directions. The whole place appeared to be panelled, including the parlour into which she was ushered.

Serena hardly noticed much beyond the dining-table set with a white cloth, and the hunting scene of a painting on the wall ahead. For Wyndham sprang up from a seat at the end of the table, and executed a small bow of welcome.

'Good morning—or rather, good afternoon.' His voice sounded stiff, his manner overly formal. 'I trust you slept well. Won't you take a seat?'

After one brief glance, Serena refused to meet his eyes. She made a business of taking the seat to one side which the maid Joyce pulled out for her, and allowed herself to be wholly distracted by the offerings emanating from the woman she recognised from earlier and who introduced herself as Mrs Pitchcott, the housekeeper.

There was coffee, and griddle cakes, with a selection of jams and cheeses to be spread upon them. 'Or if you prefer, ma'am, there's potted asparagus and pickled mushrooms.' With which Serena was offered slices from a fresh brown loaf and good country butter.

She chose at random, unable to think beyond the Viscount's pervasive presence at the end of the table. To her consternation, once she had been served and the coffee-pot left within reach, Mrs Pitchcott withdrew. Serena looked round at the closed door, feeling her stomach go hollow. Unable to help herself, she cast a flying glance at Wyndham's face.

'Have no fear,' he said drily. 'You are in no immediate danger. It is not my practice to seduce young ladies when they are attempting to eat their first meal of the day.'

Her cheeks hot, Serena dropped her gaze to her plate, staring unseeingly at its contents. She took refuge in her coffee-cup, sipping at the hot liquid.

'That is what you think, is it not?' demanded Wyndham after a moment. 'Perhaps I should rather have continued on to Gretna with you.'

Serena put down her cup. A quick breath gave her courage to look at him. 'Why didn't you?'

Wyndham hesitated. She'd had someone catch her hair up into a topknot and the change was distracting. She looked childishly young. The thought crossed his mind that green became her delightfully. Mentally he kicked himself. She had asked a question, and was awaiting his answer.

He wanted to say that he had chosen this way in hopes of repairing the damage, and mitigating the scandal. To have gone to Scotland could only have resulted in worsening it. He had already put his plans in hand, for his groom had taken his curricle to London with a letter for the Baron. But since he could be by no means certain that Reeth would obey the summons—even less that he could be induced to bring Miss Geary to play propriety—he was loath to tell Serena what he had done. He was certain that Hailcombe would try to retrieve Serena, and it was all too probable that Reeth would help him. It was evident that Serena's father was resigned to the scandal, if Wyndham was not.

'I had no wish to marry you in such a scrambling way,' he said, prevaricating.

'You had no objection before,' Serena pointed out flatly.

'The circumstances were different.'

'How?'

Again he found himself hovering over his answer. It occurred to him to wonder why he was shielding her. She must know the truth sooner or later. To withhold it was serving only to increase her suspicion of him. Yet it went against the grain with him to distress her further. Had she not borne enough? He temporised.

'If I had married you out of hand then, Serena, all that would have been said of it was that we had taken the step only because your father would not consent to our marriage.'

'Whereas on this occasion?' She looked him boldly in the eye. 'What is it that they might say now, if you please?'

He might have known her intelligence was of too high an order to be fobbed off. Fortifying himself first with a few sips of the ale with which he had been refreshing himself, Wyndham capitulated.

'Serena, you do not understand the workings of Hailcombe's mind. He had prepared things well.'

Serena frowned. 'You mean because he hired those men to fetch me to him so that he could not be blamed?'

'I am not talking of the highwaymen he hired. It is what he saw fit to put about before he went. Even in my hearing, the matter was already being speculated upon. By the time I got to you, I dare say the story he told was all over town.'

Her countenance paled, and Wyndham at once regretted having begun upon this. If he knew Serena, she would not be content with innuendo. Nor was he mistaken.

'What s-story?'

The tremor in her voice racked him, but there was no going back now. 'That Hailcombe would have you to wife within the day. What would anyone suppose, knowing you were going out of town, but that a flight to the border was intended?'

To his dismay, Serena's brown eyes grew dark with rage. Her voice shook. 'And what will they s-suppose, do you think, when I don't come back m-married? When they hear from Hailcombe that I am now with you?'

He reached out as if he would take her hand, but Serena snatched it away. Wyndham drew back, hurt. Stiffly, he answered this.

'I am persuaded Hailcombe will say nothing so prejudicial to his interests. If he shows his face, people will only think that you are at home in Suffolk.'

'Then why should I not have gone there?'

'And laid yourself open to your father's schemes?'

Balked, Serena turned away. Without realising what she did, she took another sip of coffee, thinking furiously the while. He could have taken her back to London! Why should people say anything bad of her if she returned there? She might have made up some tale to account for it. The coach had been found to require attention, perhaps. Or her maid had been taken ill. Anything.

But in London, she remembered, she would be as much at the mercy of Papa's complicity in Hailcombe's machinations as if she had gone to Suffolk. She looked again at Wyndham.

'Very well, but why did you bring me *here*?'

'Because it is the safest place I can think of.'

'Safe?'

He flinched at the scorn in her voice. 'I am aware that you believe it to be a haunt of vice, but the fact remains that it is secluded enough for a hiding-place. No one need know that you are here.'

Serena eyed him, challenge in her face. 'And now that I am here, what do you propose to do with me?'

A somewhat unnerving smile curved his mouth. 'Why, marry you, Serena. What else?'

Chapter Ten

Serena jumped so violently that she almost upset the coffee pot. 'But how can you marry me? Unless you have procured a special licence, you cannot marry me anywhere but Scotland. You know that I am under age.'

'Which is one of the reasons why I could not take you to my mother at Lyford Manor—even though she approved of you.'

She eyed him with acute suspicion. 'What other reasons had you?'

Wyndham threw up his eyes. 'For pity's sake, I should have thought that must be obvious!'

'Not to me.'

'What do you suppose my father's reaction would be,' he demanded brutally, 'if I arrived at Derbyshire—in a curricle, if you please, and with a débutante at my side!—announcing that I had intercepted her flight to the border with another man, and that I intended now to marry her myself?'

A flush rose to Serena's cheeks, and she glared at

him. 'Why do you not add that she was already living under your protection, for it is no less than the truth?'

Wyndham was tempted to tear his hair. 'Cannot you see, you little fool, that my sole desire is to brush through this with the minimum of scandal?'

'I see that you are trying to hoax me!' she retorted. 'You have already said that you had no wish to take me to Gretna Green—'

'It is not that I did not wish for it, but—'

'—and if your intentions are truly so honourable, why should you bring me to the very place where you are wont to bring those sort of women who—'

'Serena, that is the most complete—'

But Serena was on her feet, her temper flaring. 'Don't dare to tell me that I have misjudged you! I tried to give you the benefit of every doubt, my lord Wyndham. I almost argued myself into believing that it was Papa who had fabricated the whole, in order to put me against you. But now I see that it wasn't so, for—'

'*Will* you allow me to speak?'

She halted in mid-stride, her breath catching. The Viscount had risen too, and for an instant she stared at the blazing grey eyes in defiance. But the sheer fury in his voice cut straight at her heart. Dropping into her chair, Serena dumped her elbows on the table, and covered her face.

Wyndham's anger dropped right out. Sighing, he resumed his seat and reached out for the flagon of ale. As he emerged, he saw that Serena had resumed her meal, making a praiseworthy effort to behave as if nothing had happened. But her hands shook as she attempted to butter a slice of bread, and he was hard put to it to refrain from reaching out to her again. She would only flinch away!

'I beg your pardon,' he said quietly. 'You have been through a great deal, and the last thing I want is to quarrel with you, Serena.'

'No,' she agreed dully. 'Not if you wish to persuade me to become your mistress.'

Wyndham felt his temper rising again, and repressed it. 'What must I do to convince you? Why do you persist in this ridiculous delusion?'

She looked at him. 'I would not if it had been only Papa's notion. Before Hailcombe came into our lives, he had been happy enough to consider you for my prospective husband. He told me himself that until he had learned of your association with the Marquis of Sywell—'

'My *what*?'

'It is of no use to look like that, my lord,' said Serena rebelliously. 'Do you suppose I would still believe that you were one of the men he has corrupted if I had not heard it from another source?'

'Corrupted!' Wyndham's eyes narrowed dangerously. 'What other source, pray?'

'Someone who lives here. Miss Lucinda Beattie.' She brought out the name with a defiant lift of her chin. It was a name she had come to dislike amazingly, but she was not going to tell that to the Viscount.

He was frowning. 'I have never heard of her.'

'She is a friend of Cousin Laura's, and she lives in—in Abbot something, I think it is called.'

'Abbot Giles?'

'Very likely.'

'Not that it matters.' Wyndham eyed her balefully. 'So it is upon the evidence of some gossiping tabby that you choose to condemn me.'

'I don't choose to!'

'Of course not,' he agreed, with awful irony. 'You are forced to, because I have brought you to Bredington. Even though anyone with the least bit of common sense must perfectly understand my reasons.'

He rose from the table and threw down his napkin. 'Very well, Miss Reeth. Believe what you like. I have done!'

With which, he stalked from the room, slamming the door behind him with unnecessary force.

The early-morning mist made it extremely difficult to see, and the cold penetrated without mercy through the pelisse. It had not been designed for walking in an unknown forest in the middle of winter. Serena was glad she had been wearing kerseymere underneath, and not muslin, when she was captured. How had she come to forget her woollen cloak?

She was beginning to regret that she had taken this step. Only now that she was fairly into these dreadful woodlands, she doubted her ability to find her way back to the hunting lodge. She had lost sight of the river, by which means she might have trailed a route back to the point where she had forded it, close to Bredington itself. It must have been a regular crossing place, for the stones were numerous and flat, and the bed of the river visible below the clear waters.

But it was useless to think of it, for she was certainly lost. She was weary to her bones as well, having tossed and wept into her pillows for the better part of the night. What else was she to do after such a horrid day?

Wyndham had disappeared after their quarrel—ridden out, the housekeeper said. Serena had spent a miserable day, cooped up in the front parlour. She had been obliged to acknowledge the masculinity of the place with its leather-bound chairs, a chest in one corner, upon which reposed a discarded whip, several old copies of *The Gentleman's Magazine*, and a pewter tankard. On a table nearby were a number of decks of cards, and the pictures on the walls had been all of sporting subjects. There were no signs of female invasion—not that it proved anything!

The Viscount had returned only at five. By which time Serena was feeling so furious and lonely that she had announced her intention of taking dinner in her room.

Had his lordship demurred? No, he had not! Instead, he had bowed in a manner that was wholly dismissive, not to say rudely ironic. Serena had flounced off in a temper. Not that she had eaten much of the meal that had been brought to her on a tray. What she had managed to swallow might as well have been ashes, and she had wasted far too much time in listening for a footstep in the corridor beyond, in the vain hope that a tap at the door might bring Wyndham—penitent and ready to use every art to persuade her to believe in him.

But Wyndham had not come, and Serena had been wretched. The miserable counsel of the night had brought only one desire—to escape from Bredington. Which had led her to this undoubted folly.

The eerie silence of the forest was broken by the snapping of a twig. Gasping with fright, Serena froze, shrinking back against a tree and peering about her into the shrouding mist.

An indistinct shadow moved ahead of her. No, two shadows. Serena's heart began to thump with fright. They were coming this way! As stealthily as she could, she crept around the other side of the tree trunk, which was large enough for concealment. A murmur of voices approached.

'D'you get anythin'?'

'Nowt but a brace o' hares.'

'One for the pot, eh?'

'Sparse pickings. But there's winter for yer.'

Serena held her breath, not daring to peep as the men passed close. Their progress was so silent, she could almost have sworn that no one was there. But another twig or two snapping confirmed they were now on the far side.

Creeping quietly round the tree, she dared to look, and saw again only shadows. They might never have been! She set off in the opposite direction, with only one thought in her head. To get out of this horrid forest.

A couple of hundred yards further on, she saw that the mist ahead was thinning a trifle. Through it, beyond the trees, there was empty space. Lifting her skirts, she hurried, and presently came out into open country, sighing with relief.

Halting, she looked about, for the mist was clearly lifting. To one side she saw a lone cottage of a fair size, and headed towards it, intending to ask for refuge, or directions at least.

A dour-looking maid opened the door. She was of middle years and sturdy build, and her brows rose at sight of the visitor. She looked Serena up and down.

'And what might you be wanting, may I ask? Trifle early to be paying morning calls, ain't it?'

Serena was daunted. She had not thought how odd her sudden appearance must look. But before she could think how to answer, an interruption occurred. From behind the maid's broad figure could be glimpsed a screen that did not quite conceal the room beyond. A brisk voice was heard.

'Do shut that door, Janet. You are letting in the cold!'

'You'd best come in,' said the woman to Serena, and stood back to allow her to enter. Then she shut the front door and led her directly into a sizeable room that looked to be a parlour, which had been pressed into service for other purposes. An open stairway was to be seen on the far side, and a dining-table was placed by the window. The room was bright from a cheerful fire in the grate, and upon a sofa placed to catch its warmth sat a young woman with a child upon her knee. She noticed Serena with evident surprise.

'Why, what is this?'

'No use asking me,' said Janet. 'Found her on the doorstep.'

And with an air of washing her hands of the whole affair, she vanished through a door at the back, leaving Serena to make her explanation.

'I beg your pardon, ma'am, but I came from Bredington, and lost my way in the forest. I wanted to ask if you...'

Her voice petered out, for the expression had changed in the face of the young female whose house she had invaded. It was a face sharply intelligent, with eyes of an attractive green—just now showing puzzlement, or perhaps doubt? Her hair was drawn back, and partially covered with a frivolous lacy cap which tied under the chin. It was dark, in stark contrast to the abundant curling locks of the child, which were of a shining red-gold, and which the woman had clearly been in the act of brushing.

'Bredington?'

There was more than question in the one word. Serena felt herself blushing, and blurted a protest. 'Oh, I know what you must think! But it is nothing like that. At least, it was not meant to be. Only I have run away from him, and—and I don't know what I should do!'

A pair of dark brows were raised. 'Him? Is it Lord Buckworth perhaps?'

'Oh, no. I scarcely know Buckworth. It is Wyndham.'

'Viscount Wyndham? But why in the world—' She broke off, and suddenly smiled. 'Forgive me, my manners are atrocious.' Setting the little girl down, she rose and held out her hand. 'How do you do? My name is Annabel Lett, and this is my daughter Rebecca. Becky, say hello to the lady.'

But the toddler, who was clinging to her mother's skirts and staring up at the newcomer out of two wide blue eyes, only buried her face in the folds of Annabel's petticoats.

'She is shy with strangers.'

Serena smiled, said that it did not matter and introduced herself. A bustle followed, while Annabel went through to the kitchen, where she said the maid had gone, demanding tea. She was a woman of quick motions, with a trim figure and a decisive manner. When she took Serena's pelisse and hat and discovered how chill she was, she pushed her into the sofa to be warmed by the fire.

In a short space of time, Serena not only found herself partaking of tea and toast, but so compelling was the personality of Mrs Lett—a widow, as she explained to Serena—that she found herself pouring out her trials. The men in the forest, so Annabel surmised, must have been poachers.

'The villagers—in particular the tenants of Steepwood—are known to poach the forests in winter.

Sywell is so mean a landlord that one feels they have some excuse. They are not dangerous, however, and I feel sure they would not have harmed you, even had they seen you.'

The mention of the Marquis recalled the worst of Serena's troubles to her mind, and she could not withhold her upset. It was a relief to talk, especially to a female who neither exclaimed like Melanie nor scolded like Cousin Laura, as Serena related how she came to be staying at Bredington.

'You poor girl!' was Annabel's comment at the end of this agitated recital.

She had resumed her task of brushing her daughter's hair, but had given the little girl up to her maid after that redoubtable dame had brought in the tea, and the two ladies were now alone. To Serena's surprise Annabel, who was seated in a chair opposite, took her hand and held it.

'You have had a dreadful time of it, but I do think you ought to consider well before you throw away this promising solution.'

'You mean of marrying Wyndham? But I don't know that he truly means to marry me.'

'He said so, I think you told me.'

'Yes, but I don't believe him!' stated Serena defiantly. 'In any event, would you marry a man who is an intimate of the Marquis of Sywell?'

Annabel stared at her. 'Who told you so?'

'My father—whom I do not believe. Only my cousin had it from Miss Lucinda Beattie, who is her dearest friend.'

Her hand was released, and Mrs Lett sat back. 'I see. Well, I do not wish to say anything unkind of Miss Beattie. She is a worthy woman, and I have every reason to like her. But there is no denying that she lives for gossip. I cannot approve it, for gossip can be so extremely hurtful.'

She drummed her fingers on the chair arm, and Serena thought a faintly wistful expression had crept into the green eyes. But then Annabel seemed to brush it off.

'But the poor thing has little enough else to entertain her, and people around here are only too ready to condemn. One cannot blame her if she adds up two and two to make five.'

A faint hope stirred Serena's bosom. 'Are you saying that it is not true?'

Annabel smiled. 'All I will say is that I have lived here some two years, and I have never heard any ill of Lord Wyndham. Buckworth is a known rake, but even his name has not been coupled with that of Sywell. The Marquis, you must know, is an exceptionally vicious specimen. I should be astonished if the likes of the lords Wyndham and Buckworth, so far from following him, did not utterly condemn his activities.'

Serena's spirits were lifting, but still she was not satisfied. 'But were there not women of ill-repute staying at Bredington last summer?'

A little gurgle of laughter escaped Annabel. 'To my knowledge, you are the only female to come out of

Bredington. And you, it would seem, are betrothed to its owner. I see no room there for gossip.'

Wyndham had passed perhaps the wretchedest night of his life. He was forced to realise that he had supposed, in a nebulous way, that once he had Serena safe the rest would take care of itself. So much for that! Had he been so foolishly confident of her regard? Though there had been a moment, in the inn at St Alban's, when she had shown him a degree of affection.

The devil fly away with the girl, for she *did* care for him! Only she had fastened upon this ridiculous notion about his supposed association with Sywell— of all people. A man whom he had viewed with the utmost disgust from the first. Indeed there was not one of his acquaintance hereabouts who had a good word to say about the Marquis.

Well, he had Reeth to blame for it, as for everything else. His valet hovered with starched replacements while he tied his neckcloth, thinking unkind thoughts of Serena's father. In fact, where was the fellow? He had half expected him to arrive late last night.

Even as the question formed in his mind, a knock at his bedchamber door brought Pitchcott, the lodge-keeper, with a message from his wife to say that Lord Reeth had arrived, and was awaiting the Viscount in the front parlour. A surge of expectation threw Wyndham's pulse into high gear. Now they would see! Five minutes later, clad in buckskins and a blue frock-coat, he walked into the front parlour, ready for battle.

Reeth was standing by the window, looking out, the burnished head a trifle sunken in shoulders that stooped. He had not troubled to remove his greatcoat, though it hung open to reveal a wine-coloured coat beneath. Wyndham took in the change in him as the man turned. He looked haggard, his features grey, and there was strain in the eyes that searched Wyndham's face. He looked as if he had lost flesh, and if the Roman nose stood out as prominently, its arrogance was gone.

Shocked out of his antagonism, Wyndham regarded him blankly. Why had he not noticed this deterioration in Serena's father at their last meeting? Perhaps he had been too much involved in his own anxiety.

'Have you married her?' demanded Reeth harshly, but with less than his usual bark.

'Not as yet.'

'Damn your eyes!' muttered the other. 'Why not?'

Astonished at the question, Wyndham frowned. 'How could I, without a special licence? Or your permission, if it comes to that.'

Reeth seemed to sag where he stood. 'Why in Hades did you not take her to Gretna Green?'

Wyndham moved into the room. 'My object, sir, is to avoid scandal, not create it. I wrote as much to you.'

'A waste of time. We are all doomed to scandal now.'

Puzzled, Wyndham watched him cross the room

and drop into one of the heavy leather chairs, throwing up a hand to brush at his hair in a weary gesture. What ailed the fellow?

'Forgive me, sir, but I am afraid I do not understand you. When last we spoke—'

'Don't remind me!' He rubbed heavily at his forehead. 'You don't know what it cost me to—' He broke off, and looked up at Wyndham. 'But it gave me hope! If you could be induced to act—which you did!—and his plans went awry, that damned bloodsucker could not set it at my door.'

For a moment the Viscount did not take it in. The enormity of the implication was almost more than he could believe. Rage boiled up inside him.

'Do you mean to tell me, my lord Reeth, that you deliberately put your daughter through a terrifying experience in order that I should be induced to rescue her?'

Reeth glanced up at him, saying with something of his usual bark, 'It is not as bad as that. I had no hand in the arrangements. I merely tried to make it obvious that there was devilry afoot. And without rousing that fiend's suspicions.' He sighed, and a note of self-loathing entered his voice. 'I have been reduced to skulking in my house, that he might not find me, with my butler primed to say I was from home. I came with your groom in the curricle, starting out in the early hours.'

'Which is why, I presume, you have not brought Miss Geary,' suggested the Viscount.

'I couldn't. Hailcombe was bound to come looking

for me, and if we were both absent, he would smell a rat. Though he left a letter at my house, I imagine even now he believes me to be ignorant of what transpired. Lord knows I wanted to be!'

'But you were not, sir,' Wyndham pointed out acidly. 'Otherwise you would not have sent Serena out alone.'

He received a fierce glare. 'Do you think it was easy? Do you know what it has done to me to be obliged to behave to my only daughter in so savage a fashion?'

'Not only your daughter,' Wyndham said through his teeth.

The Roman nose was directed at him with some of its old arrogance. 'Yes, I attacked your character. I had to. It was easy enough. I knew Sywell of old, and you had this hunting-lodge convenient to the Abbey.'

'So you forced Serena to believe there was a connection—and painted a lurid picture that gave her a disgust of me!'

Reeth sunk into himself again, sighing. 'I didn't have to. Laura has an acquaintance here. Another old maid. I knew I could rely upon their propensity for gossip and exaggeration. Between them, they succeeded in putting Serena off.'

'You are mistaken.' Wyndham shifted to the window, and looked out. 'Even now she is fighting against her inclination. But her heart is constant.' He turned. 'Despite your best efforts, my lord Reeth!'

The elder man flinched slightly. 'My hand was

forced. You don't know, Wyndham, what a blow was promised me if I did not acquiesce.'

'No, I don't know,' Wyndham said, deliberately cold. 'I wish you will enlighten me. What hold has Hailcombe over you?'

Reeth sagged deeper into the chair, and his hands covered his face in a gesture so like to Serena's that the Viscount almost felt sorry for the man. After a moment, the hands dropped. The Baron looked more ill than ever. It was evident that he had suffered. But that, thought Wyndham, hardening, did not excuse his conduct.

'You may as well know it. The world will know it soon enough, for I have made up my mind to let him do his worst. I will not help him further.'

And not a moment too soon! 'Well, and what is his worst?'

Reeth's head drooped. 'The matter concerns my brother. He was a naval lieutenant.'

Wyndham jumped. 'Lieutenant Reeth? He was killed at Trafalgar, I believe, and died a hero.'

A fleeting glance was cast up at him. 'So the world believes. So I believed. The truth is otherwise. He jumped ship rather than face the enemy.' Disgust and pain throbbed in Reeth's voice. 'A deserter! Gerald Reeth—a man for whose passing I grieved so deeply that my own wife's death was lessened in comparison.'

'This is what Hailcombe told you, I presume?'

Wyndham held down the elation that was growing in him. He was by no means eager to put Lord Reeth out of his misery. Let the man suffer a few moments longer.

'He also served on *Neptune*. Hailcombe saw Gerald go over the side.'

'And you believed him implicitly?'

Reeth snorted. 'Do you take me for a fool? Of course I didn't believe him. At first, that is. I have contacts in the Naval Office. I made exhaustive enquiries. But you don't know these war records. They deal in essentials, they have to. The individual is sacrificed to the cause. "Missing in action." That is all they could show me. Oh, I had the usual letter at the time. Anyone who dies in battle is presumed a hero.'

A faint cynical smile crossed his face. Wyndham was conscious of a curious enjoyment in prolonging the man's agony. But it would not do.

'Many who die in battle are indeed heroes,' he began.

He was treated to another explosive snort. 'Yes, but not Gerald Reeth! You perceive the trend? I could find no evidence to refute Hailcombe. I could not allow him to besmirch Gerald's memory. The talk, the scandal, the disgrace—it was not to be borne! Dishonour is a blot that stains for ever. True or not, many people would believe him. Besides, Hailcombe claims to have seen Gerald two years ago, in a foreign port.'

'He lied!' Wyndham crossed to the fireplace and faced Reeth, who was so lost in his tale that he had barely looked up. 'Hailcombe lied, sir. Believe me, the whole story was nothing but a fabrication.'

An Innocent Miss

'Much you know! Why should you say such a thing?'

Wyndham could not forbear a smile. 'I might not have done so a few days since. Only it happens that I most fortuitously met an old friend of mine on the very day Serena left London. He is Captain Lewis Brabant, and he was also on *Neptune*.'

He had Reeth's full attention now. The man sat up. 'He was at Trafalgar?'

'He was, and knew your brother well. He spoke of him highly, and told a very different tale. In fact, if I am not much mistaken, he is likely in this area at this moment, for he lives near Steep Abbot not two miles from here.'

The Baron rose eagerly from his chair. 'Good God, man, do you say so indeed? Is it possible that he may be the means for me to confound Hailcombe?'

'He had ammunition aplenty, sir. One tithe of the articles upon which he indicted Hailcombe would serve you! The man is unprincipled beyond belief.'

'Take me to this friend of yours, I beg of you!'

'I had rather bring him here to you, for—'

Wyndham broke off, as a knock at the door interrupted them. His housekeeper entered, looking a trifle harassed.

'What is the matter, Mrs Pitchcott?'

'It's the lady, my lord!' said the woman in distress. 'I went to see if she was awake, and she wasn't in her room.'

Wyndham's heart stopped. 'Have you looked for her?'

'Joyce and I have searched the house from top to bottom, my lord. She's nowhere to be found.'

It was purely by chance that he saw her. Frantic with anxiety, the Viscount had been on horseback within minutes of hearing that Serena was missing from Bredington. He had cursed his way out of the house, ignoring his valet's shouts regarding his great-coat and hat. His first instinct had been to follow the track that led to Steep Abbot, and he had started out in a bang, riding hell for leather.

His mind had been rather on the previous day's quarrel than a common-sense approach to finding her, and he had expended much energy in cursing himself for allowing the estrangement to have been pro-longed. Serena had run away from him with nothing but the clothes on her back. Anything might have hap-pened to her. God send her steps had not taken her anywhere near Steepwood Abbey!

But Wyndham had gone only a few hundred yards when his native good sense had reasserted itself and he had reined in. She could not have been out of the house before daylight, and she must anticipate that he would search for her. It was unlikely then that she had headed down the only road out of Bredington. Which had left what? The forest of Steep Wood lay all about his hunting-lodge. Serena could not have meant to lose herself. If he had himself fled in like fashion, Wyndham reckoned that he must have cho-sen at least to navigate by following the river that ran alongside the lodge.

Turning his horse, he had backtracked, crossing at the ford, for he had calculated that Serena would have wished to put distance between herself and the lodge. His way had led him down the River Steep until he emerged from the trees and rode towards the foot-bridge that carried a pathway up via the village of Steep Ride. Surely Serena must have followed that route? What must he do? Call at every cottage, if need be.

Only a small doubt had assailed him. Had she been in a frame of mind to think logically? Could it be that she had sought a path through the forest and become lost? She might even now be lying somewhere in among the thickset trees, injured and undiscovered.

The thought had sent Wyndham hurtling up the open turf, heading back towards the forest, which he had skirted, riding a little inside it, within the trees. His eye had been trained upon the dark interior, a growing dread sending him unpalatable images of disaster. That he had turned his head just as he was passing the fateful cottage, Wyndham ever afterwards counted as instinct. For there was Serena!

Her hat was off, her pelisse unbuttoned, and she was chasing an infant around a fenced off area of garden. Even as he saw her, she caught the child, who let out a shriek of delight. Wyndham saw the toddler lifted in Serena's arms, and the sound of her laughter floated to him over the intervening space. His heart contracted, and he turned his horse towards the cottage to which the garden obviously belonged.

Breaking into a canter the instant he was clear of

the trees, Wyndham saw that Serena caught the sound. She stood still, the infant held in her arms, watching his approach in silence.

Her thoughts were suspended, and the only thing she was conscious of was the thudding of her heartbeat in her chest. Then she felt Becky being drawn out of her arms, and found Annabel beside her. She was smiling.

'I believe he has come for you.'

Serena could not speak. The Viscount was already dismounting, looking for a convenient rung on the fence where he might tether his horse. It seemed only moments before he found the gate, and presented himself in Annabel's garden.

Serena's heart was still beating like a ticking clock. What was she to say to him? How to get over the dreadful awkwardness that must attend any attempt at speech? Was he furious with her for running away?

She ventured a peep at him as Annabel introduced herself. Wyndham did not look to be irate, though his eyes were fixed on her face. Serena instantly dropped her own gaze, feeling her cheeks grow hot.

Wyndham was far from angry. He was instead conscious of a dreadful hollow feeling at his chest. She could not even look at him! Had he ruined all with his—yes, petulance!—that had resulted in her choosing to run away rather than marry him? His eye caught the female hovering to one side. She had given him her name, but he could not recall it.

'I must thank you for your kindness to my—to Serena,' he said, just stopping himself from speaking of her in intimate terms to which she might object. He wished fervently that the woman might go away!

Mrs Lett appeared to read his thought. 'I will leave you, sir.' But she did not immediately go. 'Serena!'

Serena jumped, turning quickly. 'Yes, Annabel?'

Her new friend leaned close, but her words were audible to the Viscount. 'I am persuaded that you would do well to listen to anything his lordship may have to say to you.'

With which, she settled her daughter upon her hip, and quietly re-entered the cottage. Serena was left confronting his lordship in the deserted garden. Her chest thumped unbearably and her tongue cleaved to the roof of her mouth.

Wyndham eyed her, hesitating. She was at least waiting, but her gaze shifted this way and that. How should he begin?

'Why did you run away?'

She glanced at him only briefly, but the look in her eyes reproached him. No, that had been the wrong thing to say!

'I didn't mean to ask that. I know why.'

The pansy eyes shifted again, and met his. 'Do you?'

He drew a breath. 'Because we quarrelled. Because you believe me to be a confirmed libertine. Because—' He broke off and raised helpless hands, shrugging eloquently. 'No, I don't know. I don't even know what to say to you, Serena.'

Reflecting that she was as much tongue-tied,

Serena gathered herself together. 'It was a silly thing to do.'

'Extremely silly. Lord knows what danger you might have run into!'

'I knew you were angry with me!'

He put out a hand. 'I am not, I promise you. Only you did give me a fright.'

A fleeting smile escaped her. 'Not as big a one as I gave myself. I was lucky to have happened upon Annabel.'

She was thawing, he decided. A surge of hope went through him. He took a risk. 'Serena, would you have come back?'

The blood flittered down her veins. He ought rather to ask if she could have stayed away! But before she had an opportunity to reply, Wyndham spoke again.

'No, don't answer that! What I meant to have said is—*will* you come back?' His voice dropped. 'With me.'

She wanted to say yes. She wanted to throw herself upon his chest, crying out the misery she had long been suffering on his account. Yet some instinct of her sex prevented her. A need of which she was only vaguely aware.

Her hesitation was torture to Wyndham. The devil! Did she yet question his integrity? Well, there was a new element now, he remembered. Reeth must vindicate him!

'Your father has arrived.'

Startled by the abrupt announcement, Serena stared at him blankly. 'My father?'

'He is at Bredington.'

'At Bredington!' She eyed him in something of a puzzle, feeling dazed. 'How did he know?'

Wyndham's smile was wry. 'I wrote to him yesterday—before you awakened.'

'You never told me that!'

'You never gave me a chance!'

She bit her lip, a hint of resentment in the brown orbs. Wyndham quickly flung up a hand. 'Don't let us quarrel again! I should have told you, only there was so much else to say. And to be truthful, Serena, I could not be sure he would come.'

'Indeed, no,' agreed Serena wonderingly. A horrid thought assailed her, and she paled. 'He has not brought Hailcombe?'

'By no means,' the Viscount reassured her. 'In fact, he was bent upon foxing Hailcombe—which is why he ignored my request for him to bring Miss Geary.'

In a few brief words, he put Serena abreast of the latest development, laying far more credit to Lord Reeth than he believed the man deserved. It had made Serena desperately unhappy to be at outs with Reeth, and he had no wish to widen the distance between father and daughter.

Serena listened with a resurgence of the flutter in her veins. He had not meant to hoax her! His intentions truly had been honourable. Oh, she had misjudged him terribly! She wanted desperately to tell him so, but that instinctive caution prevented her. The sense of something missing grew.

She discovered that as they talked they had turned

together without intent, walking further down the garden, a little away from the cottage.

'Is Papa then amenable to a match between us?' she asked without thinking, and then flushed as she recalled the unsatisfactory nature of their present relationship. She tried to retract, and faltered hopelessly. 'I mean—is he not...does he say that—'

Wyndham turned, catching at her shoulders. 'Serena, it is not your father's agreement that troubles me! If he could stomach Hailcombe—even to save your uncle's name—he is unlikely to balk at me, whatever he believes.'

'But has he retracted what he said of you?' asked Serena anxiously.

The Viscount let her go and dropped back a pace, wounded despite himself. 'Can you bring yourself to trust me only upon Reeth's word? Serena, this is a man, be he never so much your father, who has shown himself to be susceptible to blackmail! Must he serve as witness to my good character? Why can you have no trust in me? In my deeds, if nothing else!'

The disquieting need flowered, and all at once Serena knew just why she had run away. He might have commanded her trust at any time, had he only told her the one thing she yearned to hear! Only he had never said it. Not even yesterday, when he was trying to persuade her that he indeed meant marriage. Was she to presume it? No, my lord Wyndham, it would not do!

'Why did you rescue me? Why have you persisted all this time when you knew how I distrusted you?

You could have left me to my fate, Wyndham. I rejected you. I spurned your aid when you offered it. And you would wed me still. I don't understand. Tell me why!'

Wyndham stared at her blankly. 'Do you mean to tell me that you do not know?'

'If I knew, I would not ask you!' she retorted, snapping.

A short laugh escaped him. 'Then you are either foolish beyond belief, or more innocent that I had supposed! I love you, simpleton. Does that answer you?'

Serena's heart thumped, and her voice shook. 'It is you who is the s-simpleton! You n-never told me so b-before. If you had, I should never have b-believed those w-wicked lies I was told about you. If I did, it is your own f-fault!'

Light broke over Wyndham's countenance, and the warmth crept into his eyes. 'Serena, you unprincipled wretch! How dare you say so?' He seized her by the shoulders once again, and shook her. 'What you mean is that I am already vindicated. Who told you the truth? That woman who took you in?'

A rueful smile lit the pansy eyes. 'Annabel, yes. She said she had never heard anything bad of you, and that Miss Beattie is a dreadful gossip.'

'Exactly so.' He eyed her with mock severity. 'I don't know what you deserve, Miss Reeth!'

'For misjudging you? I cannot be blamed for that.'

Wyndham drew her closer. 'That I concede. But to

pretend that you didn't know my feelings for you, when—'

'But I didn't!' Serena protested. 'Oh, I hoped— *desperately*. Only it did not seem possible that you could truly love me.'

'Oh? What then do you suppose made me persist in trying to win back your regard, my darling little idiot?'

A shy smile crept into the brown eyes. 'Well, that was what led me to hope, you see.'

His lips twitched. 'Did it indeed? Yet when you had the opportunity to secure my affections for ever, you ran away!'

'Because you abandoned all attempts to persuade me of your honourable intentions. What else was I to do?'

Wyndham could not forbear a spurt of laughter, but he caught her into his arms. 'Your logic defeats me, my adorable innocent. But this you may depend upon. If you again mistake my caresses for those of a libertine, I shall know what to do about it!'

Serena smiled shyly up at him, and the tattoo was again at work in her veins—in pleasurable anticipation. A mixture of mischief and innocence entered the pansy eyes, reminding Wyndham irresistibly—and poignantly!—of those early days of their acquaintance.

'You will first have to give me an opportunity to make such a mistake,' she pointed out.

Which provoked the Viscount into offering her an instant opportunity that left her breathless and trembling. No hint of dismay overtook her as she became engulfed in the heat of his passion. Instead the satisfying thought flitted through her mind that the future must offer him every chance to repeat the experiment.

She opened her eyes to find his burning glance devouring her face. 'Oh, George!' she breathed, involuntarily using his given name.

'Yes, my sweet?' he murmured, nuzzling her cheek.

Serena gave a little shiver of delight, and sighed. 'Once again, if you please, for I am not perfectly sure if—'

She was not permitted to finish the sentence, and this second assault upon her senses was undertaken in a manner that left Serena so weak at the knees that Wyndham was obliged to cradle her for fear that she might fall.

He gazed down into the lovely countenance, a glow in his chest for the dreamy look that had settled upon it, and the long-sought return of pleasure in her eyes. He twined one of the gold locks around his finger.

'Now do you see why I moved heaven and earth to win you?'

She gave a deeply satisfied sigh, and smiled at him. 'Yes, and I am so glad.'

'Which means, I trust,' said Wyndham, a glint entering his eye, 'that my sentiments are reciprocated. If I did not speak of my feelings, you have certainly been reticent about yours. But I happen to know that you love me. Pray don't attempt to deny it, for I may as well confess that I heard you say so to your father.'

'When?' Serena demanded, abruptly pushing him away, her cheeks flying colour. 'I am sure I never said I cared for you within your hearing.'

He grinned, catching her back into his embrace. 'You did not know it, but I overheard you speaking with him in the summer saloon in Melanie's house.'

'Eavesdropping! Wyndham, how could you?'

'I have no compunction,' he returned. 'For I would not otherwise have known enough to be suspicious of your father's motives in acceding to Hailcombe's demands.'

Serena was outraged. 'That, yes. But you were not to know then how much I loved you.'

'And now?'

'You deserve that I should refute it!' Then she relented, sinking against him, and sliding her arms about his neck. 'Oh, George, I did care for you so much. And the worst of it was that the more I tried not to, the more entangled I became.'

'Don't I know it!' agreed the Viscount feelingly. He kissed her again, his lips lingering over hers. His voice became husky with passion. 'I am glad I had all to do to win you. I might not otherwise have recognised how very deeply in love with you I am, Serena.'

Such a gratifying sentiment could not go unrewarded, and it was some time before either had leisure for the exchange of any further words. But presently Wyndham roused himself sufficiently to suggest that they should repair to Bredington to set her father's mind at rest.

Farewells and thanks had to be said to Annabel Lett, and then the Viscount took Serena up before him on his horse, settling her in the crook of his arm. She gripped his coat with one hand, and the pommel with the other, the ribbons of her bonnet precariously clasped in her fingers.

The way was beguiled with the laying of plans. Wyndham proposed to travel to London within the day, both to obtain a special licence and bring Cousin Laura back with him—together with some much-needed garments for his betrothed. Their wedding should be celebrated in the shortest possible order— Serena breaking in to suggest that Mrs Lett should be invited to witness their nuptials—and thereafter they would travel first to Lyford Manor to break the news to his parents.

'And after?'

'There is bound to be a deal of talk, and I would spare you that,' said Wyndham, kissing the top of her head, which was resting just inside his shoulder. 'Would you care to go to Italy for a spell? And Greece perhaps?'

Serena leaned snugly into him. 'Anywhere you wish.'

Wyndham's tone became teasing. 'This is novel, Miss Reeth. Have I so suddenly become the undisputed arbiter of your movements? I had no notion I was gaining so even-tempered a wife.'

A giggle escaped Serena. 'Well, but it is not as if I had any other destination to offer.'

'If you had, I presume I might count myself lucky to have any say at all in where we went.'

'No, how can you think me so contrary?'

He drew rein, but only so that he might clasp her within the circle of his arm. 'If I have learned anything from these past hideous weeks, it is that behind the sweet innocent that originally won my heart lies a woman of courage and spirit. And,' he added tenderly, the smile warm in his grey eyes, 'I adore her in every guise.'

As his lips gave her proof of this utterance, Serena felt the last little doubts melt away. She had blamed him for not speaking of his feelings before, but in this she discovered she had erred. She ought rather to be thankful. For fate had tested their love, and found it strong.

* * * *

*What next for the villages surrounding
Steepwood Abbey?*

*Look out for more Regency drama, intrigue,
mischief…and marriage in*
The Steepwood Scandals Volume 2
featuring The Reluctant Bride *by Meg Alexander*
& A Companion of Quality *by Nicola Cornick.*

Available next month, from all good booksellers.

THE STEEPWOOD

Scandals

Regency drama, intrigue, mischief…
and marriage

VOLUME TWO

The Reluctant Bride by Meg Alexander

After her father's tragic death, India Rushford and
her sister discover that they have been left penniless and
that one of the girls must become the wife of the
hated Lord Isham.

A Companion of Quality by Nicola Cornick

Captain Lewis Brabant discovers he has to leave his
life at sea to return to Hewly Manor. Still, his friends
suggest he might be able to find consolation for his
enforced rustication—if he takes a wife!

On sale 1st December 2006

*Available at WHSmith, ASDA, Tesco
and all good bookshops*

A young woman disappears.
A husband is suspected of murder.
Stirring times for all the neighbourhood in

THE STEEPWOOD

Scandals

Volume 1 – November 2006
Lord Ravensden's Marriage by Anne Herries
An Innocent Miss by Elizabeth Bailey

Volume 2 – December 2006
The Reluctant Bride by Meg Alexander
A Companion of Quality by Nicola Cornick

Volume 3 – January 2007
A Most Improper Proposal by Gail Whitiker
A Noble Man by Anne Ashley

Volume 4 – February 2007
An Unreasonable Match by Sylvia Andrew
An Unconventional Duenna by Paula Marshall

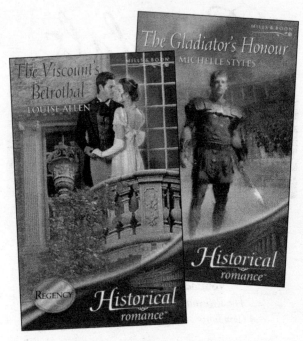

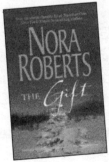

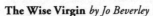

Enjoy the dazzling glamour of Vienna on the eve of the First World War…

Rebellious Alex Faversham dreams of escaping her stifling upper-class Victorian background. She yearns to be like her long-lost Aunt Alicia, the beautiful black sheep of the family who lives a glamorous life abroad.

Inspired, Alex is soon drawn to the city her aunt calls home – Vienna. Its heady glitter and seemingly everlasting round of balls and parties in the years before WW1 is as alluring as she had imagined, and Alex finds romance at last with Karl von Winkler, a hussar in the Emperor's guard. But, like the Hapsburg Empire, her fledgling love affair cannot last. Away from home and on the brink of war, will Alex ever see England or her family again?

On sale 3rd November 2006

www.millsandboon.co.uk

M&B